For Lou and Al

Enjoy

THE WGC

Dennis Flannery

Outskirts Press, Inc.
Denver, Colorado

This is a work of fiction. The events and characters described herein are imaginary and are not intended to refer to specific places or living persons. The opinions expressed in this manuscript are solely the opinions of the author and do not represent the opinions or thoughts of the publisher. The author has represented and warranted full ownership and/or legal right to publish all the materials in this book.

The WGC

v2.0

Outskirts Press, Inc.
http://www.outskirtspress.com

ISBN: 978-1-4327-6452-4

PRINTED IN THE UNITED STATES OF AMERICA

This novel is dedicated to my first editor, muse, best friend and love of my life - my wife, Zelia.

In Memory of
Aidan and Eryn, our two beautiful little angles.
All who knew you, loved you.
We will never forget.

All was as it should be. The ski conditions were textbook: the skies were deep blue, the wind was calm, it was twenty-four degrees and there were three inches of fresh powder sitting on top of a finely tuned base. There could not have been a more perfect day to begin altering the course of history.

Prologue

CENTRAL, OREGON
April 12, 1997
8:15 a.m.

The two men and two women, all fashionably dressed in colorful ski gear, flew in single file over a small rise, propelling clouds of fresh powder into the crystalline air. As they headed down a wide open, untracked slope, they separated and skied four abreast leaving, in their wake, four snake-like grooves in the virgin snow. They were still two hundred yards above the tree line when they came to a stop within a few feet of each other. All were smiling while catching their breath and taking in the beautiful view of the Cascade Mountains. Within seconds the shorter man gestured down hill.

"Last one to the bottom on this run buys lunch today." Without another word he turned his skis around and sped off.

The two young ladies laughed as they quickly followed. The second man, a good three inches taller than the first, called after them, "I'll enjoy that free lunch." He smiled to himself and confidently waited another moment before starting down the slope.

Two hundred yards below, in the cover of trees, were three sloppily dressed young snowboarders, or "shredders" as they called themselves. They weren't shredding at the moment; they were passing around a small glass pipe. One of them, after taking a last pull off the pipe, dropped it in a pocket and bent over to attach his bindings.

"Okay, chicken shits, let's get some air this time." He flipped his board around and took off through the trees at a suicidal speed. The two others quickly followed.

A little further up the hill, the lead skier was about fifty yards in front of his three companions as he raced down the groomed run between the small forests of trees. He was still smiling as he looked back to see if he was maintaining his lead when, without warning, a stoned shredder came flying out of the trees a good six feet in the air, clipping the skier on the side of his head, throwing him wildly off balance. The skier's sunglasses shattered and flew off as he shot directly toward a large tree. Further up the hill, a sickening thud was clearly heard by his companions.

"ALEX!" the tall skier screamed in alarm.

Part One

Chapter 1

INGLEWOOD, CALIFORNIA
April 12, 1962
8:20 a.m.

Prairie Avenue was still damp from sporadic spring showers causing the smell of wet pavement and exhaust fumes to mix, creating a singular aroma unique to such a day. Despite the seasonal rains, traffic was moving at a normal pace until just after 8:20 a.m. when the routine flow on this active avenue was abruptly interrupted as an ancient pickup truck came to a screeching, side-sliding stop, effectively blocking the two southbound lanes.

Within a second, a frail old man in baggy, paint-stained white overalls threw open the dilapidated truck's door and all but fell out of its cab. "He ran right out in front of me!" he cried out as he headed on wobbly legs back in the direction he had come; leaving his old truck right where it would do the most damage to the morning traffic.

Immediately horns began honking, tentatively at first but gaining in urgency as the seconds passed. Gusting breezes were blowing what appeared to be school papers and crayon drawings from one side of the road to the other, a few sticking to the shallow puddles the rains had created on the asphalt.

On the far side of the road, about two hundred feet north of where the old pickup had come to its dramatic stop, a young boy, maybe seven or eight years old, was lying on his back just a foot or two from the curb. He wasn't moving. His clothes were wet, torn, and stained with small amounts of blood mixed with grime from the road. His right shoe was missing and that sock was half off, exposing a small white heel and a nasty looking road scrape on the anklebone. The only movement was an occasional twitch of the half-covered foot.

A girl, maybe a year or so older than the boy, after precariously dodging four lanes of traffic in her effort to reach the stricken boy, quickly knelt beside him. "Alex!" she cried.

A small crowd quickly gathered. "*I called an ambulance*," a man yelled out of the front door of his hardware store, as a sudden gust of cold wind and a few drops of rain fell on the scene.

"What happened?" asked a short, slightly built teller as he rushed from a bank across the street to the back of the expanding crowd.

"Some little boy got run over, looks like," a voice yelled back, trying to be heard over the noise of the crowd and the almost constant din of horns.

There was a slight stirring and an almost inaudible moan from the prone youngster.

"Alex!" called the girl. She placed her face just inches from her brother's. "Alex, please wake up!"

The wail of a siren could be heard, still some way off. The crowd turned to look north, nearly in unison, hoping to spot the ambulance heading toward them.

The girl tried again. "Alex, can you hear me?"

Alex groaned as he reached for the back of his head. *What the hell's happening here? This isn't right*! *What's everybody doing here? Something's wrong*! *Something's wrong*! Like shouts in an echo chamber, his thoughts began reverberating in his mind. *Something's wrong! Something's wrong!*

"Alex, say something!"

Alex looked at the girl. Her nose was running and she was crying as she stared down at him with an expression of near terror. *Who*? his mind questioned. He started to get up.

"Just lie still, young man," ordered a heavy-set woman as she knelt beside the girl. She placed her hands gently on Alex's shoulders to hold him down. "The ambulance will be here soon," she continued.

Ambulance?… Nightmare, nightmare. That's what it is; it's a weird frigging nightmare. He started to laugh quietly, but stopped quickly when he saw the expression on the face of the behemoth who had him pinned to the street.

8:45 a.m.

Alex's mind was a jumble of disconnected thoughts as the ambulance sped toward Centennial Hospital. His confusion was mounting as he became more aware of his surroundings. Nothing was as it should be. *I was skiing. I was skiing with Jason… wasn't I?* His eyes became large as he came to a realization. *I've managed to ski into a tree and have brain damage. I'm hallucinating. Oh shit!… Will I wake up?… Will I live?*

Chapter 2

CENTENNIAL HOSPITAL
9:40 a.m.

Alex's body was nearly rigid from fear as the doctor finished his examination. His eyes were shifting around like a trapped animal's. His breathing was quick and erratic. He seemed unable or unwilling to talk.

"Well, young man," the bespectacled, middle-aged doctor said as he moved the light back and forth across Alex's eyes, "you're going to have a pretty sore noggin and ribs for a while. I'll give you something that will ease that pain quite a bit. Don't you worry." He clipped the tiny flashlight back in his shirt pocket. "You're a lucky boy, all things considered. You have a couple of cracked ribs and a few others are banged up a bit. Aside from those, just a couple of dandy bruises. I'll bet you'll be just fine in a week or two."

A few streaks of pink could be seen in Alex's light blond hair as it lay matted against his small forehead. The doctor gently brushed it back as he looked into Alex's blue eyes. "Can you hear me, son?" The doctor's expression was one of concern.

Is he talking to me?

"I need you to talk to me, Alex. Give it a try, why don't you?"

Alex relaxed a bit as he looked at the doctor, "What's happening to me?" His child's voice was on the verge of hysteria. He quickly brought his hand up to his throat. "*What's wrong with my voice?*" Again his breathing became quick and erratic. He brought his hand up to his vision. He looked at his little hand, made a fist and relaxed it, paused for a second, then started screaming.

The doctor was caught off guard, "What is it, Alex? Is it pain?" But one look into Alex's eyes told him this boy was on the verge of a total breakdown.

The doctor quickly turned, opened a drawer, and removed a small syringe. He opened the drug cabinet above and picked up a vial of yellowish liquid. He filled the syringe, cleared the air bubble, grabbed an alcohol swab, turned back to Alex, and without hesitation swabbed his small shoulder and gave him an injection.

Alex's screaming tapered off within seconds. His face relaxed. He again brought his hand into his vision. *I'm having a nightmare! A bad one!... Please, God, let me wake up... please.*

With the reduction in anxiety came an urge to explain to the doctor that he was, in fact, a full-grown adult and none of this was real. That he would be waking up or dying soon and this would be over. But something deep inside compelled him not to say anything. Just play along with this... whatever it is. He was calming considerably. *Thanks for the drug, doc.*

But why wasn't he waking up? Why was this continuing? He decided to see if he could interact with his hallucination and ask some questions. "What happened to me? Am I going to live?" Again he involuntarily brought his right hand up to his throat.

"I'm told you were hit by an old pickup truck while you were crossing a street just a few miles from here." The doctor smiled. "And yes, you're going to live to a ripe old age if I'm any judge."

Hit by a pickup truck?... Skiing? That makes no sense.

"Doctor, can you tell me where I am, please?"

"Why...you're in a hospital, son," responded the doctor, looking over the top of his wire-rimmed glasses.

"I know I'm in a hospital, for Christ's sake. Where am I, what town?"

This reaction surprised the doctor. "Inglewood!" he answered, as he watched Alex's reaction carefully.

"Inglewood? Inglewood, California?"

"That's the one."

Alex thought about this for a moment. "Who was the young girl in the ambulance with me?"

"I don't know; didn't see her." He was giving Alex his undivided attention; these were not normal questions, not by a long shot. A boy this age should be asking for his mother. Most boys this age would be crying out of fear and pain.

Alex failed to notice or didn't care that the doctor seemed puzzled at this exchange. He fell silent and continued trying to sort things out.

"Well," resumed the doctor, "I'd better go out and let your mom know you're going to live." The doctor smiled. "She's sure to be real upset, they always are," he chuckled, as he started replacing instruments in the drawers lining one wall.

"My mother?" exclaimed Alex, coming out of his reverie with alarm, the terrifying circumstances momentarily forgotten. He sat bolt upright, which brought jolts of pain and some nausea. "Oh damn!" he groaned and gingerly lay back down.

"Well, I don't think we could have dragged anybody else's mom out of work to come see you in the hospital do you, son?" asked the doctor, smiling down at Alex. "And you don't wanna be jumpin' around too much for a while... I guess you just figured that out for yourself."

"My mother is dead!" Alex said flatly.

"Dead? Why would you say that?"

This is a dream; this is a hallucination so don't get caught up in it, Alexander, he chided himself. But believing that was true didn't keep him from involuntarily reacting to this nightmare. *Maybe I've slipped into an alternate dimension...one that's a few decades behind... shit!*

"You don't understand." Alex was trying desperately not to interact with this hallucination, but unable to restrain himself. "My mother and father were killed in a plane crash six years ago."

Alex could still hear Jason's voice in his head. ... *Alex, I don't know how to tell you... your sister called while you were out... your parents' plane…* In his mind's eye, Alex could see the Nobel International passenger jet crashing into the ocean.

"*We expect post cards just about every day...bon voyage...call if you run out of money, ha, ha...love you…*"

I don't want my mom in this hallucination, or dream, whatever it is, Alex thought. *I don't think I can take seeing my mom without breaking down.* Tears began forming in his eyes.

"Son," the doctor's voice softened, "you've had an awful bump on the head and sometimes that makes us think and see things that aren't really true. Your mom and dad weren't killed, Alex. Say," the doctor looked at the admitting sheet, "isn't your dad's name Norman?"

"Yes?" Alex replied, surprised the doctor knew his father's name. *This really is a dream...goofy things happen in dreams; they don't need to have rhyme or reason.*

"Well then, I just had your dad in here last week fixin' that thumb he smashed with the hammer. Boy, he whacked it good."

Thumb? Alex thought. *I know about that thumb. It had a dent in the nail like a smile.* "What year is this?"

"What do you mean?" asked the doctor, surprised at the sudden change of direction.

"What's the date, you know, like it's April 10th, 19__ what?"

"Well, son, to be exact, it's April 10th, 1962 at 9:51 a.m., if that helps you any," responded the doctor while admiring his fancy new watch.

"'62, Jesus," Alex whispered. *I would have just turned eight.*

The doctor stepped over and opened the door from the examination room into the waiting room. "Mrs. Gabriel, you can come in and see your son now."

A tall, slender, blue-eyed brunette in her late twenties stood quickly and crossed the small room in three strides; her shiny black shoulder-length hair, flowing behind. She was dressed in a dark blue business suit, which purposefully did little to showcase her figure. She paused at the door to the examination room for a split second and in two more long strides, had Alex by the shoulders, leaning over him, looking into his eyes, tears forming in the corners of hers.

"How are you, sweetheart?" she managed to get out, displaying little of the anxiety she had been going through since getting the call from the hospital just an hour ago.

Ah, they did make a mistake; this isn't my mother, thought Alex. *My mother was fifty-eight when she died. This is just a kid.* Alex turned away from her. "This isn't my mother," he whispered. Then, "*YOU FUCKED UP, DOCTOR!*" he screamed at the wall, as a massive dose of adrenaline hit his heart. He began shaking.

Marian was stunned and stood bolt upright, as if slapped hard. "What? What?" She turned toward the doctor, both fear and shock on her face. She quickly turned back to Alex. "Alex, what's the matter? Why did you say that? Please look at me, please, Son...please." She again turned to look at the doctor, her eyes pleading for help.

This outburst took the doctor by surprise. Up to this point, Alex had been soft-spoken -- direct, but soft-spoken.

Marian sat on the side of the bed and put her trembling hands on Alex's shoulder and side and pulled gently, hoping to roll her son over to face her. She met strong resistance from his shaking body.

"The little fella has had a real good scare, Mrs. Gabriel," the doctor said as he moved around to the foot of the bed. "Had a real hard smack on the head and you need to watch those ribs on the left side; got some damage there." He pointed to just about where Marian's left hand was.

"Oh gosh, sweetheart, I'm sorry. I didn't realize I was hurting you," she apologized as she eased her grip and backed away, not taking her eyes off Alex.

Alex said nothing but kept shaking. He had no sense of pain now. He was just terrified.

"I'm Dr. Snider." The man extended his hand to Marian.

"Marian Gabriel." She turned quickly, taking the offered hand, and then turned back to look at Alex.

"Why don't we step into my office down the hall for a minute, Mrs. Gabriel?" He paused. "We'll be right back, Alex."

Alex's trembling was starting to subside.

The doctor walked to the door, opened it and held it for Marian. She gave no indication she had heard the doctor's suggestion. She continued to look at her son.

"Mrs. Gabriel?"

She stood, not taking her eyes off her son and nearly backed out of the examination room. The doctor followed her out and closed the door.

Chapter 3

CENTENNIAL HOSPITAL
8:54 a.m.

"Alex has a concussion," Dr. Snider explained as they entered his office. "A mild one, I would guess, by the tests I've given him and the length of time he was unconscious." He closed the door behind Marian as he continued talking. "He was only out, according to a nurse who was at the scene, for three to five minutes."

Marian could hear the doctor talking but his words were not registering properly. Little of what was going on around her was registering. Her mind was in turmoil.

Dr. Snider motioned toward a chair. "Have a seat."

She just stood looking at him.

"Have a seat, please." He again motioned toward a chair.

She walked over and sat almost trance-like. Her eyes wandered away from the doctor, absently looking at the various diplomas and awards displayed on the walls.

He took the chair beside her. "I gave Alex a thorough going-over and X-rayed his ribs and head from three angles. Three cracked ribs is all; nothing else is broken. Children's bones are soft and bend quite a ways without breaking," he smiled. "We'll keep a close eye on him overnight to make sure he has no internal injuries."

"You don't seem to understand, Dr. Snider," Marian stated through nearly clenched teeth. "Alex doesn't have a mild concussion; he has serious brain damage." *Why is this quack telling me that my son has a mild concussion and soft bones*, *for Christ's sake*? "Damn it!" she nearly yelled.

"Now, now, Mrs. Gabriel, I can assure you Alex doesn't have brain damage at all, let alone serious damage; just some mild bruising, that's all."

"I can assure you, doctor, that boy has a lot more wrong with him than some mild bruising." She continued to fight to keep her voice level. "Alex doesn't use bad language. Never has, because we don't use it around the children and we never use the 'F' word at all. Furthermore, that boy loves his mother more than anyone in the world, he would never reject me...never." She paused and took a deep shuddering breath. "A concussion wouldn't make him act this way. He's...he's acting crazy and believe me, there's never been a more stable child."

Marian was becoming more apprehensive as the minutes passed. She kept turning to look at the door, fidgeting in her seat. She wanted to return to the examination room to be with her son.

"I've seen thousands of concussions and the effect they have on all sorts of people, but I admit Alex's reaction is unique." The doctor was putting on his best bedside manner, which was legendary around the hospital.

"Unique? Yes, you could say that, that's a good word," Marian stated sarcastically.

The doctor ignored the sarcasm. "While I was examining him, he did ask...rather unusual questions."

"How do you mean, unusual?"

"Well, he is obviously confused due to the concussion, but the questions he asked were more like someone with partial amnesia."

"Amnesia?" A little hope crept into her voice.

"Absolutely. It's quite common for someone to suffer short-term amnesia with head injuries. Normally, amnesia can fog the memory for various periods of time just prior to the injury and afterward. But in Alex's case, his loss -- or misplacement, if you will -- of certain memories is rather unusual."

"Such as forgetting who his mother is?"

"That would be the biggest one for sure."

"What other memories does he seem to have misplaced?" Marian's voice was markedly calmer.

"Well, as an example, he asked where he was."

"Where?"

"Yep, and when I told him he was in a hospital, he informed me... rather impatiently, I might add, that he was aware of that, but he wanted to know what town and state he was in."

"What town and state?" She repeated, apprehension apparent in her voice.

"Yes indeed, and when I told him, he seemed quite surprised. He also asked who the young girl was who came with him in the ambulance. I didn't know the answer to that; I hadn't seen her. I assume she is his sister, now that I've seen her in the waiting room."

"Yes, that's right."

"And when I told him you were here, he nearly went into shock and informed me that you and Mr. Gabriel were killed six years ago and he believed it; he wasn't making it up."

"Oh Jesus, he thought we were dead?" *No wonder*. Tears again started to form in the corners of her eyes. *The poor kid*.

"He probably had a nightmare while he was unconscious and carried it over to his consciousness," suggested Dr. Snider. "When I told him you were alive and that I fixed your husband's thumb last week, he asked me what year it was. That answer also threw him."

"*What year*!"

"Probably all related to a dream while unconscious," the doctor assured her.

"Have you ever seen anything like these symptoms before?"

"Well, no two people act the same no matter what the circumstances, Mrs. Gabriel. Although Alex's behavior is peculiar, I wouldn't get overly concerned. The brain is a funny thing. I would bet that in a day or two, he'll be back to his old self. He might have some trouble with his memory for two or three weeks, but again, that isn't unusual. Thing to do is just keep your eye on him after he leaves the hospital and let me or your family doctor know if he takes a turn for the worse."

"All right." The reassurance by the doctor was helping Marian calm down.

"We'll keep him here two, maybe three days at the most."

"You said overnight."

"Well, with your concerns, it might be a good idea to keep him another day or so. Just to be sure."

Marian searched the doctor's eyes for any sign of actual concern about Alex. *Is he telling me the truth? Does he really believe my boy's all right?* She couldn't detect any guile.

"Despite the lack of serious bone damage, the amount of bruising around the ribs suggests he was hit really hard. Internal injuries are always a possibility." The doctor put his hand on top of Marian's. "Not to worry too much, Mrs. Gabriel. Kids have unbelievable healing powers. I suspect Alex will be up and around in a week or so." Dr. Snider paused for a second. "I gave him a mild sedative to ease his pain and apprehension."

"A sedative at his age?"

"Couldn't hurt, and seemed to be just the ticket." He walked over to a cabinet on the far side of his office and with some poking around, retrieved a small brown bottle of pills. "You might take these with you in case he starts getting overly agitated."

Marian shuddered. "Now can we go see Alex? I'll try to be more in control of myself this time," she smiled.

It was the first smile he'd seen from her, and she was dazzling. "You betcha!"

Dr. Snider opened the door and he and Marian walked back through the waiting room to the examining room.

Chapter 4

CENTENNIAL HOSPITAL
9:15 a.m.

Alex, upon seeing the doctor and his mother reentering his examination room, rolled over and faced the wall. The sight of this woman inexplicably horrified him.

Marian walked over and sat on the edge of the bed, placing a hand on Alex's shoulder. Dr. Snider stood at the end of the bed.

"Well Alexander, the doctor here informs me that you're going to live to a ripe old age, but he insists that you spend a night or two here so they can be sure you're okay," Marian explained with all the cheer she could muster. "I'll stay here for as long as they'll let me and then come back in the morning."

"You needn't bother. I'll either wake up or die soon and this shit will be over." He spoke to the wall, his voice flat, without emotion.

"Alex, sweetheart, you *are* awake and you're not going to die at all... not for a long..." Her voice broke and she paused for several seconds. "Long time," she finished. She put her face in her hands.

The doctor came over and put his hand on Marian's shoulder. "Mrs. Gabriel, please take my word for it, Alex is going to be all right... really he is."

The sound of desperation from this woman took Alex's thoughts off himself and the terrifying circumstances for a moment. *What was this young woman doing? Why was she acting like this? Why does she give a shit about me? This isn't my mother*! his mind screamed. *My mother is dead*! He turned to face her.

Marian took her hands away from her face and looked pleadingly at her son.

Alex looked deep into her tear-rimmed eyes and again began trembling. "Jesus, oh Jesus." His chin began quivering; tears spilled from his eyes. "Oh Jesus." he quickly turned away. "Go away," he choked out. "Please go away!"

Could this be his mother? The mother whom he loved so much; the mother who gave him his values; who encouraged, cared for, and nurtured him? The mother who was always asking, "*What can I do for you, Alex? What do you need, Son*?" The mother who was killed, along with his father, on a vacation trip that he himself arranged and paid for as a gift for their thirty-fifth wedding anniversary? But this couldn't be his mother. If it were, why had he suffered their loss these past six years? He couldn't take that guilt, the sorrow again; not again, not because of a hallucination. *Oh no, I'm not buying into it.* Alex's mind was in chaos. He again turned to the wall. He felt he was on the verge of screaming and once started, he might not be able to stop. He started taking deep quick breaths to stay his terror and rapid slide into insanity.

"Alex," pleaded Marian, "what can I do to help you? Please let me do something... please."

"Go away," Alex managed to choke out between breaths.

Chapter 5

CENTENNIAL HOSPITAL
APRIL 13, 1962
4:15 a.m.

"Hey, pal, wake up. You going to sleep all morning?"

Alex opened his eyes and there was Jason with a devilish look on his face. "What, what did you say?"

"Wake up! Jesus, Alex we got to go...get up and get your shit together...going skiing...going skiing!"

Alex could only stare at his best friend! What the hell was he doing with that ridiculous- looking knitted top hat on his head?

"Get your shit together, pal, we're going... "

"Shit, you wouldn't believe the dream I had... oh my God!" Alex's heart was racing, his body soaked in sweat. He was sitting behind his desk in his private office in Newport Beach. So it was a dream, after all. Alex took a deep shuddering breath.

"Hey, what's going on down there?" asked Jason.

"What? Where?"

"Looks like someone got hurt."

"What do you mean?"

"Down there, by the trees."

"What trees?" Alex was confused.

Alex turned slowly to where Jason was pointing at the carpet and found himself looking down an impossibly steep, narrow, and snow-covered slope. At the bottom was a crowd that appeared to be in the thousands.

"What the... ?"

Now they were skiing at breakneck speed, nearly straight down, huge trees whizzing past them like rows of corn. It was bone-numbing cold. Alex felt as if he was standing outside naked in a blizzard, freezing solid.

Now they were at the back of the crowd. Jason tapped a skinny old man on the shoulder, "What's the story here?"

"Some kid got run over, it looks like," the old man wheezed.

"Is he dead?"

"Not dead; just knocked unconscious!"

"Let me tell you about my dream," Alex pleaded.

"Look at him."

"Let me tell you about this dream; I need to tell you... I was eight years old..."

Jason was blatantly ignoring him.

Alex was perplexed. "Why won't you listen to me? What are..."

Now they were looking down at the body of a man lying in the snow. He was wearing a black pin striped suit that seemed to be as neat as if it were on a men's store mannequin, but his limbs were protruding at odd angles. His skis were attached to expensive wing-tip shoes, one of them half off his foot. The most startling thing, however, was that his head was horribly crushed. Blood was gushing out the top and running down several ski tracks as far as the eye could see. Spectators were just staring down at him in silence. All had blank, expressionless faces. No one was moving; there were no sounds.

"Hey shit, Alex, that's you, isn't it?"

"What?"

Now Alex was looking up at all those blank faces. His mother was in the front of the crowd. She was asking a question: "How are you doing, Son?"

Alex lurched awake screaming.

The nurse in attendance came rushing into the room. "Are you all right? Are you all right? What happened? What happened?" She was quite animated. Alex's blood-curdling scream caught her right as she was about to doze off.

"Oh shit!" Alex was soaked in sweat, heart pounding and body shaking. He quickly looked down at his hands. "Oh my God, oh my God!"

"Looks like you had a bad dream, kid." The nurse walked over and placed her hand on his forehead before picking up his left wrist and checking his pulse rate. "Better get you out of those bed clothes; they're soaked. Looks like the sheets are, too." This clearly didn't please this late-duty nurse; it was probably cutting into her sleep time.

Alex's breathing was shallow and fast. He held up his hand to stave off the nurse. "Give me a minute or two." His ribs felt as if they were on fire.

"Okay, but then I want you to use the bedpan again. Don't want you wetting the bed after I change it."

If Alex weren't in such pain he would have made a suggestion as to where the nurse could put the bedpan.

8:30 a.m.

Alex woke from his drug-induced sleep and peered around the darkened room for a few seconds. A small amount of light was filtering in from the sides of the aging curtains, allowing him to make out his surroundings; he was still in a hospital. Again he raised his a hand to his vision, he was disappointed but not surprised. *Jesus, what a dream I had -- or what a dream I'm having. God damn it!* he shuddered.

Alex had a hard time taking his mind off the nightmare. Seeing Jason that way, damn. *Thought I was back to reality for a minute. Shit, this reality is better than that one. But Jason was there, and that was comforting to a point.*

Alex's thoughts momentarily carried him back to 1980 when he had recruited Jason directly out of the Harvard graduating class. *How many years ago was that?* he asked himself. *Seventeen? I think that's right. Just two years after I opened my brokerage company.*

Terrifying thoughts of his present predicament jumped into his consciousness.

...I'd better go out and let your mom know you're going to live...

"Stop it!" Alex admonished himself aloud. "Try to think about Jason, concentrate..."

The first time he saw Jason he was quite surprised. He didn't expect him to be six foot four. He probably weighed less than 200 pounds then. Now, he was probably closer to 230. Alex smiled to himself. He remembered thinking Jason, with his height, looked like a forward on a Lebanese basketball team, what with his coal-black hair, dark eyes and olive complexion. *I liked the charming son-of-a-bitch right away*, thought Alex.

The nurse came through the door, taking Alex out of his visit to the past. Without saying a word, she walked over and yanked open the drapes. "Looks like another wet one," she said off-handedly, looking up at the gray sky, then down over the parking lot.

Alex squinted as the brighter light assaulted his dilated pupils.

The nurse inserted the stethoscope in her ears as she approached Alex's bed. She pulled back the sheet and listened to his heart for a few seconds before checking his blood pressure. All the while she said nothing. After making notes on his chart and stuffing the stethoscope in one of her pockets, she said, "Breakfast in a few minutes. You ready for it?"

"Yes, I am." Alex suddenly realized that he was hungry. He hadn't eaten since breakfast the previous day.

The nurse left the room and returned a few minutes later with his medication.

"Here, take these." She handed Alex a tiny paper cup containing three pills and a glass of water with a bent straw.

"Would you like to know how I feel?" Alex asked politely after swallowing the pills.

"Sure, how do you feel?"

"I feel like I should have a nurse who actually cares how I feel!"

This stopped the sour nurse. She looked at Alex for a second, made a sound something like a grunt, turned and left the room.

Oh well, thought Alex.

A candy striper came bouncing in within ten minutes. "Hi, young man. How are you this morning?"

"Oh, good morning," he responded belatedly, taking a second to realize that he was the subject of her greeting.

"Feel like something to eat?"

"As a matter of fact I do; stomach thinks my throat's slit!"

That amused the mildly plump young lady and she laughed as she helped Alex sit up. "You tell me if I'm hurting you, okay?"

His ribs did complain, but he said nothing to this delightful young person who Alex figured was around seventeen years old.

After swinging the rolling bed-table up to Alex's chest, she set down a tray of what looked something like an anemic omelet, a small glass of orange juice, and underdone, dry toast.

"There you are, cutie," she said cheerfully. "I'll be back in a while to take this away." With that, she bounced out of the room.

Alex began eating as if he hadn't eaten for a week. The fact that the meal had little flavor didn't matter.

As he ate, he managed to keep his mind off his horrible hallucination and on Jason. Together they built a hugely successful investment business. *Jason is one hell of a strategist, far better than I; we make a great team.*

Jason was groomed all his life to take over his family's considerable business holdings in the Boston area. But Alex knew that Jason's first love, one that he kept almost totally to himself, was journalism. He had minored in journalism and communications, but yielded to family pressure and majored in business and finance. Jason had all the good looks, intelligence, and charisma he needed to do whatever he wished. But what he wished, Alex found out early in their friendship, was to get out from under his family's thumb and "make it on his own." He was trapped until Alex came along and talked him into moving west. *The man owes me*, smiled Alex. He also remembered that Jason's parents didn't speak to him for the first two years. *I took their little boy away from home.*

THE WGC

9:35 a.m.

"All done, cutie?" asked the bouncy candy striper as she burst through the door.

Alex was startled at the intrusion into his meditation.

"Oh, I'm sorry. I didn't mean to scare you," the young lady apologized.

"No sweat," Alex responded with a smile.

"You're sure a nice boy," remarked the girl as she started removing the food tray.

"Pretty hard not to be nice to a delightful young woman such as yourself."

The girl stopped in mid-stride; her expression displayed a bit of confusion. She turned to look Alex right in the eye. "Ah, thank you; what a nice thing to say." She stood looking at Alex for another moment, then smiled as she turned and headed out the door.

Chapter 6

CENTENNIAL HOSPITAL
APRIL 13, 1962
9:45 a.m.

Marian and Norman came to see Alex the next morning, but rather than going directly to Alex's room they first stopped by Dr. Snider's office. Both were worried about Alex's condition; neither had slept well the previous evening.

Norman arrived at the hospital yesterday just in time to have his wife tell him his son wasn't doing well at all. And she advised him that it might not be a good idea for him to see Alex yet.

"Well hello, Norman," said Dr. Snider as he stood to shake Norm's hand.

"Hi, Doctor."

"Marian, how are you doing today?"

"Not sure yet, Doctor. We'll see."

The doctor nodded knowingly. "Norman, how's that thumb coming along?"

Norman was still a little embarrassed about smacking his thumb with a hammer; he turned a little pink. His complexion was fairly light and he blushed quite easily. "Coming along just fine, but it's still a little sensitive."

"Let's take a look."

Norm held his hand across the doctor's desk.

The doctor took Norm's hand, and after looking at the thumb

from a couple of angles, declared it to be healing just fine.

"You know," said the doctor after releasing Norm's hand, "it occurs to me that your son has a combination of your eye colors. The light blue of Norman's and the dark blue of yours, Marian, has made the most astounding color I believe I've ever seen. Quite striking. A handsome boy, all in all."

"Thank you, we think so too," said Marian.

"Has Marian's complexion, thank God," added Norman.

"But your hair color," offered the doctor.

"Dr. Snider, we need to know how Alex is doing." Marian had had about all the casual conversation she could take right now.

"Boy's doing fine, just fine," the doctor responded. "No signs of internal bleeding yet and probably won't be any, unless I miss my guess."

"How about his mental condition?" asked Marian.

"Can't answer that. We'll have to see how he reacts with you today."

"I'm sure he'll be fine," Norman stated with more optimism than he felt.

After a few more minutes of consultation with Dr. Snider, they headed to the third floor to Alex's semi-private room in the pediatrics wing.

Marian and Norman entered Alex's room together. Alex quickly took his eyes off his mother, but let them linger for a few seconds on his father. The sedatives prevented Alex from getting overly agitated, but didn't prevent him from turning his back. "Please go away," he pleaded quietly.

"Thought he was going to be all right for a second," Norman remarked as they headed back to Dr. Snider's office.

"I don't think I can take much more of this," Marian whispered.

10:57 a.m.

"It's the darndest thing," said Dr. Snider. "He doesn't seem to have any trouble conversing with anyone else. He is polite and mostly responsive to the nurses, if a bit impatient sometimes, I hear." The doctor leaned back in his chair, his fingers intertwined, his two thumbs rubbing his chin. "I want you to see Dr. Eagen in our psychiatry department. I'll ask her to take a look at Alex as soon as possible. I'll brief her as to his physical condition and his reaction to you yesterday and again today, Marian."

4:00 p.m.

Norman and Marian were able to get in to see Dr. Eagen at 4:00 that afternoon. After the introductions and a bit of small talk, Pam, as she asked to be called, pulled out a file folder and opened it on her desk.

"I was only able to spend a half an hour with Alex this afternoon because of time constraints." She looked down at her notes. "Physically, he's bruised and contused but will heal nicely, I'm sure," the young psychiatrist stated. "Mentally, it's another story."

Both Marian and Norman leaned forward in their chairs.

"Oh, I'm sorry," said Pam. "I didn't mean to alarm you. This is not to say that Alex has any permanent problem -- and maybe not any real problem at all."

Norman and Marian looked at each other for a second and, relaxing a bit, leaned back in their chairs.

"I haven't personally read about or run into any symptoms or a child quite like Alex. He is... well, different, for a lack of a better term."

"My wife has been telling me that since Alex was born." Norman patted Marian on the knee.

"He is bright," Pam continued, "and I can't emphasize that enough. I mean very bright. His vocabulary seems to be nearly equal to that of an adult."

"You think so?" interrupted Marian. "I hadn't noticed that." Her confidence in Pam went down a bit.

"Me neither," added Norman.

"Oh yes, it was hard to believe I was talking to an eight-year-old. He's quite articulate. But there is something more that I can't quite put into words. It's like he's holding back a great deal and I don't think that's necessarily of his choosing. The look in those beautiful blue eyes," Pam said, raising her eyebrows, "is that he knows I won't understand what he could convey if he decided to tell me." Pam looked perplexed. "That doesn't make much sense, does it?"

"A little," responded Marian. "He's always been prone to keep his own counsel."

Pam again consulted her notes. "In my interview with your son I only referred to you on one occasion. I asked why he thinks you were killed in a plane crash. His answer was simple and to the point and I quote, 'Because they were killed on June 16th, 19...' He abruptly stopped before completing the date and became very agitated, quite distraught. Didn't say another word, but I would have to be blind not to see that he was distressed. His fists were clenched, tears were running down his face and he stopped looking me in the eye. He didn't make a sound but I felt he was screaming inside. It nearly broke my heart. Had he not been sedated, we might have had a real breakdown. As it was, it took several minutes before I could continue my interview. I waited for him to calm down, feeling that this boy, your son, has tremendous inner strength. You could see him forcing himself to relax, to fight off his demons."

Marian's eyes were starting to puddle up while listening to Pam talk about her son's inner pain. She remained silent.

"We are aware that Alex's problem is directly connected to us at the moment, Pam," Norman agreed. He gave Marian's hand a gentle squeeze. "What we want from you is some sort of diagnosis as to what it could be and how we might treat the problem."

"Alex is certainly traumatized, and obviously you're the objects of his inner conflict. He believes you're dead. Seeing you might be like seeing ghosts, and that really terrifies him. The only thing I believe will cure the problem is to convince him that you were not killed, and that the accident caused him to imagine a plane crash in which you were killed."

"Obviously!"

"Another thing," added Pam.

"What's that?" asked Marian.

"He would occasionally look as his hands."

"I don't see...?"

"Not a big thing for sure, but the way he looked at them and then quickly put them back in his lap, just kind of struck me as odd."

Marian and Norman looked at each other and shrugged.

"Hadn't noticed," replied Marian, turning back to the doctor.

"Might I suggest that you stay away for a day or so and let me spend some more time with Alex? Maybe I can get to the bottom of this and help the boy back to reality. If there is any change, I'll give you a call immediately."

Chapter 7

CENTENNIAL HOSPITAL
APRIL 14, 1962
6:55 a.m.

Alex knew he was being sedated and was grateful. It reduced his anxiety to a manageable level and actually helped him think without sinking into terror. And think he did. He covered every minute from the second he awoke on a wet street until now and back again. He went back to his last memories as an adult. He was sure skiing with Jason and… two young women they had met in the lodge the night before. One was the most beautiful redhead he had ever seen; the other, a blonde that suited Jason to a tee. He didn't remember exactly what he was doing just moments prior to starting this nightmare, but felt certain he was skiing. So it had to be brain damage. There was no other logical explanation. He shuddered as he recalled the previous night's nightmare.

So, thought Alex, *assuming I have brain damage, how severe is it? The fact that I am hallucinating or dreaming might be a good sign. If my brain were smashed, as in the nightmare, I probably wouldn't be dreaming at all; I would probably be near flat-lining an EEG. My mind seems to be working normally. I can think and reason, but …I can't wake up.*

So what were his options in this reality? Few possibly, or maybe many, if he wanted to play along in this dream world. The astounding thing to Alex in this "world" was the absolute reality of it. There were no holes in the plot as there always are in dreams -- although, he knew, you didn't see the holes while in the dream, at least most of the time you didn't. But this dream was remarkable. It was so vivid, so linear. The sights, the sounds, the smells, the interaction, and the pain. The hardest to accept, next to seeing his parents and the fact that he was only eight years old, was the pain. But maybe that did make sense. After all, if he accepted the fact that he had suffered brain damage, he couldn't assume that was the only damage inflicted on his body; he undoubtedly would have other damaged parts. *Ribs and trees don't mix well. That pain could be working its way into this dream world. Again, this would probably be a good thing*, thought Alex. It might be a sign that parts of his brain were still functioning normally. *But*, Alex thought, *in any scenario, a hospital is where I would be after such an accident.*

So that's it. I am in a hospital being treated for brain and other physical damage. I'm unconscious and hallucinating while probably hooked up to EEGs, EKGs and all manner of IVs with tubes running in and out of my body. I'm probably lying quietly in an intensive care unit with 24-hour nursing care. An unsettling thought ran through Alex's mind. His sister, his uncle, his employees and his friends would be worried sick. At this moment, he was sure, there were probably at least a dozen people sitting somewhere in the hospital waiting for word on his condition, hoping to hear that he had regained consciousness and would be fine with a week or two of bed rest. Jason would, by this time, have found and consulted the best neurologists in the country. There would be no doubt that he would get the best care possible.

Alex was certain that his Uncle Walt would have taken a room at a close-by motel, if not in the hospital itself. He would be worrying himself sick. Alex would have been surprised if Walt wasn't holding his hand at this moment. He'd always been like a son to Walt. Especially after his parents were killed. If anything happened to Alex -- if he didn't make it -- it might be the end of Uncle Walt, too! *So sorry, Uncle Walt*.

"So Alexander, what are you going to do now?" he asked himself out loud. "You have to accept this scenario and play it out as it is; that's what!" he answered. "That would include accepting a role as a eight-year-old and," he paused ... "Mom and Dad!"

8:15 a.m.

It was fortunate that Alex was sedated the first time he went into the bathroom to take a pee. Being on the pediatric floor, the bathroom fixtures were lower than the normal height, to accommodate children. As he turned on the light, he was looking at himself in the mirror. For a second he was surprised and puzzled to see a young boy staring back at him. Then, with a start, he realized he was looking at himself. He gasped and looked away in shock. His heart began racing as the adrenaline hit and his breathing became shallow and rapid. "Jesus Christ!" he said as he leaned against the doorjamb for support; his ribs started burning. "Oh shit!" He didn't look back at his reflection for a full minute while he tried to gather his senses. *Okay Alexander, time to face yourself. Time to see what you look like in this reality.* He looked up into the mirror and again received another dose of adrenaline for his efforts; he again looked away. *Okay, ok*ay, he thought, *you're eight years old here; now accept that*. He looked up at his reflection and managed with some effort to maintain eye contact with his reflection. "Hi, Alex," he whispered as he continued to look at his child-self. After a few seconds, his heart rate and breathing started to slow. "Well, you are a damn good-looking boy, if I do say so myself." At forty-three, he had quite naturally forgotten his appearance at the age of eight. He, of course, had seen pictures of himself, taken at various ages; but this was completely different. With nearly white hair, eyes too big for his face, large front teeth, and two loose baby canine teeth. *And*, he thought, *no wrinkles.* He stared at the reflection in the mirror for a full five minutes. It was disconcerting yet fascinating. It was like looking at someone else. He managed to pull himself away to take a pee. He did smile after pulling up his hospital gown and seeing his miniature penis. "Well, little fella, you have bigger things in store for you...and soon, I hope," he added as an afterthought.

9:05 a.m.

Dr. Eagen entered Alex's room at 9:05 that morning. "Good morning, Alex. How are you today."

"I believe I'm much better, thank you, Dr. Eagen."

"Well," the young doctor seemed surprised. "That's good to hear, Alex. And what do you attribute the improvement to, might I ask?" She smiled as she sat on the chair next to the bed.

"Well," said Alex, "I...I want to see my mom and dad."

GABRIEL HOME
APRIL 14, 1962
9:45 a.m.

"*What...what did you say*?" Marian yelled into the phone, clearly unable to contain her joy.

"You heard me right, Mrs. Gabriel. First thing he said to me this morning was that he wanted to see his mom and dad."

"Oh, my God!"

"I just spent thirty minutes with your son and I've got to tell you, I'm impressed. He seems to have worked things out by himself. I wouldn't have believed it possible."

"I'll be right there...maybe twenty minutes tops. You tell Alex his mom's going to be there really quick. Be sure to tell him! Don't forget!"

"I won't forget." Pam smiled. "I'll tell him right now. See you when you get here."

Marian pushed the disconnect button and immediately dialed her husband. While waiting for him to pick up the receiver, she yelled toward the back of the house, "*Jennifer, get your coat on now*!"

Chapter 8

CENTENNIAL HOSPITAL
April 14, 1962
10:07 a.m.

Both Dr. Eagen and Dr. Snider were in Alex's room waiting for Marian and Norman. Alex was sitting on the edge of the bed with his feet dangling a foot from the floor. His back was ramrod straight with his palms flat on the bed beside his hips, ready to move him in any direction at a second's notice.

"So you decided that your folks are still alive, have you, Master Alex?" Dr. Snider expressed lightheartedly, trying to break the tension.

Alex said nothing but nodded slightly, not taking his eyes off the door to his room.

The doctors exchanged glances and Dr. Eagen raised an eyebrow.

"Your mom will probably bring you some clothes, don't you think?" asked Dr. Eagen in a further effort to defuse Alex's anxiety.

Alex again remained silent, hardly blinking, watching the door.

The time crept by at an agonizing pace. He sat stiffly as if waiting for someone to throw a switch, shooting a million volts through his body. He wasn't sure if he could go through with it. *You have no choice, Alexander. You either accept this reality for now or you're going to stay in this or some other "more specialized" hospital. You can do it, you can do it, you can....* The door suddenly opened and there was his mother.

Marian stopped just inside the door and looked at Alex, making no move toward him. She just stood and waited. Alex's head snapped back instantly when the door opened. He was nearly paralyzed from fear and tension. He fought hard not to turn away from the sight of this woman standing just a few feet away from him. His parents were dead; he knew that. The bodies had never been found, just some wreckage floating in the Pacific. But they were dead, all right. His mother had been just fifty-eight years old.

But here, standing in front of him was a young woman saying that she was his mother. She sure looked like a younger version of his mother; like the old pictures he kept in a special album. She had the same raven hair, same smooth beautiful skin, same height, same...same beautiful blue eyes. He could see the fear in this woman's eyes. He could see her tears welling up. *She's looking at me, and she's afraid... she's very afraid.*

"Oh God... oh Jesus!" Alex choked out. He could barely speak.

He slid down off the bed and stood for a moment, not breaking eye contact with his mother.

She smiled a small, tentative smile.

"Mom?" His chin began quivering.

"Yes Son, it's me," she nodded, tears spilling down her cheeks. She waited no longer. She took two quick strides and picked Alex up under his arms and held him to her tightly.

Alex reached up and locked his arms around his mother's neck and nearly broke down completely. Hallucination, dream, drugged or not, this was more than he could take. His emotional stability was nonexistent. He tried not to cry, but there was no way to stop; not today, not with the confusion, terror, and his mother.

Memories came flooding back in waves. Memories of his childhood that hadn't crossed his mind in twenty years or more. Memories of family dinners, vacations to South Dakota where his father was born and raised. Memories of Gabriel family get-togethers at Christmas and Easter with his father's side of the family. Thanksgiving dinners were always with his mother's side.

His memories were of a woman who, it seemed to him, dedicated her life to her family's well-being.

Alex couldn't stop crying. *Get a grip, man;* he chided himself. It was as if he were releasing all the pain and guilt he had suffered in the past six years since the crash.

"*...Alex...I don't know how to tell you this...your sister called while you were out...Jesus, Alex...your parents...*"

When Jason gave him the news of the terrible accident that killed his parents, he had gone into shock and had to be sedated. When the tranquilizers were discontinued, he went into a deep depression that lasted for many weeks. So now he just held his mother as tightly as his small arms could, and cried.

"Alex, sweetheart, it's okay; really it's okay," Marian managed to get out in a sort of half-whisper. She kept her arms around his small body and gave a little squeeze as she talked. The tremendous relief at having her son recognize her was apparent.

Dr. Snider was caught up in the emotion of the moment. He removed his wire-rimmed glasses, wiped his eyes, and blew his nose. He cleared his throat. "We'll leave you two for the moment." He touched Dr. Eagen on the arm and gestured toward the door. The two of them turned and left, closing the door quietly behind them.

"Oh God, I just don't know what's going on," Alex was finally able to choke out, "I just can't figure this out... something's really wrong here. This can't be real. This is a hallucination."

"*... the plane went down....*"

"It's all right, sweetheart. You're just a little confused right now. You'll be just fine in no time," she tried to assure her son.

"It's not all right...not at all. I've been...I've been..." He couldn't say it; he couldn't form the words. He desperately wanted to tell his mother that he had been shot back in time, a long way back. *Why can't I tell this...?* He tried again. "I've got to tell you that this.. this isn't..." *What the hell?... This is a hallucination, Alexander.*

Marian held her son for a few minutes; neither said anything.

"Why don't we sit here on the bed and talk a little?" Marian gently sat Alex on the bed and sat beside him. She looked deep into his eyes. "Dr. Snider told me that you got a really hard bang on the head. I'm sure that's why you're having so much trouble."

"I don't think that's it," he sniffled, "but I'm willing to accept that as a possibility for the time being." He continued to resolve himself to this reality.

Marian looked deeper into Alex's eyes, a puzzled look on her face. *"...his vocabulary seems to be nearly equal to that of an adult..."*

"I'm glad you're willing to accept the possibility." She smiled.

Alex was beginning to calm down and now couldn't keep his eyes off his mother.

They talked for another ten minutes. His mother told him that the old man who'd hit him had visited the hospital several times to check on him. "We finally convinced him you were going to be fine. I don't think he's been back. He was a nice old fella."

Alex had no memory of being hit, or of an old man.

Marian was observing Alex's reactions to everything she told him. She was quite concerned, but managed to hide it well.

"Oh, shoot!" said Marian, "I forgot to tell you that your father is in a meeting at work, but he'll be here a little later."

Alex's facial expression suddenly changed.

"What's the matter, sweetheart?"

Alex just shook his head; couldn't talk. Of course, he'd forgotten; his father would be part of this hallucination, too. He started to tear up again.

This time Marian was better prepared to handle Alex's emotions. "Your dad is just fine... healthy as a horse." She kept her voice as light as possible.

"His thumb is still pretty sore, though," she added as an afterthought. She watched Alex carefully. "He asked me to give you a kiss for him." Marian leaned over and gave Alex a kiss on the forehead. "There you go."

Alex had never had a confused second in his first life. Now everything was topsy-turvy. "Thanks," he managed to get out. He knew he needed time to compose himself. He knew he was getting caught up in this hallucination but couldn't stop himself.

"Oh darn," said Marian. "I forgot about Jennifer, too. Be back in a minute." She jumped up and headed for the door.

"Jennifer?"

Marian turned back to Alex, her brow wrinkled. "Your sister, Alex; your older sister."

"Oh, of course. Jen."

She turned and headed out the door. Alex watched her as she left. He was trying to gain control and figure...figure what?

Marian returned to the room in less than a minute with Jennifer.

"Hi, Alex," Jennifer said cautiously, feeling a little guilty perhaps. It was obvious that not only had her mother been crying, but her little brother as well. It was possible she had never seen either cry before. She looked from Alex to her mother and back again.

Alex looked at his sister as if he were still trying to figure out who she was. The last time he had seen Jennifer, she was going on forty-five and that was just a week ago. Now she was maybe nine or ten years old. *...This hallucination is consistent, I'll give it that. Everybody is the right age for 1962...*

"Jen?" He looked at her quizzically.

"Yeah, it's me all right."

All Alex could do was look away. He couldn't get a handle on these circumstances. Tears were still running down his cheeks.

"Do you hurt bad?" Jennifer asked with uncharacteristic compassion.

He looked back at her, still puzzled. "Some, I suppose."

"Gee, I thought you were dead for a while."

"Not sure I'm not, kid." *Maybe that's it; maybe I've been killed and I'm in some sort of purgatory, paying my dues!*

"Kid?" questioned Jennifer.

"Alex, please don't say things like that. You're not dead and you're not going to die; you're just injured, and you've had a terrible scare." Marian was clearly back in control of her emotions. Her son was at least communicating.

"Wasn't my fault, you know! I told you not to cross yet, but oh, no, you just had to go anyway. And don't call me kid; I'm older than you, ya know."

"Jennifer, it doesn't matter, even a little bit, whose fault it was," said Marian. "It was an accident. End of story!"

Alex just looked at Jennifer. He had no idea what she was talking about. The toll of the past two days, the emotions, the injuries, the drugs were having a cumulative effect. He could barely keep his eyes open. As much as he wanted to remain awake and track what was happening to him, he couldn't.

Marian saw that her son was completely done in. She caressed his cheek and said, "Why don't you lie down and take a little nap. Jennifer and I will leave you alone for a while." She helped him lie back on the bed and pulled the sheet up to cover him.

3:24 p.m.

"*Will you let go of my fucking hand*?" Alex screamed. He began to fight furiously to break the grip of this pain-in-the-ass Congressman, but to no avail. The harder he pulled, the tighter became the grip.

"Alex, wake up; you're having a bad dream...come on, wake up, wake up."

Alex awoke and saw a buxom blonde nurse. It was she who had his hand and he was still weakly trying to break free. "Oh shit!" His heart was pounding so hard that he could hear it in his ears. His breath came in short gasps. "Please let go of my hand."

"Oh sure." She let go immediately. "I'm sorry."

"It's all right; just part of my nightmare," he gasped. His rapid pulse began subsiding quickly, his breathing slowing. He brought his hand up and took a look; dropped it back to his side.

The nurse had an odd expression; she probably hadn't heard the "f" word -- or for that matter "shit" -- from someone so young. He was asleep at the time; nevertheless, it took her by surprise.

The dream was still vivid in Alex's mind. He suddenly realized why he'd had the nightmare. It was a flashback to the last bit of business Jason and he had done before heading to Central Oregon for their ski vacation. In fact, he remembered, it had happened just last week. The meeting with the Mayor and the Congressman had left a bad taste in Alex's mouth. He couldn't tolerate corruption and this Congressman was corrupt. Alex, Jason and F. C. Guyot, the CEO of a large brokerage house, were representing the West Coast Investment Counsel in an attempt to garner support for a bill before Congress. The bill would effectively eliminate about a year's worth of red tape when trying to rewrite poorly written and archaic securities rules. The Congressman didn't understand the first thing about securities, nor had he bothered to read the bill, but for a substantial contribution to his "re-election campaign," he would sure vote for that "dandy" piece of legislation. The best government money could buy, Alex thought with disdain. The Congressman kept holding Alex's hand during the dream as if he were a father with an unruly child.

The nurse put her hand to Alex's forehead, which was a bit clammy. She checked his pulse, walked to the end of the bed, took the chart from the hook, and made notations. "Looks like it's time for a couple of pills, young man. How do you feel?"

"Like I was picked up, shaken hard and dropped from a tall building, as a matter of fact," he managed to get out without groaning.

"Is that so?" laughed the rotund, blonde nurse. She had a much better attitude and bedside manner than the grouch in attendance the previous morning. "That was pretty funny. Are you always this funny?" she asked as she again looked at his chart. Her eyebrows rose when she saw that this young boy was being given a tranquilizer, and a fairly strong dose at that. She replaced the chart on its hook.

"Only the times I've been critically injured," Alex smiled.

"Critically injured, are you?" She smiled back while putting a pain pill and tranquilizer in the tiny paper cup. After handing them to Alex, she went over to the sink and put some water in a plastic cup, added a bent straw, and returned to Alex's side. She helped him sit up to take the pills.

"Ouch, oh shit!" exclaimed Alex. He was in pain again. It_was worse than it had been before he'd gone to sleep. He paused to let the sharp pain in his ribs subside somewhat before taking the pills. "Thanks," he said as the nurse helped him back down to the pillow. "May I have a little more water, plea...?"

His mother walked into the room. She was wearing different clothes and had refreshed her makeup.

Alex smiled broadly at his mother. How long had he been asleep, he wondered?

"Hi, Mom."

"Hi, sweetheart."

He hadn't remembered how pretty his mother had been at this age. She was so young and strong. Her black hair was thick and shiny and hung just past her shoulders. She was nearly five foot eight, and it seemed that a great deal of that height was her legs. She always had a great deal of class.

"Geeze, I'll bet your mom is the prettiest in school...like a movie star," Alex remembered his friend, Teddy, saying more than once.

She had changed from the dark blue business suit she was wearing when last he saw her. She was now in a pair of tan slacks, and a white blouse with a maroon Gaucho-style jacket. *Professional- looking,* he thought. In another decade or so she would definitely be considered a yuppie.

"I'm sorry I wasn't here when you woke up. As exhausted as you were, I figured you'd be out for another couple of hours." Marian sat on the edge of the bed. "How are you feeling?"

"Physically, I have a great deal of discomfort, but mentally, I believe I'm making great strides forward," he responded seriously.

Marian cocked her head. "I'm sorry you're hurting, but I'm delighted you're making great strides in the mental department."

Alex could see that his mother was puzzled. "Something wrong?" he asked.

Marian smiled at her son. "Nope, I don't think so."

Alex had always been proud of his parents. His mother, at this point in her life, was an executive secretary for Dan Duvia, Executive Vice President of SARC, Scientific and Aerospace Research Corporation, one of the leading space research companies in the west. At the age of twenty-nine, she was the youngest woman to hold such a position in the huge company. Alex remembered SARC had paid his mother well, and remembered Dan Duvia treating her with a great deal of respect. Dan apparently knew that he would not be where he was without Marian.

His father was a scientist with SARC, doing research in pressure hull design. SARC was, as a matter of fact, where his parents met.

Marian had always been a take-charge kind of person and pretty much ran the Gabriel household. His dad was no wimp, by any means, but decision making for everyday, mundane matters was not something that particularly interested him. The key to the Gabriel home, Alex felt, was the deep love that his parents had for each other.

Chapter 9

CENTENNIAL HOSPITAL
APRIL 15, 1962
9:30 a.m.

"He's going to be sleepy for a day or two and that's normal; not to worry. Keep him down for a week or so, if you can. I imagine those ribs will be sore for at least three weeks. Feed him light foods for a few days, soups and such," Dr. Snider went on. "Tell him that if he sees any blood when he goes to the bathroom, to tell you right away. You hear that, Alex?"

"Yes, sir," replied Alex.

"Yuck," remarked Jennifer, displaying an expression of total disdain.

Assuming this whole thing was a hallucination caused by head trauma, Alex was amazed at how well he was able to play along with it. Tranquilizers or not, he should, by all rights, be in a mental institution secured by a diminutive straight jacket.

"I've written three prescriptions. One is an antibiotic, one is to control the pain, and the other should keep him calm. Be sure he takes the entire dose of the antibiotic, but you might cut back on the pain pills in a day or two. You'll have to play that by ear. We try to get people off pain pills as soon as possible. Not good for anyone, especially young people, to take them for too long. You need to keep in contact with Pam Eagen about the tranquilizers." Dr. Snider nodded at Marian and then handed her three prescriptions.

Alex had overheard the conversation between Dr. Eagen and Marian about the tranquilizers. *Better keep him on the tranquilizers for a few days, Mrs. Gabriel. They are a lot stronger than I would normally recommend for a child but they seem to be the right thing for now.*

"Thanks, Dr. Snider; you've been wonderful." She took the doctor's hand. "I want to apologize for being such an emotional wreck when we first met; I'm usually better in a crisis."

"No apology necessary, Mrs. Gabriel. This has been a traumatic experience for a mother to go through." He shook her hand with both of his.

"I'll keep in touch." She smiled brightly at the doctor, and then she looked over at Alex. "You ready?"

"As ready as I'll ever be, I suppose."

The blonde nurse helped Alex into a wheelchair and proceeded to push him past the door into the hall.

"This is a funny young man you've got here. Has he always been so funny?" the nurse asked Marian as they wound around the corridors heading for the front door.

"I don't know about funny, but he has always been clever...quite clever."

"Alex isn't funny," stated Jennifer. "Teddy's really funny, though.

"Yes he is," agreed Marian.

"*Teddy*?" thought Alex. *Something about Teddy?* He became completely confused again for a brief moment. He knew that this couldn't be real, yet somehow it couldn't be more real. He was amazed that he was not, at this time, terrified, or for that matter, even frightened. Here he had been hit by a truck, shot back thirty-five years, and regained consciousness lying in a gutter on Prairie Avenue in Inglewood. He was confused and in mild pain yes, but not terrified, just a little frightened.

They exited the hospital and, with help, Alex managed to get out of the wheelchair. He took his mother's offered hand.

"Alex, tell me how you feel," Marian said as they walked slowly toward the parking lot.

"How do I feel?" Alex thought for a moment, grinned and

responded, "Painful bewilderment would pretty much sum it up, I believe." He continued looking at the world around him.

"Painful bewilderment?" asked Marian.

"Alex is talking kinda funny," remarked Jennifer.

"So I've noticed," replied Marian as they entered the parking lot.

Other than the pain that, excluding his ribs, had subsided considerably, Alex was actually starting to enjoy this experience. *I don't seem to be in any real danger right now, may as well enjoy this while I can. Bound to snap out of it sooner or later.*

"Well, get in, kids. Jennifer in back and Alex, you're in front," Marian instructed. "And both of you buckle up in those seat belts. We paid extra for them, you know."

"Why do I always have to get in the back?" Jennifer whined.

"Jennifer, you can sit in the front if you want," Alex offered with no rancor.

This statement apparently took Jennifer and Marian both by surprise. They looked at each other with furrowed brows. Not that Alex was mean or selfish as a rule, but when it came to his sister, he could be and was pretty cold most of the time. Marian tried to make peace between them, but Jennifer would have none of it and Alex would always say, "It's up to her." From the time Alex was born, when Jennifer was almost two, she displayed excessive jealousy. Marian realized that Alex sensed this hostility from an early age. His sister was the only person whom Alex would treat badly and would do so just about every chance he got, and he was good at it. Jennifer had given up playing dirty tricks on her brother. Every time she did, he either caused it to backfire on her or somehow got even.

Jennifer just stood there now and stared at Alex, her mouth open. Then her eyes narrowed, "What are you gonna do, Alex, slam the door on me before I get all the way in the car?" she spat out.

"Good Lord no, Jen; why would I do that?" responded Alex, really taken back. *Jesus, was I that mean to my sister at this age*? he thought sadly.

As they drove by the spot where Alex was hit by the old pickup truck, Jennifer yelled, "That's where it happened, Alex!" pointing to the place where just three days before, he lay unconscious in the street.

"I found your shoe on the other side of the street," said Jennifer. "The top part was torn nearly off the bottom part," Jennifer went on. "Mom picked up a bunch of your school papers off the street and out of some bushes, too. You're probably gonna have to do em over, ya know." Jennifer turned and gave a nasty little smile to her brother.

"Jen, sometimes you really try my patience," Marian muttered as she took a left on 112th Street and headed to their home two blocks away.

10:37 a.m.

Marian helped Alex walk into the house, and got him undressed and into bed.

"Well, sweetheart, looks like you're out of school for a week or so. I'm sure that's going to break your little heart," she whispered as she tucked him in.

"School?" he expressed sleepily, hardly able to keep his eyes open.

"Yes, school, Sweetheart, you know the three Rs, readin', 'ritin', 'rithmatic?"

I can't go to school with a bunch of eight-year-olds, thought Alex. *Hey, get serious... Jesus Christ!* It hadn't occurred to him that school was still part of his life at this age.

"Your dad will be home in about ten minutes; I'll send him in to see you and then you're to get a lot of sleep."

"Dad?"

"Yes, you know the parent that shaves, deep voice, stuff like that?" she teased Alex, and gave him a little peck on the cheek.

Alex was asleep in two minutes and his father did not to wake him.

Chapter 10

GABRIEL HOME
APRIL 16, 1962
4:20 a.m.

Alex woke up early the next morning, still in pain, but less than the previous day. His mind had cleared considerably and he immediately began running though the possibilities of his predicament. *If I don't have a massive skull fracture and brain damage, wasn't drugged, and this isn't a dream, then maybe I am eight years old and I dreamed an entire lifetime to age forty-three.* He pondered that for several seconds. *I have way too many detailed memories for that. What the hell, could it be..insanity? Is my drum off cadence with the world?* In the dim light provided by a street lamp, he looked around his room

Alex wondered for the hundredth time how long it would be before he snapped out of it. Or *would* he snap out of it? If he didn't, how long would it be before his folks realized that there was more wrong than a concussion; a lot more? How long would it be before they forced him to face endless tests? Therapy? Shock treatments? "*Oh shit*!"

He wondered if he were forced to live his life over again, would it be a different challenge from the first time around? Or would it be a replay? Would he again start a brokerage firm, branch into investment banking and venture capital, and develop other companies as the years went by? Would there be Gabriel Industries? Would Jason be his best friend and partner again in the future?

Alex was the CEO and President of Gabriel Industries, or at least he had been in his past life. With Jason's help, he had created one of the most successful investment brokerages on the West Coast. Their peers, in fact, referred to them as the "Golden Boys." Alex smiled to himself as he remembered how they were forced to turn away potentially valuable clients for lack of time and help. Jason, in the early years, spent ten to twenty percent of his time recruiting the best and brightest securities people, investment bankers, and analysts from around the country. A job he did extremely well, Alex remembered fondly.

Alex recalled clearly the day he opened the doors and plugged in his phones: It was November 11th, 1980. It was after college and a short apprenticeship in his uncle's brokerage firm in downtown Inglewood. But his experience in investing began long before that. Since the age of eleven, he had an absorbing interest in the "investment world." He remembered clearly that life-altering day in 1965...

"Alexander, my boy," said his Uncle Walt, "your mother tells me you have quite a nice bank account from money you earned on your paper route."

"Yep, have nearly three hundred and twelve bucks and getting three percent interest on it." Alex remembered being quite proud of his "small fortune." "Compounded weekly, you know!"

Walt smiled. "What would you think of letting me invest it for you?"

"What about me, Uncle Walt?" Jennifer jumped in before Alex could answer. She wasn't about to be left out of anything. If it was good for Alex, she had to have it, too. "I've got baby-sitting money."

The three of them were sitting at a round white table in the local ice cream shop.

"Oh sure, Jenny, I'm sorry. I guess I didn't realize you were gainfully employed."

"What do you mean, invest it?" Alex was all ears while ignoring his sister's interruption.

As it turned out, Alex, as a boy, saved more than half of every penny he ever got his hands on, which was represented by the "small fortune" he had in the bank.

Jennifer was not at all frugal and spent most of her money on movies, records and such things that pleased thirteen-year-old girls. When it came time to actually hand over their money to Uncle Walt, only Alex still had the cash. Jennifer never said anything more about it.

Alex recalled that from the time he put his first money in the market in the summer of '65, he had a new and totally engrossing hobby. He lived and breathed the investment world. He remembered his parents and Walt talking about his unique abilities from that time on. It was clear to them and Alex that he had found his true vocation at an early age.

Starting in his junior year of high school, Alex had worked summers in his uncle's brokerage firm. At first he did odd jobs, janitorial mostly, then worked his way into filing and then to clerking. In his spare time, which became limited, he studied every facet of the business. By the time he graduated, near the top of his class at UCLA, he had a BS in economics and was just a year away from earning his master's. At the end of the following year, his net worth was over two million dollars. At the age of twenty-three, he was fully capable of running his own brokerage, but decided to acquire two more years of experience with his uncle's firm, much to his uncle's delight.

"*Marian, my nephew - your handsome son - is a genius, an absolute genius*!" Alex smiled at the memory.

He was a genius, not only in his uncle's opinion but in time, by all accounts. Alex had an uncanny ability to recognize the potential in newly formed companies and up-and-coming management. He also had the courage of his convictions and invested heavily in these new offers. He generally avoided investing in the safer "blue chip" stocks, except when he felt something was "in the wind" that might dramatically effect these relatively passive investments. His ability to remember hundreds, if not thousands, of successful companies from their stock issue dates, to the size of the issue, to opening prices and highs and lows, bordered on the supernatural. By the time he was thirty, he was considered one of the top investment minds on the West Coast. Alex smiled as he brought himself out of this nostalgic trip to his past. *That was then, but this is before any of that happened.*

5:30 a.m.

Alex lay there in his old familiar child's bed. Looking around the room in the pre-dawn light, he could make out his chest-of-drawers, a hand-me-down from his sister. His sister got their parents' complete bedroom set after his parents bought new furniture.

His closet door stood ajar, but it was too dark to see inside. He spotted his baseball bat with the small first baseman's glove sitting on top. They were right where he'd always kept them, leaning in the corner by the door; the wicker hamper next to them. Everything still looked to be nearly new. *Must not have had them long at this point.* That glove was pretty beat up the last time Alex had seen it. His mind again drifted back to his childhood. His fondest memories were of his best friend, Teddy, whom he hadn't seen for what, twenty-one years? What had become of him? Why hadn't they kept in touch? What was he doing now? *Jesus, Alexander, what are you doing now? Here you are back in '62, eight years old, lying in your old bed and thinking about your past, when you had better start thinking of your immediate future, if there is to be any.*

Can it be that Jason is only, what, five or six years old? Jesus! Alex thought about all they had accomplished together; all the long hours, the planning, the sweat, the sacrifice each went through. *Gone? No, not gone… just hasn't happened yet.* He thought about their brokerage firm, the philanthropic organization, the political arm. *Is it possible that none of it has ever been? How could that be?*

Alex's mind kept churning for hours, sorting and filing his limited information. Although he kept telling himself that this was an elaborate dream, that he would wake up and laugh about it, he really was beginning to doubt that was the truth. *I just don't have enough information,* he thought. His big question remained how something like this could happen. This wasn't a movie with some sort of weird retrogression plot; this was damned serious and somehow quite real.

Well, Alexander, unless something changes things back to the right time and place, he mused, *and for some reason, I'm beginning to think it won't, you'd better figure out how to make the best of an... untenable situation.*

The age old question is, "If I had to do it all over again... and it looks as if I might, what would I do differently?" he asked himself; then thought, *Differently? Not much. If I just had more time...I might...* Alex switched thoughts. *It's beginning to look like I might have a lot more time!*

8:05 a.m.

Alex had a great deal to think about. First thing was to develop a plan that would keep him out of school. In a week or so, he would be back in third grade and that would be ridiculous.

There was a light knock on the door and Marian came in quietly. She knelt by his bed and whispered, "You awake, sweetheart?"

Okay, take it easy, he admonished himself. "Yep."

"How do you feel?" she asked, concerned.

"Have pains all over the place. Geeze." *Geeze?* thought Alex. *Haven't said that in...?*

"I'll bet you do. I'll get you a pain pill." Marian walked over to Alex's dresser and retrieved a pill from one of the three small bottles lined up in front of the mirror. "If this doesn't work soon, I'll call Dr. Snider and see if there is something stronger he would recommend for a little kid like you."

There are no other little kids like me, thought Alex. *None at all.*

His mother and father were the part of this hallucination or phenomenon that was confusing him more than anything. His life these past six years without them had seemed so incomplete. He had never fully accepted the fact that they were gone. At least if he had been able to see the bodies, there could have been closure. After the crash, whenever something good happened or a major hurdle was overcome, he found himself mentally sharing the news with his parents, as he would have done by phone or in person had they still been alive. More than once, he said aloud, "Boy, I wish you two were here to see this."

Alex had little memory of what a beautiful woman his mother was at this age. She, of course, was always beautiful to him, but he was now looking at her more objectively. There were his treasured old pictures, but they didn't begin to do her justice; didn't show the sparkle. He couldn't recall her appearance as she was in her late twenties, other than bits and pieces of scattered memories. His most vivid memory was how she looked when she and his father boarded the plane to Hawaii. It was a mental image forever imprinted in his mind. An image of a beautiful and distinguished looking fifty-eight-year-old woman, smiling and waving as they entered the jetway.

"...Your sister called while you were out... your parents.. The plane..."

"Is there any place that hurts worse than your ribs, for instance?" She was talking and Alex was looking at her. But not his usual way; he seemed to be distracted.

"Well?"

"What?" Alex had drifted.

"Does any place hurt worse than your ribs?" Marian's brow furrowed. She obviously wasn't used to repeating herself with Alex; he had always paid close attention to everything she said, unlike Jennifer. This would take a bunch of getting used to if it continued.

"Oh, I'm sorry, no. My ribs pretty much lead the pack of pain," he responded, "closely followed by my head."

"Lead the pack of pain?" She laughed. "That's pretty cute, Son."

That was pretty cute, Alex thought. *Maybe too cute for an eight-year-old.*

"Boy, my side over here really hurts," Alex almost moaned,

pointing at his lower left rib cage.

"I guess that's where the old truck smacked you one. That's going to be sore for a few weeks, I bet. Let me take a look at it."

Alex rolled to his side and lifted his pajama top.

"Wow," exclaimed Marian. "That's colorful! Darn near see the bumper marks on your ribs." She pulled the top back down. "Anywhere else hurt a bunch?"

"I'm just real sore all over."

"I'm sure you are." Marian put her palm on Alex's forehead. His skin felt a bit clammy, but not too bad. "Your dad really wants to see you. I'll see if I can pull him away from his morning paper." she smiled, patted Alex on the shoulder, stood and walked over to the door.

"Norm, sweetheart, come on in; he's awake."

Alex could hear the rustling of papers and his father's recliner squeaking.

"Hi, Son; how you doing?" Alex's father inquired as he came into the room. He had that big ingratiating smile on his face.

Alex tried hard not to tear up at seeing his dad. He'd seen him briefly in the hospital but he was in a completely different frame of mind at the time. To see him now so young and healthy with a look of concern and love on his face almost shattered his reserve. His eyes welled up and he could feel his chin twitching, but he didn't cry. His thoughts momentarily flashed back to his memories of his father at this time in history.... *time to teach you to play catch, Son.... keep your eye on the ball...don't look away... See what happens when you don't keep...*

"I'll be okay, it just hurts a little," Alex half croaked as he wiped away the tears with the back of his hand.

Alex then reached his hands out and his father bent over and picked Alex up out of the bed, embracing him in a gentle hug.

Oh my, this is my father holding me again...oh...

"I hear you're a pretty tough little kid," Norman said softly. "Your sister tells me you played Superman and flew all the way across Prairie Avenue." He held Alex out at arm's length and looked him in the eye. "Shoulda landed on your feet, though. I found it doesn't hurt as much that way," he teased as he held Alex against him again. "But I suppose that takes quite a bit of practice," he said, resuming a softer, more concerned tone.

Alex could feel his father shiver just a little.

"Don't think I want to practice that anymore." He almost said, "Pop" but caught himself and said "Dad." He didn't start calling his father Pop until he was in high school.

"No, I don't suppose you do, kid." Norman gently returned his boy to the bed. "Your mother and I love you a lot, you know? You had us both so worried."

Alex nodded, "I know." He looked deep into his father's eyes. "I can't tell you how wonderful it is to see you again." Alex nearly choked up.

Norman's brow furrowed. "It's only been a couple of days, kid."

"A couple of days," Alex whispered quietly. "Just a couple of days." His voiced trailed off as he looked away. Tears started flowing again.

"Well, tell me all about it. What happened?" Norman asked with as much cheer as he could muster.

"*What happened*?" Alex didn't have a clue.

Chapter 11

GABRIEL HOME
April 19, 1962
7:30 a.m.

This was the seventh day after the "accident" and most of the pain was subsiding, except for his ribs. They still hurt. He had developed a small cough that managed to elevate that pain to a new level.

Alex was getting used to the circumstances in which he found himself. Although his confusion was still enormous, he found that he could remember more and interact better with his past childhood than he would have thought possible. He chalked it up to his memories being unlocked by the old and familiar surroundings.

10:10 a.m.

"Alex, Teddy's here to see you," Marian called from the front room.

"Who?" Alex yelled back from his room.

"Teddy, and he's heading your way."

"*Hi, Alex*!" Teddy Oldaker shouted cheerfully as he burst into Alex's room. "Geeze, let me see where you got run over." This was apparently quite exciting to young Teddy.

"Teddy?" Alex said with a quizzical smile on his face. Then he inexplicably began to tense up. He hadn't seen Teddy since they had graduated from high school. *Is that right? Was it high school? Or was it after that? Can't remember.* Alex's mind began to spin. He thought he remembered the Oldakers moving to Arizona shortly after high school graduation, but could not remember anything about them after that -- nothing at all. Teddy had been his best friend all his life through high school. They were inseparable until...until what? Until they moved? That didn't seem right. Now, here was his dear friend again, but ten years younger than he was the last time Alex had seen him.

"*...movin to Arizona... June.*"

"Of course, it's me, whatdidyathink?" asked Teddy with a big toothy grin. "You sure don't look like I thought you would after you gettin runned over." Teddy was looking Alex over from top to bottom.

"*...going to miss you, old buddy...been like brothers...we'll get together in...*"

"Teddy?" Alex repeated to himself, trying to instill the thought solidly in his mind. He was having trouble comprehending this new circumstance. Tears began to form in the corners of his eyes. *Teddy Oldaker!* his mind screamed, then screamed the name again. A barrier came down.

"Teddy!" Alex's mind suddenly and inexplicably cleared. "Oh my God! It's great to see you after all this time," Alex exclaimed as he grabbed Teddy and gave him a big hug, regretting that move instantly, but gritted his teeth and continued to hug his best friend. His tears were dampening Teddy's right ear where their heads met.

"All what time, Alex? it's only been a week since I seen you. And what's this huggin' stuff?" Teddy pushed Alex away. He could see the tears in his best friend's eyes. He could feel them on his ear, but he said nothing. Alex was never a crybaby.

Alex started laughing as he released Teddy. The pain in his ribs seemed to increase tenfold. *Jesus, this has gotta be one of the cutest kids on the planet.*

Teddy's Dodgers baseball cap was "on lock." The bill looked as if it were pulled straight down to the eyebrows and then torqued about 45-degrees to the right, not quite to his ear. Mother Nature had replaced his baby teeth with the biggest, whitest teeth in the history of the world and Teddy had a huge grin, accented with perfect dimples, to show them off.

"I've got to tell you, Teddy... I'm so happy to see you," Alex managed to get out while holding onto his ribs, slightly bent over. *Oh shit, no more hugging for a while.*

"You're acting kinda funny, Alex. Maybe you better take a nap, or maybe you forgot to take some pills or somethin'. I'll go tell your mom. She'll probably know what to do," Teddy said sincerely, and started out the door.

"...is a bad cut, Alex...I'll go get your mom...she'll know..."

This statement started Alex's mind whirling again, long-ago emotions being forced to the surface. A mixture of pain and joy, laughing and crying at once, and again the pain.

"Wait, wait, Teddy," Alex choked out. "I'm fine really. It's just that things seem a little strange...today. I got knocked on my head, ya know. It screwed up my brains a little, but the doctor said I'd be all right after a while."

Teddy turned back and looked at Alex for a second, obviously not quite sure what he should do. Apparently, he had never known Alex to act like this. "It doesn't look like you're havin' much fun. I'll go get your mom."

"It's okay, Teddy, really. Just give me a second."

Alex could nearly feel the force of his friend's scrutiny. Teddy actually cocked his head while looking into Alex's eyes, looking for something, some clue to his friend's odd behavior.

"Can you go out and play, then?" ask Teddy after a second, his face brightening a little, probably hoping this question wouldn't make Alex act funny again.

"....Mrs. Gabriel, can Alex come out and play?... me and Freddie.."

"I don't think so today, Teddy. I really did get hurt when that truck hit me and I'll need to take it easy for a while," Alex responded as he managed to straighten up a bit. "Why don't we play here for a while and I'll try to get out in a few days?" *Jesus,* thought Alex, *this kid should be in movies.* He didn't remember Teddy's extraordinary facial expressions. Right now, Teddy's expression was one of complete confusion.

Chapter 12

GABRIEL HOME
April 22, 1962
9:15 a.m.

"Your mom says it will be all right for you to go out for a little while," Teddy exclaimed as he ran into Alex's room three days later.

Again he had on that Dodgers baseball cap, and again it was on lock. To complete his ensemble, he wore an orange, brown, and yellow horizontally striped t-shirt, about a size too small, and a pair of old blue jeans so large they had to be hand-me-downs from his overweight older cousin who lived just a short block away. The waist was so big around that an oversized belt was required to pull the belt loops close together, which left shallow pleats running around his waist like drapes. The legs of these hand-me-downs were rolled up about five times, leaving a heavy looking three-inch cuff sitting atop his worn-out, high top black Converse sneakers.

Alex took one look at Teddy and began giggling; then after another look, started laughing so hard that sharp shooting pains began radiating from his damaged ribs, but he could not stop.

Teddy turned and ran out of the bedroom. *Uh-oh*! Alex could see that his abnormal behavior was scaring his young friend.

Teddy headed straight to the dining room where Marian was helping Jennifer with her homework. Alex was right on his heels. The two found Marian in more or less the same condition as Alex.

He surmised that she'd had the good fortune of answering the front door when Teddy knocked and could only imagine her reaction. He could see that his mother was trying desperately not to laugh, but was having about as much success as he'd had. She kept wiping her tears with the back of her hand while trying to stifle her chuckles.

Jennifer took a quick look at Alex's best friend and couldn't help but laugh herself; something she tried to avoid when it came to anything to do with Alex or his friends.

Clearly Teddy was now totally perplexed. All he could do was stand there and look up at Marian with considerable confusion in those huge, soft brown eyes.

Marian smiled warmly as she bent down to give Teddy a big hug.

"We're all right, Teddy," she said softly, while sitting back on her heels, her eyes level with Teddy's. "It's just that sometimes when someone you love gets hurt like Alex did, and everyone is real worried for a long time, you tend to act silly over almost nothing." She paused as she again wiped her tears with the back of her hand. "Then you come in here looking as cute as anyone can possibly look and we just have to laugh." She gave him another hug. "I really want to thank you for cheering Alex up, Teddy. Nobody else could have done it as well."

Alex could see Teddy pondering this for a moment before his face brightened. Marian's words seemed to have pacified and pleased him immensely. He turned and gave Alex a big smile.

Alex smiled back. "Okay Teddy, let's hit the road." Alex was determined not to laugh at Teddy again if he could help it.

As they headed for the front door, Alex was thinking what a wonderful person his mother was. He stopped and gave her a kiss and whispered, "Good job."

As they started out the front door, Alex looked back. "See you in a while."

"Okay, Son. Be careful with that banged-up little body of yours," she called after him.

Alex was apprehensive about stepping into the world of his past.

He didn't know what to expect, or what eight-year-old boys did.

He and Teddy stopped on the front porch for a second, giving Alex time to get his bearings. He was still on pain meds and tranquilizers, causing him to look around in a mild daze. He could smell the smog. It was mixed with the aroma of a freshly cut lawn and just a whiff of ocean thrown in. The smell instantly shot him back to his childhood. *This is my childhood,* he thought. *This is my childhood...damn!*

The boys both turned and looked west at the same time toward a sudden, god-awful racket. It was old Mr. Eshbach, from across the street, barreling down 112th in his 1938 Ford coupe. Black smoke was shooting out the rear while gray smoke or steam exited from around the hood. The old junker sounded like it had a hole in its muffler about the size of a grapefruit. To top it off, Eshbach, about a year before, had hand-painted his vehicle Kelly green with a thick bristled house brush. You could actually see the brush strokes from a hundred feet or so. Mr. Eshbach, as usual, swung into his driveway too fast, making the front suspension appear to be made of pogo sticks, bouncing the front of the car up and down, while bottoming out three times before coming to a halt about a foot shy of the closed garage.

Alex and Teddy laughed spontaneously.

Boy, that takes me back, thought Alex as he brought his left hand up to his ribs.

"Bet Mr. Eshbach is drinking again," stated Teddy, still giggling. "My dad says he'll run through that garage door some day."

"Wouldn't be surprised, Teddy."

112th street in 1962. Damn, hard to believe this area is rated as one of the most dangerous areas in southern California in 1997, and there will be a lot of dangerous areas down here, thought Alex. *Seems kind of peaceful now, but the smog is horrible. Can't see a half a mile.* Alex knew it would be a few years before they started cleaning up the air enough to make a difference. *Makes a person want to quit breathing, or move.*

"Let's go over and see what Fred is doing. Maybe we can play with his trains if they're set up," suggested Teddy enthusiastically.

"Great, Teddy, right on," Alex responded with forced enthusiasm. *Gotta see what Fred looks like at eight years old.* Alex smiled to himself as they stepped off the porch and cut across the Gabriel's front yard, heading east toward Yukon Avenue.

"Right on what?" ask Teddy as they walked slowly toward Yukon Avenue. Alex still had a slight limp.

"Right on the mark, you know... good plan."

"Oh!" Teddy shot a sideways glance at Alex.

...Your friend Teddy is a smart kid, you know...

Alex felt that if he was going to be stuck in the past, even if it was a hallucination, he had better get used to everything and everybody connected with it. He wondered if it would be as much fun seeing Fred as it was seeing Teddy. Fred, as he recalled, started hanging around with the artsy set in high school and became somewhat of a beatnik. The last Alex had heard, Fred had headed east and was living in a loft in Greenwich Village, trying to take a bite of the Big Apple.

"Hi, Teddy, hi Alex," called Joanne and Eileen from the Buyers' front yard. The two neighborhood girls, about a year younger than the boys, were sitting on a blanket playing with a tiny black and white kitten.

Alex turned and stared at them for a second before he recognized who they were. "Well, I'll be damned," he exclaimed and started up the slight rise in the yard.

"Where you goin', Alex?" asked Teddy.

"I'm going to go see Joanne and uh...uh?"

"Eileen!"

"Yeah right, Eileen!"

"They're girls, Alex. Let's go see Fred. Come on." Teddy apparently held girls in somewhat lower esteem than dog-doo on his shoe.

Alex looked over at Teddy and smiled. He realized young boys wanted nothing to do with girls. “Just be a second, just want to say hi...haven’t seen these two for years.”

“You mean days, and who cares anyway, they’re girls, come on, let’s go.” Teddy had no patience at all.

“OK, Teddy, we’re going. See ya, ladies.”

“Ladies? They’re just girls. Don’t ya know that?” Teddy again looked sideways at Alex. “That bash on your head made you a little goofy.”

“A little, I guess.” Alex smiled. He knew Teddy wasn’t trying to be insulting; he was just offering an opinion.

12:05 p.m.

Alex hopped up on a stool located at the pass through counter which separated the kitchen from the dining room. Jennifer was already there. She had her chin cupped in her hands, her elbows on the counter; she looked bored. Marian was in the kitchen, making peanut butter and jelly sandwiches, as she hummed along with a song playing on the radio.

“Hi, Jen; hi, Mom.”

Jennifer said nothing and didn’t bother to look in Alex’s direction.

Marian turned and smiled. “Hi, Son. How was your first morning out?”

“Eventful, I would say.”

“Really?” Marian continued putting the sandwiches together.

“Really. I assume most days around here don’t produce quite so much excitement.”

Marian stopped what she was doing and looked at Alex. “Most days?” Her brow furrowed. “What happened?”

“Nothing too serious. First, we watched Mr. Eshbach nearly drive through his garage door.”

“That’s nearly a daily occurrence,” remarked Marian.

“So I gathered. Then we spotted Joanne and Eileen. I was surprised to see them again after all this...” Alex abruptly stopped.

"All what?" asked Marian.

"Time. I don't think I've seen them for weeks," said Alex in a recovery effort.

Marian was studying Alex. "I wouldn't think you'd care too much about seeing some girls."

Jennifer looked at her brother.

"That was certainly Teddy's attitude." Alex smiled.

"I could imagine," said Marian as she finished making the sandwiches. "That's all that happened?"

"Oh, no! That was just the beginning. Right after we left the girls we ran into three punks sitting on a retaining wall over on 111th."

"Oh?"

"I'd guess they were about twelve or thirteen. I assume they're neighborhood bullies. One of them was a pudgy red-headed kid; Teddy called him 'Rotten Ronny.' Not to his face of course," Alex smiled.

Marian put the plate of sandwiches in front of Alex and Jennifer. "You're the one who named him 'Rotten Ronny,' you know?"

"I did? I don't remember that."

"You did, I remember," said Jennifer.

"Really?" Alex paused for a second, trying to remember, but nothing came to him. "Well, at any rate… When we came up to them they were passing around a cigarette and acting about as cool as they could."

"Hey, don't Bogart it, Lew, you dick," Rotten Ronny admonished the tall, skinny, stupid- looking kid.

These three punks were all sporting greased-back hair, khaki cotton pants a bit too long, wool plaid long-sleeved shirts worn outside the pants, and black leather pointy-toed shoes. Lew's shoes were scuffed and beat-up so badly; it was hard to tell exactly what they started out life as.

"Uh-oh," Teddy muttered under his breath.

Alex looked over briefly at Teddy, wondering what prompted the expression of dread.

"Hey punk," Ronny said to Alex. "What's the bandage for? Your big sister beat the shit out of you?" Ronny smiled at his friends, showing how clever he was.

"Nope, I got hit by a truck," Alex responded as they started to walk by the punks.

"Hit by a truck? You must be stupider than you look," Ronny said as he reached out and grabbed Alex by the arm. "I think anyone as stupid as you should pay a toll to walk down the street. You got any money, stupid?"

"No I don't, butthead, and if I did, I wouldn't give it to a jerk like you."

This cracked up Ronny's friends. "Did you hear what he called Ronny? The little kid has some big balls."

Teddy quickly looked over at Alex, then back at the punks. "He didn't bring any balls..."

"Shut up, punk," said Lew.

"Okay."

Ronny was not nearly as amused as his friends over being called a butthead and jerk and was about to take some revenge on this big-mouthed kid.

Teddy also was not amused. His black high-top Converse sneakers were starting to vibrate up and down seemingly on their own. "Let's go Alex," he whispered giving Alex's sleeve a slight tug.

Ronny was just about to slap the shit out of Alex when Alex held up his hand, palm forward, as if he were a traffic cop.

"Wait a second, Ronny," said Alex as he stared up directly into this pudgy bully's eyes. "I don't think you really want to fight me because even if you win, everybody will think you're a big fat chickenshit for beating up a little kid."

"What do you mean, even if I win, you little turd?" replied Ronny with a malicious grin, but momentarily stalled.

"Well, you don't know how tough I am. I might be a Black Belt in Judo for all you know." Alex seemed unconcerned about the situation he and Teddy found themselves in. "And even if you do manage to whip a kid a third your size and already injured, I'll see to it that you spend a great deal of time…"

"In jail?" interrupted Ronny with a smirk on his face.

"In the hospital," concluded Alex. "You, being as dumb as you are, probably think that all my family are my size, but believe or not, there are some big and real tough members of my family. The ones who come immediately to mind are my cousins who live in East LA. Since the stabbing the rest of the family doesn't talk about them much anymore, but I still like the guys, and more importantly to you, they still like me."

"I suppose you're going to try to make me believe that your cousins would come over here just to kick my ass if you asked them to."

"I guarantee it," stated Alex, maintaining eye contact with Ronny.

Teddy looked as if he were about to wet his pants, but stayed by Alex's side.

"I'll tell you what," the third kid remarked without getting off the retaining wall. "Why don't you bring your cousins by and we'll kick their asses for you. How's that sound, piss-ant?" He took a final drag off the filterless Camel and flicked the butt at Alex. It passed within an inch of Alex's left ear, but Alex didn't even blink.

"Hey, watch out; you can burn somebody like that, ya know!" Teddy objected mildly.

"Shut up, punk." The kid glared at Teddy.

"Okay."

"That sounds great," Alex cut in. "As a matter of fact, I believe Hector and Manuel will be coming over next weekend with my aunt and uncle so why don't we set up a time for you to kick their asses? How about noon at the basketball court at Center Avenue School?"

"Hector and Manuel? You're not Mexican, shithead," proclaimed Lew, turning his attention back to Alex.

"Well, no shit, Lew. Say, you're not nearly as stupid as everyone says. Next time someone tells me how stupid you are, I'm going to tell them how, after just a brief look at my blond hair and blue eyes, you concluded that I wasn't a Mexican," Alex smiled. "My aunt isn't either, Lew, but my Uncle Manny sure is."

Ronny and the kid on the wall thought this was pretty funny, but now Lew wasn't smiling.

"You're full of shit," said Lew.

"You're right, Lew; I'm lying to you." Alex was still smiling. "I guess you figured me out, so I suppose you and these other two brave dingleberries had better go ahead and pound me."

Teddy looked at Alex as if he was just about to step off a cliff. After a short pause, Teddy spoke up. "Alex, don't start lying to these guys. I met your cousins just a couple of weeks ago at your mom's birthday. Remember? Geeze." Teddy had just a slight tremor in his voice.

"I'll tell you why, Teddy," Alex replied without taking his eyes off the tall skinny Lew. "I figure these three dipshits won't kill me if they slap me around a little, but I also know that if they lay a finger on me we'll never have to worry about them again."

"But Hector told me that he and his brother had to stay out of trouble for a while or they would go to jail for sure. The guy they stabbed almost died, I guess." Teddy was getting into the spirit of the moment.

For the first time, the three greasy punks had nothing to say, they just stared at Alex. You couldn't tell if they were thinking about the situation or not; their eyes had a perpetual vacant look.

"I don't think you have any Mexican cousins in East LA," stated the boy sitting on the wall. "And even if you do, they gotta be cool for a while."

"Me neither," added Ronny with little conviction in his voice.

"Even if he does," piped in Lew, "we'll just kick their asses too."

"That's the spirit, guys," Alex said as he made eye contact with each one in turn and gave them a little smile. "Hey, there are only two of them, how tough can they be? I guess you'll just have to go ahead and beat me up."

"I'm going to let you slide this time," Ronny remarked as if he were losing interest, "but if you keep mouthing off, I'm going to have to smack you one."

"I'm waiting!"

"Screw you," said Ronny and pushed Alex aside. "Let's go guys, before I'm forced to step on this dog turd."

With that, the kid on the wall slid down and the three of them crossed the street and headed north on Yukon Avenue.

Alex and Teddy watched as the three walked away. They could hear Ronny saying quietly that he didn't think Alex had Mexican cousins and Lew saying that he thought he did. The third boy said nothing.

"Thanks, Teddy," said Alex as he turned toward his young friend and put his hands on Teddy's shoulders. "You were very brave to stay with me and I'll never forget it."

"Alex." Teddy's voice was breaking a little. "I was really scared, you know." Tears were welling up in Teddy's big puppydog eyes.

"I know you were -- me too, my friend," Alex said sincerely. "That's what makes what you did so brave."

"I wasn't brave, I almost ran away," admitted Teddy as he looked down at the ground in front of him, clearly embarrassed.

"That's what bravery is, Teddy. It's when you're scared and don't run. There's nothing brave about doing something scary, if you're not scared."

Teddy thought about this a minute. He raised his head up and looked at Alex and smiled that big toothy grin. "Really?"

"Really! And boy, would I have had my butt kicked if it hadn't been for you! Nice going!"

Alex could see Teddy was elated by what he had said. He could tell his friend felt very proud. It was the first macho thing Teddy had ever done and today's experience would probably stay with him all his life.

"You don't have any Mexican cousins do you, Alex?"

"Nope."

Alex took a bite of his sandwich, chewed and swallowed.

"That was clever of Teddy, very clever," said Marian.

"I'll say," agreed Alex. "Teddy's a smart kid."

"You're just a kid too, ya know?" remarked Jennifer, none to pleasantly.

"I know I'm a kid, Sis."

"Well you sure don't act like it, sometimes," Jennifer replied. "And you sure don't talk like it."

Marian remained silent but was paying close attention to what was being said. "*...has the vocabulary of an adult...*"

Alex didn't know what to tell his sister. He made a mental note to try to cut back on his vocabulary. "I don't know why that is, Jen, I really don't."

Marian wasn't missing any of this conversation. "I guess you did have an eventful morning," she remarked.

"Not over yet," said Alex. "From there we walked to Fred's house. After I was through showing Fred my injuries, and explaining, as best I could, how the accident happened, it was Teddy's turn."

"Turn to do what?" Jennifer asked with a mouth full of sandwich.

"He told the story of our encounter with the punks."

"Teddy's good at telling stories," said Jennifer.

"He sure is," added Marian.

"Good? He's remarkable. His rendition of the event was absolutely fascinating. With few exceptions, he had every word, inflection, and posture of the punks down pat. He switched from one character to another, effortlessly. It was, without question, the single most amusing and amazing thing I've ever seen. My friend Teddy is a natural born entertainer."

"Teddy's always been like that, Son. You've just forgotten."

"Yeah, your memory is rotten," added Jennifer.

"Jennifer! Finish your sandwich."

Chapter 13

GABRIEL HOME
April 22, 1962

It was tough to act like an eight-year-old for any prolonged period of time. Occasionally, Alex would inadvertently lapse into an adult mode. Most of the time he was with his family and they chalked the odd behavior up to the concussion, but if his lapses were around Teddy; it was a different story.

Teddy would either question him immediately -- "You're talking funny again, Alex" -- or he would watch him carefully for a few minutes. It seemed that Teddy sensed, more than anyone else, that Alex was not right.

Alex did not miss this scrutiny. He knew Teddy was insightful for an eight-year-old, or any age, for that matter. He assumed that character trait was probably tied to his uncanny ability to mimic people. Any deviation from normal behavior stuck out like a sore thumb to Teddy.

The person who was the least affected by Alex's unusual behavior was his father. If he did see the change, he didn't seem concerned. Alex on one occasion overheard his father say to his mother, "Is Alex acting different lately or is this normal for his age?"

His mother replied, "Norm, sweetheart, if you were any less observant, I swear I could farm the kids out for a week before you'd notice."

"What do you mean? Have I missed something...what?"

Alex was spending a lot of time trying to figure out the best way to integrate himself into this new reality. He had painstakingly come to the conclusion that he might be here, in this time and place, to stay. Why and how, he had no idea. Some of the possibilities scared him. Brain damage was, by far, his worst fear. Or maybe he had been slipped a hallucinogenic drug and instead of being in a hospital, he was in a mental institution. He could be in a corner of a padded cell talking to himself, talking to his mother, talking to Teddy, mumbling incoherently, or screaming... *Shit*!

So it was time to bury these thoughts and circumstances as completely and deeply as possible. He had gone over them time and again and hadn't gained so much as a trace of insight. They only added misery to this life.

Alex possessed a remarkable ability to categorize his thoughts completely and place them in separate "files" in his mind. He credited this gift for his astounding success in the investment market. This unique ability allowed him great clarity of thought and memory. He wasn't confused by unrelated thoughts or emotions spilling into the mix. He simply opened the desired "file," spread the contents out in proper order, and took a look. Now, he decided, it was time to "file" the horrible uncertainties concerning his physical and mental condition and place them in a remote, dark corner of his mind. It would be a tough file to bury, but in time, it could be done. Alex had little doubt that there would be times when these negative and disturbing thoughts would jump uninvited into his consciousness. On those occasions, he would have to deal with them the best he could, but in the meantime, the file was to remain closed.

The upside to this scenario was, the longer he was in this reality, the more natural it became. He felt he hadn't lost any of his forty-three years of memories and this time period's memories were becoming sharper by the day. He was starting to believe he could survive and thrive in this reality and quite possibility get to enjoy it.

April 24, 1962

The only logical way Alex could devise to stay out of school and accomplish his other major goals would be to become a genius, a child prodigy, someone way beyond the need for formal education. He needed to convince his parents that the bump on his head had somehow elevated his IQ by twenty or thirty points. They would have to be persuaded that sending him to grade school would be a complete waste of time and much more importantly to them, he reasoned, it could be detrimental to their son's emotional stability. Alex knew he would have to play hardball on that point.

April 25, 1962
11:55 a.m.

Norman, Alex, and Jennifer were sitting on stools at the pass-through counter connecting the Gabriel Kitchen with the dinning room. Marian had just set a tray full of sandwiches in front of them.

"Think you'll feel well enough to get back to school Monday?" Marian asked Alex.

Alex stopped chewing for a second. Then mumbled, "Are you talking to me?"

"Who else has been out of school?"

Alex continued to chew his sandwich as he prepared his response. *Okay, now's the time to put school behind me.* "I don't think I need to go back to grade school."

Norman and Jennifer stopped eating and looked at Alex. Maybe they hadn't heard right.

"I'm sorry! You don't think… what?" asked Marian.

"Well, I've read all the books Jen brought home for me, and I know everything in them. So I won't be needing to get back to school… for at least the rest of this school year."

Norman quickly entered into the conversation. "Well, first off, you are going back to school! And secondly, I doubt you can prove to us that you know everything at your grade level."

Alex took another bite of his sandwich and continued to eat as he made a show of thinking about this predicament. Norman, as well as Marian and Jennifer, were staring intently at Alex.

Playing hardball as expected. Time for the test. "How about testing me? If I pass, to your satisfaction, I can skip the last two months of the school year."

Norman thought about Alex's proposal. Marian and Jennifer continued to eat in silence. Alex acted as casual as possible.

"Let's just see how smart you are before we start pulling you out of school, young man." Norman took a bite of his sandwich but didn't take his eyes off Alex.

"Tell you what. You design and ask as many questions as you wish, based on my school books, and if I get any wrong; I'll go back to school with no further argument. But if I get 100 percent right, I'm off the hook for the rest of the year. Deal?"

Norman unconsciously rubbed his chin. Then he addressed Marian. "What do you think, sweetheart?"

"Before you answer, I would like to point out that the single most stated reason for kids to hate school and do poorly is boredom. I am quite certain that putting me back in the third grade would literally drive me crazy."

Marian thought about that for a moment before answering Norman. "I think you ought to design a tough test for our little genius here. If he passes it with flying colors we can leave him out of school for a couple of months."

Norman looked at Alex. "You have a deal. But just one wrong answer sends you back to school Monday."

Alex put out his hand, "Shake on it, Pop."

Norman hesitated for a couple of seconds before he took Alex's hand. "Pop?"

"You call your father 'Pop.' I like it."

Marian smiled. "A rose by any other name."

April 26, 1962
7:35 p.m.

All the Gabriels were sitting in the living room. Alex had a self-satisfied look on his face. Norman, Marian, and Jennifer had looks of disbelief on theirs.

Norman seemed bewildered. "How in the hell…? That's amazing."

Marian is bemused. "That was pretty good, Son. I didn't even see you studying."

"Geeze, Alex." Jennifer was shocked; she thought for sure her brother would fail the test.

Alex knew this was only his first hurdle. He would, in the near future, need to convince his parents to let him do many things that kids simply do not do. The first phase might not be too tough, but as years went on, it could become a lot tougher. He would have to somehow enlist his mother as his ally. If what he had in mind worked, he felt his father wouldn't be able to handle the pressure.

Chapter 14

GABRIEL HOME
April 29, 1962
4:35 p.m.

"Hey, Mom, where's Russia?" Alex called out.

"It's in the Far East, pretty much on the other side of the world, Alex." Marian replied from the kitchen. "Why do you ask?" The radio was on in the kitchen and Alex could hear Elvis singing *Heartbreak Hotel* in the background.

"Just wondering. Looks like a lot of Americans don't like Russians testing atom bombs."

Marian walked into the adjoining dining room to see Alex with the newspaper spread out on the table, studying it intensely. To Alex, this was like finding thirty-five-year-old papers in an attic. It was fascinating.

"What are you doing, sweetheart? Isn't this kind of unusual reading for you?" Marian asked, doubtless amused and puzzled at the same time.

...Slow and easy...make it gradual...make it believable.

"I can read most of the words all right and can figure out almost all the others," Alex responded without looking up.

"I know you can, Alex, but the newspaper is a little past *Captain Marvel* comics, you know." She patted him on the shoulder and walked off.

"I was past comics when I was six, ya know," he called after her.

4:05 p.m.

"Mom, what's a stock?" called out Alex, half an hour later.

"What do you mean, stock?" she called back.

"Well, it says, 'stock market up.' What's that?"

Marian came back into the dining room to see Alex with papers now spread all over the table and floor. He was looking at the financial page with great intensity.

She could see what he was looking at and she raised an eyebrow. It was not only a giant jump in reading ability, but quite a leap in subject matter. Other than school work, Alex had pretty much stuck to comics.

"Well, Son, I don't know a great deal about the stock market, but I'll see if I can explain it to you a little bit."

Alex looked up from the paper and stared into his mother's eyes, a trait that always amused her. Whenever anybody talked to him, he looked straight into their eyes and paid close attention to what they were saying. This was unusual for young children and unfortunately, for a lot of adults, too. She never had to say, "Look at me when I talk to you," as she had seen so many other parents do. The one exception to this was that Alex seldom looked at Jennifer when she talked to him.

"Well, let's see now," Marian started. "Suppose you want to start a new business but you don't have enough money to do it. Let's say you need a thousand dollars. You could sell pieces of your new company to other people. These pieces are called shares or shares of stock. Kind of like when I bake a pie and cut it into six pieces so everyone gets their share, except your dad, he usually gets two shares." She smiled and so did Alex. "You would probably make two thousand shares," she continued. "Keep one thousand for yourself because it's your idea for the company and you're going to do all the work. You sell the other thousand shares for one dollar each. That will give you the one thousand dollars you need."

"So you need to get a thousand people to buy a share in your company?" Alex asked with a serious look on his face.

"Not necessarily. Some people might buy a hundred shares or fifty or maybe one person will buy the whole thousand by himself. Just depends on how much money they have, I guess."

Alex made a show of mulling this over.

"What do people do with the shares of stock?" asked Alex with a furrowed brow. The way he handled this next series of questions was critical.

"Well, they hold on to them for a while and hope they go up or pay dividends or both."

"Go up and pay dividends?" he said, staring intently into his mother's eyes.

Marian took a deep breath. "Let's say you and Teddy want to start a lemonade stand on a busy corner like Crenshaw and Imperial where they're building a new bank..." Marian went on to explain how the boys could sell stock to buy lemons and sugar. How they would pay their stockholders a dividend when the profits exceeded their costs; how their stock would go up because of all the profits they were making and how they might have to liquidate their assets when the bank was completed and there was no one left to buy their lemonade.

Alex was impressed by how well his mother understood the concept and how adeptly she was able to explain it to an eight-year-old.

"I get it," Alex proclaimed in a triumphant tone. *I couldn't have explained it much better myself,* he realized.

"Do you and Pop buy stock?" Alex asked with great excitement.

"Yes, we do a little. Your Uncle Walt is a stockbroker and sometimes he knows about a company that might do well. We gave him some money a few years ago, and he invested it for us."

"...Alex, my boy, why don't you take some of your paper route money and..."

"What's a stockbroker?" Alex knew he had to continue this line of questioning in order to establish a solid interest in the subject. "And what's 'invests'?"

"A stockbroker is a person who helps other people buy and sell stocks. People pay him to do this."

You're doing great, Mom, Alex was thinking. *I'm afraid I'm going to keep you at it for a while.*

"Invests?"

"That's what you call things like buying stock. An investment is a way of taking some money today and buying something that you hope will be worth more money in the future. Buying a house is also an investment. People invest in all sorts of things like art, stamps, and real estate. People invest to make money and some get rich doing it."

"That's what I want to be, rich," exclaimed Alex. "Can I buy stocks, too?" he asked, maintaining his excitement.

"I think you're a little young for that kind of activity, young man," Marian replied with a smile.

"I found my old bank book in a top dresser drawer. I've got $34.52 in the bank. I could buy shares of something," Alex stated hopefully.

"Your old bank book?"

Oops! "Yeah, I haven't seen it in a long time, nearly forgot about it."

Marian looked at Alex for a second before continuing, "There's another part of this I haven't told you about, Son. Sometimes the shares you buy go down and you can lose your money."

"Lose your money?" Alex pretended to be shocked.

"Sure, sometimes the business that you buy shares in does badly and goes broke and all the shares they sold aren't worth anything."

"Oh." Alex acted as if someone had let some of the air out of his balloon.

"I have an idea, sweetheart. Why don't you wait and ask your Uncle Walt all about this the next time he comes over?"

"Okay," he agreed after a moment of feigned thought. *Perfect, Mom. That's exactly what I'd hoped you would say. I doubt, however, that Walt will see it that way*, he thought with some amusement. *I can hear him now. "Thanks Marian, I would really love discussing high finance with an eight-year-old*."

Alex continued asking both his parents questions totally unrelated to his past interests. He tried not to make too big a nuisance of himself, but he read everything he could get his hands on; things that kids wouldn't read under any circumstances, such as *Time* and *Newsweek*. He would then ask his mother or father about their opinion of a certain article. He occasionally caught them glancing quizzically at each other, and smiled to himself.

"Jesus, Marian, what the hell is he doing reading *Newsweek*?" asked Norman as Alex left the living room. He heard his father clearly as he walked down the hall. "He hasn't read anything like this before. Hell, he *couldn't* read anything like this before." It seemed that his dad was finally starting to take notice of the changes his son was going through. "And what's with these questions? Why would an eight-year-old want to know about segregation?" Alex smiled as he entered his room and closed the door.

Chapter 15

GABRIEL HOME
April 29, 1962
10:15 a.m.

"Hi, Jennifer; whatcha doing?" Alex asked cordially as he walked into his sister's room.

"None of your beeswax." Jennifer's attitude toward Alex had been deteriorating at a steady pace since the accident. Her little brother was getting all the attention, and she didn't like it one bit.

In the short period of time since the accident, Alex had come to realize that it had to be Jennifer's extraordinary jealousy, from the beginning of his life, which had caused the rift and continuing animosity between them. Something he, as a child, simply couldn't and didn't understand. But now, as an adult, he had the opportunity to mend that unfortunate part of his and his sister's early life together. He needed to convince Jennifer that he had changed a great deal because of the accident and that he no longer wished to be her enemy.

"I didn't come in here to fight with you, Jen. Actually, I thought we might play together a little while." Alex was using his friendliest demeanor.

"You don't want to play; I know you. You just want to trick me some way, so go away or I'll call Mom."

"Honest, I don't want to trick you, Sis." Alex was sincere. "Actually, I want to talk to you about something. Maybe you could help me."

Jennifer looked at Alex with a somewhat blank expression for a few seconds before regaining her snotty posture. "Oh, no you don't, Alex. I know you're gonna do something bad to me, so go away," she responded, with a little less conviction in her voice. She would have had to be really stupid not to see the changes in her brother, and she certainly wasn't stupid.

"Well, I was really hoping I could talk to you about something that I can't talk to Mom and Pop about." Alex started out the door.

"Wait a minute," she said quickly. "What do you wanna talk about?... and you better not trick me, Alex."

Alex paused at the door for a moment. "Okay." He stepped back in and quietly closed the door, creating the impression of secrecy. He walked over and hopped up on the edge of the twin bed across from his sister and the array of dolls she had neatly laid out on the other. Neat would be an apt description of Jennifer. Alex had noticed with some amusement and pride that she took great pains with her appearance, particularly for a ten-year-old. Her curly blond hair was always combed neatly with colorful ribbons placed just so. She would never be seen in wrinkled or stained clothes. *A bit of a priss,* Alex smiled to himself. Her pretty blue eyes were alert, maybe too alert. *Looking for faults in others, especially in me, I suspect.*

"Well?" she demanded impatiently.

"Oh yeah," Alex started. "Since I was hit by the truck, I've been feeling different somehow. I don't feel the same about things the way I used to. Like my toys aren't any fun anymore and I don't want to read comic books -- stuff like that."

Jennifer was clearly puzzled. "Why are you telling me this? Why don't you tell Teddy or Fred?" Jennifer stared into Alex's eyes for a moment, doubtless searching for the truth. Searching for some sign of deceit.

Am I telling her the truth? Or am I just setting her up for some pain? "Because they're not my family. They're not my big sister," Alex replied sincerely.

Jennifer looked away; she was clearly and deeply affected by

Alex's statement. More so, by far, than Alex had expected. She began silently straightening the hem on one of her dolls' dresses; a hem that was already straight. She said nothing.

This little girl has been deeply hurt over our horrible relationship, Alex thought with sadness. He could see her chin quivering.

Alex slid down off the bed, stepped over and put his hand on top of his sister's. "I want to be your little brother and your friend, Jennifer. I love you, ya know?"

Jennifer paused for a moment before saying softly, "Okay."

Chapter 16

GABRIEL HOME
May 20, 1962
4:20 p.m.

Marian and Walt were sitting at the kitchen counter enjoying a cup of coffee. It was Saturday afternoon and Norman, Jennifer, and Alex were out of the house. Walt was very fond of his niece and nephew. For the past two years or so, he called every two weeks and asked to take them to dinner or a new movie. To Marian's eye, Walt seemed slightly fonder of Alex than Jennifer, but unless you were close to the situation, you couldn't tell. He covered it well. Even Jennifer, who was more than a little sensitive when it came to being slighted, wasn't aware of it.

Walt had always been one of Marian's favorite people; they were close friends. Although only two years younger than her husband and raised in the same family, Walt was totally different. Walt's lifestyle was 180 degrees from Norman's. He was at his office no later than 6:00 a.m. Monday through Friday and stayed out late most weekends. Marian often wondered how he'd managed to remain single. Walt was a little shorter than Norman but with a similar build. His hair was a strawberry color as opposed to the pure blond of Norman's, but there the similarities ended. Walt was outgoing and personable while Norman was friendly but stoic.

Walt and Marian could talk for hours on just about any subject. Today's subject was Alex.

"I tell you, Marian, your handsome son -- my genius nephew -- has to be the brightest eight- year-old in the world," Walt stated with considerable wonderment in his voice.

"He's a pip, all right," agreed Marian.

Walt continued to beam. "I spent four hours going over stocks, bonds, interest, corporations, investment in gold and silver and commodities with that eight-year-old yesterday and I believe he may know as much about them now as I do." He paused for a second as if in wonder. "I didn't have to go over anything a second time. He just absorbed everything like a sponge. You wouldn't believe the insightful questions he asked me."

"Oh, yes I would, we're getting them all the time. It's causing me to go through periods of anxiety and a little depression, mixed with periods of pride and elation," Marian paused for a second. "His dramatic change has me on an emotional roller coaster, Walt. I want my cute, bright, pugnacious little boy back… I miss him."

"He has changed, no doubt about that."

"Did you know that he easily went through the entire curriculum of grade school in the past twenty days?"

"I didn't know that…. That boy is going to amount to something special someday; you mark my words."

"Yes, he will. I know that as sure as I'm sitting here. It's an unshakable feeling I've had for some time now. Makes me anxious for some reason."

"The boy has a good heart. No reason to be anxious about anything he might do in the future."

"The school principal and Alex's teacher were quite reluctant to graduate him three years early," Marian paused. "I can understand their reluctance. I could hardly believe I was asking them to do so."

Walt nodded.

"Somehow the local newspapers got hold of the story and wanted to interview Alex and his family. We put them off with various excuses long enough to cause most of them to lose interest. Except for one persistent young reporter."

"Who?"

"A freelancer. Jack Calloway's his name."

"Haven't heard of him." Walt finished off his coffee before asking, "Alex doesn't want to be interviewed?"

"I'll say not."

"Might give the boy a little fame."

"I told him that, but he informed me he didn't want to be famous."

"He said that?"

"Yep."

Chapter 17

GABRIEL HOME
July 3, 1962
8:00 a.m.

Alex had been up for a couple of hours, showered, dressed, and eaten breakfast by the time his parents were up. It was the custom at the Gabriels' to sleep late on Sundays. Alex enjoyed this custom during his first childhood, but not this time around. He was an early riser every morning, an unbreakable habit created by spending over twenty years as an investment broker, on Pacific Time.

"Good morning." Marian looked up from the paper as Alex walked into the room.

"Hi, Mom." Alex walked over and kissed his mother on the cheek, something he did every morning since the accident.

"What is so important that you can't sleep late once in a while?"

"Nothing really... just can't seem to sleep past six."

This was another change in Alex's personality. Changes had continued to manifest themselves on a regular basis since the accident. There had been so many that Norman and Marian had started prefacing Alex's behavior with BA for "before accident" and AA for "after accident."

"Whatcha got there?" Marian gestured toward some newsprint Alex had in his hand. She put the Sunday paper on the end table and picked up her coffee.

"Order forms."

"For?"

"The *Wall Street Journal* and *Baron's*."

Marian looked at Norman, then at her son for a second before saying, "Really?"

July 18, 1962

"Mom, gotta send away for some prospectuses from a few companies," Alex said as he walked into the kitchen, savoring the smells of the meatloaf baking in the oven.

"Is that so? How many companies are you investing in with your thirty-five dollars?" She turned to hide her smile and selected another bowl from the cupboard.

"Well, I don't know; maybe not any. But I'll need to read up on them in order to figure it out." He stuck his finger in the cake dough. "Want to send away for about fifty right now." He sucked the dough off his finger and jumped up on a stool.

"Fifty? That's about two bucks in stamps."

"I'll pay you back."

July 29, 1962

Alex, in fact, knew hundreds of companies in which he wanted to invest. Not necessarily now, but in the future for sure. But he still needed the prospectuses. They would be used to stimulate his memory -- the foundation for his detailed files that eventually would encompass thousands of companies. He had no idea when or if his memory would decline, so he decided that while his past life memories were still vivid, he should record everything he could recall on future investments. As a side benefit, maybe the people around him would assume he was making a lot of money because of diligent study and hard work. That would certainly be part of it, but he didn't want people to think he possessed a crystal ball.

Although he recognized many of the stocks listed as good solid investments, and some would show a nice return in a short period of time, he had only $35.52 to invest. He needed to find a low priced stock that was due to take off. He assumed buying a hot stock would go a long way toward accomplishing two things. It would create a great deal more capital to invest and it would set a precedent of high earnings that his parents would be seeing a lot of in the future.

To this end, he was looking for real hot "penny stocks" in the research and development category. He thought he would recognize what he was after when he saw the names of the managers, officers or the companies. He was already starting to write down names and had started charts and graphs for future use. He knew this would get cumbersome in a hurry.

Boy, would I love to have my PC for this task. He knew the first generation Univac, the first somewhat practical computer, was developed in the '50s and second generation in the early '60s. They were huge machines designed for corporate use, and as such, would be totally impractical as far as he was concerned for at least another ten years. He might be forced to acquire a second generation Univac as soon as they were available. *Time will tell.* Stone Age equipment compared to what he was used to, but the Univac was a useful tool in its day. It was going to be at least ten years before any really usable PCs would come into their own. Gates wouldn't develop DOS for IBM for another ten years.

For at least four hours a day for the past few weeks, Alex had sequestered himself in his room making charts, writing notes, studying prospectuses and financial magazines of every description. Fortunately, his uncle was able to provide much of the material and information Alex requested. Alex, however, would not accept week-old or, for that matter, day-old *Wall Street Journals* or *Baron's* magazines. He insisted on his own subscriptions. "Old stock reports are of little use," he argued. He was careful to call his uncle only after the markets closed, but he called almost daily with a list of questions and requests. He knew his uncle would be talking to his parents and would undoubtedly keep them abreast of his activities, but that was all right. It all fit into the plan.

August 1, 1962

While Alex was out playing with Teddy and Fred, Marian took Norman into Alex's room to show him what their little boy was up to. There, on an old oak coffee table Alex had discovered in the garage and subsequently dragged into his bedroom, were notes, graphs, and calendars. The calendars were nearly filled with various symbols neatly printed under various dates, past and future. Norman walked over and picked up some of the material.

"What the hell?" he exclaimed after a couple of minutes of scanning the material.

"I ask you," responded Marian, "how could our relatively normal eight-year-old little boy change so radically? How could he possibly know or care anything about sophisticated investing? Have you ever heard or read about anything like this?"

"Nope."

"Do you think we ought to tell somebody about this?"

"Like who?"

"I don't know. Maybe a child psychologist?"

Norman's eyes continued roaming over the material on the coffee table. "I don't think we should share this with anyone. It's not like the boy is building bombs or drawing dirty pictures or anything like that."

"But something has happened to him, for Christ's sake, and it scares me. Remember what Walt said yesterday?"

"...actually look forward to our daily conversations. He has never asked a stupid question nor asked the same question twice. Couple of times I told him I'd have to get back to him with an answer and then called someone a hell of a lot more astute than I am, for the answer..."

"Yeah, I remember," replied Norman.

"And then there's the matter of how he and Jen have become close friends. That's damn near as spooky as this stuff."

Norman nodded his head knowingly.

Chapter 18

GABRIEL HOME
AUGUST 2, 1962
9:00 a.m.

Norman and Marian were lounging in the living room Saturday morning in their pajamas and robes. Marian was sitting crosswise in an overstuffed wing chair with her legs hooked over one arm and her back wedged between the wing and back of the chair. Her shiny black hair was pulled back into a short ponytail and her face looked freshly scrubbed.

Norman hadn't bothered to run a comb through his hair that morning; just raked it back with his fingers. He, as usual, had his recliner leaned back as far as it would go and had his steaming hot coffee handy on the oak end table; newspaper in hand.

"Looks like they're going to raise the minimum wage to $1.30 an hour."

"I found the stock I want to invest in," Alex announced as he walked into the living room. He was, as usual, fully dressed and looked as if he had been up for hours. Since the accident, he had taken to showering every morning as he had done as an adult. It took a little effort to get his father to build a stool to set in the tub so he could use the shower properly.

"What's that, Son?"

"I've found a stock that I think will go up in no time and I want to buy it right away, first thing Monday morning. I'll make a fortune!" Alex answered enthusiastically, looking first at his father, then his mother. He was getting good at maintaining the façade of an eight-year-old.

"Well, tell us about it. What kind of company is it?" Marian closed her book and placed it face up next to Norm's coffee cup.

Alex saw with amusement that she was reading *Peyton Place*.

"This is a company that has been inventing and designing new electrical appliances for the kitchen. The name is Sunshade. There is talk of them merging with Great American Electronics in the near future. This, I understand, will give them access to unlimited development capital and immense manufacturing capabilities," Alex declared matter-of-factly.

"Unlimited development capital, immense manufacturing capabilities?" Norman repeated. "Really?" He looked quizzically at Alex, then over at Marian.

Marian just raised her brow ever so slightly at her husband, then turned her attention to Alex.

"Yep," said Alex without acknowledging the looks exchanged. "They have designed and patented an electric kitchen knife and they say if the merger goes through, they will start production right away. I think when they do, their stock will go way, way up."

"An electric knife, Son? What's it do, burn the food apart, or is it more like a skill saw?" Norman was attempting to be funny.

"I think it's more like a guillotine. You just stick the meat in the hole and watch the big blade chop the heck out of it," Alex kidded back.

"How many shares do you want to buy, Alex?" asked Marian, smiling.

"1000. It's selling for three cents a share and I have $34.50 saved up. You can't buy odd numbers of shares when it's selling for under $1.00 per share, ya know."

"As a matter of fact, I didn't know that."

"Mom, I'm going over to Jackie's for a while," Jennifer announced as she walked into the living room. In one hand she had a small cardboard suitcase she used to pack her collection of dolls, in the other, a jump rope.

The conversation stopped abruptly.

The carefully designed "reports" from Alex to his sister on a near daily basis kept Jennifer from going off the deep end whenever Alex was the center of attention. If the conversation stopped, when she walked in, she didn't get upset the way she would have before she and her brother became friends.

"Okay, honey, be back at noon for lunch and don't forget you promised to finish your homework today."

"I will. See ya, Alex." Jennifer smiled at her brother, turned, opened the door and walked out.

Marian looked at Norman, saying nothing.

"I can't believe a stock selling for just three cents would be a good investment," Norman returned to the previous conversation.

"You're right, Pop. I guess most of the time they're not, according to everything I've read, but some of them are great investments and I believe this is one of them. Actually, you might want to consider buying some shares yourself."

"Are you sure you want to spend all your money on just one stock?" Norman asked. "Maybe you should buy two or three different stocks and spread the risk a little." He took a sip of coffee.

Alex would have been surprised if his father hadn't offered some advice. He knew that he would be listening to "advice" for years to come if he didn't get some rules set now. Alex had picked today to get past a couple of major hurdles. He had the next set of exchanges mapped out as best he could. There would be a little planned give-and-take, but if all went according to his script...

Alex knew his dad was ultra-conservative and had a lot of trouble taking any risk at all financially. "Spontaneous" was not a word Alex would have used to describe his father. He was a scientist/engineer by both nature, and professionally. He wanted to know every detail, every angle, and all possibilities before making almost any decision. Alex was surprised to learn that he had actually given money to his brother to invest. There could be no doubt that his mother had to force that concession out of him. Alex would also have been willing to bet the amount given to his uncle was considerably less than he could afford to lose.

"No, Dad, I have spent a lot of time studying these stocks and this is the one I've picked to start my fortune with."

"Your fortune, eh?" Norman smiled.

"Yep. I talked to Uncle Walt about it and he suggests we set up a separate trust account for me, with Mom's name on it as trustee," Alex explained. He knew it was critical that he keep his father's name off his account or the next thirteen years would be spent clashing with his father every time he wanted to buy or sell. He knew he would have some disagreements with his mother, but felt that in a relatively short period of time, he would have her confidence.

"Why just your and your mother's names on the account?"

"I plan on doing a lot of buying and selling and Uncle Walt says that we'll save a lot of time and trouble if just one person has to do all the signing and stuff like that. Also, Uncle Walt says if we set up this kind of trust, it won't affect your taxes, no matter what I earn." Alex knew his father had a great deal of respect for his younger brother's opinions and the word "taxes" would certainly be a hot button.

"A lot of buying and selling you say?"

"Yep, a lot!"

Norman looked at Marian and gave a little smile and wink.

"Well, I guess that's a good idea. I think between your mother and you, you should be able to handle all this high finance."

"Thanks, I think so, too." *That's "one,"* thought Alex.

Marian remained quiet throughout this exchange, a fact that didn't escape Alex. He could see she was paying close attention. She was chewing on her bottom lip, an unconscious habit she employed when deep in thought.

...Watch her here... he admonished himself.

"There is another related matter I think we should talk about now, if you have time," Alex pressed on.

"It's my day off, Son. Got plenty of time," smiled Norman.

"It is possible I'll be making a bunch of money over the next few years, and I would like for us to come to an agreement now to forestall any serious disagreements in the future." Alex was maintaining his innocent little boy demeanor as best he could. Guile wasn't something he had practiced in his former life. The one thing he couldn't do was reduce his vocabulary to that of an eight-year-old. Every time he tried, he sounded like an idiot. He could see the effect his extensive vocabulary had on adults and to a lesser extent his friends, except Teddy, but that's the way it was going to have to be.

"What possible 'serious disagreements' should we be 'forestalling'?" asked Marian, shooting a glance at Norman.

"Especially if you're making a bunch of money," smiled Norman. "Can't see disagreeing with that. Be able to help with your college expenses."

"Well, supposing that I turn my $34.50 into say, $10,000 in the next year or so? What would you suggest I do with all that money?"

Norman jumped right in on this one, as Alex knew he would. "Well, I would probably suggest that you put a lot of it in the bank for your education. I guess I wouldn't care if you bought some toys or whatever you wanted with some of it."

"I see." Alex smiled as he turned toward his mother. "Mom, what do you think I should do with it?"

"I suppose I would have to weigh all the circumstances at that time and make my judgment then."

Alex paused for a long moment feigning deep thought. "The agreement I would like you two to agree to now, is that no matter how much money I make, you won't interfere with my buying and selling," Alex said seriously as he looked from one parent to the other. "I know if and when there is a lot of money involved, you're going to worry I'll lose it." Alex paused again. "Keeping in mind that I'm the one who created the fortune in the first place, and I couldn't have done it by being stupid."

Alex could see his mother's eyes narrow slightly.

"I don't think we can agree to that, Alex," Norman responded. "You can't expect us to sit back and let you lose hundreds, maybe thousands of dollars if we see you are about to make poor investments." He paused for a few seconds, "But I don't think we'll have to worry about that for a few years."

Marian was again nibbling on her bottom lip. She looked over at her husband, then back at Alex, but remained silent.

"Hum....Okay, what do you think of this idea?" he paused another moment as if to put the final pieces together, then, "I'd like to make this bargain with you. Say I agree to put ten percent of all my earnings, after I earn $100,000, into a college fund until that fund reaches a total of $50,000?"

"After you earn $100,000, you say?" Norman took a sip of coffee. "What happened to the $10,000 you were up to just a few minutes ago?"

"It may be millions for all I know, Pop; maybe billions. Just thought we might come to an understanding now before the big bucks start to roll in." Alex gave his father his biggest smile.

"Billions, you say!" Norman declared with mock joy. "Well now, I don't think we'll have to worry about our future at all, Marian. I believe we'll just call in Monday morning and resign from SARC. Say, Son, just to be sure, how long do you think it will take you to come up with a billion dollars?"

His father was attempting to be humorous; Alex hadn't expected this. *But this is good*, he thought. He began acting as if his father's ribbing was upsetting him. He stopped smiling and looked down at the carpet as he answered quietly, "Ten or fifteen years...I guess."

The ruse seemed to be working as Marian and Norman exchanged glances and then leaned slightly forward toward their son.

"Well, I personally think this brilliant boy can earn a billion dollars, Norm, and I think we should support him one hundred percent in this endeavor." Marian wasn't about to throw a wet blanket on her son's ambition...no matter how lofty.

...Atta girl, Mom...

"If anybody can do it, it's Alexander Gabriel; that's for sure!" Norman didn't want to damage Alex's enthusiasm any more than Marian did. "But how about putting ten percent of all your earnings into a college fund right from the start?" Norman smiled. "Why wait until you've earned your first $100,000?"

"Because," Alex returned to a happier posture, "I will need all the capital I earn to reinvest until I get to $100,000. Actually, I would rather not take ten percent out after $100,000, but I'm willing to do that to strike a bargain with you right now."

"Norm, it occurs to me that all Alex is risking is $34.50. I think we are jumping the gun a long way when we start worrying about tens of thousands of dollars that may or may not be earned in the future," Marian offered reasonably. She again looked deep into Alex's eyes; her own eyes again narrowing slightly. "I think we ought to agree to this bargain. What can it hurt?"

"Sure, why not!" Norman went back to reading his paper.

...That's all I need today...perfect.

August 5,1962

"Hey, Mom, I wonder if you would take this with you to your office tomorrow and type it up for me?"

Marian had just finished changing out of her work clothes and was heading to the living room while still in the process of buttoning up her well-worn jeans. After work she enjoyed watching the early evening news on TV.

"What's this, Alex?" ask Marian, finishing the top button. She continued toward the living room but reached over and took the sheet of notebook paper from Alex.

Alex followed closely behind, waited until the TV was turned on and his mother walked to her chair before he started. "It's the agreement we talked about Saturday. I thought I'd better write it down while I could still remember what we agreed to. You can probably fix it up a little -- correct my spelling; stuff like that."

Alex remembered his father saying several times in his life... *never renege on an agreement, son...a man's word...*

Marian started reading the paper before she sat down. "You're not missing a beat, are you?" she remarked as she read.

AGREEMENT

The party of the first part, Alexander J. Gabriel, hereafter called Alexander, hereby enters into the following agreement with the parties of the second part, Norman J. Gabriel and Marian A. Gabriel, hereafter called Norman and Marian.

After Alexander has accumulated a net worth of $100,000, he hereby agrees to set aside ten percent of all future earnings, to a maximum of $50,000, into a college fund of Norman and Marian's choice.

Norman and Marian hereby agree not to interfere with Alexander's investment choices including, but not limited to: What and when to buy, and what and when to sell. Norman and Marian also agree to let Alexander have full control of his method of investment, including, but not limited to: buying on margin, buying warranties, selling short, or buying contracts on commodities, futures, precious metals, real estate, real estate development, etc.

Regarding the purchase or sale of margins, warranties, short selling and contracts, Alexander agrees never to risk more than fifty percent of his actual capital available, excluding any moneys in his college fund.

Alexander J. Gabriel ______________________ Date ________
Norman A. Gabriel ______________________ Date ________
Marian A. Gabriel ______________________ Date ________

"Where in the world did you come up with this, Alex?" Marian was bewildered.

"Well, a lot of the stuff Uncle Walt gave me had a bunch of contracts and agreements in them, so I copied some of it and called Uncle Walt and read him what I wrote. I thought he was going to quit breathing before he stopped laughing. Said he would like to see the look on Dad's face when he reads it," Alex said with some amusement. "He had me rewrite most of it."

"I would have helped you, you know." Marian seemed hurt. "After all, I read and write contracts and agreements five days a week for SARC."

"Oh gosh, I didn't mean to hurt your feelings. It's just that I thought Uncle Walt could help me because he is a stockbroker and investment counselor. Actually, he's the one who put in the stuff about margins and things like that. He said it might save further discussion," Alex explained in an apologetic tone.

"I guess I can't be too upset, kid. There is still a little work to be done, spelling and such. I'll fix it up for you."

"Would you mind making four copies?"

Chapter 19

GABRIEL HOME
August 22, 1962
11:30 a.m.

"...and finally, after a marathon session in London on the SALT accord, British Prime Minister Harold Macmillan and USSR's Communist Party leader Nikita Khrushchev, have come to an agreement. For further news, stay... "

"Time to sell Sunshade Corp." Alex was beaming as he walked out to the back yard where his parents were lounging under their corrugated fiberglass patio roof. Sunshade had performed just as he remembered. This successful first test put Alex in a euphoric state that was nearly impossible for him to conceal. It meant this reality coincided with the real world, as he knew it. If it continued to hold true, the possibilities would be endless.

The radio helped mask some of the neighborhood noises and for some reason, despite the heat, today seemed to be a day of hyperactivity. The Beckers, two doors down, were having a shouting match again. Hard to believe that people continued to be married when they obviously hated each other. Mr. Jones, next door, was busy, as usual, in his garage shop. Today he seemed hell-bent on wearing the blade off a skill saw. The only noise missing was the almost constant barking of the black lab that resided at the home behind the Gabriels. The heat must have forced him to find a cool shady spot.

It was a blistering afternoon in Southern California. The Santa Ana winds were blowing not only heat but also smog from the deserts of eastern Los Angeles County to the normally more temperate western side. Alex, along with everybody else, was miserable. The temperature had been hovering between 91 and 102 degrees for the past ten days and it wasn't cooling off more than 15 degrees at night. To make things more uncomfortable, the smog was so bad it was impossible to take a deep breath without coughing.

"Sell? You just bought the stock," Norman remarked after taking a big gulp from his iced tea. "What's the matter, did you decide it wasn't such a hot stock after all?" Norman seemed peeved, due mainly to the uncomfortable weather, and was about to give an "I told you so" spiel when Alex cut him off.

"Oh no, it's done just about what I thought it would and I think it will continue to go up for quite a while," Alex explained, looking from his father to his mother and back again.

"If you think it will continue to go up, why do you want to sell it?" asked Norman, wiping the sweat from his forehead with a napkin and swatting at flies that seemed to use only him as a landing field.

"Because..."

"What's Sunshade selling for now, Alex?" Marian interrupted. She, too, was suffering from the weather, but she didn't have the tendency to go Jekyll and Hyde in the heat like Norman.

"Great American Electronics has tendered an offer to merge with Sunshade at 58 cents a share and it looks like Sunshade is going to go for it," Alex replied with a big smile.

Norman was just in the middle of taking another gulp from his iced tea when Alex said, "58 cents." Some of the tea made it back into the glass, some of it splashed on the cement patio floor, but most of it was absorbed by Norman's shirt and cut-off Levis.

"Are you kidding?" Norman choked out. "That's a gain of..?"

"Just over nineteen hundred percent," Alex offered, stifling a laugh.

"Nineteen hundred percent!" Norman repeated as he jumped

out of the patio chair and proceeded to try to pat his clothes dry with a paper napkin. "Damn it!"

"Congratulations, Son. I'm really happy and proud of you," declared Marian as she walked over, picked Alex up and gave him a big hug and kiss on the cheek. She spun him around about three times before setting him back down. Then she sat down again. "Give me a sec," she said as she picked up a pencil on the patio table and quickly started writing some numbers on a napkin.

"Nineteen hundred percent!" Norman stepped over, picked Alex up and gave him a big squeeze. "That's great, Son -- what are you going to do with...how much money is that?

"$638.00." Alex's smile was about to split his face.

"No kidding! Wow! So what are you going to do with it?"

"Reinvest it in two other stocks tomorrow morning," Alex answered matter-of-factly.

"Don't you think you ought... "

"Norman!" Marian cut in. "Let's remember the agreement we have with Alex. It's official, you know, and we're going to keep it. We cannot give him any advice concerning his investment capital, that was the deal."

"But... "

"No buts, Norm." She turned to Alex. "We'll call Walt tomorrow and get your order in to sell Sunshade and buy the two other stocks."

"Norm, sweetheart," Marian said as she lifted her bare foot and gently kicked Norman in the knee. "I have a little confession to make and I hope you won't be too upset with me."

Norman looked over at his wife as he continued to swat at flies.

"When I had Walt buy Sunshade for Alex, I asked him how our portfolio was doing. To make a long story short, one of the stocks we owned was just kind of sitting there doing nothing. We only had about $1200 worth so, after having Walt assure me that there wasn't too great a risk with Sunshade, I had him sell Southern Cal Gas and Electric and buy Sunshade." She raised her eyebrows, opened her blue eyes as wide as she could, put on a great big smile, looked down at the numbers on the napkin and yelled. "*That $1200 is now worth nearly $23,000.*"

"*Holy shit*!" exploded Norman. The heat and the flies were no longer a problem.

October 21, 1962
6:50 p.m.

Alex, Norman, Marian and Walt were sitting at the Gabriels' dining room table Saturday evening having just finished dinner. Jennifer had taken off to spend the night with a friend.

Alex was trying to talk his father out of paying off their mortgage, and investing the money instead. "Why pay off a four percent mortgage when you have averaged over 600 percent on investments?" he argued.

"A bird in the hand, as they say," was Norman's answer.

"Alex, I can assure you that my frugal brother, your cautious father, will not be swayed from his course by the logic of your argument."

Marian nodded in agreement.

Alex smiled. "Okay, I give up."

"However I do think we had better discuss fame and fortune," suggested Walt. "I believe we had better consider keeping our sudden gains in wealth a secret. More than that, we had better keep Alex a secret. If the newspapers and television get hold of a story that an eight-year-old is some sort of financial genius, we'll have a hard time keeping them away from every facet of our lives." He had their attention. "Quite frankly," Walt went on, "I'm surprised that you were able to suppress the story on Alex's academic achievement. Not often that a third grader goes through grades one through six in six weeks. If word gets out that Alex has now become a financial wizard, whether true or not, it'll be tough to fend off the news media."

Walt paused for a second. "I would suggest that we agree, here and now, that we do not discuss any of Alex's gifts with anybody for any reason at all. We had better disguise our little wizard like a miniature Clark Kent and keep his powers secret."

Alex sat for a second. He really hadn't given much thought to what other people's reactions would be to his success in the stock market. But having his uncle voice his concerns on the subject made him think. "I have to agree with Uncle Walt," he acknowledged. "No point in drawing attention to ourselves."

Chapter 20

GABRIEL HOME
November 20, 1962

"John Steinbeck is getting the Nobel Prize for Literature." Norman was again reading notable news aloud.

"That's interesting," Marian responded automatically.

Norman looked over the top of the paper, "By the way, am I allowed to ask how our son is doing with his investments?" he asked with some humor.

Alex had just started down the hall to the living room when he overheard his father's question. He stopped and listened for a few seconds.

"He's doing just fine, Norm," Marian replied. "I don't know exactly what the figure is today but, if you promise not to go gunny sack, I'll give you the figure for last week."

"You have my word."

"How does about $61,000 grab you?"

"Jesus Christ, I..." he started, but fell silent.

Alex smiled. *Pop's an honorable man; he won't renege on his word.*

Marian resumed reading her magazine, making sure it covered the amused look on her face.

Alex had just returned to his room when there was a knock at the front door.

Jennifer ran out of her room and opened it. It was Teddy. "Oh, it's only you." Jennifer was expecting a friend of hers.

"Sure it's me, Jen. I'm always coming over here, don'tcha know?"

Jennifer was about to tell Teddy to come on in when he slipped by her and headed in the direction of Alex's room.

"Hi, Teddy," said Marian.

"Hi, Mrs. Gabriel," Teddy called over his shoulder and continued into Alex's room.

"Hi, Alex," he said as he entered the room. "Whatcha doin?"

Alex wasn't expecting Teddy and had been working on his investment files. Alex really didn't want Teddy to know about this part of his life; he couldn't possibly understand. "Well, I'm just trying to figure out some stuff." Alex answered while he systematically began to put papers away in file covers and then in drawers.

"What kind of stuff?" Teddy's eyes took in the tabletop full of unfathomable papers.

"Well, investment stuff."

"Investment stuff?" Teddy was confused. "Where'd ya get it?"

"A lot of it, my uncle gave me."

"Why?"

"Because I kinda think it's fun to play with." Alex finished putting everything away and stood up. "Why don't we go over to the school and play some four-square?" Alex was trying to change the subject.

Teddy looked at his friend for a second. "That's fun?" he asked, nodding toward the table and now hidden papers.

"Kinda."

December 20, 1963

It was over a year and a half since the accident and the Gabriel family had settled into a routine that wasn't much different than before the accident -- the one exception, of course, being that Alex was not in school. He spent each morning from about 6:00 to 9:00 working on notes for his present and future investments. Lately, he'd begun spending time reading scientific journals and magazines. He started making notes and saving clippings from a multitude of publications. These were kept in a separate area from the investment material. After his reading, he had the rest of the day to kill and usually spent time on his bike cruising the neighborhood alone or reading novels.

Much to Marian's delight, Alex started spending more time with Teddy and his other friends once the school day was over, something he'd been avoiding.

"Where've you been, Son?"

"Biking around with the guys; throwing grass clods at the girls -- stuff like that."

"I thought you were too sophisticated to be playing with your old friends, eh kid?"

"Really, I hadn't noticed," Alex remarked offhandedly. "I did notice my energy level dropping, probably from lack of exercise. Kids need a lot of exercise."

"So you're only spending time with your old friends because you need exercise?"

Alex paused for a second. "No, not really," he replied. "I actually enjoy their company as much as I did the first... " Alex stopped abruptly.

"The first?"

"I mean before I quit playing with them."

Marian took a long look at Alex.

Oops, thought Alex. *I just set off another alarm.* He wondered when or if she was going to call him on them. *She and Teddy never seem to miss my slip-ups*.

It had taken some time for Alex to convince his folks that he didn't need a babysitter while they were at work. "Do you really think I'll get into trouble if left alone? Do you think I might play with matches or take to drinking."

Alex knew his parents were aware that there would be far less chance of problems with him than with most teenagers, but still they argued that the law stated that children under the age of twelve couldn't be left alone.

"We just won't tell anyone." Alex eventually won out.

Chapter 21

GABRIEL HOME
JANUARY 15, 1964
7:45 a.m.

"You want to do what, Alex?" asked Walt.

"I want to margin this one to the hilt. I don't see the problem," Alex spoke into the phone. His table had five separate files stacked neatly on the top, leaving little room for anything else.

"You can cover the margin but Jesus, Alex, you haven't done anything like this before." Walt switched the phone to his other ear and began writing with his free hand.

"Haven't had the money to do it or the need to, up 'til now, Uncle Walt," Alex replied. "This stock is marginable and it is going to go way up. I could buy $100,000 worth outright or I can buy $500,000 worth on margin. To make you and Mom feel a little safer, you could maintain a stop-loss at $1.00 below the bid price. That way, I can't lose more than I can comfortably cover."

Walt was speechless for a second.

Alex could just about picture the look on his uncle's face. "Further, I want this buy kept at maximum margin. With the stop-loss at a buck below, it will be quite safe."

Walt found his voice. "Do you realize that if you lose your money, your mom and dad will have my butt for supper?" Walt was beginning to sweat.

"Uncle Walt, I appreciate your concern, but think about the

investments we have made in the past year and a half. They probably wouldn't have been considered a great investment by most brokers, and in most cases, you would have recommended against buying them because they were highly speculative...and rightly so, I might add," Alex paused. "This is just another transaction that has a certain amount of risk involved... actually, this one isn't as speculative as some of the others we've chosen. This company has been around for years and has a good record. I can't see how it could possibly go down any."

"How many shares would you like me to buy, Alex?"

"Seventy five thousand at $6.75 per."

There was a long silence.

"...I'll have to get your mother's signature on the papers, you know?"

"I know." Alex smiled. "I'll put her on the phone... hold on a sec."

Alex returned to the living room ten minutes later to find his mother staring at the phone.

"Well?"

"Just finished talking to your uncle," she replied soberly. She had been transfixed on the phone since hanging up five minutes before. "I asked him how I could let my nine-year-old son risk a half a million dollars, and you know what he said?"

"Nope."

"He said it scared the hell out of him, too, but reminded me of your perfect record, and of course, 'The Agreement.'"

Alex walked over and put his hands on his mother's shoulders and looked into her eyes. "It will be just fine, Mom. I know it's a big jump but I guarantee, it's a good one."

"This scares me, Son."

Chapter 22

WALT'S OFFICE
March 12, 1964

Alex was in Walt's office for just the second time in his life. This time he had to suffer through the introductions to the two accountants and one beautiful secretary/assistant.

"Look at those beautiful blue eyes and those lashes. Boy, are you going to be a lady-killer when you grow up. Wow!" an incredibly attractive young redhead named Colleen exclaimed, leaning over and pinching him on the cheek.

Alex remembered his uncle telling his parents about the new girl he'd hired. *Walt said she was the prettiest woman he had ever seen.* Alex smiled to himself. *And then Walt corrected himself with, "Next to you of course, Marian."*

Norman and Marian joked that Uncle Walt might have hired this eighteen-year-old woman at first sight, before he had even read her employment application. Well, Colleen Keefe was in fact, breathtaking. She had the most dazzling emerald green eyes, incredible red hair, and a figure that was, for lack of a better description, perfect.

"Well, if you'll just wait eight years or so, we'll get something going, Miss Keefe," Alex answered as he gently took hold of her pinching hand and held it in both of his. *My God, look at that alabaster skin.*

"Why wait eight years? What are you doing tonight, Master Gabriel?" she came back with a big beautiful smile.

"My mom won't let me stay out late on a school night, unless it's a special occasion," Alex continued, losing himself in her green eyes. "But you might call and explain to her how special an evening with you could be to a young, innocent boy like me. She's pretty understanding."

Colleen stood straight up, clearly caught off guard by the clever response. She smiled again. "You win. I'll see you in eight years." She winked, turned, and walked off.

"It's a date," Alex called after her. *Would you look at that tush?*

"If you're done flirting with my help, maybe we could jaw a little in my office." Walt put his hand on Alex's shoulder and walked him toward the back of the fair-sized room, which held three desks and a bank of file cabinets.

The door to Walt's private office was left open most of the time. His employees had access to him at any time. Alex noted his uncle's office had gone through a makeover since the last time he saw it.

"Had this redecorated two months ago, thanks to your 'insights,' Alex," Walt remarked as he closed the door and scanned the room with obvious pride. "Sit down." Walt patted the back of one of the two big avocado-green, overstuffed chairs in front of his desk.

The whole office was done in shades of green except for the moldings, book cabinets, and Walt's large desk, which was a highly polished cherry wood. The light fixtures and lamp on the desk were of Tiffany design. The plush carpet was also avocado green, but several shades lighter than the big chairs.

"This is really beautiful, Uncle Walt." Alex sat down and looked around the office. "Have you asked Colleen out yet?" he asked out of the blue.

Walt was clearly surprised by the question. He'd been asked the same question by his friends and peers, but obviously didn't expect it from Alex. "Nope, for two reasons. One, I'm too old for her and two, she works for me. Can't be dating the help, Alex."

"Horse pucky, Uncle. One, you're only about ten years older than Colleen and two, if I felt like you do about hired help I'd fire her, and then ask her out."

"Would you now?" Walt laughed.

"In a minute; you bet I would. That is the prettiest woman I have ever seen," Alex paused for a second. "Next to Mom, that is."

"Got a little crush, do you, Alexander?"

"What able-bodied man... boy wouldn't?"

Walt smiled. "Aside from her physical appearance, young Alex, the girl has a head on those beautiful shoulders."

"Always a plus, Uncle."

"Just turned eighteen, you know? She's attending a junior college in the evenings with plans to switch to UCLA in a year or two."

"I just can't see what you're waiting for, Uncle."

"Can't be dipping your pen..." Walt stopped before completing the old adage.

"In company ink," Alex finished for him. "I know and agree; it's a sound principle."

"You've heard the expression before?"

"Who hasn't?"

"Most kids your age, I would think."

Oops, thought Alex. "I think I read it in a novel."

That seemed to satisfy Walt.

"How about we get down to business for a minute?" said Walt, changing the subject.

Alex could see that his uncle was uncomfortable talking about women with him and understandably so. The vast majority of the time, his uncle treated him as an adult. *But being ten, I shouldn't have much of an opinion when it comes to women.*

"Okay, but I still think you're missing a nice bet," Alex finished.

"How did you know, Alex?" Walt asked as he sat down in his executive chair, a perfect match for the cherry wood desk.

"Know what?" Alex still had his mind on Colleen.

"That American General was going to more than double in a short period of time?"

"It's all there if you read and pay attention, Uncle. This is the electronics age. Almost any company that produces or can produce some sort of helpful electric gadget is going to make money. When you find an established company with a good reputation that is looking for expansion and development capital, it's usually a good, safe investment. Now, add to that the fact that they're expanding to produce a new line of attractive home electronic equipment, and it's got to be a winner. This company has made great use of television advertising for years. Put this together with everything else -- how can it lose?"

"How indeed?" smiled Walt.

Alex, on occasion, could see his uncle's countenance change. He knew that once in a while it would dawn on Walt that he was having an intelligent conversation concerning stocks, bonds, or high finance with a young kid. He could see his uncle's face briefly get a kind of puzzled look. Sometimes Walt would actually do a modified double take. *I'm sure if I were dealing with a tow-headed kid, his feet in Converse sneakers, feet just barely touching the floor from the chair, my face would get a little goofy now and again too.*

Alex dressed and acted like any ten-year-old would in 1964. His gifts were unknown to all but his mom, dad and uncle. Jennifer, of course, knew that her brother was something special, but didn't begin to suspect just how special. For his part, Alex tried to maintain the young boy façade, but occasionally there were lapses, such as flirting with the stunning Colleen.

"I didn't play along with you on this one, you know," Walt explained, somewhat exasperated with himself. "I have always covered your play some, but for some reason, not this time."

"It's probably the bigger numbers that threw you off. Actually, the stock price didn't go up that much in comparison to most of our other investments, but the margin buy makes up for that." Alex was trying to mollify his uncle.

"American General will be declaring a dividend next week. Do you want to hold on to it until then?"

"I think so, yes," Alex replied. "I think we'll see a slight increase until then, but it will start dropping off after that." Alex paused in thought for a few seconds. "Better sell it all Wednesday, the day after the dividend."

"You realize this transaction makes you a millionaire, don't you, young Alex?" Walt remarked seriously.

Alex paused for a second. "Before taxes I'm afraid, Uncle," he replied with a slight smile.

"Before taxes, sure, but doesn't making that much money get you a little excited? Most kids your age haven't earned a legitimate dime in their lives, for Christ's sake."

"I guess I don't think about it that way, Uncle. Making money is the name of the game, but it's the game itself that I'm enjoying, not so much the money."

Walt thought about that for a second, shaking his head slightly. "Okay, kid. What are we going to do next?"

"Here's what I have in mind to do with the proceeds of American General."

Alex could tell Walt remained perplexed, but he said nothing as he wrote down the new buy orders.

A few minutes after Alex was picked up by his mother, Colleen entered Walt's office."You've got one handsome, clever young nephew there, Mr. Gabriel," Colleen remarked as she sat down ready to go over the daily reports. "There is something unusual about him... I can't quite put my finger on it, but there is something."

"Your new acquaintance -- my brilliant nephew -- is a genius, you know."

Chapter 23

GABRIEL HOME
August 1, 1964
9:00 a.m.

Alex was just about to the front door when Marian called to him. "Hey, Alex, your dad and I would like to have a word with you if you have a minute."

"Sure, just heading over to Teddy's to see if he wants to go for a bike ride," Alex responded as he turned and plopped down in an overstuffed chair. "What's up?"

His father was sitting on the edge of his recliner. He had on his usual hot weather cut-offs and a t-shirt, perspiration covering his face. His mother was sitting on the edge of the coffee table and was similarly dressed. This wasn't the warmest part of the summer and so far the Santa Ana winds hadn't begun. The temperature was staying in the mid 80s.

"We've been thinking about selling this house and buying a new and larger one… maybe with air conditioning," he added as an afterthought. Norman started mopping his forehead with a paper napkin.

"I think that's a great idea, Pop," responded Alex. "What do you have in mind?"

"Not sure, but because of your investment advice, we can afford to improve our lives a little."

Alex said nothing for a few seconds while he thought about this new idea. "I'm sure you two have discussed this plan in great length and probably don't need any input from me, but I might offer a thought or two."

"What's that?" asked Marian.

"Well, I'll bet you're thinking about buying close by, if not in this same neighborhood. You wouldn't want Jennifer to have to change schools, lose friends, and stuff like that. But I might suggest that you think about Orange County."

"Orange County! That's out in the boondocks! Out of the question, Alex."

"To say nothing of one heck of a long commute to and from work," added Marian. "I'll tell you right now that Jennifer will attempt to desert the family if we try to move her away from her friends."

"I would like to stay close to Teddy, too; he's my best friend," Alex said matter-of-factly. "But Orange County is not the other side of the world. Sometimes I think we have to be more far-sighted and practical."

"What could be practical about moving out to the farm country and driving thirty miles to work and back?" Norman had his back up.

"Several things," replied Alex, undaunted by his father's obvious and logical objections to Orange County. "First, I doubt that you can find a house in this immediate area to fit our needs. Second," Alex ticked off the points on his fingers, "if that is the case, you would have to try finding a vacant lot and building the home you want. Third, if you do find a suitable lot to build a house that fits everyone's needs, you will have overbuilt for the area and won't be able to get the cost back when you sell. Fourth, we live in a middle-income neighborhood in which we are already seeing a slight decline due to light and heavy industry moving in and around the airport. Because of this, and the fact that newer and much more modern homes can be bought for less money in Orange County, property values will start to drop in areas such as ours. Fifth..."

"Stop... have you been thinking about this already, Son?"

"Not really."

"Then how in the hell...?"

"Norman! Let's let the boy finish and then we'll make the best decision we can. Sometimes he comes up with some pretty sound ideas."

Marian apparently had come to grips with the radical change in Alex. She seemed to enjoy her "new" son and his exceptional insights. Before the accident, Alex had only one personality trait that was cause for concern: his relentless obsession to get even when he felt he had been treated badly. The bad treatment was usually at the hands of his sister, but not always. But he and his sister had remarkably "buried the hatchet," so apparently, that was no longer a problem.

"All right, Son; go ahead."

"Well, let's see. Where did I leave off?" Alex continued. "Also, I believe Orange County will be the place to be in the not-too-distant future. I think that most of Jennifer's friends' families, along with many others who can manage it, will be moving down there. The 405 freeway is being connected way down south to Interstate 5 and that will give access to all of Orange County. The thirty-mile drive will only take about half an hour."

"Alex, where did you get all this information? And more to the point, *why* do you have all this information?" asked Norman, becoming more confounded by the minute. "I just don't get it." He got up and walked over to the living room window just in time to see Teddy and Fred heading up the driveway on their small bikes.

"He reads everything, Norm. You know that," Marian said to Norman's back.

He turned to face his wife. "I know, and I realize that he remembers almost everything," Norman replied and turned back to Alex. "But how can you assimilate so much and put it to such practical use with no apparent prior thought?"

The doorbell rang.

"It's your friends." Norman walked to his favorite chair and sat down.

Alex got up to open the door, but stopped halfway there. "Pop, I do have prior thought. I think about everything I read when I read it, and then add new information to the old. Everyone does the same thing."

"But not nearly as well as you."

The bell rang again.

"Some do and some don't, I suppose." Alex opened the door. "Hi guys; be right out." He closed the door without waiting for a reply and turned back to his parents.

"The *Times* and *Harold Examiner* have been running feature stories on the developments and long-term plans for Orange County for months. For quite a while I've been exposed to everything we have talked about." Alex paused and smiled, "Besides, I'm a smart little shit."

"Alexander!" Marian exclaimed, trying not to laugh. "I'll thank you not to use that word."

"Sorry, thought it would fit in pretty well right there."

"Okay, kid. It's just that I sometimes get overwhelmed," Norman responded with a smile. "Go ahead and play with your buddies. You can give us the rest of your thoughts later."

11:10 a.m.

Alex returned two hours later, looking a little sweaty. "We rode up to Hollywood Park and then to downtown Inglewood. These kids are in good shape."

"Kids?"

"Yeah, you know Teddy and Fred."

"You don't consider yourself a kid?" Marian was watching Alex's eyes.

"Of course I'm a kid; just ten, you know!" *Damn, did it again.*

Marian watched Alex's eyes for a second. "Well, go wash up for lunch, Alexander!" She patted him on the head and walked toward the kitchen.

"Think I'll shower; got a little grimy on the ride."

"Didn't you already take a shower this morning?" Norman asked.

"Yep."

Norman looked at Marian. They said nothing.

Alex hopped up on a stool at the kitchen counter about fifteen minutes later, looking clean and neat as usual. "What's for lunch? I'm starved."

Jennifer came in and took her usual place at the counter.

Marian set a plate of tuna sandwiches on the counter, put a glass of milk in front of the children, and a beer in front of Norman. Although there was a fourth stool, she seldom used it, preferring to stand, facing her family. "It's easier to wait on you hand and foot if I'm on my feet," she would say good-naturedly.

"Well, Alex, have you given any more thought to our moving to Orange County?" Norman started and took a big bite of his sandwich.

"Orange County!" Jennifer's eyes got big and then narrowed as she looked first at her father, then Alex.

Alex was surprised his father had brought the subject up in front of his sister. Jennifer wouldn't be offering any positive thoughts, that was for sure.

"Jennifer, we're just talking about buying a new, bigger house that's all, sweetheart. Don't get in a snit."

"Don't get in a snit? We're moving to Orange County and you don't want me to get in a snit? I'm not moving anywhere! That's all!" She jumped off the stool and headed straight to her room. They waited for the predictable slamming of the door and then continued.

"That wasn't smart of me, was it?"

"No, Norm, I think you could honestly say that wasn't smart."

Alex remained silent and went about eating his sandwich, as did his dad. Marian just tapped the side of her plate with her forefinger, staring at her husband.

Alex took a gulp of milk. "I might point out that Jennifer, sooner or later, would have to be let in on the fact that we're moving." He took another bite, chewed and swallowed. "It might be a good idea to let her participate in the planning; it might help her attitude...

once she cools down, of course."

Marian wasn't one to stay angry for long. She finished counting to sixty, took a deep breath and picked up a sandwich.

"Okay then," said Alex, seeing the tension had lifted some. "What do you think of buying a beachfront lot and building in the Balboa Island or Newport Beach area?"

"Now it's beachfront?" his father asked.

"Why not? But before you answer, I want you to consider the fact that within two years, you'll be retired and not have to worry about any commute."

"We'll be retired, will we?"

"Absolutely, if you want to be. If not, it will be just a few years before most major aerospace companies and related industries will be all over Orange County. You'll probably be able to get a job closer to home. But instead of living in an area that's going downhill, we could be living in a beautiful custom home with an incredible view, in an area that will do nothing but appreciate for decades."

"I guess there is no doubt at all about this eh, Son?" Marian was back in the conversation and again she watched her son carefully.

I'm displaying a bit too much insight here, Alex realized. *Better soften up a bit.*

"Not according to what I've been reading. Of course, I'm just guessing and hoping about some of it."

Chapter 24

GABRIEL HOME
August 2, 1964
1:30 a.m.

Alex walked by several people whom he thought looked familiar, but none seemed to notice him. About halfway down the hall, he turned to the right and walked into a nicely decorated reception area. Without stopping or slowing, he continued past a dowdy receptionist until he stood before a polished mahogany door. He couldn't quite make out the name on the brass plaque; the lettering was quite fuzzy, but after a moment, he turned the knob and walked in without knocking.

"So you want to move to Orange County, do you, my friend?"

"What?" Alex looked around. He was standing in Jason's old office. The room was sweltering.

"I asked if you wanted to move to Orange County."

Alex could see that his friend was a bit upset and sweating profusely. "Well, it's cooler and easier down there, ya know?"

"What about our business? You just going to fold your tent and head south?" Jason wiped his face with a large paper napkin.

"What business, I don't have a business; I'm only ten years old!"

"Who told you that you were ten years old, for Christ's sake?"

"What are you, blind?"

"A little near-sighted maybe, not blind."

"Well then, look at me; look at me. I'm just a kid!"

"Horse shit! You're two years older than I am." Again Jason wiped his face, but this time the paper napkin was soaked to the point of dripping. "Got to get back to business, Alex."

"We don't have a business! I'm a kid." Alex could feel sweat trickling down his face. It felt like his shirt was glued to his back.

"Really? How soon we forget, how soon some of us forget."

"I haven't forgotten anything... have I?"

"Does the name Jason Gould mean anything to you?"

"Sure, you're my close friend and business partner."

"What business is that, Alex?"

"What do ya mean?" Alex became confused. "You're the one who asked about our business."

"And you're the one who forgot about it."

"So, I'm just a kid now."

"How can you forget?"

"I think I need to forget. Can't think about that anymore. I've put that stuff away."

"Where'd you put me, Alex? Where'd you put me?"

"I know where to find you, Jason. I'll find you when I'm not a kid any..."

Alex woke up in his hot, dark room, "Damn!"

He quickly reached over and turned on the lamp, looked at the clock; it was just 1:35 a.m. *Jesus Christ!* He shuddered. *Haven't had one of those for a while.* He sat up in bed. *Goddamn, it's hot.*

He could see the sheer white curtains hanging limp at the sides of the window; there wasn't even a slight breeze. Alex had another dream, but this one, as with the others he'd had in the past year, weren't the horrible nightmares he'd suffered right after the accident. This one, however, was damned unsettling and, maybe, revealing. He got up and started for the kitchen. His throat was dry, he was sweating and he really needed a cold glass of water. He drank the first one and carried a second to his room, setting it on the night-stand. He got back in bed and lay on his back on top of the sheet.

There was no way he was going to get back to sleep for a while. *Jesus, it's hot*! He began thinking about his dream while melting in the heat of the early morning hours. He hadn't thought about his past life for over a month now and he knew, as time went by, he was thinking about it less and less. After twenty minutes or so he came to a conclusion. *I believe I've actually lost the desire to return to my old life*. This revelation came as a surprise to him. *This life is exciting*, he smiled to himself, *and it has unlimited possibilities*.

Chapter 25

GABRIEL HOME
November 3, 1964
10:45 a.m.

Marian and Alex were heading out the door for the Spouse Reitz department store in the Imperial Village just as the phone rang. Marian hurriedly placed her handbag on the coffee table and picked up the phone.

"*Mrs. Gabriel?*"

"Yes!"

"I'm Jack Calloway. I'm a reporter for the *Herald Examiner* and I would like to talk to you about interviewing your son Alexander for the human interest column in our paper."

"Why would you want to interview Alexander?" questioned Marian as calmly as she could, signaling Alex to listen in. He put his ear next to the phone with her.

"You may recall, you and I talked briefly a few times a couple of years ago when Alexander successfully managed to pass all the tests in grades three through six in just a few short weeks. As I recall, you managed to put me off long enough for both me and my paper to lose interest in the story," Calloway said lightly.

Alex smiled at this.

"Yes, I do recall talking with you, Mr. Calloway."

Alex also remembered. The man was tenacious; a trait Alex appreciated.

"Surely you're not still interested in that story?"

"Not specifically no, but possibly as part of another story that I just happened to stumble over at lunch a couple of days ago."

"What story might that be, Mr. Calloway?"

"Well, it seems there is a young boy who has a Midas touch when it comes to picking stocks. This boy, with the name, coincidentally, of Alex, has managed to become a millionaire in the stock market in just a couple of years."

Alex turned to look at his mother with big eyes as if to say, "Uh-oh."

"Why would you think our Alex is the same one you heard about?" Marian lightly pinched Alex.

"Well, from what I overheard, I assumed the people talking worked for a stockbroker so, being the nosy fellow that I am, after lunch I followed them back to their office building. Lost them after they entered the building, but a quick check of the building marquee showed only one stockbroker: Walter Gabriel and Associates."

"I still don't see why you think..."

"Because," Jack Calloway interrupted, "I have a pretty good memory and the name Gabriel rang a bell in the back of my mind. Thought I recalled a bright kid by the name of Alexander Gabriel. Went back to my office and reviewed an old file and sure enough, there was the unfinished story on Alexander." Calloway paused for a second. "It didn't take a lot of checking to find out that Walter Gabriel is Alex's uncle."

Shit, thought Alex, *he has us*. He gave his mother a panicked look. *Must be careful not to get caught in a lie here,* he thought.

"You have come to the conclusion that because Walt Gabriel is Alex's uncle and that employees of Walt's have said that Alex is picking the stocks, he has a Midas touch?"

"Yes, that pretty much sums it up, Mrs. Gabriel."

"Do you think there could be a possibility that a ten-year-old might not know a great deal about buying and selling stocks, but his parents and uncle might? Has it occurred to you that Alex and his sister both have investment trust accounts overseen by their parents and uncle? That the family may have several investment accounts and that they may all be doing quite well?" Marian asked casually.

"Again, yes, Mrs. Gabriel, all that occurred to me. Had I not remembered Alexander Gabriel from two years ago, I probably would have dropped the story. But putting two and two together, i.e., very bright kid versus the stock market -- hey, I have no choice but to check it out."

"Well then, I'll have to commend you on your intuition and memory and tell you that you're partially right. My son Alexander is quite bright and does know a great deal about the stock market."

"Really!" Calloway was apparently surprised by this admission.

"Yes, we're proud of him. He has, on a number of occasions, helped pick stocks that have done quite well. If he keeps up on his studies, his uncle thinks he may become a real financial wizard someday."

"Is that a fact?"

"Absolutely. Some of his stock picks have been incredible. I'll bet he has been right on the money sixty or seventy percent of the time."

"Sixty or seventy percent?" There was a noticeable drop in Jack's enthusiasm.

"Well, he'll try to slip in a real clunker once in a while, but his uncle checks out everything before we jump on it, so to speak."

"Oh?"

"He has fine potential, mind you. If he'll just stick with this pursuit for a longer period of time than usual, he'll have himself a fine career someday."

"What do you mean?"

"Alex is like most, if not all, gifted children. He has the propensity to become bored with things after a while, a short while, normally. Although I will admit that he is sticking with this hobby longer than he has stuck with most."

"Most?"

"That must have sounded like Alex flits from hobby to hobby all the time and I don't want to give that impression, Mr. Calloway. He has actually only been seriously interested in two or three other things.

"What might they be?" asked Calloway, a tinge of disappointment creeping into his voice.

"His first love was astronomy. He was really into that for a while. We bought him a huge telescope and he must have read fifty books on the subject and that led him to physics."

"Physics?"

"Yes, you know he actually read Einstein's 'Theory of Relativity' and Newton's books on gravity. He said he understood them, but I don't think he did. He sometimes exaggerates his abilities a little."

Alex could see his mother was on a roll and he found it interesting the way she was leading this reporter down the garden path.

"Do you think I could possibly have a short interview with Alexander?" asked Calloway. "He would make a good human interest story."

Alex got his mother's attention and nodded yes.

Her eyebrows went up in surprise. "Well, I guess it would be all right, Mr. Calloway. I'll have to talk to Alex about it first, but as he pretty much likes to be the center of attention, it should be no problem."

"That's great, Mrs. Gabriel. What would be a good time for you and Alexander?"

"Alex isn't here right now, but why don't you give me your phone number and I'll call you later and let you know."

"Orchard 1-2862. Call anytime, and thanks."

Marian hung up and looked at Alex, cocking her head.

"I think we need to satisfy Mr. Calloway's curiosity or he may never let go of the story."

"What do you plan on doing, Son?"

"I'll think of something. By the way, nice going."

November 6, 1964

"You must be Mr. Calloway," Marian smiled at the man standing on the front porch.

"Yes, I am, but please call me Jack." Jack returned the smile as he held out his hand.

"Pleased to meet you, Jack." Marian shook the offered hand. "Won't you come in?" Marian stepped aside, allowing Jack Calloway to enter the Gabriel living room. She closed the door behind him.

"Please have a seat," Marian gestured toward the recliner that was normally used by Norman.

"*Alex, Mr. Calloway is here!*" she called down the hall.

"*Yeah, yeah. I'll be there in a minute*," Alex yelled back in an unpleasant tone.

Marian's eyebrows went up, momentarily. But she recovered quickly. "Can I offer you some coffee, Jack?"

"That would be nice, thank you."

There was an uncomfortable five minutes of small talk before Alex finally made an appearance. When he did, his hair wasn't combed, his shirt was half tucked in and his jeans were filthy.

"Hey, my room's a mess, you haven't cleaned it in two days," Alex said as he entered the living room. He didn't even look in Marian's direction. He proceeded to the couch and flopped down, flat on his back.

"I'll go clean it right away, sweetheart." Marian looked embarrassed. "This is Mr. Calloway, by the way."

Alex briefly looked in Calloway's direction. He said nothing.

"Pleased to meet you, Alex," Calloway said cheerfully.

"Before you clean my room, bring me a Coke, will ya?" Alex rudely ignored Calloway.

"Okay," Marian said meekly. "Jack, would you like a refill?"

"No thanks, Mrs. Gabriel. I've had my limit today."

Alex spun himself into a sitting position and turned toward Jack Calloway. "So, now what can I do for you?"

11:15 am

"Well, we all thought it was Teddy who was the budding actor," Marian remarked as she turned back into the living room after seeing Jack Calloway out.

"Do you think he bought it?" asked Alex.

"Hey, I bought it!"

"Yeah, sure ya did," Alex smiled at his mom as she sat on the coffee table in front of where he was sitting.

"Why would you want that nice man to think you were an egotistical, spoiled brat?"

"People don't want to spend any more time around such an, excuse the expression, 'pain in the ass't han they have to. If Mr. Calloway hears more rumors about me, he may be inclined to pass on the story."

Marian stared into her son's eyes for a moment then said, "Jesus, Alex," as she stood and walked into the kitchen.

Chapter 26

GABRIEL HOME
NEWPORT BEACH
November 12, 1965
10:15 a.m.

It was the day after the Gabriels had moved into their magnificent new home, and Alex had just taken a break from organizing his bedroom, a chore he'd been at since six a.m. He walked through the kitchen, grabbing a cinnamon roll on the way, and exited the kitchen via the French doors. The marine layer hadn't yet burned off and it was still a bit on the cool side as he strolled west across the expansive patio to the ocean side. He could see, off to the west, a helicopter heading toward their new home. As it passed, it swung right and headed down the coast. Alex's attention went back to the ocean view while eating the roll. He found himself looking down and about sixty yards to the left at a spit of rocks jutting nearly fifty feet into the harbor. He'd been aware of this natural jetty since they were first shown this extraordinary piece of property nearly a year before. The tide was quite low this morning, exposing more rocks on the jetty than he'd previously noticed. It looked like it might be easy to hike out to the large rock at the far end. He decided to do just that. As he turned back toward the house, he saw his mother on the other side of the pass-through window in the kitchen. "*Hey, Mom*," he called out.

Marian looked up from whatever she was doing, spotting Alex by the edge of the patio. She slid open the window, "What is it, Alex?"

"Going to walk down to the beach; be back in a while."

"Okay."

Alex turned and walked over to and down the stairs that had been cleverly constructed in a natural fissure in the cliff face. At the bottom, he traversed a narrow stretch of sandy beach, proceeded across a small span of tide pools to the beginning of the jetty. He stopped there for several seconds studying the best way to proceed. It was going to be more difficult than it appeared from the heights of their patio. He made his decision and stepped up on the first of the rocks and began jumping from one rock to another. Halfway to the end, he found that the next jump was more than he was comfortable trying so he backtracked three rocks in order to circumvent the problem spot. From that point on, he had little trouble making it to his goal.

Alex was delighted to find that the large rock at the end provided a near perfect place to sit. The rock, just below its pinnacle, had a small flat spot, maybe two feet square. It was reasonably smooth on top and had a nice place to put one's feet further down. He sat down facing away from the Gabriel home. He looked across the mouth of the harbor to the blue Pacific. *I like this*, was his first thought. The sound of the small waves breaking on the base of the rocks, the smell of the ocean, the light breeze keeping the temperature comfortable, even the myriad noises associated with a small harbor, he found comforting. *Yes, I like this*! he repeated in his mind.

After sitting for nearly fifteen minutes letting his thoughts wander, he turned and faced in the direction of the house. From where he sat, he could only see the top half of the great-room section of their home as it shined brightly above the short cliff.

We're actually here, he thought. *Damn, it's only been a year and a half since we first discussed the possibility of moving out of Inglewood. Incredible,* thought Alex.

"*Wow, look at that*!"

The loud voice startled Alex. He quickly turned around in time to see a charter fishing boat about fifty feet off his rock, heading out of the harbor. The small party aboard had all moved over to the port side and were looking up at the Gabriel home. Two reached for their cameras as the other four gawked and pointed. "That has to be the prettiest house in Newport," exclaimed a buxom redhead as she raised her camera and started taking pictures.

"House, my ass. That's a mansion!" proclaimed another.

"Look at the size of that thing. Be nice to be that rich," added a third.

"Probably assholes," offered a potbellied middle-aged man as he took a swig of his beer.

Not assholes, smiled Alex. *Damn nice people, actually*.

Alex watched the boat continue out of the harbor, the passengers' attention diverted elsewhere as they joined the dozens that were out enjoying an unseasonably warm day.

As he watched the variety of boats from trawlers to sailboats burst through the swells of the Pacific, he found himself recalling the steps it had taken to get here. *Had three major hurdles to overcome*, he mused. First, he had to convince his parents to move to Orange County. He thought that would be the hardest part, but it wasn't. That took less than a week. The sheer practicality of it won them over. His next chore was the property itself. He smiled when he thought of the realtor they worked with. *Colorful, but efficient*, remembered Alex. Alex's challenge came when, after viewing dozens of properties, they had pinned it down to four finalists, all of which would cost far more than their present home would sell for. The objection this time surprisingly came from his mother.

"Do you realize, Alexander, this piece of property costs nearly twice as much as our house is worth?" Marian stated emphatically.

Alex remembered countering with, "Well, we could buy a 50 by 100 foot lot three miles inland, build a house, put a cinder block wall around it and live pretty much as we do now or..." Alex smiled when he thought about how the realtor actually took notes on his arguments. "Bright boy you've got there," she said more than once.

Alex remembered standing on the cliff right about where the stairway was now. *It was warmer than it is today*. There had been a gentle inland breeze and the ocean had just a slight swell. Alex remembered a large flock of gulls screeching, diving and swooping around the back of a medium-sized trawler, grabbing whatever scraps the crew of the fishing boat were throwing off the stern. There was a flight of pelicans flying gracefully and quietly in single file at what seemed to be no more than a few inches off the water. He remembered that his father seemed transfixed by the sights and sounds of this place. Alex recalled him walking slowly back and forth along the cliff looking in every direction. Alex and his mother had watched his father pick up some small rocks, tossing them one at a time over the cliff into the harbor.

"Just look at him," Marian said warmly. "Like a kid at a carnival. The man's walking around like he just discovered his own Garden of Eden." There was no doubt by the look on his father's face that the man had found where he wanted to live. At that moment, Alex knew he'd gotten past the second hurdle.

Then came the big one -- the size of the home itself. Alex recalled with amusement the reaction of his parents when he'd shown them the rough sketches of his ideas on the preliminary floor plan...

"You want how big a house?" His father was incredulous.

"I know it seems like I'm going way overboard, Pop..."

"The damn living room, excuse me, 'great-room,'" his father had corrected himself, "is going to cover more square feet than our entire house including the garage, for Christ's sake." Alex remembered his father waving his arms out wide to illustrate the size of their present home. *Not only was I trying to convince them to build a huge house, but wanted no expense spared.*

"Can you tell me why the ceilings have to be twelve feet high instead of the normal eight? Except for the living room ceiling, of course; you've got that one at twenty feet."

"Windsor Castle wouldn't cost this much a foot," his father exclaimed more than once.

Then came Leon Brochette. Alex smiled broadly. Leon was the architect they, with Alex's prodding, had decided upon to design their home. *Talk about a personality conflict.*

Leon was, to say the least, flamboyant. But he was also brilliant. He was only twenty-three, but already had won several prestigious design awards. Alex knew that as the years went on, Leon would become one of the most celebrated architects, not only in this country, but most of the free world. But, of course, his father couldn't know that.

"You must be the Gabriels," were the first words his family heard Leon speak.

Alex remembered his father had all he could do to keep his jaw from dropping to his chest.

"Yes, we are. I'm Marian." Alex remembered his mother found her voice first. When his father shook Leon's hand he made some sort of grunting sound and avoided eye contact.

Alex remembered that the ride home after that first meeting wasn't all that pleasant. "The man's homosexual, I'm sure of it! I've had stronger handshakes from my Aunt Hilda and she's eighty-seven, for Christ's sake," his father had said, obviously disgusted. "Who in the hell would dress like that..? Jesus!"

"You find a tweed coat, jodhpurs, and riding boots a bit affected, do you sweetheart?" his mother had kidded his father.

"And the fucking pink scarf!"

That was the first time Alex or his sister had ever heard their father use that word.

Jennifer, of course, couldn't let that go. "Ooh, Daddy said a real bad word."

Alex remembered his mother shooting a fast glance at his father. They drove the rest of the way home in silence.

But to his father's credit, by the time Leon completed the home's design, his feelings toward Leon had softened considerably. The day Leon presented the final drawings to the family was the day his father's respect for Leon became quite apparent. *That was just over a year ago*, Alex recalled. *That's when the plan came together.*

"Thought we would start with the outside elevations," Leon said as he placed the first of approximately twenty drawings on the easel. It was an outside drawing showing what the house could look like as seen from the mouth of the harbor.

All four Gabriels gasped at once. "Look at that, will you!" Norman exclaimed as he leaned forward in his chair.

"My God," exclaimed Marian looking quickly over at Norman, then back to the drawing.

"*Whoa*!" added Alex.

It was spectacular -- more magnificent than even Alex had expected. Leon had designed their home to fit perfectly atop the low cliff that overlooked the mouth of Newport Harbor. It didn't overpower the cliff, but managed to be every bit as imposing. The basic design reminded him of a contemporary Tudor. The nearly white stucco exterior contrasted with the dark gray slate Tudor-style roof with its many high peaks and angled lines. The home differed from the traditional Tudor primarily because of the extensive use of glass. Almost every room had a view of the harbor, the Pacific Ocean, or both. Each room had a large bay window arched at the top to take advantage of the views and light, except the living room. The west wall of the living room contained six windows side by side, each eight feet wide and sixteen feet tall. The south wall had four similar-sized windows. All this glass would let an immense amount of light into what would be one of the most spectacular great-rooms to be found in Southern California.

Norman looked over at Alex with a sheepish smile and gave a slight nod. Alex understood. His father was apologizing for his angry outburst after the first meeting with Leon. Alex nodded back with a smile.

Leon placed drawing after drawing on the easel. With each, came a chorus of approval. This was obviously Leon's greatest pleasure, his reason for being. He was clearly in heaven as he placed one of the last outside drawings on the easel...

Just over a year ago, who'd've thought?

Chapter 27

GABRIEL HOME
March 25, 1966
10:20 a.m.

Alex and Uncle Walt were sitting on the west side of the Gabriels' patio, which afforded them a perfect view of the yachts and various other boats as they passed by the Gabriel home on their way in and out of the harbor. The harbor was busy this morning. The sounds of the many different engines, from huge diesels to small two-stroke outboards, were mixed with people laughing and yelling and gulls screeching. It all made for a festive atmosphere.

"Before I forget, I want to thank you for talking me into moving my brokerage firm down here. It's been great!"

"You're welcome….We couldn't have you driving back and forth to Inglewood."

"Thank God I was able to bring Margaret with me. Wouldn't have moved without her."

"The woman certainly knows how to keep books," Alex nodded.

"And keep the other accountants in line," added Walt.

"I don't believe I've ever seen her without a cigarette hanging from her lips. A spinster, I assume?" asked Alex.

Walt smiled, "Well, she'd have to take the cigarette out of her mouth to say, 'I do.'"

"I'd bet you might have stayed in Inglewood if the beautiful

Colleen hadn't also agreed to move down here."

"Don't think I didn't think about that possibility." Walt smiled slightly. "She's become my right arm and taken a huge load off my shoulders."

Alex nodded in understanding.

Walt changed the subject. "You know, Alex, I've gotten so busy with the Gabriel investments I've decided not to solicit any new accounts."

Alex smiled at his uncle. "I think that's a good idea. I'm sure in time, they alone will take up about thirty-six hours of your day."

"That'd be most of it."

"And a good part of someone else's."

Alex and Walt continued enjoying the view from the Gabriels' patio while engaged in light business conversation. There was an incredible variety of watercraft on this particularly busy Saturday morning. There seemed to be dozens of boats all wanting to exit the harbor at the same moment. An occasional bumping of boats would bring either good-natured laughter or sporadic profanity, depending on who ran into whom or who ran into what, with what. The boats ranged from small unkempt dinghies to immaculately maintained sailboats approaching eighty feet or more. At this moment, a particularly beautiful motor yacht was passing in front of them.

"That must be over a hundred feet long. Is that impressive or what?" Norman exclaimed as he returned with a tray laden with two cups of coffee, iced tea and rolls.

"Hey, if things keep going the way they are, maybe I'll get one like that for myself," Walt declared. "I believe a bachelor like me could do real well around here with a rig like that."

"Quasimodo could do real well with a rig like that," Norman remarked as he set the tray on a small table.

"The Oldakers are here!"

The three looked back just in time to see Marian's head retreat from the kitchen pass-through window, presumably to greet the Oldakers at the front door.

"Great!" Alex jumped up and headed into the house.

He caught up with the Oldakers just as they were about to enter the great-room.

"Teddy!" yelled Alex.

"Hi, Alex!" Teddy responded with a huge grin. At times like these, Teddy seemed to be all puppy dog eyes and sparkling white teeth. Alex himself, grinning from ear to ear, hurried over and gave his friend a big hug and pat on the back.

Marian and Sandy Oldaker smiled at each other.

Norman and Walt walked into the great-room and greeted Sandy and Bob Oldaker.

"Ah, Teddy, how are you today?" Walt reached down and shook Teddy's hand. Walt had known Teddy nearly as long as the Gabriels had. Walt's smile broadened as he looked at Teddy.

"Nice to see you again, Mr. Gabriel," Teddy replied cheerfully, looking straight into Walt's eyes, something Alex had taught him to do.

"...If you look people right in the eye, you can see what they're thinking...and it's the polite thing to do..."

"Well, let's get something to drink and head out to the patio and enjoy a fabulous day," suggested Marian.

"If you don't mind, Teddy and I will do our own thing," Alex responded.

"Have fun, kids. Just be back in time for the party at one o'clock."

With that, the boys, with Alex in the lead, headed toward the kitchen.

Teddy still couldn't get over the kitchen. "Geeze, this is bigger than the one in my uncle's restaurant." Teddy hopped up on one of the stools arranged around the large center island. "Hi, Maria," he said happily.

"Señor Teddy, how are ju today?" Maria smiled, revealing all her gold caps. She just couldn't contain herself and walked over and pinched Teddy's cheek. "Looks jes like my son when he was thees age."

"What would you like to drink, Teddy?" Alex asked.

"I'll have me a, a, a, sarsaparilla, barkeep," Teddy responded a wonderful imitation of Jimmy Stewart.

"Uno sarsaparilla coming up, muchacho," Maria giggled and shook her head as she walked to the refrigerator. She retrieved a Coke for Teddy and a Dr. Pepper for Alex, carried them back to the island, and opened them.

The boys headed for Alex's room. Upon entering, Teddy walked quickly to the bay window. "Man, you can see everything from here."

Alex walked over and stood beside his friend. Off to their left they could see their parents and Walt sitting around a glass-topped patio table at the far side of the patio. They were in the shade of a large umbrella, sipping various beverages and talking animatedly. Teddy looked to the east to the interior of Newport Harbor and then west to the mouth of the harbor and on to the Pacific Ocean.

"This is too cool," exclaimed Teddy.

"Pretty cool all right," responded Alex.

Teddy turned to see the rest of the room. His eyes swept past the impressive oak desk sitting in front of the other large window and then quickly glanced at the bookshelf.

There were recent copies of every newsmagazine, including *Time*, *Newsweek*, and *Life*, etc. Also current copies of *Popular Mechanics*, *Popular Science,* and half a dozen other science digests and trade journals. An entire wall of Alex's large bedroom was taken up with bookshelves, from floor to ceiling, and was about half full of loose-leaf binders, books, and charts. Books and novels Alex had read and didn't need for reference went into the library off the living room where there was ample room for thousands of books. It was here at his desk that Alex meticulously recorded every investment he and his family had made, presently owned, and would be investing in at sometime in the future.

Teddy hadn't really paid any attention to this *inner sanctum* before. Teddy began looking from the bookshelf back to the desk before walking over and examining the material stacked neatly on the desktop.

"What's all this stuff?" he asked.

"Oh, just some things I've been reading."

"This?" Teddy was comically gesturing from the desk to the large bookshelf. A person would have had to be quite myopic not to see the confusion on Teddy's face. "Glad it's you who likes this stuff and not me."

That was the only time Teddy remarked on his best friend's inexplicable fascination with the most boring "stuff" Teddy could imagine. "Let's go take a look at some boats."

Chapter 28

GABRIEL HOME
June 20, 1966
8:00 a.m.

Alex had the phone stuck to his ear holding it with his shoulder. He was walking around his room pulling the long phone cord as he went, stopping occasionally to look out at the harbor.

Alex never tired of the view from their home. It was at the same time peaceful and busy. He could watch the gulls circling in their constant search for food, or watch fishing boats rigged to go out of the harbor for a day or a week of fishing. On most days, today being no exception, he could witness dozens of sailboats with their bright white sails billowing in the winds, sailing gracefully across the gentle chop of the Pacific. Occasionally, people could be heard laughing and carrying on as their boat headed out of the harbor bound for who-knows-where. Alex recognized many of the boats when they returned to the harbor, and in most cases the partiers were a great deal more subdued. Eight hours of sun and fun would remove the starch from most sails.

"I think we are going to have to do it soon, Uncle Walt. It won't be long before people are going to start wondering who these people are who can't seem to lose in the market."

"Our own mutual fund?" Walt was saying into the phone as he jotted notes on a yellow legal pad on his desk.

"We will, of course, be the only investors. A small closed-end fund doing well and investing heavily in the various markets will draw far less scrutiny than individuals will. You come up with the articles of incorporation and bylaws and we'll get to it." Alex was staring absently across the harbor while talking to his uncle. "Make yourself chairman of the board and CEO, Mom President, Margaret Treasurer, and Colleen Secretary."

"All right, this is probably the ideal time for us to make a change. I'll be closing the sale of my brokerage probably within the next sixty days. All the audits, IRS, and SEC examinations have been completed to everyone's satisfaction and the buyers are anxious to take over."

"Good. In the meantime, sell Consolidated Fabricating and Penrose Glass. Use part of the proceeds to buy thirty percent of a new issue called Comutec Inc. and the balance to leverage as many soybean futures as we can get our hands on." Alex's eye caught a medium-sized motor yacht heading out with what looked to be five or six couples on board. All held a beverage of some sort and were quite animated. About the time they were passing in front of the Gabriel home, two of the young ladies took off their bikini tops, much to the delight of the men on board and Alex, too. He grabbed a pair of binoculars and zoomed in on the ladies.

"Soybeans, Alex? You've never gone into commodities before. What's the deal?"

"What was that?" Alex asked without putting down the binoculars. *Wow, very nice!*

His uncle was right; he hadn't ventured into the commodities market before. Not in either life. He'd be walking the commodities high wire without his usual safety net of advance knowledge. But if he lost some money, it might be a good thing. No one should be perfect.

"I've been studying the commodities market for some time. It's astounding what drives the prices. A lot of emotion, and guessing, goes into that kind of trading. But, to make a long story short, I believe, based on facts, soybeans are going to do well in the next few months."

"If you say so. So, on to Comutec," remarked Walt, searching for and finding a piece of paper with his notes. "Why don't you buy the whole issue while you have the chance?"

"I simply don't want to have controlling interest in anything until I see a real need or big advantage in taking control. It could bring too much attention to us at this time."

"Okay, you're the boss, kid."

Chapter 29

NEWPORT HARBOR
November 1, 1967
9:30 a.m.

Alex was sitting on the large rock at the end of the jetty on this chilly morning, a place he could be found almost every morning. It had become his daily routine. He had already spent up to three hours reading and making notes in his room and, depending on the day, another ten minutes to a half an hour talking to his uncle. He found sitting out on the end of the jetty, after those three hours, relaxing, giving him a chance to just let his mind drift without direction.

More often than not, he went into what seemed like a trance-like state that lasted from a half-hour to as long as two hours. From time to time, he took the ever-present note pad from his back pocket and jotted down some thoughts. Following his time on the rock, he headed back to the house and transferred whatever he wrote on his note pad into the proper file or loose-leaf notebook. Then it was time for his daily exercise.

Today, while sitting at the end of the jetty, he reviewed what he had accomplished in the past five years and began formulating what he needed to put into motion in the near future. Unrelated thoughts began creeping into his consciousness -- unpleasant thoughts he managed to keep locked away for longer and longer periods of time. He thought about how absurdly easy this all was. How there had been only minor hurdles to overcome these past five years. Nobody, for instance, said anything to him about returning to school. Why not? None of their friends ever questioned -- at least not that he was aware of -- what he was doing home all the time. Why wasn't he in school? He realized they knew of his academic feats five years ago, but why had nobody questioned that since? Why, he wondered, would anyone give a child such leeway in the financial markets? It made no sense. None at all! He started to become anxious, as he had many times in the past. He suddenly began to feel that he was not really in this scenario. He could feel his pulse rate increasing. *Jesus, could it be I've been dreaming all this time? If that were the case, I'd have to be in a coma. I'd still be in a hospital...*Alex's breath started becoming shorter and faster. *Stop it!* his mind screamed. He forced himself to start taking slow, deep breaths. *Put those thoughts back away, Alexander.* After a minute or two, he began to regain control. His pulse rate came down and his breathing returned to normal. He leaned his head back and looked straight up into the blue sky, took a final deep breath and slowly let it out. *Damn, if it is a dream, it's sure a good one. It's been an incredible five years*, he concluded, *no matter what the cause.*

His and the family's net worth was approaching seventy five million. Alex knew he probably wouldn't be able to maintain that rate of growth indefinitely, but felt certain that in another four years, that fortune would be increased at least tenfold. He had a great deal of what and when to buy mapped out for the next decade. His three hours of keeping completely up-to-date on national news, scientific discoveries, trends, fads and political changes etc., allowed him to add to the list of future acquisitions, almost daily.

Today, instead of taking a long bike ride up the Pacific Coast Highway, or jogging to the harbor or maybe swimming at the exclusive Newport Bay Club, Alex hurriedly jotted notes on his pad, jumped up, and jogged back to the house. He transferred his notes to various loose-leaf binders and headed for the kitchen. Marian and Norman were sitting at the island sipping coffee and reading the paper.

"Good morning, Mom, Pop."

"Hey, Son."

"Whatcha doin', Alex?"

"Got something to run by you and was wondering if you could join me at Walt's office in an hour or so?"

"What's it about?" Norman asked.

"Be better if we can all be together so I will only have to go through it once... if you don't mind."

"I've got nothing planned. How about you, sweetheart?"

"As a matter of fact, I'm free this morning," Marian replied.

11:35 a.m.

"Jesus, Alex are you serious!" asked Walt. "You want to form a holding company? What are you going to do with a holding company, for Christ's sake?"

The four of them were sitting in Walt's office in a new high-rise office building on MacArthur Boulevard in Newport Beach. Walt had a gorgeous corner office near the top floor with a clear view northwest over the Orange County Airport. Since selling the brokerage and forming a mutual fund, Walt found he needed three more employees immediately and, based on the Gabriels' investment growth rate, would require more in a short period of time.

"I'm serious, Uncle. Not only that, but with everyone's permission, I want to use just my assets to form it."

Walt, Norman and Marian sat and waited for Alex to conclude his thought.

"If my numbers are correct, those assets amount to sixty-six million and change."

"Sixty-six million!" Norman nearly jumped out of his chair. "Are you kidding?" he exclaimed loudly, looking first at Alex then at Walt.

"Norm, darling, I thought you knew or had a good idea what Alex is worth," responded Marian, sounding surprised. "Did you know that you and I have around three million?"

"About three point two actually," interjected Walt.

"We have, really?" Norman paused and looked over at Walt. "I thought we had our money in conservative investments?"

"Most of it is and you're probably making about nine percent gain on that portion," Walt smiled. "The amount that isn't is invested along with Alex's and my funds."

Norman thought about that for a moment. "Last I heard, Alex had somewhere around eighteen million...before taxes." Norman was calmed down some and looked over at Marian as if waiting for an answer.

"Brother," said Walt, "maybe we'd better go over Alex's investment strategies again."

"Please do," prompted Norman, sitting back down. "It's not that I object to Alex having sixty-six million; it's just that it comes as such a surprise, a shock... I just don't understand how... Jesus!"

Alex was puzzled at his father's reaction. He thought Norman accepted the fact that he was going to continue to accumulate a great deal of money. *I guess he just wasn't ready for today's figure.*

"Alex margins everything that is marginable to the hilt and buys big, really big," Walt explained. "As an example, last month, Georgia Container Company tendered a new issue of ten million shares at $8.50 per. Your handsome son, my brilliant nephew," Walt added with great pride, "bought two million shares for $3,440,000, which is 20 percent of the total value. He, in effect, borrowed 80 percent of the value, using the stock itself as collateral." Walt was making some calculations on his adding machine as he talked.

"Are you saying someone loaned a thirteen-year-old boy..." Norman was trying to calculate exactly how much money that would be, but wasn't sure where the decimal point should be.

"$13,560,000," Walt offered as if it weren't too big a deal, although it was, in fact, the single largest transaction made on behalf of Alex to date. "We've been investing like this for five years now."

"You're throwing million-dollar figures around as if we we're playing Monopoly," protested Norman. "Who would lend a thirteen-year-old boy that kind of money, for Christ's sake?"

"They're not lending to a thirteen-year-old boy. They're lending to an investment account that has more than sufficient assets to cover any margin call. An account, I might add, that has the single most successful investment record in history. They would probably crap if they knew who was brain behind this outfit."

"Marian, did you know how Alex has been investing? How risky buying on margin is?"

"Of course. Being trustee I have to sign every buy and sell order. The first time Alex bought on margin, I was a nervous wreck; didn't sleep well until he had liquidated that stock. Since that time, margin buying, warrants, commodity contracts, short selling, and every other conceivable method of making money has been and is being used by Alex damn near daily. I've gotten used to it. The only thing that changes is the amount being risked. Every week it seems to be a much greater amount than the week before."

"As an example," Walt cut in, "if Georgia Container Company goes up a dollar, Alex is two million richer."

"And if it goes down a dollar, he is two million poorer. Jesus, Marian, the boy could be wiped out investing like this."

"No, he couldn't. Alex has stuck to the agreement we made over five years ago; that he would never risk more than 50 percent of his net worth on any one transaction."

Walt clicked on his intercom. "Colleen, what's the quote on GCC this morning?"

"Give me a sec," her pleasant voice replied.

Walt looked around the room for a moment.

"Eleven and a quarter," Colleen came back.

"In the past thirty days," said Walt, looking up from his adding machine, "Alex has made $5,500,000 on that single transaction. And that's just one of many."

"Pop," Alex joined in, "supposing next week I do indeed lose half my assets, or say $33,000,000? That would leave me $33,000,000, which is a much greater amount than I was worth even six months ago and nearly twice as much as you thought I had when you came into this meeting."

"I might add, brother, that Alex has been right on 99 percent of his investments. Loses on one or two once in a while, but that's to be expected," offered Walt.

"Loses once in a while?"

"Not much actually, but once in a while we buy a dud."

Alex smiled to himself. A couple of years back, he figured perfection could lead to suspicion so he'd better pick a loser now and again just to keep everyone thinking everything was normal. He chalked the losses up to the cost of doing business.

Norman sat quietly for a moment. "Just exactly how much money do you want, Son?" Norman asked in a low voice.

"I don't have a figure in mind, Pop, but whatever it is, I haven't reached it yet."

Alex could see that his mother was in her deep thought mode; her bottom lip was getting worked over.

"Maybe I just better not know what you three are doing from now on," Norman suggested solemnly. "I'm obviously not emotionally equipped to handle these kinds of numbers."

"Pop, if it will make you feel any better, the $50,000 I promised to set aside for college expenses, if investing my $34.50 turned out to be successful, is sitting in a safe interest-bearing account." Alex smiled.

Norman looked over at Alex, shrugged his shoulders, and gave a small grin. "Guess sometimes we tend to lose sight of our humble beginnings."

"I might suggest that we get back to what we're here for," said Walt.

"Pop?"

"Sure, why not," sighed Norman.

"Unless the three of you object, I would like to be the sole stockholder of the holding company. We will continue to invest as we are now, but I think in the future things will be easier if I have sole possession of the holding company from the beginning."

Marian, Norman, and Walt just looked at each other for a

moment and shrugged their shoulders.

"What would you like to name this new company, Son?"

"Nothing fancy... how about Gabriel Industries?"

"That's got a nice ring to it."

"Let's hear about it, Alex," said Marian.

"There really won't be much difference except that the holding company takes the place of my stock trust account. Uncle Walt will be chairman of the board and CEO. Mom, you'll be President, Margaret will be Treasurer, and Colleen the Secretary."

"I doubt anyone will object, Alex," Walt remarked. "If you wish to do this, I'm sure you have a good reason. There are only the three accounts to be concerned with. Your folks', yours -- with your mother as trustee -- and mine. With you as sole stockholder of the new company, your mother will have to remain as trustee for a few more years."

"That's correct," agreed Alex. "Secondly, we put the mutual fund, along with all my other assets, under the ownership of Gabriel Industries, which of course, you run, Uncle. Third, we form a real estate brokerage and a commodity brokerage firm. We hire two people to head up these operations and let them pick their staffs." Alex paused for a moment, seemed to come to a decision and continued. "In a few days, I will have the names of some people we can interview for those positions. These two new companies will be wholly owned by Gabriel Industries."

Norman sat staring at Alex, clearly in awe of his son's business acumen.

"Been giving this some thought for quite a while, have you, Master Alex?" Walt inquired in his best southern accent, the mood now lighter in the office.

"Yep." *About twenty-five years*, thought Alex.

"Then, once we have Gabriel Industries on line, I would like to begin plans to build our own corporate headquarters building, down closer to the beach. Probably on the Pacific Coast Highway, overlooking the ocean and harbor. It will be a prestigious address and have a great view."

"Build our own building?" asked Norman, again surprised.

"You bet." Alex smiled. "The biggest, best, and most visible in all of Orange County."

"Why would you want to build an office building when we can lease beautiful space like this?" Walt motioned around his office.

"Several reasons. First, space like this will become costly in the future, probably equal to or exceeding rents paid in downtown LA. What are you paying now, about fifty cents a foot per month?"

"Fifty-eight."

"I would be willing to bet that future rents will be up to three dollars a foot for this same office."

"Nobody could afford that, Alex," Walt disagreed.

"Not at today's economy and money value, no; but in the future."

"You think so?"

"Just about sure of it."

"Well, go on!" Marian was clearly anxious to hear the rest of the plan.

Alex smiled. "Secondly, a prestigious office building will pay for itself in rents in a relatively short period of time." Alex, as usual, was ticking off the points on his fingers. "Third, building costs won't be getting a bit cheaper and the longer we wait, the more it's going to cost to build, and the longer it will take to recover my capital investment. Fourth, we will not be paying someone else's mortgage payment for them; our tenants will be paying ours."

"Damn, Alex, do you have any idea what this is going to cost?"

"Oh, probably about eighty to ninety dollars a foot for what I have in mind."

"Eighty dollars a foot!" exclaimed Norman.

"That'll probably build us a nice building," explained Alex.

"And how big a building are you thinking about?" asked Walt.

"Thirty or forty stories, a million square feet."

"Jesus, Kid," Norman muttered.

"That'll cost you over a hundred million dollars -- more than your net worth, Son."

"I think I can get it done for twenty percent down and borrow the rest at a nice interest rate. Can't go wrong. It will end up costing nothing and actually make a lot of money."

The four sat for a minute saying nothing.

Walt was first to break the silence. "Are you going to let me in on exactly what you have in mind with this major change in the way we have been conducting a successful investment strategy?"

"Yes, and in one word.... image."

"Image?" the three said, almost in unison.

"Yes. In order to get big things done, you need a great deal of clout. Clout comes from money, connections, and image. If, for example, you want to get the powers in the city or county government to say, change zoning or bend or change building codes, relax city ordinances and such, you need clout. Money we have, but we're pitifully short on connections, and our image is nonexistent. Image can be and usually is, created. It is my intent to make the Gabriel name a household word."

"Why, Son? We're doing great. We have more money than we will ever be able to spend and we're making more all the time."

"It's not the money, Pop."

"And, as I recall, Alex, you have been the one to insist we keep a low profile. Many times you wouldn't even buy all the shares you could because, you said, and I quote, 'We don't want to draw too much attention.'" Walt paused, obviously perplexed. "Now you want to make the Gabriel name a household word?"

"Not only that, but I'm going to start to make substantial financial contributions to various local and state politicians, for starters." Alex was being contemplative. "This helps fill the need for connections. When a Gabriel or an associate of ours walks into a county or city council meeting or into the Mayor's office, I want people to take serious notice."

"You want to be famous -- is that it, Alex?" asked Walt.

Alex looked over at his uncle, his face displaying a little disappointment. "No! I don't want to be famous. To the contrary, I really don't want Alex Gabriel's name on anybody's lips; but I want the Gabriel name to be well-known and highly respected."

"What is it you want to do?" Marian asked quietly.

"I have no idea; I wish I did." Alex looked at his mother and sensed her apprehension. He knew she was seeing beyond his dad's and uncle's concerns.

"But when I figure it out, I definitely don't want to be short of money."

Chapter 30

GABRIEL HEADQUARTERS
November 27, 1968
10:00 a.m.

It was the day before Thanksgiving and Alex was eagerly waiting for Teddy to show up at his office. Teddy knew nothing of the Gabriel Building, and little about Alex's business life. Today would be a real eye-opening experience for his friend. Alex swiveled in his chair and looked west across Balboa Bay while pondering the wisdom of what he was about to do. He had decided to tell Teddy almost everything about what he'd been doing in the six years since the accident. He felt guilty for concealing most of his life from his best friend, but Teddy was intelligent and mature for a fourteen-year-old and Alex felt certain he could trust him not to betray a confidence. He smiled as he contemplated Teddy's reaction. Hard to tell with Teddy; he had an amazing repertoire of reactions for almost any situation. This one ought to be a pip.

Alex's plan was to have his mother invite the Oldakers over for the long weekend, dropping Teddy off at the Gabriel Building on their way to the Gabriel home. He'd told his mother to have the Oldakers leave Teddy at the front entrance to the building, letting him find his way to Alex's office from there. Alex left instructions for everybody working in the lobby reception area to be on the lookout for his friend. When Teddy asked where he might find Alex, they were to politely give directions to the executive floor. The receptionist in the penthouse would buzz Alex upon Teddy's arrival.

"You're sure this is a good idea, Alex?" Marian asked.

"I hope so. I'd like to spend more time with Teddy, but it's impossible as long as I have to conceal so much of my life. He needs to know what's going on."

10:12 a.m.

"A Mr. Oldaker is here to see you, sir."

Alex smiled as he held down the intercom button, "Show him in please, Janice."

Within five seconds, one of the large side-by-side mahogany doors opened and Janice, followed by a grinning Teddy, entered his office.

"Hi, Teddy!" said Alex. He met Teddy halfway across the office and gave his friend a big hug. Janice smiled, turned and closed the door on her way out.

"Boy," Teddy began as he looked around the office. "This is bitchen."

"Bitchen, is it?" Alex smiled. He hadn't heard that expression for a couple of decades.

"Yeah, geeze," Teddy replied as he continued looking around. "And the lobby, wow! Got restaurants and everything. I wasn't even sure I was in the right place."

"You're in the right place, all right. Did you have any trouble finding it?"

"Naw, my dad is good at that kind of stuff. My mom spotted the building first. Then we saw the big Gabriel name at the top, but we figured that was just a coincidence."

"You figured that, did you?"

"Yeah, I told my dad that your uncle was pretty rich, but he said you'd have to be more than pretty rich to have a building like this. Said he'd read in the paper that this was the biggest building in Orange County."

"He's probably right."

"Boy, did ya see the girl down in the reception booth? Her

name's Bobbie. Read it on her name tag."

"I've seen her, yes."

"She's beautiful."

Alex could see his friend was excited.

"She called me 'sir' right off the bat. That was cool. When I asked if she knew where I could find you, she said, 'Why, you must be Mr. Oldaker.' I thought my dad must have followed me in, so I turned around real quick to see. Made her laugh."

"I can imagine." Alex was enjoying his friend's excitement.

"She's the one who told me to go up the elevators, all the way to the penthouse. Cool!"

"Cool, all right," Alex was mimicking his friend.

"We're on the top?"

"Fortieth floor, yes."

"Wow….Looks like a big emerald. It's all green glass."

"Sea green, actually," Alex smiled.

A puzzled expression appeared on Teddy's face. "How did Bobbie know my name, anyway?"

"She was told to keep an eye out for you."

"Who told her?"

"I did."

"You did?"

Alex nodded.

Teddy's face became a mask of confusion. His smile faded a little as he looked around the beautiful office again. "What are you doing here, Alex?"

Here it comes, thought Alex. "I work here," he responded with a slight smile.

"Work here? You mean you help your uncle or somethin'?" That would probably make some sense to Teddy. "Is this his office?"

"Nope, this is my office, believe it or not."

Teddy again looked around the expanse of the room, "Okay," he smiled. "What's the joke? This is going to be a good one, isn't it?"

"Oh, it's going to be a good one, all right," Alex agreed. "Why don't we sit down over here and I'll tell you a story that'll answer your questions." Alex turned and headed to his desk in the southwest corner. Teddy followed.

"Sit." Alex pointed to one of the two comfortable chairs sitting in front of the large cherry wood desk. He walked behind his desk and sat.

"Boy, this is a nice office. I've never seen anything like this, even in the movies." Teddy was relaxing a bit. "This office looks bigger than my house."

Alex looked around his office. "Not quite." Actually, Alex thought, if he included his private bath, this office was close to half the size of the Oldaker home. The office looked bigger because of its high ceilings.

"Hey, look at that view." Teddy quickly walked over to the west-facing windows that ran the entire length of the office, from floor to ceiling. "Wow, you can see everything from up here. Geeze, look at all the yachts down there. They look like canoes from here." Teddy walked quickly to the north corner and looked northwest along the Pacific Coast Highway. From this height, he could to see the many beachfront towns and the Palos Verdes Peninsula in the distance.

Alex watched Teddy walk around the office. He made his way to the northeast corner, past the board table.

Teddy turned. "I've never been this high up before."

"Glad you like it," Alex responded.

Teddy walked back to Alex's desk and plopped down on the chair. "Okay, tell me what you're up to." Clearly, Teddy was expecting a great story.

"Need to go back a few years, to start the story."

"Okay."

"Do you remember when you came into my old bedroom one time and I had all sorts of papers, charts and notebooks lying on top of my desk?"

Teddy wrinkled up his face for a minute. "A little bit maybe; back in your old house. A bunch of numbers and letters all over 'em."

"That's right, my old house."

"I've seen a lot of stuff on your shelves in your bedroom in the new house that didn't look like a lot of fun to me."

"Same kind of stuff, too. Just more of it now than there was back in Inglewood."

"So, what is it?"

"All kinds of investment information, mostly on stocks, some bonds, commodities, real estate, that sort of thing."

"You mean kinda like the stock market?"

"Not kinda," said Alex. "I've been investing in the stock market since I was eight. Since the accident."

"Investing in the stock market. They don't let kids invest in the stock market... do they?"

"My mom has to sign everything."

Teddy was getting more confused by the second. "Okay, so you buy stocks and other stuff; what's that got to do with being in this office today?" Clearly the fun had gone out of this conversation for Teddy.

"This is my office; I'm in here every day. It's where I work."

"Work?"

"Yes, work," Alex repeated. "Something happened to me in that accident six years ago, Teddy. My mind was altered. All of a sudden, I became smart about stocks and investments, stuff like that."

Teddy looked at Alex for a few seconds, his face suddenly acquiring a stern expression. "I knew it; I knew it!" He sat forward in his chair and pointed his finger at Alex. "Ever since you got hit by that truck, you haven't been the same. That's when you went kinda nutty; I remember you weren't the same after that. You were never the same after that." Teddy was becoming agitated.

"You're exactly right, Teddy." Alex wouldn't have guessed this reaction.

"Why didn't you tell me?"

"I didn't think you'd understand then; you were too young."

"I was the same age as you!" Teddy paused. "Still am!" Teddy was actually angry.

"I'm sorry but I couldn't tell you then; you wouldn't have

understood. The only people that know are my mom, dad, and uncle. My sister doesn't even know." Alex paused for a second. "I had to think a long time about telling you."

Teddy sat looking at Alex for about ten seconds. "I won't tell anyone, ya know?" Teddy's voice was cracking a little.

"I know you won't."

Teddy suddenly got up and walked to the far side of the office and looked north; his hands in his pockets. After a few seconds, Alex could hear him sniff quietly.

Shit, I've hurt my friend. "Teddy!"

"What?" said Teddy without turning around.

"I have something else to tell you."

Teddy turned to face his friend. The anger was starting to dissipate. "Now what?"

"I own this building."

Chapter 31

GABRIEL HEADQUARTERS
September 9, 1970
9:00 a.m.

Alex and Walt were in Walt's office finishing up the monthly and weekly reports.

Alex leaned back in his chair. "Times are changing, Uncle. I think we need to diversify and start investing outside this country."

"Really?"

"Yes, sir."

"Doin' pretty good where we're at, you know."

"Yes we are, but I think we will start to develop tunnel vision if we don't broaden our horizons a little. Need to get our fingers on the pulse of the rest of the financial and political world."

"Political world?"

"Well, politics has a great bearing on economics. We'd better get up to speed on the political climate in more countries than just ours. Our future investments depend, in part, on what other nations or regions of the world are doing."

"That's true," agreed Walt. "I assume you're not thinking about Third World countries?"

"Oh hell, no! The political corruption in Third World countries is, of course, why they remain Third World countries. We'll be staying out of such places for the foreseeable future."

"Good to hear you say that."

"It's tough enough dealing with corruption in so-called civilized countries, including this one."

"You're not implying that some of our elected officials are bent a little, are you?" Walt remarked lightly.

"I'm not implying anything," Alex smiled. "I'm saying it outright."

"I guess there are a few bad apples in our political barrel, but it's always been that way."

"A few bad apples? If I had to guess, I'd say that over ninety percent of our congressmen and senators are on the take in one form or another."

"Jesus, Alex, when did you become such a cynic?"

"I'm not a cynic; I'm a realist. As an example, what's a person's chance of getting an audience with a US senator if they haven't contributed a substantial amount to their campaign?"

"Slim to none."

"How many votes are cast in favor of legislation that benefit a large contributor?"

"Many."

"How many pork barrel projects are enacted to benefit the politician and his constituents at the expense of the rest of the nation's taxpayers?"

"Again, many."

"How many votes are cast, right or wrong, along party lines to simply gain favor with the party leaders? Or who sell their souls for an appointment to a powerful committee where they can demand even larger bribes, or as they like to say, campaign contributions."

Walt sat back and looked at his nephew for a moment. "So you think only ninety percent of our politicians are corrupt?" Walt laughed.

"I was being kind."

"I get the picture. So what 'first world countries' would you like to take a look at?"

"What do you think of sending Robert Chin over to set up and run a Hong Kong operation?"

"I guess that means we're starting a Hong Kong expansion first." It was more of a statement than a question.

"I think that would be a good place to start. Hong Kong is the financial center of Southeast Asia and, no doubt, will be until the Chinese take back control in 1997. The amount of money that flows through that island in one day is truly mind-boggling."

"I understand there are some serious sharks in that area of the world and Robert Chin is only twenty-six, with limited experience, Alex. I would think you would want someone with a great deal more experience to captain a ship in those waters."

"A point well taken, but to continue the metaphor, I think we can provide Robert with a pretty good bite. We'll put a substantial deposit in the Bank of Hong Kong to help establish credentials. We'll also hire a local shark to help guide young Chin through those treacherous seas. We can get some excellent introductions from our contacts here."

"We'll need to find out whether or not Robert would be willing to take on such an adventure," Walt added.

"Robert is bright, hard working, half Chinese, speaks fluent Mandarin and is ambitious. I'll bet you a case of good scotch against a six pack of Grape Nehi that he'll go for it without a minute's thought," replied Alex.

"Having a Chinese surname should be a leg up," said Walt pensively. "I don't suppose you had this in mind when we hired this kid a year ago, did you?"

"The thought crossed my mind."

Chapter 32

GABRIEL HEADQUARTERS
January 4, 1971
9:30 a.m.

Colleen Keefe worked her way into becoming an indispensable part of Gabriel Industries. When they first moved into the new building, she was in charge of office operations and took care of all hiring and firing except for executive staff. Three months before, she was appointed to fill the position of Executive Secretary and her salary doubled.

"I had a feeling sticking with you Gabriel boys would be the right thing to do," she kidded.

Alex felt her crush on Walt, that began the day she went to work for him and had grown over the past seven years, had more to do with her decision to "stick with the Gabriel boys" than her successful climb up the corporate ladder. Alex and everyone close to them could see she held deep affection for Walt. Alex couldn't understand why Walt didn't or chose not to see the obvious. He knew his uncle had strong feelings for Colleen, but he managed to hide them well. He also knew his uncle would never make a serious pass or ask Colleen out, believing as he did in "not sticking your pen in company ink." He and Colleen would banter back and forth with all sorts of innuendoes, sexual and otherwise, but that's as far as it went.

Alex, for his part, maintained a mild crush on Colleen, but never let on to anyone, except Teddy.

It was a gray day in Southern California. The long New Year's weekend was over and things were running a bit slow in the office. Walt, Alex and Colleen were sitting at one end of the board table, doing a little first-of-the year planning, concentrating mainly on staff commitments and future office allocations.

Colleen seemed quite distracted for most of the morning. She wasn't prepared for a lot of the questions that Walt and Alex were asking about vacancies and staff requirements. This was not characteristic of this competent woman.

"How much more space do you think we'll need?" Walt directed his question at Colleen.

Colleen was thumbing through a file sitting on the table in front of her. She looked flustered.

Alex turned his attention to Walt. "It's hard to believe we're going to require more of this building's space. It's been less than three years since we moved in."

"We now occupy what? Thirty percent of the space? Is that right, Colleen?"

Colleen looked up from her fruitless search of the files, "I don't know, I guess so… something like that."

Walt looked at Alex then back to Colleen, "Perhaps we had better do this another time. We all seem to be running a little slow," Walt remarked as he started gathering his papers together.

"You mean I'm a little slow, don't you?" Clearly, Colleen was not happy.

Alex had never seen Colleen like this, but instinct told him to let Walt handle it.

"Well, it's been a long weekend, Colleen. I'm not sharp today, either," offered Walt. "We'll just get at this tomorrow afternoon, after the market closes.

Colleen abruptly stood up and started for the door, leaving her files on the table.

Walt was surprised and stood quickly. "Colleen, are you upset with me? What is it? What did I do?"

Alex just sat and watched. Like Walt, he had never seen Colleen act petulant in any way.

Colleen turned back to face the Gabriels. She had tears in those beautiful green eyes.

Uh-oh, thought Alex.

"We've got to have a talk," she said.

"I'll be going now," declared Alex. "I have a feeling this has nothing to do with me." Alex got up from his chair and headed for the door.

"I'm afraid it does have to do with you, too, Alex."

"Whatever I did, I apologize; I didn't mean it and I'll never do it again," Alex responded rapidly.

"No, no, Alex, you sweetheart," Colleen said smiling a little. "You didn't do anything wrong. Neither of you have; it's me. I've made a terrible mistake."

"Whatever it is, we forgive you and that's the end of it -- right, Alex?" Walt expressed, looking quickly at Alex, getting an enthusiastic nod, and then back to Colleen. He was clearly intent on putting whatever this unpleasantness was behind them as quickly as possible.

Alex could see that his uncle was starting to panic; he could hear the tightness in his voice and could see a large vein on Walt's forehead pulsing rapidly.

Colleen's face was starting to contort as if she were about to lose all restraint. She steeled herself and gained some composure. "I'm afraid I'm going to have to tender my resignation."

"*What*?" both the Gabriels exclaimed at once.

"I don't know what else I can do," she replied. "I spent the entire New Year's weekend alone, going over my options and came to the conclusion that I must get away from... " There was a long pause while Colleen fought with herself about what to say. "From Gabriel Industries."

Alex could see the pain that this wonderful woman was going

through, but he remained silent. This, he still felt, was Walt's business.

"Why, for Christ's sake, Colleen?" Walt was beside himself. He walked over and was about to put his arms around her. She backed off a couple of feet.

"*You, God damn it*, you big blind son of a bitch." The dam broke; tears were pouring down her cheeks.

Alex came out of his chair. "I get it, and I'm out of here. Your resignation is not accepted… 'Aunt Colleen.'" Alex headed to the door, stopped and turned. "Uncle Walt, I don't want to hear another damned word about company ink!" Alex went out the door and closed it behind him. "Hold my uncle's calls; no interruptions at all… I'll take any urgent calls," Alex instructed Carol as he walked by. He walked back to his office, a big smile on his face. *This is going to be a great year.'*

April 11, 1971

It was a beautiful spring day for a wedding and a finer, more lavish wedding had not been seen in Orange County. The Laguna Chapel was rented because of its size and location overlooking the Pacific Ocean. Over four hundred invitations had been sent out and nearly everyone invited had accepted. The guests ranged from officers and employees of Gabriel Industries to local and state politicians whom had become friends over the last couple of years. The Gabriel and Keefe families were represented to the fullest.

Norman was to be Walt's best man, as Walt had been at Norman's wedding. As one of the groomsmen, Alex stood next to his father, reflecting happily on the confrontation three months before that preceded this wonderful occasion. *What a day that was*!

He found himself absently looking across the aisle at the bridesmaids. The three, including Jennifer and two of Colleen's sisters, were dressed in emerald green silk floor-length gowns with sunbonnets of pale yellow trimmed in emerald. The gowns were somewhat low-cut and exposed a little cleavage. One of Colleen's sisters, Aidan, must have been ten years younger and nearly as beautiful as Colleen. In a couple of years, she might even catch her sister in the beauty department. The other sister was just over a year older and married with two children. She didn't have the striking beauty that Colleen and her younger sister possessed, but was a handsome woman nonetheless. Her husband was also a groomsman and stood on Alex's left as they faced the rear of the chapel. He, Alex understood, was a successful general contractor in San Diego. Alex's eyes were continually being drawn to the younger sister, Aidan. This young lady was definitely a Keefe. Although a full inch shorter than Colleen, she had the same beautiful Irish skin and green eyes. Her hair, although red, was darker than Colleen's by a shade, but her figure was, like Colleen's, impeccable.

Alex had seen Aidan only once prior to the rehearsal dinner held two nights before, and that was about five years earlier when Colleen had brought her into Walt's office for the day. It seemed that Aidan, as Alex recalled, had been requested to stay out of school for a few days to contemplate the error of her ways. Apparently, among other things, she had a major problem with the school dress code. She would have been about ten or eleven at the time. Alex remembered her as a pretty little girl dressed in ripped blue jeans, dirty sweatshirt, and the most trashed sneakers he had ever seen. He also remembered, with some amusement, Colleen's embarrassment over her younger sister's appearance. *Well, she isn't dressed in blue jeans and sweatshirt today, and she isn't a little girl anymore, not by a long shot.*

At the rehearsal dinner, she and Alex hadn't gotten a chance to speak, other than a brief greeting, but Alex planned on rectifying that today. At the meal two nights before, Alex remembered Aidan wasn't wearing any makeup and wore a plain, nondescript dress. Even so, he thought her extraordinarily pretty. *She's wearing makeup today and has gone from pretty to gorgeous.*

Alex found himself reflecting on the conversation that he and Colleen had the morning after the rehearsal dinner...

"Aidan and I talked about you last night."

"Really?" remarked Alex, finding this somewhat arousing. "What was said?"

"Well, she thought you were as skinny as the proverbial rail."

"I'll fill out someday," Alex replied matter-of-factly, hiding his disappointment.

"I told her that."

"That's all that was said?" Alex probed.

"Oh no. She also said she thought you had nice hair and," Colleen paused a second, "the most incredible eyes she'd ever seen."

"She said that?" *Cool!* he thought.

"She did."

Alex's smile broadened.

"I told her that she would have a great deal of trouble keeping up with you."

"Why would you tell her that?"

"My little sister has always taken to challenges."

Alex thought about that for a second. "What did she say?"

"She said that she'd never seen a boy she couldn't keep way ahead of," Colleen answered with a trace of a smile.

"Really?"

"Yep, but I told her she'd just seen one."

Alex looked deep into Colleen's dazzling green eyes, "It seems to me," he said, "you're playing Cupid."

"You think so?" Colleen feigned innocence as she turned and walked out of the office.

Alex again looked across the aisle at Aidan and found himself anxious to have the wedding itself over so he could get a much closer look at this particular Keefe at the reception.

The twenty-piece band suddenly stopped what they were playing, paused briefly and began the Wedding March. All eyes turned to the back of the church. Colleen appeared on the arm of her father and the place went abuzz. It was hard to imagine a more beautiful woman in the world.

My God! was all Alex could think.

The two photographers hired to record the wedding and a dozen or so in the pews began taking pictures as fast as they could. Alex looked over at his uncle and smiled when he saw the look of total wonderment and love on his face. One of the experienced photographers caught and recorded that magnificent expression for the following generations to see and enjoy.

Great shot! thought Alex.

The wedding went off without a hitch, thanks to Marian's organizational skills and Colleen's eye for detail. The two of them together were a force to reckon with.

The reception was held at the Balboa Bay Club's great hall.

Following the reception line, the guests meandered around the hall, many heading directly for the bar, others talking and sipping a non-alcoholic punch. Alex found himself talking to Teddy on one side of the hall while Aidan and two of her friends were on the other side of the room. The three young women were corralled by five young men, ranging in age from thirteen to twenty.

"Did ya see the redheaded bridesmaid?" an awestruck Teddy asked.

"Am I blind or what?" replied Alex.

"Guess that was a stupid question." Teddy was smiling widely.

"Pretty hard not to notice that girl." Alex continued to watch Aidan from across the room.

"She's almost as pretty as Colleen," Teddy proclaimed.

"As hard as that is to comprehend, I believe you're right."

"Think we could go over and talk to them?"

"I don't think any of them are packing a gun, so I'm willing to take the risk," Alex responded with a smile. "Let's go!"

About halfway across the hall, Teddy muttered under his breath, "You do the talking, okay?"

Alex smiled. "If you insist."

As they approached the young women, Alex put out his hand. "Aidan, it was a beautiful wedding, wasn't it?"

Aidan took Alex's offered hand. "I've never seen a prettier one." She held his hand for a moment.

"I have to tell you," said Alex, "that your sister was the prettiest bride I, and I suspect everyone in attendance, have ever seen."

That statement seemed to delight Aidan. "What a nice thing to say." She came forward and gave Alex a nice hug.

"Well, if that fact earns me a hug, let me say you are the most beautiful bridesmaid I've ever seen."

"That will earn you another hug, all right." Aidan put her arms around Alex's shoulders, pushed her body into his and held on for a few seconds.

"I'll second that," remarked the oldest of the boys while nudging his friends to one side. He opened his arms for a hug.

"Sorry, I only hug for original flattery." Aidan smiled radiantly as she released Alex.

"Geeze," Teddy uttered under his breath.

"And your friends are?" Alex looked over at the two girls at Aidan's side.

"Oh, I'm sorry," she turned toward her friends. "This is J.J." she motioned toward a petite young lady with flowing silky brown hair.

Alex shook her hand. "Nice to meet you, J.J." *Teddy's going to like this one*, thought Alex.

"And this is Eryn." Aidan introduced the brunette dressed in a hot pink micro-mini.

"Nice to meet you, too, Eryn," Alex smiled while shaking her hand.

Eryn, and J.J., much to Teddy's delight, looked even prettier close up.

"This is my oldest and dearest friend, Teddy." Alex introduced Teddy to the girls.

The band on the far side of the hall started playing a nice dance tune.

Chapter 33

GABRIEL HOME
March 25, 1972
7:00 p.m.

The Gabriels were sitting at their dining room table just finishing up Alex's birthday cake. Alex had already opened his presents and colorful wrapping paper littered the floor around his chair. His mother had given him three nice sweaters and two new tennis outfits. Jennifer bought him a nice pair of sunglasses, the new fad aviator type. After these presents were opened, Norman left the room and returned, toting what had to be a large picture or painting by its size and shape. It was wrapped in conservative but expensive looking paper.

"For your office, kid. I hope you like it." Norman seemed nervous.

Alex was surprised his father would give him such a present. He took the package from his father and sat it on an empty chair with the top leaning on the back. He tore the paper away. There, in an impressive gilded frame, was an oil painting of Alex at the age of nine or ten, sitting on his rock in the mouth of the harbor, elbows on his knees and his chin cupped in his hands, looking out at the blue Pacific. If you looked closely, you could see the ever-present notebook sticking out of his back pocket with a ballpoint pen stuck into the spiral wire binding. Everything was depicted perfectly, from the sailboats to gulls to the sea foam, running off the rocks. The painting had to have been done by a master and captured the feel of Alex's special place so well that Alex was completely speechless.

"Do you like it, Son?"

All Alex could do was nod. He couldn't take his eyes off the painting. He turned to his father and gave him a hug. "It's the nicest present I've ever had -- I don't know how to thank you for it."

"I think you're doing an adequate job," his father responded cheerfully as the anxiety drained from his body.

Marian knew Norman was apprehensive about this gift.

"*... but he may hate it. He may feel it's an invasion of his privacy or something*," Norman had been quite concerned.

"*Norm, he's going to love it, especially if it's from you,*" she had tried to reassure him.

Alex let go of his father and looked again at the painting. "This is wonderful," he said.

Norman looked over at his wife and gave her one of the most loving and proud looks she'd ever seen from him.

Walt and Colleen walked around behind Alex and were also taken by the painting. "That's just incredible," Colleen remarked, without taking her eyes off the painting.

"Well, that's going to be a real tough act to follow," added Walt, who was also caught up in the moment. He smiled, "I guess we'll save our present until your next birthday."

"Oh no you don't, Uncle." Alex acted alarmed. "I'll be having it now if you don't mind too much." Alex reached over and squeezed his father's arm. "Thank you, Pop."

Walt smiled as he walked to the serving table. He picked up a small box wrapped in shiny black paper and a small gold bow; he handed it to Alex. It measured no more than three inches square and an inch deep. Alex removed the paper and opened the box. Car keys!

"In the garage, Master Alex." Walt grinned as he reached over and took Colleen's hand.

The six of them, with Alex in the lead, quickly made their way to the garage.

There it was in the first stall. A brand new shiny black Shelby Cobra with silver racing stripes, wrapped with the biggest gold ribbon and bow Alex had ever seen.

"That's a 427-cubic-inch engine with 450 horsepower, my young nephew. I figured a high-powered young man like yourself needed a car to match. Hope you enjoy it."

"Oh my God!"

Now, twenty minutes later, Alex was still smiling as he looked over at the painting. He couldn't wait to hang it in his office. And he couldn't wait to drive his new car. He put the last bite of cake in his mouth as Walt started to stand. He had a champagne glass in his hand.

"I would like to propose a toast to Alexander J. Gabriel," Walt said as he stood, not too steadily, and raised his champagne glass, "the brightest, handsomest, and newest eighteen year-old *billionaire* on the face of the planet."

"*Billionaire?*" both Norman and Marian chimed in at once.

"Yes, you heard right, and after taxes, by God." Walt was just beaming, having already had several glasses of the bubbly. "We decided to break the news to you on the kid's birthday. Actually, he passed the mark a couple of weeks ago, but we thought today would be a nice time to tell you."

Norman was looking at his son as if he'd just grown a third eye, and Jennifer's mouth dropped open. Marian stood and walked around the table, took Alex by the shoulders, pulled him to his feet and gave him a big hug. "Congratulations, Son. You're really something."

"Thanks, Mom," Alex replied as he held her by the shoulders at arm's length. "As I have said before, I couldn't have done it without your understanding and trust."

Alex knew his net worth was going to come as a big shock to his father, and he had tried to talk Walt out of the announcement.

"*...Your father, my slightly narrow-minded brother, needs to be yanked into reality once in a while...*"

"You are looking at a young man who ran $34.50 to over a billion dollars in just ten years," Walt went on. "I, for one, cannot wait to see what this fella will accomplish in the next ten years." Walt's smile looked as if in might split his face. He took another sip of champagne.

It was clear by Norman's demeanor that he was more disturbed by Alex's extreme wealth than delighted that his son was doing so well.

"As I recall, that's just what you said you'd do ten years ago when we made the 'agreement.' We assumed that prediction was just a little boy's fantasy -- but it wasn't then, and it's not now... is it?" Norman paused for a brief moment. "Just how much money do you think you'll need?"

"Not really sure, Pop. I'm sure I don't have nearly enough to do anything yet. But if I have a God-awful amount of money by the time I figure it out, I'll be able to get right to it," Alex replied with some humor.

"Do you think ten billion would allow you to do -- whatever?" Norman wasn't being snide; he was serious.

"Ten billion would probably allow me to do almost anything." Alex was trying to remain casual.

"*Almost*? Then I have to assume you'll be accumulating a great deal more than ten billion. How about a hundred billion? Or maybe a trillion, for Christ's sake." You could practically see the adrenaline pumping into Norm's veins. "Just what are you going to do, Son?"

"I'll need guidance…" Alex suddenly stopped. His face lost all expression; his eyes glazed over. He reached over and unsteadily took hold of the back of his chair. "Need guidance," he repeated in almost a whisper. "I'll need… oh… what… "

"Alex?" said Marian with some alarm.

Alex's forehead broke out in sweat and he started swaying slightly. He was in trouble. Norman sprang up, knocking over his chair, and was at Alex's side within two seconds; he took Alex by the shoulders, steadying him. Walt, Colleen, and Jennifer sat, transfixed.

Alex's face became animated. It looked as if he was watching something he didn't understand, couldn't comprehend. His brows furrowed and he cocked his head slightly as if to get a better look. "What is that? Why are all those… people…?" he whispered, all the while looking off in the distance. "I can't… no, I … so many… " His voice was choking, tears started to form in the corners of his eyes.

Marian put her face just inches from her son's. "Alex!" she yelled.

That startled Alex. His eyes cleared some and he regained his balance. "What the hell?" he said, clearly confused.

"What the hell is right!" said Norman.

Alex looked at his chair and sat down, heavily. He sat for a few seconds, slowly looking around. "Where am I? What day is this?"

Marian looked at Norman then back to Alex. "You're at home, it's your 18th birthday."

Alex looked up at his mother. "Oh?... really? Alex remained confused for another minute. "Oh, okay…. Good!" he said, while attempting a smile. "I guess I went away for a while."

"Where in the hell did you go?" asked Norman as he bent down to pick up his chair.

Alex sat contemplating that question for a couple of moments. "I think I went everywhere."

"You didn't have time to go everywhere, Son," said Marian.

"Oh, yes I did. I was gone… quite a while."

Again Marian looked at her husband. She was frightened.

"What did you see?" asked Norman.

"Oh, I saw… dead bodies… chaos… all over the world." Alex's brow furrowed. "I can't remember why."

Chapter 34

GABRIEL HOME
April 11, 1974
8:20 p.m.

Alex looked across the Gabriels' dining room table to his aunt and uncle. It was obvious that their marriage agreed with them. *It's hard to believe it's their third anniversary.*

This wasn't an anniversary that would normally be celebrated, but Marian was going to have a small dinner party anyway to introduce Jennifer's new boyfriend to the family, and the timing was right. She, as always, invited Teddy to join the party. She considered him one of her own, and he was a great guest. He kept any function lively; he was an entertainer.

"I understand that you and my pretty sister have been seeing a lot of each other, lately, Alex," Colleen remarked.

"Yes, we have," Alex smiled broadly. "Plan on seeing more of her, too."

Teddy looked up from his dessert. "The girl is dazzling, darn near as gorgeous as her older sister."

"She is indeed." Alex winked at Teddy.

"You're a lucky man," Teddy smiled.

Colleen turned her attention to Teddy. "Aidan tells me you've been seeing a lot of Eryn."

"Yep, I am. She's going to college in Washington, but we get together whenever she gets a break."

"Anything serious there?"

"We're having some serious fun, if that's what you're asking," Teddy said with a big grin.

"That's not exactly what I meant."

"Chuck, what field do you plan to pursue when you graduate?" Walt turned the attention to Jennifer's boyfriend.

Jennifer's newest beau had potential that most of her past boyfriends lacked. He was twenty-two and, according to Jennifer, would be graduating with nearly a four-point average from the University of California at San Diego.

Chuck seemed apprehensive about the evening and remained quiet unless asked a direct question. His friends at college continually teased him about dating the richest girl in Orange County, but had he known the extent of this wealth, he might have been even more nervous.

"Well, sir," Chuck began, "I want to get into research in the field of projected optics." His palms were beginning to sweat. A person didn't have to be a student of body language to see that Chuck really didn't want to be the center of attention. "I'll be getting my BS soon. Two more years for a master's and who knows how much longer for a doctorate." He put his hands under the table and wiped them on the napkin. "Then I will apply to a research facility such as TRW or maybe SARC."

Alex was all ears as he looked over at this neatly dressed young man. Given the times, it was refreshing to see a college student with close-cropped hair and no beads. Alex knew Jennifer had always been drawn to men with dark hair and olive complexions. Chuck was all that, but a bit shorter than her other "friends," and a great deal neater-looking.

"Projected optics?" inquired Walt.

"Yes, sir. Lasers, fiber-optics, heavy particles… that field. I believe this is a growing industry, unlimited in scope."

"Who, in your opinion, is the top dog or dogs, if you will, in that field?" asked Alex.

Chuck looked at Alex. "There are a number who are doing

remarkable research right now, Alex. Dr. Julius Brown at Stanford, Sam Plummer at MIT, and a number of lesser-knowns. There is a professor at the University of Tokyo who has some really exciting ideas using heavy particles."

"Hiro Takanara?"

"Why… why yes." Chuck was clearly puzzled.

Alex smiled inwardly, seeing the surprised look on Chuck's face. "I know that Hiro Takanara is doing some astonishing work with heavy particles." Alex took a sip of his iced tea.

"I didn't realize you were interested in light physics, Alex."

"I've read a few articles on the subject," Alex acknowledged. "I would like to spend more time talking to you about this. It's a field that has interested me for some time."

Chuck's forehead had begun to bead up to the point of dripping.

Norman apparently noticed and picked up his napkin, blotting his own forehead. "Anybody getting warm in here besides me?"

"Yes, sir," responded Chuck as he quickly wiped his forehead before it actually dripped.

Marian looked over at Norman and gave him an almost imperceptible smile. She turned her attention back to Chuck. "Jennifer tells me that you're a real brain, and getting top grades, but I assumed she was a little prejudiced." It was obvious Marian had taken a liking to Chuck.

"Don't start on me, Mom," Jennifer said lightly.

"I have to study quite hard to maintain good grades, Mrs. Gabriel." Chuck continued to wipe his hands on a napkin under the table.

"No shame in having to study hard," said Norman.

"Chuck, what's your schedule for the coming week, if you don't mind me asking?" Alex interjected. There was something about this young man that struck a chord in some deep recess of his mind.

"Dead week coming up; I'll be studying for finals in between work schedules."

"Is there a day we might have lunch?" Alex pressed on.

"I suppose any day really," offered Chuck. "How's Tuesday for you?"

"I'll have to check my calendar, but I believe that will work. I'll give you a call tomorrow to confirm."

"Okay."

"Would you mind bringing some information on lasers and heavy particles with you?"

"What sort of information would you like? There is literally tons of printed material on those subjects."

Alex could nearly read Chuck's thoughts, almost see what he was thinking. He was a little like Teddy as far as facial expressions were concerned. *He's having trouble comprehending the fact that he's talking to a man two years his junior,* thought Alex. *And he's wondering why I have any knowledge of light physics*. "I would like what you think are the best and most promising theories on both subjects," Alex replied. "Ideas that you would like to pursue when you get into research. The volume of material you bring is up to you. I will tell you that I'll read everything you are able to leave with me. I do quite a bit of reading."

"That would be a mild understatement," remarked Norman to a chorus of affirmatives.

"And be dammed if he doesn't remember just about everything he reads," Walt added.

"And understands it all, to boot! That's always been the tough part for me," Teddy jumped in. "If I started reading some of the crap that Alex reads, I wouldn't remember my name by the fifth page."

"Whoa," said Alex. "Enough, enough!"

Within minutes, the conversation switched away from Chuck and light physics. But Alex recalled what Jennifer told him about Chuck. Chuck had lost his mother to cancer in his freshman year of college. He and his father had both lost the most important person in their lives that day three years ago. What had been difficult, before his mother's death, apparently became almost impossible after. Jennifer told him Chuck was able to get several small grants and made up the rest of the expenses through student loans and work-study programs. *He knows what it is to work,* thought Alex. He liked Chuck now that he had met him. Liked him a lot. Alex had a thought; actually it was more like a revelation. *I'm going to need this man in my future.*

Chapter 35

GABRIEL HOME
October 20, 1974
7:30 p.m.

Marian was enjoying the early evening with three of her favorite people: her husband, Walt, and Colleen. The four were enjoying a glass of wine out on the patio after a leisurely dinner; something Marian and Norman made part of their daily routine. The sun had all but dropped below the vast Pacific horizon and it was a relatively quiet time in the harbor. It was a beautiful evening.

"Alex's twenty-first birthday is coming in just over five months and it's time we made some plans," Marian remarked.

"God, that's right; the boy's coming of age." Walt put down his wine glass. "Chronologically speaking, of course… the boy's been of age mentally for what... thirteen years?"

"Thirteen years is about right...since the accident." Marian looked melancholy. "Since the accident," she repeated quietly as she stared at her wine glass.

The four sat in silence for a few seconds.

"We lost our little boy in that accident," Marian acknowledged softly, betraying the loss she still felt. "But God immediately replaced him with Alexander." She smiled. "At any rate, we have to make plans."

"Agreed," said Walt.

CONNOR BUILDING
March 25, 1975
2:00 p.m.

The birthday celebration, much to Alex's surprise, started midday in his office. A dozen senior Gabriel executives were led in by Carol, followed within seconds by Walt and Norman. Marian and Colleen came in last, carrying between them a miniature steamer trunk. They set the trunk on the board table and all broke into a ragged version of Happy Birthday.

"Thank you all. I would recommend voice lessons but I don't believe they'd help." Alex couldn't take his eyes off the trunk. "What's this?"

"It's your birthday present," answered Marian.

"Really?"

"This diminutive trunk, my young nephew, was painstakingly designed by your creative father, my talented brother, a year ago, and made in China under the direction of Robert Chin, of your acquaintance."

"Really," he repeated. He smiled at his father, and then bent over to take a closer look. The trunk was made of polished ebony and deeply engraved in an intricate design. Instead of the normal brass, the corners, latches, and fittings were made of solid gold, inlaid and engraved. It was an absolutely stunning piece of art. "Wow!"

"Open it up, Son," said Norman. "The real treasures are inside."

Alex smiled, bent over, released the latch and opened the trunk. He put his hand on three rich- looking leather folders. "And these are?"

Walt, without saying a word, reached in and picked up the first folder. He opened it with some flourish and held up single stock certificate for all to see. It stated, SUNSHADE CORPORATION, 1000 SHARES.

Alex instantly realized that his uncle had saved this cancelled stock certificate for the past thirteen years. He smiled brightly.

"This is the actual stock certificate from Alex's first venture into the stock market," Walt explained to the people gathered around the board table. "Alex bought this at age eight for just over $30.00 and sold it for a gain of 1900 percent just six weeks later." Walt grinned. "He's been making investments like that ever since."

Marian stepped up and retrieved the second folder. "This," she announced, "contains the documents that effectively remove my name from all your trusts and turn total control of the Alexander J. Gabriel fortune over to you. You no longer need my signature."

"I hadn't given that a thought," said Alex.

"Last, but not at all least," said Walt as he held up the last folder, "these documents, when signed by you, will make you Chairman of the Board and Chief Executive Officer of Gabriel Industries and Gabriel International. I hereby officially turn the reins of the two largest corporations in the world over to you."

"I didn't expect anything like this. It's a little overwhelming. Thank you very much." Alex looked at the people around the table. *So much for my anonymity.*

The actual birthday party was held that night at the fabulous Newport Marriott. It was a party the likes of which few in attendance, had ever seen. Marian had pulled out all the stops.

March 26, 1975
4:30 a.m.

Alex was lying on his back in bed; his face held a satisfied smile that threatened to become a permanent fixture. *Wow,* he thought, that *was some party.* His smile increased. *It was the most fun I've ever had. The entire evening was perfect… and continues to be.*

He moved his head just slightly to look down at Aidan, who was lying in the crook of his arm with her face and right hand on his chest. Her red hair spread across her gorgeous face and the pillow. She was sleeping soundly. *What an incredible woman. She was and is the topping on my cake.*

During the previous evening, Alex noticed that the passion in

Aidan's sparkling green eyes grew as the party wore on. And he noticed the passion emanating from her perfect body as they danced. It was difficult, at times, to pull himself away to speak to the guests as they came up to congratulate him. Alex's smile widened.

Chapter 36

GABRIEL HEADQUARTERS
May 12, 1975

One of the men in the meeting was growing flustered. "Mr. Gabriel, are you saying that you expect to buy our wheat at $1.00 a bushel?"

"And pay the shipping."

"You're a smart young man and I'd be surprised if you didn't know exactly what it costs to grow and harvest a bushel of wheat."

"If memory serves, the costs average about $2.75 per."

"That's close enough, sir."

"But," added Alex, "unless my information is incorrect, Mr. Voyce, the American wheat growers have managed to produce so much wheat that there isn't an empty silo in the continental United States. In fact, there are hundreds of thousands of tons stored in huge piles on the ground beside those silos and on farms all over the nation. Is that not correct?"

"Yes, sir."

"Is it not also correct that wheat is presently selling for less than $3.00 per bushel because of this glut?"

"Yes, sir. But it's not selling for $1.00."

"Is there a lot of profit at $3.00?"

"None really."

"Okay then, let's get to the facts. I propose to buy a great deal of your wheat and ship it out of the country. Your farmers will get

$1.00 per bushel and be able to take a huge tax loss. My buying this wheat will lower the glut considerably and, therefore, raise the price of your remaining wheat. You should be able to get a somewhat higher price for your remaining wheat than what it's presently selling for. Is what I've said true or not?"

"Yes, sir."

"Then what's the problem?"

"The $1.00 a bushel, sir. Our fixed markets around the world will naturally wonder why they're paying, say $3.00, when we're willing to sell it to you for $1.00."

"Because, Mr. Voyce," Alex smiled, "you're willing to take a beating on price in order to help the starving people around the world. The PR for the American wheat growers will benefit your organization immeasurably. And, one has to assume that there will be droughts, floods, or disasters of one kind or another followed by famine somewhere around the world every year."

"Then we can expect you to try and slip it to us every year from now on?" Mr. Voyce half-smiled.

Alex smiled. "What we're going to do, Mr. Voyce, and the rest of you gentlemen, is to set up a permanent organization dedicated to helping distressed and starving peoples around the world. What we're doing here in this room, this week, might actually be historical. It is our intention not only to supply food, but also medical assistance, and shelter wherever needed, for a time. But we sure as hell don't want to supply food, medicine, and shelter for tens of thousands of people every year. That would do neither them nor our wallets any good."

Alex looked at each of the people in the room. "So you know, we at Gabriel Industries are considering setting up training colleges in various parts of this country. We assume we will eventually train thousands of people. The trainees will be recruited from third-world countries around the globe. We are going to ask for your assistance, gentlemen, in this endeavor."

"Assistance? How?"

"Don't know exactly," Alex replied, "but possibly something

like finding volunteers to teach courses on irrigation or fertilization. Maybe work-study programs for agricultural students. Give them credits for teaching. As an example, Mr. Thomas, we would appreciate your suggestions as to where, when, and how to train these people in the growing of rice. Mr. Voyce could help in the same way for wheat production, etc. The same would go for the rest of you.

"Give 'em some basics on herbicides, pesticides, food processing, stuff like that?" offered Mr. Thomas.

"That's it!" agreed Alex. "Then our trained experts will head back to their native countries, taking with them food, medicine, and above all, knowledge. They, in turn, will begin setting up training schools immediately. We may need twenty or more instructors per school here in the States. Each an expert in one field, teaching everything from farming to bread-baking, well-drilling, irrigation, plumbing, and first aid to treating diseases. In short, we are going to teach them to be self-sufficient."

"Seems like I've heard similar plans many times before," said Mr. Bowley. "The fly in the ointment in each case has been their governments. Or should I say, their corrupt or ineffective governments."

"We're not going to deal with their governments, gentlemen," stated Alex. "The only way we'll go into a country is with the understanding that our people operate on their own. Help from their governments will not be solicited, required, or accepted."

"Why then would any government give you permission to enter their country?" asked Mr. Ramstead.

"We have to assume some won't, but if they don't, they're going to get some really bad press, worldwide. Press that can disrupt all sorts of aid. Aid, that in one form or another, virtually all Third World countries require to remain viable."

"That would be money in most cases," offered Bowley.

"That's for damn sure!"

"Sounds like the Peace Corps combined with the Red Cross!"

"You bet! It will have elements of those organizations and then some."

Mr. Voyce was anxious to get back to the price of wheat. "I'll have a job selling this to my members."

"Well," reasoned Mr. Thomas, "the reduction of surplus will increase the price of the remaining produce, be it wheat, rice, oats, or chickens. That benefits the American farmer. The fact that the American farmer is willing to "lose money" in order to help less fortunate people around the world is great public relations, which, in turn, benefits not only the farmer, but America's image around the world."

Alex briefly looked over at his mother. She gave him a knowing smile. She and Alex had talked at length about the philosophy, cost, and pitfalls of such an enormous undertaking. But it seemed the men in this room, although reluctant at first, were warming to the idea.

"You people represent some of the major food producers in this country," said Alex. "Mr. Herberger with the beef growers of America; Mr. Bowley, the pork producers; Mr. Thomas, the rice growers; Mr. Ramstead, the poultry producers. Each of you here represents a segment of the farmers and ranchers of the nation. If my studies are correct, all your organizations overproduce from time to time and in doing so create massive stockpiles of one product or another. Next year, maybe wheat will be in short supply and rice will be in abundance. Then I'll pick on the rice growers, Mr. Thomas..."

This first meeting, for what would become the largest and most encompassing disaster relief organization ever created, lasted for the rest of that day and would continue weekly for the next several months. The working name given to the project was Gabriel Relief International, or as it was already being called, "GRI."

Alex convinced his mother to take over the helm of the massive project until the basic structure was in place. She had carte blanche authority to hire all personnel, sign contracts, and commit the Gabriel resources to whatever she felt necessary. He knew her organizational skills were a huge benefit to such an enterprise. He assumed this organization would become huge and cumbersome within ten years, but one had to start somewhere. Even Alex couldn't foresee the need, in the future, for building modern hospitals and creating a private army to protect them, but the need would arise.

Chapter 37

GABRIEL HEADQUARTERS
December 1, 1975
8:30 a.m.

It was cold and wet in Orange County. The wind gusts were reaching forty miles per hour, causing the rain to blow in sideways. It had been like this for six days now and the Southern California area had received well over five inches of rain. Los Angeles and its myriad suburbs were not designed nor equipped to handle this much moisture. Flooding and landslides were being reported all over.

"Can you believe this weather?" Colleen grumbled as the receptionist helped her off with her raincoat. She paid little attention to Walt and Alex as they approached her on their way to Alex's office. "If I wanted weather like this, I'd move to the flippin' Amazon for Christ's sake," she continued her tirade while proceeding to pull off, with some effort and a few expletives, a pair of rubber galoshes. Her foul mood might have been due, in part, to the weather, but Alex assumed the majority was due to her six months of pregnancy.

"Morning, sweetheart; traffic must have been a bitch. You're running a little late." Walt walked over and gave his wife a big kiss and a pat on her behind.

Colleen was still obviously disgruntled and after muttering something about a drowned rat, she remarked, "Other than having two feet of water at each intersection and no boat, I think I made exceptional time."

"Good morning, Auntie," Alex smiled.

"Just what is good about it?"

"Just seeing your face brightened it up for me," Alex responded.

Colleen managed a slight smile.

"Get yourself some hot cocoa; you'll feel better in no time." Walt smiled. "While you get warmed up, I've got to track down Mallory in legal for a short meeting. Why don't you sit in; you'll find it interesting." Walt turned and headed toward the elevators.

"What are you up to today?" She looked over at Alex. "Don't you know it's raining out and you're not supposed to do business in a storm?"

"Didn't know that," Alex responded lightly. "Why don't you come into my office and we'll see if we can't make you more comfortable."

"Okay," she agreed, then turned toward Walt as he stood waiting for an elevator. "Then we'll go to lunch and do some new baby shopping, right?"

Walt did not reply; just raised his hand in acknowledgment.

11:45 a.m.

"Let me review what we just discussed," remarked Bill Mallory as he looked down at his notes. "First, you want me to charter a company that is to be wholly owned by Gabriel Industries and name it Global Media Incorporated. Second, Global Media is to buy a small liberal newspaper in Berkeley that has just been put on the market and goes by the name of *The Berkeley Gazette*. Third, you would like me to keep an eye out for other 'liberal papers' to absorb as time goes on. Is that about it?"

"Not just liberal papers, all the papers we can acquire," responded Alex as he reached over and retrieved a column he'd cut out of the newspaper. "Here is a name you might explore for the position of Managing Editor."

Bill leaned forward and took the long slim piece of paper from Alex. It had a picture and byline at the top, followed by an article exposing a local politician's indiscretions with a wad of campaign funds. "I know who this is. I've read his stuff for years. He's quite good."

"Who is it, Bill?" asked Walt.

"Jack Calloway."

"Calloway?" Walt looked pensive for a moment. "CALLOWAY! Isn't that the son of a bitch who wrote the nasty article about you when you were just a kid?"

"That's the man, but don't think harshly of him. His impression of me and what he wrote was exactly what was needed at the time."

"What do you mean? I remember being so pissed off after reading that piece of crap that I damned near went to see the lying son-of-a bitch to kick his ass."

"I do remember you getting a bit upset."

"A bit! Well, that son-of-a..."

"Walt, sweetie, you're getting agitated all over again. That happened more than fifteen years ago." Colleen reached over and patted Walt on the knee.

Alex smiled. He could see that his Aunt Colleen was starting to feel better. "Actually, Calloway was being kind at the time. What you didn't realize was that I sandbagged the guy. Had the roles been reversed and I'd been the reporter, the article would have been a lot nastier."

"Sandbagged him?"

"Yep."

"Be that as it may," interrupted Bill Mallory, obviously not wishing to reminisce with the Gabriels, "I have a question. Who is going to head up Global Media Inc.?"

"You are -- for the time being, anyway," Alex replied. "Shouldn't be too big a job, being only one paper and all. Especially if you get a good managing editor."

"I am?" Bill wasn't expecting this news.

"Yes, indeed, but if we can get him, I want Jack Calloway to be groomed for the job of managing editor. He and I had several conversations over the past few months and I believe we're reading off the same page. In the meantime, we'll keep an eye out for someone to run Global permanently."

"Knowing you, Alex, I suspect newspapers won't be Global's only acquisition," Colleen remarked.

"Absolutely not. Eventually, I want Global to be the biggest media company in the world."

"Then that's what it will be, I have no doubt," said Walt.

"Then I assume part of my new duties will be to be on the lookout for additional properties for this new enterprise?" responded Bill.

"That's right, but you'll have help. I'll be putting out feelers to our friends in the media business and anyone else I feel can help."

"Is it your intent to turn liberal papers to the right?"

"Not on your life, Bill. I want this paper and all future papers to remain politically as they are."

Bill shook his head, "You're the boss!"

"Is that it?" asked Walt.

"Not quite," said Alex. "I also want to start acquiring radio and TV stations as they come up for sale, both here and in other countries."

"What other countries?"

"All of them."

Chapter 38

ORANGE COUNTY GENERAL HOSPITAL
March 25, 1976
5:38 p.m.

Alex returned to the waiting room after spending forty-five minutes on the phone to his office. "Nothing's changed?"

"I believe your uncle has, if you can believe it, become even more unstrung," Marian answered.

"Uncle Walt, a little nervous, are ya?"

"Christ, I think I'm starting to hyperventilate."

Jennifer walked into the waiting room carrying a shallow cardboard box loaded down with hot drinks and rolls. "Here you go, Uncle Walt, hot chocolate. You don't need any more coffee," she remarked as she placed the box on the coffee table.

"Good thinking, babe." Norman walked over and picked up a steaming paper cup of coffee. "Cream and sugar, sweetheart?"

"What? And mask the taste of this gourmet roast?" Marian responded with little humor.

"That was sarcasm, right?" Norm proceeded to doctor the coffee.

"Happy birthday, brother," Jennifer smiled broadly as she walked over and gave her brother a hug and kiss.

"My God, in the excitement of the moment, I forgot it's your birthday." Marian jumped up and gave Alex a big hug. "Sorry, Son."

"I didn't forget," smiled Jennifer.

"Happy birthday, Son. We do have presents for you at home."

Norman gave his son a warm hug.

"Hey, don't give it another thought. My last birthday party will carry me for a few years."

"Looks like another Gabriel might have the same birthday," Norman suggested.

"Not at this rate," remarked Walt.

6:50 p.m.

Walt was in the middle of several hot laps around the waiting room, as the nurse returned. "Would anybody like to see the new mama and baby?"

"Oh my God!" Walt exclaimed while nearly tripping over the coffee table. He would have fallen had Norman not grabbed him.

"Why don't you follow me, Mr. Gabriel," the nurse suggested, obviously suppressing a laugh. She turned and addressed the others. "Let's give the new parents a few minutes alone with their new baby before the rest of you go in. Is that okay?"

"Of course."

"Sure."

"No problem."

7:15 p.m.

Walt was sitting in a chair on the far side of the bed when the rest of the Gabriels came into the room. In his arms was his new daughter.

"How you doing, Sis?" asked Marian. She had been calling Colleen "sis" since she and Walt were married.

"Pooped, real pooped." Colleen smiled weakly.

The others, after greeting and congratulating Colleen, walked around the bed to see the new arrival.

Walt's face was about to split from his grin. "Seven pounds, nine and a half ounces and twenty inches long, by God," he exclaimed as he proudly displayed his new daughter to a chorus of approving sounds.

"A beautiful new Irishwoman is born to the world," stated

Norman. "My God, look at that hair!"

"A beautiful redhead," smiled Alex. "Jesus! That's some mane."

"I've never seen so much hair on a newborn," laughed Jennifer. "Wow!"

"Congratulations, Aunt Colleen, Uncle Walt. I'm real happy for you. She's a beautiful baby," added Alex. He really wanted to touch the baby, but wasn't sure he should. He'd wait.

"Well," asked Marian, "what are you going to name this future heartbreaker?"

Colleen and Walt looked at each other for a moment and then Walt looked at Jennifer and Alex. "Your cousin," he said and turned toward Marian and Norman, "your niece, and our new daughter's name will be," he proclaimed as he looked lovingly at Colleen, then back at the family, "Alexandra."

Chapter 39

GABRIEL HEADQUARTERS
December 18, 1978
11:45 a.m.

"Excuse me a second." Walt reached over and pushed the intercom button. "Carol, will you ask Huff in acquisitions to look up all commercial and light industrial-zoned property in this area, including what we own, and give me a buzz when he has it?"

"*Yes, sir*," Carol came back.

Walt turned his attention back to Alex. "How big a facility are you going to put together?"

"I don't know." Alex paused for a second. "Maybe something about half the size of SARC's main building, with plenty of space to grow in the future."

Walt thought about that and smiled. "Thought we'd be using just a small portion of this building during my lifetime."

"And now we're about out of space," Alex added.

"Hard to believe."

"Maybe it's time to build a second tower on this campus," suggested Alex.

Walt smiled and nodded. "Which one first?"

"The research center."

"Okay. What sort of research are you thinking about?"

"Propulsion, light-physics, fusion, matter, anti-matter, pressure hull design for starters."

"Planning to leave the planet soon, are you Alex?" asked Walt.

"What?"

"You said, among others, 'propulsion and pressure hull design.' Those two could equal a spaceship."

"Oh, that's not what I had in mind," Alex smiled. "But these subjects have always fascinated me, except pressure hull designs; I added that as an afterthought. I want to get my dad involved."

"I see."

Alex realized that after these past sixteen years together, Walt assumed his nephew never did anything on a whim. Although Alex, himself, wasn't sure this one wasn't just that.

"Where are you going to get the scientists and engineers to staff your center?"

"Believe if we build the most modern facility without government oversight and provide unlimited funds, we will attract the greatest minds in each field from around the world. I plan on putting out feelers right away."

"*Mr. Huff on line two, sir.*"

Walt reached over, pushed the blinking button, picked up the receiver and said, "Ron, what have you got for me?"

After a two-minute conversation, Walt hung up. "Well, it seems most of the desired land around here is owned by one company... ours!"

"Really?"

"I don't think the man would lie to me."

Chapter 40

GABRIEL HOME
December 20, 1978

"Hi, Mom, Jackie, Sis. Trying to hold off a winter pallor?" Alex was in his usual good mood as he crossed the patio heading to where the ladies were sunning themselves by the pool.

Alex hadn't seen Jackie for a couple of months and that was probably a good thing. Jackie, Alex was certain, was hot for his bod, as they say. She might well have been hot for any "bod" but his was the only one he was concerned with. It made him a little uncomfortable. Not from the lurid attention so much, but because he wasn't sure he could, or would want to, fend her off if she became any more aggressive. Jackie was a very sexy woman. Not the kind you want to spend a lot of time with, or, God forbid, marry, but the kind that almost any man would love to have unbridled, animal sex with. Just seeing her now caused a sudden warmth deep in his groin.

"Hi, Alex. We were just talking about you. Why don't you go put on your bathing suit and join us?" suggested Jennifer.

"Yes, please do," added Jackie with a warm smile.

Marian looked up from under the large straw hat she had across her face. "Hi, sweetheart."

The three were lying by the pool that had just been completed in May. The temperature was in the low 80s for the third straight day and all around the harbor, one could hear and see all sorts of "summer activities" going on. Alex had just returned from a morning of tennis with Teddy and was heading for the shower.

"That's what I had in mind. Teddy will be here in a while; he got stuck on the phone. We plan on lying around the pool and relaxing the rest of the day."

"Gosh, I haven't seen Teddy since your big birthday party. It's been over a year." Jennifer was always happy to see Teddy. "Thought he was in a play in New York that was doing well?"

"Teddy was, but apparently the play wasn't. He has another year at Julliard and then he'll decide if he wants to make a career of the legitimate theater or motion pictures."

"Who's this you're talking about?"

Alex could see that Jackie's interest in the conversation was now piqued. Jackie, it seemed, among other things, was a closet thespian. Marian and Jackie had become friends, despite a nearly twenty-year age difference, while serving as volunteers on a local community theater board. Jackie was married to a man twice her age and the two of them, as it turned out, lived no more than a quarter of a mile from the Gabriels. Alex, at this moment, was looking at Jackie lying face-up in the briefest bikini he'd ever seen. *Oh boy*!

"Alex's lifelong friend, Teddy Oldaker, is a natural entertainer. Great gifts in acting, dancing, and singing," Marian offered. "He and Alex have been like brothers all their lives."

Two lives, thought Alex. *But in my first life I wasn't living here and Teddy wasn't attending Julliard.*

"And wait until you see how cute he is," Jennifer added.

Alex could see that this subject would keep the ladies going for quite a while. He tore his eyes away from Jackie. "Let me clean up and I'll be back out; fifteen minutes, tops." He leaned over and gave his mother a peck on the cheek. As he stood up, he pinched his sister on the arm and headed toward the house. He could feel Jackie's eyes following him.

Alex returned to the patio wearing a bathing suit, with an oversized light blue beach towel draped over his shoulder and a huge glass of iced tea in his hand. His wet blond hair was combed straight back. Alex was filling out. He had put on more than twenty pounds in two years and although he was still slim, he had left the awkward teenage body behind.

"You and Walt look a lot alike, don't you? But you're quite a bit slimmer." Jackie's interest in Alex was becoming less guarded. "You have a tennis player's body."

"He looks a lot like his father when I first met him -- a couple of inches taller, though," offered Marian, seemingly oblivious to her friend's interest in her son.

"Your eyes are really something," Jackie went on. "Look like a combination of your mom's and dad's. Never seen such a penetrating blue."

"Yeah, he's quite the lady-killer all right." Jennifer came into the conversation. "Half the girls at the club make passes at him on a regular basis." She rolled over, swatted at a fly and took a sip of Coke. "The other half, he has already taken out."

"That's a bit of a stretch, Jen," Marian remarked as she turned over on her stomach. At forty-seven, Marian was still a beautiful woman. Her figure remained as nice as any woman ten years her junior. There were fine crows' feet at the corners of her eyes and when she smiled, the laugh lines were more pronounced.

"Actually, I've taken out just two young ladies from the club," Alex remarked. "And I still see Aidan whenever she's in town." *Wish she would move back to California*, he thought.

"Are you ever in a bad mood, Alex?" asked Jennifer, changing the conversation.

"To tell you the truth, Sis, other than crime, graft, poverty, famine, wars, disease, ecological disasters, pollution, and the generally horrible state of the world, what's to put me in a bad mood?" Alex replied. "I don't have a lot of things happen in my personal life that upset me. I have a wonderful family, a beautiful home, loyal friends, and a good paying job." Alex smiled as he took a sip of tea and leaned back on the lounge.

"A good paying job?" both Gabriel women repeated and laughed.

"So, what's up?" asked Alex as he lay there with his hands behind his head, watching a row of pelicans flying overhead. The onshore breeze was perfect for sunbathing.

Jackie shifted and was now lying on her side, facing Alex, her head supported with her hand. The straps to her bikini top were recklessly undone and her breasts were dangerously close to being totally exposed. She was watching Alex with a faraway look in her eyes.

Alex hadn't noticed, but Jennifer did, and thought it amusing. Even women five years older thought her younger brother was sexy.

"What is Pop's greatest love in life, other than you, Jennifer, and me?"

Marian thought about that for a minute. "Well, it was design work, you know -- engineering, drafting."

"And just how much of that has he been doing lately?"

"None, since he retired."

"I'm thinking of building a research facility and asking Pop to run it."

"He's retired!" Marian stated quickly.

"But he's bored doing nothing. He needs to do something meaningful."

"*Señora Stein, Señor Stein would like to talk to ju*," Maria's voice could be heard over the intercom that served the pool area.

"Oh damn!" Jackie quickly rose to a sitting position on the lounge, carelessly letting her top drop below her now erect nipples.

Alex happened to look over just in time to see the exposure.

"I forgot to leave his car keys. I'll be back in a few," she said as she started to stand up. "Oops," she exclaimed as she realized her exposure. She smiled at Alex as she casually pulled the strings behind her neck. She smiled at him again as she stood, walked the four steps to the phone, and pushed the blinking button. "Sorry, honey bun; I'll be right there," she said without preamble and hung up the receiver. "I'll be back in a bit, don't want to miss this sun." She wrapped a sarong around her waist and headed for the house.

Alex was following her departure with his eyes just as she looked over her shoulder and caught him at it. She smiled and winked and continued on her way.

Damn, that woman does have a body...and that was a dandy little display. More than my twenty-four-year-old hormones can take, thought Alex. He quickly rolled over on his stomach. *Damn* it!

None of this scene was lost on Jennifer.

"Coincidentally, Sis, your friend Chuck is going to work there also."

"He hasn't said anything to me about it. That's strange." Jennifer seemed a little put off, the flagrant flirting of Jackie now forgotten.

Jennifer and Chuck had been a steady item for over four years now. The family liked Chuck a lot and so did Jennifer. They were quietly talking about getting married right after Chuck earned his doctoral degree. He no longer had to work, however, as he and Alex made some sort of bargain a couple of years back and Alex was now underwriting his education.

"He doesn't know about it yet."

"Oh? I guess it hasn't occurred to you that maybe Chuck wouldn't want to go to work for you?"

"I'll make him a real good offer, Sis."

"Has anybody turned you down for anything in your whole life, Alex?"

"Of course… just this morning as a matter of fact. Asked a new member to join me for lunch and was informed, quite coolly, she had other plans. Damn shame, too; she's a looker."

"What's her name?"

"Julie," Alex thought for a second. "Julie Bashford, I believe."

"I just met her," said Jennifer, "She's younger than most of my friends but a lot of fun and quite outgoing. She might be perfect for Teddy."

"You think your father will come out of retirement?" Marina asked.

"Yep, because I'm also going to throw in a lab dedicated to pressure hull-design."

"This sounds like make-work, to me," said Marian.

"Not at all." Alex had a self-satisfied look on his face, even with his eyes closed.

Teddy's voice could be heard as he loudly greeted Maria on his way through the kitchen, heading for the patio. "Oh, Señor Teddy!" Maria responded and a few giggles could be heard from them both.

Teddy pinched her on the butt again, thought Alex. "Hi, Mrs. Gabriel, Jennifer," Teddy said in a cheerful voice as he walked through the kitchen door onto the patio. "What the hell?" he expressed, as his eyes fell on the new pool.

"Like it?"

"What's not to like? Geeze, you Gabriels don't do anything in a small way, do you?" He looked over the pool quickly. "I'll get back to this in a minute." He put his towel and glass of tea down and turned toward Marian and Jennifer. "Got to give my two favorite girls a hug first."

He walked over to Marian as she stood to give him a hug.

"Good afternoon, Mr. Oldaker," she responded with exaggerated politeness and put her arms around Teddy's shoulders. He gave her a big hug and a kiss on the cheek. She had tried, on numerous occasions, to get Teddy to call her Marian, but to no avail. Teddy just felt comfortable addressing her as Mrs. Gabriel.

"Hi, Teddy. How's Julliard and the Big Apple treating you?"

"Love Julliard; not too crazy about New York." With that, he grabbed Jennifer in a big bear hug and swirled her around the patio. "There is no weather like this in New York, not *ever*." He continued spinning Jennifer.

"Stop, you're making me dizzy," she giggled.

He stopped and carried Jennifer back to her lounge, still in a hug.

It was obvious that Jennifer adored Teddy. "Well, tell me more."

"Should absorb everything Julliard has to teach me in about another year, if my best friend here wants to continue to pay the bills." He still had that big toothy smile.

"As long as you need, Teddy."

"Thanks, Alex, couldn't do it without you." Teddy looked over at the pool. "Give me a minute here."

Teddy walked over to the pool to get a better look. The pool's northwest corner was built right up to the cliff's edge. A person could actually look almost straight down to the beach, thirty some feet below, while still in the pool. The pool itself was designed to look like a river pool in a rainforest. There was not one bit of concrete showing. The entire area around the pool was made up of large flat rocks all at different elevations, interspersed with huge boulders, plants, and trees. A staged waterfall fell from an elevation of some twenty feet above the surface, starting at the top of their property close to the road and cascading down to the pool. The diving platform was a huge boulder at the deep end next to where the waterfall entered. Two smaller pools were located in the rocks and served as hot tubs complete with Jacuzzi jets. Exotic trees and plants completed the illusion of the tropics.

"I have never seen anything like this, not even in the movies... my God! Where did you get the idea for this?"

"The movie *Bridge on the River Kwai*," smiled Alex.

Teddy's face turned into a study in concentration, then recognition. "Ah sure, geeze!"

Teddy returned and sat on the edge of his lounge and picked up the glass of tea.

"You may not be aware, Jen, but your brother just completed setting up ten scholarships with the top ten colleges and universities in the state," said Marian, displaying great pride in her son.

"You're kidding! Why haven't I heard about this before now? I think it's wonderful. What kind of scholarships, Alex?" Jennifer was really excited. Her wealthy brother was now a philanthropist.

"All kinds; depends on what the particular school is best at. I gave them guidelines such as ability, grade point average and need, and will let them handle the rest."

"How big are the scholarships you're giving?"

"Full ride, Sis. Room, board, books, tuition, and a weekly allowance. The recipients must have and maintain a 3.5 GPA or better. If they do, the scholarship will continue for four years. Drop below that in any one term and they're out...forever."

"I didn't know that," said Teddy as he set his glass of tea down next to Alex's. "Doesn't surprise me, though. Your brother is a generous man." Teddy's admiration of Alex had always been obvious.

"Hey, let's not forget damn good-looking to boot," Alex added.

"Well, you betcha, big guy," Teddy responded, using gay inflections in his voice.

"Well, I'm back," announced Jackie as she came through the kitchen door. She took off her sarong as she walked and dropped it on her lounge. "And this must be Teddy."

"Teddy, I'd like you to meet our friend, Jackie," said Marian.

Teddy stood up and took Jackie's hand. "Hey, any pretty friend of the Gabriels' is... well you know the rest." Teddy smiled at Jackie.

"My God, you were right. This is the cutest man I've ever seen!" Jackie was nearly gushing.

"She's not only pretty," remarked Teddy, "but has a damn good eye." With that, he pulled Jackie to him and gave her a big hug and kiss on the cheek.

"Oh my God, I'm in love!" responded Jackie.

"Teddy, you are something!" Jennifer laughed.

Apparently, Teddy has gotten over his fear of pretty women, thought Alex.

Teddy released Jackie, smiled, and sat back on his lounge.

Jackie dropped down on the lounge, fanning herself with her hand. "I've got to come over here more often."

Teddy had changed over the last year. Like Alex, he had put on weight and was losing the boyish look.

"Where'd you get that tan, Teddy? If your hair was darker, you'd look Mexican or maybe Italian." Teddy's tan made his big beautiful white teeth look even bigger and whiter.

"Not much sun in New York, so when I get out here I soak it up."

Marian smiled under her hat. She was enjoying the day and the company of her children, which included Teddy.

"You have a steady girlfriend, Teddy?" asked Jennifer. "There's a new girl at the club who would be perfect for you."

"Watch out here, my friend; I sense a Cupid buzzing the area."

"Stay out of this. Teddy is full-grown. He can take care of himself," Jennifer responded in mock anger. "Her name is Julie."

Chapter 41

GABRIEL HEADQUARTERS
January 5, 1979

"There are a couple of items that I would like your thoughts on, Uncle," said Alex as he walked into Walt's office.

"Give me a sec here, Alex. Just need to finish this up and get it to Carol."

Alex took a seat in front of his uncle's desk and waited.

Walt nodded and continued working on a stack of invoices. In less than a minute, he reached over and pushed the intercom button. "Carol, the invoices are ready whenever you are."

"*Thank you*," her voice came back.

"You ready?" asked Alex.

"You have my undivided attention."

"Okay. One, I believe we had better consider chartering a bank here and buying a bank in Zurich."

"Here and in Zurich?"

"Yes, sir."

"If you feel we need a bank out of the country, I hear it's much simpler to charter a bank in the Grand Caymans."

"Oh, I'm sure that's true, but I'm thinking of expanding into Europe and Zurich is where Europe does its banking."

"Expanding into Europe… really, why?"

"Europe has millions of sophisticated and relatively affluent consumers. They also have modern factories and for the most part, stable governments. Their potential for growth is in place."

Walt shrugged his shoulders. "Okay, I guess."

"What do you think of going into Japan and maybe Hong Kong?"

"Japan is a whole different ball game. They don't do things the way we do. Hard to figure them out."

"We would need to hire someone who knows the Japanese inside and out to head up our operation there, that's for sure," agreed Alex. "That country has already started on the road to becoming an international economic power. The Japanese are an extremely industrious, ambitious, and highly disciplined people. That's a winning combination. We need to help them along their prosperous path and share in their growth."

"You going to want another bank over there?"

"No, not yet," Alex smiled.

"Okay."

"Chartering a bank here shouldn't be much of a problem."

"It shouldn't be." Walt replied. "It seems to me that when we built this building, you insisted on putting a gigantic safe in the sub-basement."

"That's where we keep all the goodies. Stock certificates, bonds, deeds, and all manner of financial instruments. We won't be needing actual bank space. And we already have the bookkeepers and accountants."

"I have no idea how to go about acquiring a bank in Zurich, but it wouldn't surprise me if you do."

"Actually, I haven't the slightest," said Alex, "but I'd suggest we start with a list of every bank in the country and see if we can talk to a few of the owners and management of the smaller ones."

"I have the feeling that the Swiss won't be too receptive to Americans owning a bank in their country," suggested Walt.

"Massive amounts of money will lower a lot of barriers, Uncle."

"Can't argue with that. I'll get the acquisitions department started on a list and we'll take a look at them. What next?"

"Let's get a team together to study the best ways to set up bases of operation in Europe and Japan."

"You haven't got the world covered yet, my aggressive nephew. How about South America and Africa?"

Alex paused for a few seconds before answering. "South America and Africa certainly have abundant resources and huge numbers of cheap labor, but their major problem has always been weak, ineffectual, and corrupt governments. Someday we'll change that."

"Really! you're not planning a coup d'état are you?" Walt said in mock alarm.

Alex looked puzzled for a few moments. "I don't know why I said that."

Chapter 42

ZURICH, SWITZERLAND
November 2, 1979
8:00 a.m.

"*Mr. Auchland, the Gabriels are here for their appointment*." Otto pushed the intercom button. "Show them in please," he said in accented English.

As Alex and Walt were being shown into Otto Auchland's office, Alex's mind flashed back to what this banker had told him the first time they'd met. "*This bank has been in my family since 1873, Mr. Gabriel. There are more than fifty family stockholders. Even if I wanted to accept your offer, it would take a two-thirds majority vote to force the stockholders to sell*."

"Alex, Walt, nice to see you again." Otto shook Alex's, then Walt's hand. "Please sit, gentlemen."

"Nice to see you again, Otto. And it's always a pleasure to visit your beautiful country," said Alex.

"I'll say," agreed Walt. "There is no prettier place on the planet."

"You are kind, Walt. You wouldn't be trying to butter me up, as you Americans say, would you?"

"Maybe just a little." Walt smiled.

It was Walt and Alex's third trip to Zurich in their ongoing effort to convince Otto and the Auchlands to sell the family bank.

Alex, before approaching Otto, had been made aware, through

rumors in the Swiss banking community, that Otto had decided to break with family tradition and push for a major expansion in the bank's assets. The old line and traditionally large Swiss banks knew that the Auchland Bank would have a great deal of trouble breaking out of their small shell and were discreetly laughing up their sleeves at the prospect. Otto was aware of his peers' attitudes, so when Alex approached him, he was in somewhat of a receptive, if not an open-minded, mood.

Otto Auchland looked to Alex like the epitome of a Swiss banker. *I'll bet he can barely see his hand in front of his face without those glasses*, Alex was thinking. *The lenses must be half an inch thick*. Alex also noticed that Otto was wearing a beautifully cut suit, conservative but quite stylish. Alex gathered from extensive research that this man was literally born to be a banker. His uncle, upon retiring three years ago, had turned the reins of this conservative family bank over to Otto, as his uncle's father had done for him some thirty years before. Alex probably knew more about the family lineage and the Auchland Bank than most of the Auchland family stockholders themselves.

10:00 a.m.

Two hours into this third face-to-face meeting, they were still at an impasse.

"Would you be willing to bring in the major family stockholders and let me tell them personally what I have in mind for their bank?" Alex asked, out of desperation. He didn't want to insult Otto, but the man seemed to have trouble making this monumental decision. *Emotionally, this was too close to his heart,* Alex thought.

Otto got up and walked over to the window overlooking downtown Zurich. He stood there with his hands clasped behind his back and stared off into the distance for what had to be five minutes. Neither Alex nor Walt made a sound during that time.

"*He who talks first loses,*" Alex kept repeating to himself.

Otto turned and slowly walked back to his desk and sat down while looking Alex in the eye. "I will let you do that, Mr. Gabriel."

The offer Alex had made Otto would immediately thrust the small bank above many of his detractors' banks in size. Otto would remain president and CEO of the bank, and the family would retain twenty percent of the outstanding stock. In addition, the Auchland Bank would become the major bank for the European operations of Gabriel International. Just for starters, Gabriel International would be depositing a half billion dollars. This proposal was more than Otto and the rest of the Auchland family could resist.

Chapter 43

HUNTINGTON BEACH
December 20, 1979
11:00 p.m.

"Have another glass of champagne, sir?"

Alex turned to see the bartender smiling at him from the other side of the exquisite mahogany bar.

"Don't know if I should." He turned to his right. "What do you think, Aidan, darlin'?"

"If yer as drunk as I em, I tink we should."

"Should what?"

"Have another drinkie, silly."

Alex could only laugh. He didn't recall being this smashed or having ever seen Aidan Keefe walk around with her beautiful green eyes crossed and out of focus. They were, by any standards, having one hell of a good time.

Aidan had invited Alex to her company's Christmas party. The two of them were spending as much time together as possible since Aidan secured a position with a public relations firm in Century City, moving her back to Southern California. But both were busy people and seeing each other more than six times in a month was unusual. This actually worked out well for them both. Neither wanted to be tied down to a serious relationship, but both enjoyed the other's company immensely.

"Can I buy you another drink, gorgeous?" asked a tall man as he rudely inserted himself between Aidan and Alex. He, along with several other male associates from her department, was sitting in a booth close by for most of the evening, telling each other what they would do to Aidan if they ever got her in the sack. The more they drank, the louder and more vulgar they became. Alex saw and heard some of this, but chose to ignore it. After all, they were drinking and Aidan was one sexy lady.

"No thanks, Ray, I've got this handsome devil here to handle that."

Ray glanced at Alex with a bit of disdain. "How about we dance then?" he looked back at Aidan.

"Same answer as before, Ray." Aidan leaned around Ray and kissed Alex on the cheek. "Huh, sweetie?"

"Absolutely," Alex smiled broadly. "As a matter of fact, let's go show these old folks how to boogie right now." With that, he slipped off his barstool, took Aidan's hand, and started toward the dance floor.

"Wait a second, prick! I'm not done talking to this 'I'm too good for you' bitch yet!"

"What did you say?" asked Alex as he snapped back around. All good humor had vanished in a heartbeat.

"You heard me, asshole."

"Yeah, I did. So why don't you and I head out to the parking lot so I can teach you how to be a gentleman?"

"You got it, rich boy," he replied sarcastically. "You just wait here, bitch. I'll be back before you can say...."

"Is there a problem here, sirs?"

All three looked over to see a well-dressed man standing just off to the right side of Ray. The man wasn't tall, maybe five ten, but he was stout with the broadest, meatiest shoulders Alex had ever seen. He looked to be carved from an oak stump.

Alex said nothing but kept staring daggers at Ray, at the same time trying to clear his head.

"When there gets to be a problem, buddy, I'll be sure to look you up. I'm just going to take this spoiled, rich asshole here out to the parking lot, and spank him."

"I'm sorry, sir. We can't allow that here; we have a reputation to maintain."

The bartender had a puzzled expression as he witnessed this exchange.

Ray looked down into the light brown eyes of this bulldog and saw nothing but... cold. This, under normal and sober circumstances, would have been enough to cause Ray to reconsider his options. But Ray still had adrenaline pumping through his veins along with a good percentage of alcohol. "Hey, fuck you and this dump, I'm goin'..."

The bulldog's left hand shot out and latched on to Ron's arm just above the elbow. "I'm sorry, sir. I'm going to have to escort you out of this establishment," the man said in a conversational tone.

No one would have believed how big Ray's eyes could get. The look of pain was almost comical.

"Excuse me, sir, miss," said the fireplug, as he led the cooperative Ray past Aidan and Alex.

They stepped aside quickly.

Ray wasn't putting up any resistance. He was literally walking on his tiptoes, not making a sound. The two of them, the oak stump and the light-footed Ray, went directly to the front door and exited. The other men at Ray's table, after some macho talk to bolster their courage, decided to go out and help their friend kick this bouncer's ass. They scrambled out of the booth as quickly as their wobbly legs would take them and headed out the front door and into the parking lot.

"Well, that was kinda exciting, don'tcha tink?" exclaimed Aidan.

"Interesting, to say the least." Alex was concerned. "Why don't you wait here for a minute while I take a look outside. It looks like Ray's friends are drunk enough to hurt that guy."

"O-kee-doe-kee," said Aidan as she more or less slithered up on a barstool, only one cheek of her perfect derriere actually gaining purchase. Her green eyes were now completely out of focus. "I'll have another drinkie, Mr. Barteendoor."

Alex patted her on the knee, turned and headed to the front door.

As he exited into the brightly lit parking lot, he saw that the four men had nearly surrounded the well-dressed bouncer. The bouncer was standing with his hands together at his belt line, taking a vast amount of verbal abuse as Alex approached the group. He bouncer wasn't, as far as Alex could tell, even upset. He just stood looking straight ahead, taking the harassment.

"Thought I might be able to even this confrontation up a little," Alex said as he approached the group.

"Oh, that won't be necessary, sir," replied the oak stump, maintaining a conversational tone. "But thank you anyway."

"Yeah, git the fuck outta here, rich boy," said Ray, "or you'll be taking a trip to the hospital along with this piece of shit!" Ray was sobering up quickly and was now fixing to take some rage out on the man who caused him such pain and embarrassment.

"I don't think so, dickhead," Alex replied.

Ray didn't pause a second before starting a punch in Alex's direction.

There was a loud smacking sound and Ray was on the ground writhing in pain, his hands holding his face.

"What the fuck?" exclaimed one of his friends looking down at Ray.

"You motherfuc..." started another as he swung a looping right at the head of the bouncer.

Alex could barely see the bouncer move, but move he did. He deftly blocked the punch with his left forearm and caught Ray's friend in the mouth with his right elbow. Two assailants were down within five seconds.

The remaining two backed off several feet while each rattled off a string of expletives. As drunk as they were, it was clear they had seen all they needed to see.

Alex was amazed to see the bouncer still standing with his hands clasped at belt level as if nothing had yet happened. Had Alex been sober, he might have seen more of the action, but it was all just kind of a blur.

"I would suggest," said the bouncer in a calm voice, "that you two waddies take your friends to get some medical attention."

"Jesus Christ," exclaimed one as he kneeled down next to the second casualty. "He's unconscious."

The other friend walked over to Ray and tried to help him up, but Ray was still rolling around on the pavement holding his hands over his mouth. It didn't require good vision to see the blood dripping from between Ray's fingers.

The bouncer, apparently seeing the threat was over, nodded to Alex, turned, and walked back into the restaurant.

"Jesus," Alex said quietly. He turned toward the four men, "Let me help you get these guys into your car."

"We can handle it...Mr. Gabriel," replied one without the slightest trace of rancor.

"Okay, fine!" Alex turned and walked back into the restaurant. He found Aidan right where he'd left her, sitting crookedly on a barstool happily sipping a glass of champagne.

Aidan smiled as he approached. "Hi, handsome."

"Hi, yourself." He kissed her on the cheek, and then began looking around the restaurant in an attempt to spot the beefy bouncer. The man was nowhere in sight. Alex turned and signaled the bartender. The young man came right over.

"Can you tell me where your bouncer is? I'd like to thank him for his help."

"That would be a problem, sir," responded the young man. "We don't have a bouncer."

Chapter 44

BOSTON, MASSACHUSETTS
April 10, 1980
9:30 a.m.

Alex had mixed emotions; he was quite excited, and at the same time, nervous. This was the day he was going to meet Jason Gould for the first time... again. It had been eighteen years since he had last seen one of his best friends. He smiled to himself as he recalled what Jason was wearing that first day, *a Harvard sweatshirt and faded jeans*.

Alex wasn't sure how he'd react or if in fact he could keep the meeting on a professional level. He'd purposely avoided contacting Jason for all these years. He realized because of his massive investment activities, he'd altered the timelines of tens of thousands of other people, but he didn't want to change a thing in Jason's life until he was out of college, just as it had been the first time.

Alex had reserved a suite at the same five-star hotel, the Boston Marriott, where he met Jason in his first life. *Was that thirty-five years ago? Is that right, thirty-five years? Met him in 1980, worked with him until 1997, took the trip back in time to 1962. It's been eighteen years since then –thirty-five years. I've known Jason for thirty-five years and he's about to meet me for the first time.* Alex reflected for another moment. *This is one of the few times my first and second lives are coming close to intersecting. I'm in the same spot, at the same time, that I was thirty-five years ago but I'm not the same as I was…I'm older… a lot older….Christ, I've been alive for fifty-nine years…but by my current life's calendar I'm only twenty-six... STOP!* his mind screamed. *Now is not the time to try to sort out that conundrum*. "Put it away, put it away," he said aloud.

There was a knock, bringing Alex all the way back to reality. He quickly walked over and opened the door. "You have to be Mr. Gould," Alex smiled. "I'm Alex Gabriel." Alex extended his hand. *God, I'm glad to see you, my friend.* Alex was a bit surprised to see how young Jason was; he didn't fit Alex's mental picture. His last memory of Jason was when he was forty-one; now he was twenty-three, no gray hair, thirty or forty pounds lighter and... dressed in a suit and tie?

"I've been looking forward to meeting you, Mr. Gabriel."

ORANGE COUNTY
November 30, 1980

"How's Jason Gould doing at Global?" Alex asked Bill Mallory. "I assume you've been having him spend time with different papers?"

Walt, Bill Mallory, Jack Calloway, and Alex had just been served a variety of sushi at a popular Japanese restaurant off MacArthur Blvd. Walt and Alex considered sushi among their favorite foods. Bill Mallory was, on the other hand, reluctant to try any sort of raw fish. Jack Calloway could take it or leave it.

"That's one bright and aggressive young man. What the hell is this crap?" Bill was using his chopsticks to poke a sushi roll that was topped with a nasty looking yellow-brown mush of some sort.

"Uni... sea urchin roe to you, round eyes. It's damned tasty. Give it a shot," Walt suggested.

"Not in this lifetime, thank you." Bill picked up a piece of uni with his chopsticks and placed it on Walt's serving board and the other on Alex's. He proceeded to eat the more Americanized items he was assured were cooked. "Jason, as we speak," Bill went on, "is spending a few weeks at the *Berkeley Gazette*, the best-run and most profitable paper in Global, thanks to Jack here."

Jack smiled and grunted while he held up a finger, his mouth full of sushi. He swallowed and took a sip of beer. "Started him in the mailroom, then the printing plant and every other department for two or more weeks, for indoctrination. We plan on doing the same thing with him at three of our other properties. Want to give him an idea of what an efficiently run operation is like before taking him into our newer acquisitions." Jack motioned to the sushi chef. "How about another order of California roll and a couple more pieces of shrimp."

"Hai!" acknowledged the chef with a slight bow.

"You think Global will be a home for him?" Walt asked Alex as he picked up a piece of yellowtail and dipped it into a soy and wasabi sauce.

"He's a natural," Jack interjected. "Taking to the media business like he was born to it."

"Is that so?" Walt responded.

"Yes, sir! Came into my office with about half a dozen written suggestions on how to improve the operation of each of the departments he'd spent time in." Jack put an entire piece of sushi into his mouth at once. "Boy, I do like these," he mumbled.

"How were the suggestions?" asked Alex.

"Most were damned good; a few were not practical at this time, but might be in the future. Jason will be a force to be reckoned with in a few years." Jack took a sip of beer.

"I agree with Jack," said Alex, "I think Jason will end up running Global someday."

"How about we make him my administrative assistant? Maybe give him a title, like Assistant Vice President, Administration. It would be good experience for him and take a big load off my back," suggested Bill.

"Let's give him another three or four months. A little more experience will do him good," suggested Alex.

"You're the boss."

"You, for some reason, have taken this young man under your wing." Walt directed this statement at Alex. "A fact, I might add, which seems to be the topic of much conversation around the water cooler."

"I suppose I have," Alex responded matter-of-factly.

"Where'd you find him?" asked Bill.

"I've known his parents for some time," Alex stated truthfully.

Walt cocked his head slightly. "Really?"

Alex could see his uncle was puzzled. *If I know the Goulds, why wouldn't Walt*? "Met them quite a few years ago in Boston."

"You know," said Walt, "somewhere in the back of my mind, it seems like I know something about Jason and his family, but I just can't bring up the circumstances."

Chapter 45

GABRIEL HEADQUARTERS
October 10, 1982
8:05 a.m.

"Good morning, Uncle." Alex looked up from the newspaper, folded it and put it on top of his desk.

"Good morning." Walt was pensive as he walked over to Alex's desk and sat down. "Have you ever heard of a man by the name of Victor Kula?" asked Walt without the normal pleasantries.

Alex leaned back in his chair. "Sounds vaguely familiar, but I can't put a face or place to him." He could see his uncle was grappling with something.

"The man has been making a lot of money the last couple of years; a lot of money."

"Good for him; so have we."

"Hmm."

"What?" Alex smiled a little.

Walt was drumming his fingers on the edge of the desk. "Well, it seems like he's buying most of what we're buying just about the same time we're buying it."

"Oh?" The smile faded.

"It may be nothing more than a coincidence, I suppose, but I have an uneasy feeling for some reason."

"Really?" Alex was now a bit apprehensive. "What are you thinking?"

"I think we had better put a man on him for a while."

"You think so?" Walt wasn't one to jump to conclusions. "Do we know who his broker is?"

"Not yet, but I've put out feelers."

"If it were a West Coast broker, I believe we would have known about this some time ago."

"I agree."

"Hmm." Now it was Alex's turn to feel a bit uneasy. "Be interesting to see when he's selling."

"I'll say!"

October 17, 1982

The weekly staff meeting had just broken up and Alex and Walt were at the board table sorting various reports. Walt looked up to see that the last of the department heads leave the room.

"There's one more report you'd better take a look at," said Walt.

Alex could tell by his uncle's demeanor that this was not going to be pleasant. Walt had been uncharacteristically distracted all morning.

"I assume you have more knowledge of Mr. Kula?"

"Indeed I do, and none of it is good."

Walt retrieved two files from his briefcase and handed one to Alex.

Walt said nothing as Alex opened the file and began reading. Alex had no need to look up buying and selling dates or prices, so he read, not uttering a sound. When he finished the final page, he put it back and pushed the file toward the center of the table. He sat and stared at it for a few minutes.

"We've got a problem!"

"I'm afraid we do," agreed Walt.

"Has to be someone in this office; someone close to the action."

"Yep."

"Any ideas?"

"A couple. I'll keep my man on it and at the same time, you and I will see if we can't come up with a way of routing out our rat." Walt was solemn.

"Your man, by the way, is damn good at what he does. This is a thorough report." Alex motioned toward the report lying on the board table. "Private eye?"

"Nope, security."

"Security?"

"Yep."

"Who's he work for?"

Walt paused for a moment. "Us."

Alex knew his uncle better than anyone did, with the possible exception of Colleen, and had seldom seen him evasive.

"Would you like to expand on that a little?"

"Not really, no." Walt raised his left eyebrow and gave an almost imperceptible smile.

Alex stared at his uncle for a moment. He didn't recall Walt ever holding anything back from him, so he had to assume it was for his own good. He smiled. "Okay."

Walt got up and headed for the door, but turned around about halfway across the room, "His name is Vance...Vance Youngblood."

Alex shrugged his shoulders, "Okay," he repeated and smiled again.

October 20, 1982

"I can't believe it's one of these two." Alex dropped the report on his desk. "Shit!"

"It really can't be anyone else, considering the time frames. There could be many other possibilities if the purchases were made at least a day after ours. However, these two are the only people, other than you and me, who are involved in the transaction within minutes."

"But Margaret, for Christ's sake. She's been with us for fifteen years. She was the first person you hired after Colleen." Alex was perplexed. "The woman's got to be in her seventies."

"We don't know that it's Margaret; it could be Carol."

Walt, like Alex, was more hurt than angry. The sense of betrayal by one of their long-time, trusted employees was weighing heavily on both of them. The violation of trust was depressing. They never required loyalty; they just assumed it.

Proving that there was indeed a leak within Gabriel Industries was a relatively easy matter. With the cooperation of the phone company, Vance Youngblood and his team laboriously searched all the phone records from the previous month for calls from any phone in the Gabriel building to Victor Kula's office in downtown Santa Ana. There were as many as three a week coming from various pay phones within the building. Then Vance, using a different source in the phone company, managed to get Kula's phone records. The records revealed calls originating from Kula's office to a phone number in Miami, all made within minutes of calls received from the Gabriel building. A simple check of that number found it to be a stockbroker. Miami was a good choice of locations, all things considered. Because of the vast numbers of affluent retired people, a lot of buying and selling was going on in that part of the country. Also, being located on the opposite coast, it afforded autonomy from the high-rolling and loosely knit West Coast brokers.

"So how do we pin it down so there can be no doubt?" Alex couldn't keep his eyes off the condemning report. He knew it was the timing that would finger Kula and his informer. If the informant had waited a day or two to relay the information to Mr. Kula, or if Kula waited a day or so before acting on it, the leak might not have been discovered -- or if discovered, hard to pin down to a single culprit. But as it was, there were only two names typed at the bottom of the page. Margaret Wallace, head of the accounting department; and Carol Bowman, Walt and Alex's private secretary.

"We separate the two long enough to give buying information to one of them without the knowledge of the other," said Walt.

"But we still wouldn't know when Kula is buying or selling," Alex paused momentarily. "Do you think your man, Vance, could put phone taps on Mr. Kula and his broker?"

"Phone taps are illegal, Alex," Walt replied.

"I know. But I can't think of any other way to track Kula's activity. We need to know exactly when he receives the information."

Walt looked at Alex for a second or two. "I'll talk to Vance about it."

"Maybe he'll know of a legal way to find out what we need to know. We need to make these people suffer a little."

"Suffer?"

"Suffer!"

"I assume by that, you don't intend to turn the matter over to the proper authorities?"

"Been my understanding the 'proper authorities' will take months or years, if ever, to convict and punish the offender, and the punishment for white-collar crimes is usually minimal. Punishment for crimes of this sort usually amount to a piddly fine and a short, unsupervised probation."

"I think we'd better give this to the authorities, Alex. We're not in the punishment business."

"No, we're not, but I'll bet if we take this out of house, we'll have a team of government investigators and accountants pouring over our books and disrupting a number of our departments for who knows how long. I think we can handle this ourselves."

"I don't think it's a good idea to take what amounts to industrial espionage into our own hands, Alex. Why don't we just fire the informer, when we find out who it is, and let it go at that?"

Alex got up, walked over to the window and looked north to where the Pacific Coast Highway joined MacArthur Blvd. *What would be the most fitting punishment for this crime?* Alex asked himself. After a minute or two, he turned back toward his uncle. "We'll need to know Mr. Kula's exact net worth!"

"Why's that?"

"We'll see how much of it we can cause him to lose."

"Jesus, Alex!"

October 21, 1982

Walt was obviously depressed as he walked into Alex's office. "Just had a call from Vance," he said as he sat down.

Alex could see his uncle was upset. "What'd he tell you?"

"Guess what Margaret's sister's married name is?"

Alex looked at his uncle for a few seconds. "Ah, shit!"

After that, with Vance's help they completed a thorough investigation of Mr. Kula. He was Margaret's only nephew; one she doted over since he was born. They also discovered that he had been in trouble with various authorities starting in grade school. Among his questionable accomplishments was the fact that Victor Kula was a convicted con man and embezzler. They could only speculate why Margaret would risk losing everything to help this piece of shit make a fortune.

November 3, 1982
9:15 a.m.

"You heard right, Margie," said Walt.

"Let me confirm then. You're selling all Data Industries and half your gold futures to cover this buy?"

"That's it," agreed Walt. "And it's likely we'll buy a great deal more in a week or so."

"Must be a good one," said Margaret.

"You'll be amazed." Walt looked at Alex.

"All right, I'll get the funds transferred," finished Margaret.

"Thank you." Walt reached over and pushed the off button. He looked over at his nephew. "Jesus, I can't stand this, Alex, any part of it."

Alex knew his uncle hated to put a sting on this trusted longtime employee and friend. Alex almost capitulated to his uncle's wishes to just fire Margaret, but held his ground. Although he felt betrayed by Margaret, he really didn't want to cause her any more grief than to give her retirement papers. It was Victor Kula he wanted to punish. Alex disliked him immensely for taking advantage of a loving old aunt. Him, he wanted to hurt.

This instruction and conversation with Margaret was just the final part of the plan to relieve Victor Kula of his fortune. For the past week, both Alex and Walt had contacted eight broker associates and placed buy orders for large blocks of TTI stock. All brokers involved were close friends of the Gabriels and could be trusted to remain tight-lipped when necessary. Only two asked what the hell was going on. The other six involved assumed that Walt and Alex knew what they were doing and besides, there were big commissions to be earned here. The two who questioned this unusual transaction were satisfied with, "Let's just say we're trying to catch a crook and let it go at that!"

Each broker was given a varying number of shares to buy, from a low of 30,000 for the smaller brokers to 90,000 for the larger traders.

"Why don't we just buy all 600,000 shares ourselves?" Walt asked during their first planning meeting.

"Because it will take a few days, to a week or so, to acquire that number of shares, and Mr. Kula, in all likelihood, would be buying at the same time we are. When Kula starts buying, we'd better be selling."

"Of course. That was a stupid question. Sorry."

"Not to worry; I know your heart isn't in this."

They -- or to be more exact, Vance Youngblood -- had ascertained that Victor Kula's two-year- old company had a net worth of approximately $9,000,000. This came as a big surprise to both Walt and Alex. Victor must have borrowed or conned a goodly sum prior to beginning his investment career. This assured the Gabriels that Kula hadn't stumbled on a scam; he'd created it. It might mean that Mr. Kula had partners with money.

"Better find out if anyone is backing this shithead, and just what the connection is!"

"Vance is busy gathering that info as we speak."

Alex sat back in his chair and smiled at his uncle. "When do I get to meet this resourceful Mr. Youngblood?"

"I'd rather you didn't for a while."

"Any particular reason?" *What the hell is it about this man that causes Walt to keep him away from me?*

"I don't want to talk about it right now."

Alex stared at Walt for a moment, and shook his head, "Okay, let's get back to the plan."

TTI was presently selling for $38.50 a share, which meant the Gabriels had to gain control of just short of 600,000 shares. TTI had 12,000,000 shares outstanding, so the total purchased would amount to only five percent of the outstanding stock. Although a trade of five percent of a company's stock in a single week would probably cause the stock's value to increase, it could also bring some scrutiny from astute analysts. The Gabriels assumed spreading the buys over several brokers would thwart any serious investigation. The plan included having the eight outside brokers purchase a total of 400,000 shares. Each broker was to contact them the minute they had acquired the prescribed number of shares. It was five days before the last of them confirmed their buy.

The Gabriels, at this point, put in a buy order for the balance of 200,000 shares, using their own brokerage with Margaret's knowledge, assuming Margaret would contact her nephew within a short period of time, possibly just minutes. As soon as Victor Kula contacted his broker and placed his order, they would contact the other brokers and have them sell their TTI. Timing was critical to make the sting work. To that end, Vance's people had phone taps on all Victor's phones and his Miami broker's phone. If Victor Kula didn't take the bait and purchase 600,000 shares of TTI, the Gabriels stood to lose a great deal of money.

November 3, 1982

Walt quickly walked into Alex's office, holding two cassette tapes in his hand.

"What have you there, Uncle?" asked Alex.

"The proof. Vance just sent these over to me. They're only thirty minutes old."

Alex leaned over and opened the bottom drawer on the left-hand side of his desk. He reached in and pulled out a portable cassette recorder, setting it on his desk.

Walt leaned over and put in the first tape. "You ready?"

Alex nodded.

Walt pushed the play button.

The two of them listened for about two minutes before Walt reached over to turn off the machine.

"Let's hear the rest of it," said Alex.

Walt leaned back in his chair.

"Thanks, Aunt Margaret. Maybe now I can pay off my old car and think about getting married."

"I sure hope so, dear. I've never seen Walt so excited about a stock."

"Really?"

"Oh yes, dear. He told me he and Alex have been talking about it for a couple of weeks now."

"So they bought a bunch themselves, you say?"

"I'll say, and they sold some profitable investments to do it..."

There was a moment's pause.

"You know, dear, it's illegal for me to give you this information. I hope this will help you get on your feet. I feel guilty about helping you this way."

"Gosh, Aunt Margaret, I don't think the few shares I buy will really bother anyone, do you?"

"I suppose not, but it's still illegal."

Again there was a pause; this one a little longer.

"When do I get to meet this fiancée of yours?"

"Soon. We don't want you to see our apartment until we can afford to get it furnished. Don't want you to think your nephew is a bum."

"We could have dinner out some night. I could meet your lady that way, you know. My treat, of course."

"You've got a deal. I'll call you for a time and place after I talk to Sherry."

"Okay, dear; I'm looking forward to it. Got to go now. Love you."

"Thanks again. Love you, too."

The recorder went silent.

"That son of a bitch," Alex responded angrily. He reached over and pushed the rewind button.

Walt was upset. "I don't want to hurt her, Alex. Shit, she's just trying to help her nephew."

"I agree," replied Alex. "Let's listen to the other tape and then we'll decide what to do."

Walt nodded.

Alex removed the first tape and replaced it with the second.

The first thing they heard was Kula's voice.

..."*What a dumb bitch*!"

"*She may be dumb*," said a female voice, "*but she's making you a rich man, Vic*."

"*And about to be a lot richer, God bless her wrinkled old ass*."

Alex and Walt could hear some rustling noise then the sound of a phone being dialed. It was long distance judging by the amount of numbers dialed. They could hear the phone ringing. Alex was thinking how efficient this Vance Young was. He had the asshole Kula completely wired for sound.

"*Volkman, Hoyt*," a female voice could be heard.

"*Connect me to Herb, and make it fast*." It was Kula's voice.

"*May I tell him what this concerns*?"

"*No you can't... just put me through to him, now*!"

After a few second's pause. "*Yes, sir*!"

There was a buzz, then a male voice came on the line.

"*Herb Volkman here*."

"*Herb, this is Victor*."

"*Yes, Victor, what can I do for you*?" The voice sounded quite solicitous.

"*You can buy me all the TTI you can; that's what you can do for me*."

"*TTI*?"

"*You heard right; I want all I can get. And I want it right now*."

There was a short pause.

"*I think I've heard rumors about TTI. I'd better do a little investigating before you buy this stock.*"

"*How long will that take?*"

"*No more than two days, I promise you.*"

Alex looked at Walt with mild alarm.

"*Two days, are you out of your fucking mind? The stock will probably go through the roof in the next two days and I'll lose out on some God-damned big gains.*"

"Thank God for greed," Alex remarked.

"*What's it selling for right now?*" Victor continued to talk.

"*Hold on.*" There was a full minute's pause before Herb's voice came back on. "*Well, it's gone up from $38.50 to $41.25 in the past five days.*" There was another pause. "*Christ, somebody's buying a lot of it!*"

"*Well, God damn it, that should tell you the shit's going up, so fuck the rumors.*"

"*Okay, don't get so excited. How much do you want to buy?*"

"*Everything I can get a hold of!* "

"*What do you mean?*"

"*What, are you, deaf? I want you to sell every fucking stock I own and buy me all the TTI you can.*"

"*I would strongly advise against that, Victor.*"

"*Are you my stockbroker or not? If not, I'll find someone who can take orders without handing me a bucket of bullshit.*"

Another pause.

"*I'll place the order, Victor.*"

"*I thought you would!*"

The sound of the phone being slammed was heard. Then a few seconds later, Kula's jubilant voice could be heard, "*My partners are going to think I'm a god.*"

November 3, 1982

"I appreciate that, Levi. We owe you one," said Alex into the phone.

"You owe me nothing, my friend. The business you've sent me over the years put my kids through college and kept me and my

Sara living in a manner that we're still becoming accustomed to. I thank you."

"Okay, old friend. Say hi to Sara for me."

Alex had just placed what would be Levi Goldberg's largest buy and sell orders of his career in the stock market. It was at a reduced brokerage rate, to be sure, but Levi would still make a tidy sum.

Alex had just bought back, through Levi, all the good stocks they had sold through their own brokerage earlier in the day to deceive Margaret. Then he instructed Levi to sell not only the 60,000 shares of TTI he purchased for the Gabriels, but also the 200,000 shares the Gabriels purchased through their own brokerage just under two hours ago. This was the last of the transactions of the "sting" operation. The other seven brokers already received their sell orders. The only thing to do now was to sit back and wait.

Alex was still a bit apprehensive about TTI. He hadn't spent much time, in either life, studying companies that went in the dumper. But TTI stuck out in his mind because of its size and the scandal that surrounded its collapse. As he recalled, a young financial reporter from a minor newspaper was responsible for breaking TTI's back. What he wasn't sure of was exactly when the shit hit the fan. He was sure, however, it was in November of `82. Alex also knew that whoever was investigating TTI would notice the large buying, and subsequent selling, these past two days and might assume the cat was out of the bag. If he did assume that, he would want to disclose the results of his investigation before someone scooped him.

November 12, 1982

"Margaret's here to see you, sir," Carol's voice came over the intercom.

"Give us a few. I'll buzz you." Walt released the intercom bottom.

Alex could see that his uncle was distraught. "So that's it, then. We're out of TTI and actually made a little profit."

"Yeah, just about enough to pay the brokerage fees."

Alex felt badly about how this was affecting his uncle. Walt's normally high spirits were at an all-time low. Now, to top it off, he had to fire Margaret.

"I would rather take a severe beating than to face Margaret today," Walt said solemnly.

"I know you would, Uncle, and I'll offer again to handle this for you."

Walt just shook his head, took a deep breath and pushed the intercom button.

Chapter 46

GABRIEL HOME
November 19, 1982
9:05 p.m.

"Alex. It's Colleen."

"How's my favorite aunt?" Alex asked cheerfully.

"Terrible. We just got a call from Margaret's sister..." there was a pause.

Alex felt a jolt of adrenaline and sat straighter in his chair.

"They found Margaret dead in her condo this evening."

"Oh no!"

"It's worse than that." Colleen's voice broke. "It looks like she was beaten to death."

Alex nearly dropped the phone. It felt as if his heart had stopped. "Oh my God! What have I done?"

Colleen said nothing for a few seconds and when she spoke, her voice was flat. "Can you come over? I'm sure Walt needs you to be with him right now." It was clear at that moment, Alex was not Colleen's favorite person.

"I'll be there within twenty minutes." Alex's hands were shaking so badly he could hardly hang up the phone.

"What's the matter, Alex?" asked Marian the second she saw her son's face as he entered the TV room.

"Margaret Wallace has been killed," Alex choked out.

"Oh no! Was it a car accident?"

Alex just shook his head, "I've got to get over to Walt's right now... oh, Jesus, Mom; I've really screwed up." He couldn't stop his hands from shaking.

"*You* screwed up?"

9:15 p.m.

Alex could barely maintain a coherent thought as he drove to his uncle's home five miles to the south. *Shit, shit, shit*! The shock of Margaret's violent death kept running around in his brain. He could see her in his mind's eye, battered and bloody, a look of shock on her old wrinkled face. He imagined the pain she must have gone through. *I'm so sorry, Margaret, so sorry.*

"...Why don't we just fire the informer?"

Why couldn't I have listened to Walt? Why did I have to inflict my own punishment on these people? Was it to show them it wasn't wise to fuck with Alexander Gabriel? Is that it? What makes me so FUCKING SMART?

...First we need to pin down the guilty party... make them suffer...

Well, Margaret, how do you like that for suffering? Alex drove like he was a zombie. He saw nothing around him. He didn't notice the dark green nondescript Ford, maintaining a discreet distance behind him. He noticed nothing at all of the real world. What was he going to say to his uncle? *I'm sorry I got you into this, dear uncle. I'll try to be more reasonable next time. SHIT!*

November 22, 1982
10:10 a.m.

All the Gabriels were in a black limo that held fifth place behind the hearse carrying Margaret's remains to her final resting place. They were heading to a cemetery near the city of El Toro in southeast Orange County. There was a total of twelve cars in the procession. In last place was a nondescript dark green Ford, containing two men properly dressed in black suits.

The past three days had been tough on everyone, but no one was more devastated than Alex. Walt was saddened and guilt-ridden, despite the fact that Alex spent hours trying to convince him he had done his best to talk Alex out of "punishing" Margaret and her nephew.

"Had it been up to you, we wouldn't have done it, you know that. So let's put the blame where it belongs, right here," Alex pointed to himself.

"I could have voiced my objections stronger. I could have worked harder to talk you out of it."

"Uncle Walt, when was the last time you talked me out of anything?" Alex replied quietly.

Walt shook his head, tears forming in his eyes, "I wish I would have won this one."

"Me too," Alex almost whispered.

The police homicide unit had interviewed Walt and Alex at some length. They had learned from Margaret's sister that she had been fired from Gabriel industries just three days prior to the murder. The detectives wanted to know the circumstances behind the dismissal of such a long-time employee. They were told the truth. Margaret had been caught giving company secrets to her nephew and had subsequently been fed false information in order to bring down her nephew's operation.

"What sort of false information?"

"Let's just say we led her to believe a stock was going to go up when, in fact, we believed it would go down. We felt she would relay that information to her nephew and he, in turn, would invest in it and consequently lose a great deal of money."

"How much money?"

"Don't know exactly."

"Do you believe it would be enough to cause," the detective looked at his notes, "Victor Kula to retaliate against his aunt?"

"Without question!"

"Really!"

"I would think, Detective, that Victor Kula should be at the top of your list."

"But why kill his aunt over it? Seems to me you two would be the targets of his wrath."

"We agree, but we're probably not dealing with a rational personality."

"Just the same," said the detective, "if I were you, I'd take some precautions until we get our hands on Mr. Kula."

"We have that covered," responded Walt.

Alex looked at Walt but said nothing.

The funeral procession arrived at the Heavenly Angels Cemetery. All the attendees exited their cars and stood around, not quite sure what to do next. Most of the mourners were employed at Gabriel Industries in one capacity or another. Of those, most were from Margaret's accounting department. The men stood with their arms around or holding the hands of their loved ones. Those who were alone just stood with their hands clasped in front, or in their pockets, and waited. The chosen pallbearers, after some mumbling among them, gathered around the back of the hearse. The funeral director, after a few moments, gave instructions as to how to carry the casket and where to take it. Walt and Alex were not asked to be pallbearers. As the procession gathered behind the pallbearers, the Gabriels took up the rear. Walt and Colleen, holding hands, went first, followed by Marian, with Alex on one side and Norman on the other. Jennifer and Chuck followed them.

The two men in a dark green Ford quietly exited their vehicle after the procession had moved fifty yards up a small hill toward the gravesite. The shorter, stocky one walked to the left; the other to the right.

It was a blustery cold day and few other people could be seen in the cemetery. Over to the right and down a way, another small funeral was in progress. To the left and further up the hill, a lone mourner was kneeling beside a gravesite. A large bouquet of fresh flowers could be seen lying on the ground in front of him.

The ceremony at the gravesite was quite short. It consisted of a brief eulogy and, as the casket was being lowered into the grave, the minister led the group in two prayers. Margaret's sister, dressed in black with a black veil covering her face, stepped to the edge of the grave, bent, picked up a handful of dirt, and dropped it on top of the casket. She stood there sobbing quietly for a few moments, then turned and started walking down the hill with a close friend. Other mourners followed; some threw in a handful of dirt, and others dropped flowers on top of the casket. Some paused for a moment, then turned and started down the hill toward the parked cars.

The Gabriels were last. Walt and Colleen approached the grave and dropped their flowers, followed by Norman, Marian, Jennifer and Chuck, and then Alex. As the others started down the hill, Alex stood looking into the grave, tears in his eyes. He had never felt so miserable. He was responsible for another person's death. The guilt was all-consuming. He could think of nothing else.

Walt looked back over his shoulder and saw that Alex was still there. "Wait here for a second, will you?" he said to his family.

"Sure," Norman replied. They all stopped and looked back up the hill as Walt headed back to console his nephew.

"Alex is taking this hard," said Marian.

"I'm afraid I've been a lot harder on him than he deserves," Colleen remarked. "I should have known he would be devastated by what happened. I owe him an apology."

Most mourners were already in their cars and starting to drive off. Five or six others were talking to Margaret's sister. Nobody noticed the lone mourner picking up the large bouquet of flowers and starting down the hill toward Alex and the approaching Walt. Nobody noticed that the two men, properly dressed in black, had also begun to head toward Margaret's gravesite at a fast pace. The shorter one was reaching inside his coat.

"Alex," called Walt as he approached.

Alex turned his head toward his uncle.

"HEY, ASSHOLES!" someone yelled from a short distance up the hill.

The Gabriels by the gravesite, and those further down the hill, looked up in time to see the lone mourner drop the large bouquet of flowers and reveal a nasty looking, short-barreled shotgun.

"Thought you motherfuckers would like to know who killed you. I'm Victor Kula." With that single statement, he raised the gun.

Alex stepped in front of his uncle just as a loud swack, like a hanging rug being hit with a baseball bat, filled the air, and Victor Kula's head seemed to expand grotesquely. His left eye exploded outward and blood gushed from his nose. The shotgun in his hands fired and Alex felt a slamming blow just above his right knee. Victor Kula fell face forward, still holding the shotgun. Alex's body twisted violently to the right as he fell.

There was a brief moment of terrifying silence; then came screams from Marian and Colleen, and shouts of confusion from those mourners still gathered around Margaret's sister. Norman was first to react. He dashed straight up the hill; terrified his son had just been killed. Walt stood shocked, no coherent thoughts in his mind.

The shorter, stocky man ran up and stood over Kula's body with a pistol pointed at his deformed head. He kicked Kula hard in the side just to be sure there was no movement. He uncocked his pistol and returned it to its holster.

Alex lay still on the ground; his thoughts were a confused mess and he had an intense numbing pain in his right leg. He momentarily couldn't figure out why he was on the ground or why there was so much yelling and screaming. "What the hell?"

Norman was down on his knees beside his son within seconds of the two shots. "Alex, lie still; just lie still."

Walt snapped out of it. "Oh, Jesus Christ!" He spun to his right and saw Alex on the ground with blood spurting out of his ripped pants above his right knee, the leg bent unnaturally to the side. "Oh, Jesus Christ!" He jumped to the other side of Alex and quickly knelt down.

Both Colleen and Marian were now beside Alex, Marian at Alex's head and Colleen next to Walt.

"Excuse me," said the stocky man as he nudged Norman, none

too gently, out of the way. He immediately reached down and ripped Alex's pants nearly to the crotch and down to the cuff. After studying the gushing wound for a brief second, he looked up at the other Gabriels. "May I?" He reached over and snatched the scarf from around Colleen's neck, then wrapped and tied it tightly around Alex's leg three inches above the wound. The blood flow nearly stopped. He looked up at the other man in the black suit. "Jake, get down to the car and call an ambulance and the police."

"Yes, sir," and off he went at a dead run.

"Just lie still, Mr. Gabriel. You're going to be fine."

"Who are you?" Alex asked between clenched teeth; his face displaying a great deal of pain.

All but Walt were wondering the same thing. Who was this man who had just killed Victor Kula, and had now taken over the care of their beloved Alex?

"Vance Youngblood, sir."

Margaret's sister walked back up the hill with a few others to see what had happened. She first stopped to see Alex on the ground with the other Gabriels kneeling beside him. "Oh, my God, what's happened?"

"Oh, Jessie, you shouldn't be here," said Walt as he looked up.

"What do you mean?" At that point, she looked thirty feet up the hill where Victor's body lay. She started to walk over when Walt jumped up and restrained her. "Who's that?"

"You don't want to go over there, Jessie."

"Why? Who is that?"

Walt had her by the shoulders and looked her in the eye. "It's your son, Jessie."

"My son! Is he all right? Let me go help him!" She tried to pull away from Walt but he held her tight.

"He's dead, Jessie," he whispered to her.

Her eyes grew large and round as the horrible news seeped into her mind. Then she began screaming.

Alex spent two hours in the operating room. During that time, the police questioned all witnesses at the gravesite except Marian who was at the hospital with Alex. They started with the remaining Gabriels and after about half an hour and repeated pleadings the police let them go to the hospital to be with Alex.

"Alex is going to be all right," the doctor was telling the Gabriels and Vance Youngblood. They'd all been nervously waiting in the reception room. "Had the buckshot hit him just an inch to the right or down two inches, he would have lost his leg for sure. As it is, looks like one ball struck the inside of the femur four inches above the knee, breaking it at that point, but remarkably not causing a great deal of bone damage. It looks as if another ball tore through the main artery, which caused a large loss of blood and some soft tissue damage. Had someone not applied a tourniquet soon after he was hit, he might have died. He was lucky."

"If he was lucky, he'd a had a better bodyguard," remarked Vance.

Everybody turned and looked at Vance, clearly puzzled.

"You saved our lives, Vance. What the hell are you talking about?" asked Walt.

Norman cocked his head. "I didn't know Alex had a bodyguard."

"I let that demented son of a bitch get way too close. I didn't spot him until he was nearly on you. I can't tell you how sorry I am."

"Be that as it may," said the doctor, "Alex is going to need about two months to recuperate and probably some continuing therapy for a while after that."

"Is he going to be able to walk all right?" asked Marian.

"Oh yes; no reason he shouldn't. He'll have a limp for a spell, but there shouldn't be any lasting effects."

November 25, 1982
8:10 a.m.

Alex lay flat on his back in a hospital room for the second time he could remember. It had been over twenty years now. But this time, he wasn't confused. This time he knew when, where, why, and who he was. The circumstances, on this occasion, were clear-cut. He had been shot; someone had actually tried to kill him.

The itching had already begun under the oversized cast, adding a new element to his misery. The cast extended from his toes nearly to his crotch on the right side. The cast itself hung from four separate wires attached to a framework suspended above his bed. He had a glucose IV dripping into his left arm and various electrodes leading from his chest and right arm. He was miserable.

The room itself was nice by hospital standards and was crammed so full of flowers that the normal hospital smells were completely masked.

Jason and Walt hadn't been gone five minutes when Vance Youngblood made an appearance. "Good morning, sir."

"Morning, Vance," Alex responded.

"How's it going today, sir?" Vance walked around to the far side of the bed, allowing him to keep an eye on the door.

"Still wounded, I suspect," Alex answered as his eyes followed Vance's progress.

Walt had formally introduced Alex and Vance the previous afternoon. Alex remembered the introduction, but not much of the conversation. He recalled believing that Vance's apology was sincere and heartfelt. But he remembered little else of the previous two days because of the morphine. But the doctor had cut back on the morphine the night before. "*You should be able to get along with a lower dosage*," he remarked as he made a note on Alex's chart.

Now Alex wasn't nearly as fuzzy as he looked closely at Vance, a powerful looking man with cold brown eyes and thick dark wavy hair above his low forehead. This was the toughest looking man Alex had ever seen. Vance was well-dressed, very well-dressed, but he clearly didn't buy his suits off the rack, not with those shoulders. It was as if he was a GQ model in a `house of mirrors`, perfectly dressed, but oddly distorted. A strong feeling of deja vu suddenly struck Alex, "Have we met before, Vance?"

"Not formally; no, sir."

"Informally then?"

"In a manner of speaking, you might say we've had a little interaction, sir."

Alex kept looking at Vance, but nothing was coming to him; the moment had passed. "Can I order you some coffee or something, Vance?"

"Oh, that won't be necessary, sir. But thank you anyway," Vance responded.

Alex cocked his head a little...*Thought I might be able to even this confrontation up a little....*

...Oh, that won't be necessary, sir....But thank you anyway...

"That's it, I've placed you," Alex exclaimed, obviously pleased with himself.

"Sir?"

"Three years ago at a Christmas party, you were a bouncer. You knocked the shit out of a couple of guys who were giving my lady and me a bad time. Right?"

"Never been a bouncer, sir," Vance responded evenly. "But you do have the rest of the circumstances essentially correct."

Alex's smile faded and then disappeared. "Christ...how long have you been protecting me?"

Vance gave the slightest of smiles. "Something over four years now, sir."

2:10 p.m.

"You've had private security on me for four years?"

"I have. Started by retaining Vance's security company and then after a couple of years, talked Vance and his men into joining Gabriel Industries as employees."

"You didn't think I should know about it?"

"Frankly, I'm amazed you never spotted them, not even once," smiled Walt. "Vance's organization, by all accounts, is the best in the business."

"You didn't think I should know about it?" Alex repeated.

"Well, at first I thought about it; then after a while, it kind of slipped my mind. Vance's men blended so well, it just didn't seem to matter."

Alex didn't know whether to be angry or grateful. "What prompted you to hire security in the first place?"

Walt's brow furrowed a bit. "I believe it was around the time of your twenty-first birthday party. I remember thinking any of us, given our circumstances, would be prime candidates for kidnapping, you in particular. So I thought about it for a while, asked around and came up with Vance's name."

Alex shook his head in disbelief. "What hours do they work?"

"Twenty-four, every day of the week. And by the way, it's not just you that Vance has covered. Got the office and our homes under twenty-four-hour coverage."

"Jesus," Alex muttered. "Guess I'm not too observant."

"I'd chalk it up to your not having a suspicious or paranoid personality. You tend to do your own thing with little, if any, notice of what others do around you."

"Sounds like I'm quite self-centered."

"I wouldn't say that at all. Dedicated and focused would be a more apt description."

"I'm sure you're being kind."

"Not at all."

Alex thought about that for a few seconds. "Well, tell me about Vance Youngblood."

"Okay," smiled Walt. "Just happened to bring along his dossier today."

"Thought I might have a question or two, did you?"

"I was sure of it."

"I'll give you what it says here and what I have found out over these past few years."

"Over four, actually," corrected Alex.

"I see you've gotten some info from Vance."

"Not much -- the man's certainly not a blabbermouth."

"Well, I'll fill you in a little." Walt opened the file. "Vance is in his early forties. He was born in South Central LA to what, I gathered over the past few years, was a dysfunctional family. He has one older brother and a younger sister. Apparently, he had another brother, the oldest, who died of a heroin overdose." Walt paused for a second. "You know, I've been in Vance's office on a few occasions and have seen pictures of his family on the wall. I've got to tell you he looks nothing like his siblings or parents," Walt reflected for a moment. "I understand his parents originally came from Arkansas and, no slight intended, his family looks like they are, for lack of a better description, from Arkansas. Vance, on the other hand, looks like he could be found chopping the shit out of opposing gladiators in a Coliseum; definitely looks Roman or Greek to me. You would never guess they were related."

"That's odd. Adopted, you think?"

"Not a chance. Could be a throwback to an ancestor I suppose," Walt said thoughtfully. "His father was kind of a drifter and a drunk; a mean drunk as I understand it."

"Really?"

"That's what Vance has alluded to in the past. Didn't care much for his father, I've gathered."

"That's too bad."

"Apparently young Vance was born with some gifts," Walt went on. "His scholastic record is in the top five percent throughout high school and college. He was captain of the UCLA wrestling team and was all-state heavyweight champ two years running."

"That doesn't surprise me one little bit."

"That wasn't even his long suit. It was football that earned him a full ride at UCLA. Played halfback, and in his senior year shattered the eight-year running record. Must be awfully quick for his mass."

"I've seen him in action... let me rephrase that; I've been there when he was in action and saw little. It was just a blur."

"I got a report on that incident," Walt smiled.

"I might have seen more if I hadn't been so smashed, but I doubt it," Alex reflected.

"Joined the Navy after graduating," Walt went on. "Went through officer's training and graduated near the top of his class. Apparently 'Ensign Youngblood' caught the eye of a SEALs commander and he joined that lethal branch of the service."

"Jesus, he's a SEAL?"

"A good one by the looks of his record. Three bronze and two silver stars for bravery in Vietnam and a Distinguished Service Cross. Attained the rank of captain before resigning his commission in June of 1971. Went into private security shortly after that."

"Jesus Christ, a trained killer.... No purple hearts?"

"Not a one!"

"I like the man a lot," Alex said pensively. "I feel safe around him."

Chapter 47

NORMAN RESEARCH CENTER
October 5, 1983
10:45 a.m.

"Hey Pop, how's it going?" asked Alex as he walked into his father's office at the Norman Research Center.

"Hi, Son. What a pleasant surprise," Norman responded cheerfully as he got up and walked around his desk.

Alex walked over and gave his dad a hug. Then he turned and sat in one of the chairs located in front of his father's desk. "How are things in the labs?"

"Great, as a matter of fact." Norman smiled. "I hear you're finally going to meet Dale Isley."

"Yes, this afternoon. Looking forward to it. I've read some of his papers; he's certainly an abstract thinker."

"That he is. The young man is a genius; doctorates in both microbiology and quantum physics." Norman paused for a second. "Need to warn you, the man's a hippie. He may not have bathed, shaved, or changed clothes for several years. If ever there were a man who cared not one iota about his appearance, this would be that man. You can actually smell him, but…"

"Smell him?"

"I'm afraid so, but he has as good a mind as I've ever seen."

October 5, 1983
2:45 p.m.

"Dr. Isley is here for his appointment, Mr. Gabriel." Alex looked at his watch and frowned. Isley was over an hour and a half late. He reached forward and pressed a button.

"Show him in please, Carol."

Within a few seconds, Carol opened the door to Alex's office and escorted Dale in.

"Dr. Isley, meet Mr. Gabriel," Carol said as she rolled her eyes back in her head just for Alex's benefit.

Holy shit! Alex was already pissed, now he was disgusted. *Pop told me this man was a walking trashcan… but shit!*

"Dr. Isley," Alex extended his hand.

"Mr. Gabriel," Dale responded as he shook hands with Alex without making eye contact.

"Please have a seat," Alex motioned toward one of the over-stuffed chairs in front of his desk. Alex sat back down and wiped his right hand on his pant leg.

"I'm sorry it has taken so long for you and me to meet, Dr. Isley. You've been with Norman research - what, six months or so?" The more Alex saw of this man, the less he liked him. *He does have BO, for Christ's sake*.

"I guess...I don't pay much attention," answered Dale as he scanned the office.

"Are the facilities to your liking? Are you given everything you need to conduct your research?"

"Yes, sir, the best I've seen." With this, Dale spun nearly 180 degrees in his chair, allowing him to view the rest of this opulent office.

"Is there anything else we can provide you with that we haven't?" Alex was becoming more aggravated by the second.

"No, sir."

"Would you like to continue to work for Norman Research, Dr. Isley?"

"Yes, sir?" said Dale again, but this time there was a slight question in his voice and he briefly looked at Alex.

"For you to continue working for Norman Research, Dr. Isley, you will be required to make a number of changes." Alex's voice had a slight chill.

"What?" This got Dale's attention and he again looked up quickly at Alex and then away.

"I said that if you wish to continue your work with Norman Research, you will be required to make a number of changes in your mode of operation."

"I don't understand, sir." Dale's voice displayed some concern.

"Well, let me explain, Dr. Isley." Alex's voice held a slight but distinct edge. "First, when I talk to someone, I fully expect them to look at me. I would strongly suggest that you do so now. If you choose not to, we can consider this conversation and your employment terminated."

Dale's head shot up. He looked at Alex, his face a mask of shock. He was clearly having trouble maintaining eye contact. If one was not in the habit of maintaining eye contact with people, Alex was not the person to start with. "You would fire me for not looking at you when you're talking?"

"Absolutely! And I expect you to look at everyone in this company when you're in a conversation with them." Alex was staring into Dale's eyes and could see the man had a real problem. "How is anyone supposed to know that you're even paying attention to what they're saying if you're rudely looking away?" Alex held a level voice with just a trace of rancor.

"I could get a job in almost any research facility in the country, if I want. And I don't think they would make it a requirement that I look at them when we're talking. I'm into research, Mr. Gabriel, not communications."

"Then I suggest you do that, Dr. Isley." Alex started up from his chair.

"Wait, wait! I said I could get another job; I didn't say I wanted to," Dale replied quickly. He was maintaining eye contact with great difficulty. A casual observer might think Dale was looking into the face of Medusa for the trouble he was having.

Alex sat back down. *If he'd just been on time, I wouldn't be so pissed. But I am pissed, God damn it*!

"Second thing, Dr. Isley, is your appearance. Quite frankly, if I took as little time as you apparently do in personal hygiene and dress, I would have trouble looking anybody in the eye; I would be too damned embarrassed. Not only do you look like someone found sitting in a doorway on Skid Row, but you smell the part."

Dale Isley was clearly having trouble comprehending what was being said to him. He probably expected to have a brief conversation with the "Big Boss" and then be on his way.

Genius or not, I can't have someone like this working for Norman. The other employees will avoid him like the plague. "In my companies, I expect everybody to work closely together and exchange ideas. This, we've found, is the best way to get tasks accomplished. I suggest to you that few, if any, of your associates will be able to spend any time in your immediate presence, and that is not acceptable."

Dale was clearly at a loss for words. His lips were moving slightly, but no sound was coming out.

Alex paused for a few seconds, then leaned forward a little. "I don't give a shit, Dr. Isley, how long your hair is. I don't even give a shit how long your beard is, but they both will be clean and combed, every day. Further, if you wish to continue employment with Norman Research, you and whatever you choose to wear will be clean. I suggest you wear sneakers or whatever instead of those sandals, but that is not a requirement. Lastly, when you have an appointment with me or anyone in the company, by God, you-will-be-on-time." Alex stopped for a moment, leaned back in his chair and softened his voice. "If these requirements are more than you can or are willing to comply with, we can part company, right now, with no hard feelings on my part."

Dale just sat for a few seconds, obviously stunned, probably embarrassed, but he managed to maintain eye contact. "Nobody has ever talked to me that way." He paused, looking down at the desk for what seemed like a full minute and then suddenly back up at Alex. "Either no one has given a shit or they just didn't have the balls to call me on it...I don't know."

Alex could see the confusion and hurt in Dale's face. *I bet I could have done that more diplomatically*, he thought, feeling a tinge of regret and quite a lot of empathy for Dale.

Dale was looking at the top of Alex's desk, and then he looked back at Alex, not quite making eye contact. "I'm going to need some time to think about this."

"Take all the time you need, Dr. Isley," Alex said gently.

Dale sat with his eyes focused on a crystal paperweight sitting on Alex's desk. " I'm going home now," Dale muttered as he pulled his eyes away from the paperweight and stood.

"Okay," said Alex.

Dale started walking toward the door, then stopped and turned. "This doesn't mean I'm quitting. I just need time to think."

"Dr. Isley, just so you know, we would like you to stay with Norman," Alex said sincerely.

Dale nodded, turned and walked out of the office.

Pop is not going to be happy with me if Dale quits, was Alex's first thought. He sat back in his chair trying to imagine what sort of upbringing caused Dale Isley to be the way he was. Had he not been disciplined at all? What the hell kind of people were his parents?

October 10, 1983
11:30 a.m.

"Dr. Isley is here for his appointment, Mr. Gabriel."

Alex looked at his watch and smiled. *One minute early*. He reached over and pushed the intercom button. "Show him in please, Carol."

A few seconds later, the door opened and Dale Isley walked into the room.

Alex was momentarily stunned and leaned back in his chair, an almost comical expression on his face. "You gotta be shitting me!"

Walking across his office was a dapper young man, dressed in tan worsted wool slacks, a powder-blue cotton sport shirt open at the collar, a dark blue blazer with brass buttons and expensive-looking huarache-style shoes. His hair was rather long, but obviously styled, and his beard was close cropped and neatly trimmed. This was a good-looking young man.

"You gotta be shitting me!" Alex repeated.

"Am I on time?" asked a smiling Dr. Isley, looking directly into Alex's eyes.

Alex stood, leaned over the top of his desk and shook Dale's hand. "You're on time." Alex smiled, "Please sit down."

"Thanks." Dale sat down, not taking his eyes off Alex.

"I assume, from your appearance, you've decided to stay with Norman Research?"

Dale looked down at his hands for a moment, then back at Alex. "I need to say something, Mr. Gabriel," Dale said, obviously nervous. "It's going to be a little tough for me to get through it."

Uh-oh, thought Alex, thinking Dale might be about to quit. "Take your time, Dr. Isley."

Dale broke eye contact for a few seconds, cleared his throat, then looked back at Alex. "I didn't like you much after I left this office the other day," Dale paused before continuing, "and for the next couple of days, actually."

"I want to apologize to you, Dr. Isley. I had no right to, for lack of a better word, scold you."

"No, sir! Don't apologize, please. Your scolding may be the best thing that ever happened to me."

"I...why don't you continue; I'll listen."

"I won't go into any of the gory details, but just so you know, sir, I was raised in foster homes, a lot of foster homes. In a nutshell, I guess I didn't take to discipline or criticism well, so my various foster parents would quit trying and just pass me off to another family. I... " Dale paused as if re-thinking what he was going to say; he took a deep breath. "I've had no permanent friends or, I guess, any real friends at all. The only consistent thing in my life has been books. I could and did hide in them... to the obvious exclusion of everything else."

"I see."

"I guess what I'm trying to say is that no one ever seemed to care enough to point out my social inadequacies."

Alex said nothing while waiting for Dale to continue.

"I spent the last few days looking in the mirror, both literally and figuratively. Your cruel words kept coming back to me."

"I'm sor.."

Dale quickly held up his hand, palm forward, stopping whatever Alex was going to say. He cleared his throat again. "Two days ago, I came to see what you and everybody else was seeing...and smelling. I cried a lot that day." Dale looked down at his hands for a few seconds. When he looked up, he had tears built up in the corners of his eyes. He quickly wiped them with the back of his hand. "I decided to do something about my condition."

"I can see that."

"Found myself a barber and a men's store. Hadn't been to either one for as long as I can remember."

"You've found some good ones," Alex remarked. "What you've done about your appearance and attitude is nothing short of remarkable. I don't ever remember being so impressed."

"You mean that, sir?"

"With all my heart." Alex stood and walked around his desk, extending his hand. As Dale stood and took Alex's hand, Alex pulled him in and gave him a hug. As he stepped back, he continued to hold Dale's hand. "I hope you've decided to stay with Gabriel Industries, Dale."

"It may be hard to explain this to you, Mr. Gabriel, but you'd have to fire me before I'd leave your company."

Chapter 48

GABRIEL HEADQUARTERS
April 1, 1984
9:00 a.m.

"All in favor of dispensing with the reading of the minutes from the last meeting please signify by saying aye...opposed nay. The ayes have it." Alex scanned the agenda he had before him.

"We will begin with the treasurer's report on Gabriel International. Mr. Elsner, if you would, please."

This was the quarterly meeting of Gabriel International's executive officers. Aside from Alex, Walt, Bill Mallory and Sam Elsner, and a recording secretary, in attendance were Robert Chin, head of the Hong Kong-Taiwan operations, Douglas Ito, head of Japanese operations, Guenter Schmitt, head of German and Western European operations, and Otto Auchland, president and CEO of Zurich's Auchland Bank. Two of the attendees had brought their second-in-commands to the meeting, making a total of ten sitting comfortably around the board table in Alex's office.

Robert Chin was accompanied by his executive vice-president and chief financial officer, a Mr. Lowe, a dignified, elderly Chinese gentleman, whom Robert treated with a great deal of deference and respect. Mr. Lowe was the "local shark" Alex and Walt had found to lead Robert Chin through the treacherous Asian waters. Mr. Lowe's presence did not reflect any shortcomings on Robert's part, but Alex felt Mr. Lowe's vast experience in that area of the world would be a great benefit to the group.

Guenter Schmitt was a wealthy man in his own right and had just joined Gabriel International in January. Alex was somewhat surprised that Guenter had accepted Walt's and his offer to oversee Gabriel's European operations. Guenter had a reputation for being aggressive and a bit cold-blooded when it came to business. Because of this, Alex had done extensive checking but could not find a single report that Guenter was in any way dishonest -- just shrewd.

Otto Auchland had become a close friend of both Alex and Walt, and a member of the board in the years since Gabriel International acquired eighty percent of the Auchland Bank's stock. The Auchland Bank had seen its assets, over these past five years, grow to rival the largest of banks in Switzerland. All Gabriel's European and Asian funds were being processed and held in this bank.

Douglas Ito could only be described as the quintessential Japanese businessman. By all accounts, Douglas had few friends and a small family, but he was highly skilled at doing business in the cutthroat Japanese inner circles. Douglas was greatly respected for his intellect and clarity of thought. Douglas and Alex had become close friends over the years.

The meeting lasted throughout the day. The subjects ranged from future acquisitions to employee benefits. It was approaching dinner time.

"For the last order of business," said Alex, "I would like to announce the promotion of Jason Gould to President and CEO of Global Media Inc."

All in attendance looked at Bill Mallory sitting on Alex's left. Mallory obviously was not unhappy about this decision.

"Bill, will you give a rundown of Global's activities as of this date?" said Alex.

"Of course." Bill stood up, holding a couple of legal-sized papers. He put on his reading glasses and read from his notes. "Global Media has, since its inception six years ago, acquired twenty-three newspapers, three television stations, five radio stations and five weekly magazines in four countries. Each of these properties was suffering either stagnant or declining readership, viewers, or listeners -- and many, quite frankly, were on the brink of collapse. All, I am happy to report, have been, due to infusions of cash and good management, restored to a healthy, profitable state." Bill looked over at Alex. "Jason Gould, whom many of you have not met, has had a hand in much of this success."

"As you are all aware, Bill Mallory has been heading up Global Media, with Jason as his second in command for the past two years," Alex interjected. "Bill, quite frankly, would rather be in on the challenges here in the corporate office. It was never his wish to run a media conglomerate."

"As you are all aware," added Mallory with a slight smile, "it is difficult to say 'no' to Alex."

There was a chorus of agreement around the table.

"I suspect," Mallory went on, "that Jason will take Global Media to heights that even Alex could not foresee. He has one of the finest minds I've ever come across. There is, in my opinion, none more capable to take the helm of Global Media." With that, Mallory sat down.

"Thanks, Bill; I appreciate your saying that," said Alex.

"No sweat," replied Mallory. "If you're not careful, Jason will have your job someday."

"I wouldn't be surprised," smiled Alex. "Jack Calloway," he went on, "has been with Global since its inception. We put him in as Managing Editor for our first property, *The Berkeley Gazette*, and after a couple more acquisitions, made him Managing General Editor for all our newspapers. He has done an excellent job. I suspect Jason will want to keep him close by his side."

April 4, 1984

Alex sat behind his desk reminiscing about his sister's wedding to Chuck the day before. He smiled when he thought of Walt and Colleen's daughter, Alexandra, as the flower girl. *Boy, she's a serious child.* Alex didn't recall seeing her smile much the entire day.

"*She's taking her responsibilities as the flower girl very seriously*," Colleen told him. "*She had to be assured she had enough rose petals to go the distance to the altar. She actually wanted to do a practice run the day before. We eventually agreed to put twice as many petals in the basket as were needed before she was happy*."

Practice run, for Christ's sake! thought Alex.

And that curly red hair, Alex mused, *my God*!

"*She looks like a miniature Bozo when she gets up in the morning*," Walt told him. "*Scared the shit out of me more than once... bless her little heart*."

But it was her stoic personality that had Alex and everyone else baffled. Alex had overheard a young girl call his niece "Alex." This hapless child was immediately and sternly corrected, "My name is Alexandra; my uncle's name is Alex!" Nobody could understand where those genes came from. Oh well, it was a wonderful wedding. Chuck surprised everyone by holding up much better than expected, considering his aversion to crowds. Alex suspected his new brother-in-law had a couple of shots of a strong 'elixir' before walking down the aisle.

"Mr. Mallory on line two, sir."

Alex pushed the blinking button, as he picked up the receiver, "Bill, what's up?"

Again Carol's voice came over the intercom, "Mr. Gould is here to see you, sir."

"Hold on a second Bill, he's here now." Alex switched the phone to his right hand and reached over to press the intercom button. "Send him in, Carol."

Ten seconds later, Jason entered the office and walked down the two steps to the sunken room and across to Alex's desk. He seemed to enjoy coming up to the executive floor at the top of the Gabriel Building. Paintings and sculptures were placed strategically around the walls and floors. He was like a wide-eyed kid when he entered Alex's office.

"Just love this place," he remarked as he crossed the room.

Alex motioned to one of the chairs in front of his desk and

Jason, after taking another scan of the office, sat down.

"Okay, Bill, I'll tell him. Talk to you later," Alex hung up.

"Bill asked me to give you his congratulations," Alex said as he looked up and smiled at Jason.

"Congrats for what?" Jason had a doubtful look.

Alex stood up and started around his desk. "At the board of directors meeting Friday, you were promoted to President and CEO of Global Media." Alex stuck out his hand as he approached Jason. "Congratulations, my friend."

Jason just sat there looking up at Alex. He slowly raised his hand to take Alex's and stood. "*What*?" he inquired while looking Alex in the eye.

"You're the honcho at Global, that's what."

"But... I've only been with Global three years. There are people who have been working their asses off since... and what about Bill or Jack?"

"Bill never wanted to run Global in the first place; I railroaded him into it. Jack can't do the job you can... But if you'd rather not take the job, I bet we could find some..."

"I'll take the job, I'll take it!"

"Thought you might." *It's yours, my friend; take it and do what you will with it.*

Jason was quiet for a moment, "How about bringing Jack up to corporate with me? I could learn a lot from that man before he retires."

"You're the boss."

Chapter 49

WALT'S YACHT
May 12, 2985
10:10 a.m.

"Bout time to throw a line in the water, isn't it?" asked Jason as he took another pull off his beer.

"A few more miles, I'd guess," answered Walt, squinting under his Angels baseball cap, as he looked aft toward the receding Catalina Island.

"Be hard-pressed to find a more perfect day," Alex remarked. He was lounging comfortably on a cushioned deck chair.

"Or a more perfect place to be on such a day," added Jason.

Five men were heading out on Walt's seventy-two foot Grand Banks to do some tuna fishing. This weekend was for the boys; no women or children allowed. It was a rare occasion when all five were able to get away at the same time and just relax.

The three, hearing Vance's laugh, looked up in time to see Teddy in the lead with Vance following him down the stairs that connected the flying bridge to the rear deck. Vance had managed, in the past two and a half years, to go from an employee in charge of the Gabriel's security, to becoming Alex's close personal and trusted friend.

"Captain wanted me to ask you buncha slack-jawed pussies if yer ready to go fishin'?" Teddy asked with a semi scowl on his face, mimicking Vance's when mildly upset. His voice and inflections had Vance down pat.

Jason spat a mouthful of beer on the deck before he chuckled. Alex nearly knocked his beer off the deck table as he and Walt laughed ecstatically. Vance, who wasn't known for his sense of humor, laughed as he shook his head. His stoic demeanor all but evaporated any time he was around Teddy.

"We'll be back in a few. Looking for a pair of binoculars." Teddy and Vance headed belowdecks.

"It never fails to amaze me," said Jason.

"What's that?" asked Alex.

"Vance's change of personality whenever Teddy is around. I remember the first time those two met at your Christmas party a couple of years ago. How we kept an eye on Teddy every time he got within striking distance of Vance. We thought those two would mix like Arabs and Jews."

Alex nodded.

"Thought, for sure, Vance would have Teddy by the ankles, hanging him over the edge of your patio within seconds of their meeting," Jason went on.

Walt smiled."Just the opposite occurred -- within minutes, Teddy had Vance laughing so hard he was nearly doubled over. They became friends instantly."

"Vance was the single most scary person I'd ever met before that," interjected Jason. "I don't believe I ever saw him smile before that day. Teddy broke through his crusty shell in a hurry."

"Teddy has that effect. There's something about him; always has been," offered Alex.

"It's his loving aura," said Walt. "The man just doesn't have a malicious bone in his body… and it shows. He really cares about everybody he meets. I've never seen such a personality."

They presently were motoring beyond Catalina, looking for tuna that were reported running about thirty miles west of the island. Teddy was in an expansive mood, even for him. Over the past two years, Teddy had appeared in three movies, and the parts had been getting better with each succeeding film. He had consistently received wonderful reviews from the critics so it had to be simply a matter of time. Last week, he had completed shooting a movie in which he had the leading role. Judging by the rumors floating around Hollywood, this new movie, "*Tangle Foot*," was shaping up to be a blockbuster. It was to be Teddy's breakout role.

Teddy spent most of this fishing trip describing the making of the movie. He did takeoffs on nearly everybody connected with the picture, using, of course, the voices, inflections, body language, and personalities of all concerned. He particularly loved doing takeoffs on one of his co-stars, a well-known actor who usually played a "hard case" in westerns and war films. Jeff Pallon was, among his more notable talents, a skirt chaser. "Jeff just couldn't keep from making moves on every woman on the set. It was hysterical when he hit on Julie."

"Would that be Julie Newman?"

"It would," Teddy smiled, put his foot up on the rail resting his forearm on his knee and then said, in Jeff's slow drawl, "Did ja ever screw a man while sittin on top of a trottin' mustang, Miss Julie?"

Teddy switched to the female lead's irritated voice, "No, but I'll bet you have… you pervert."

By the time the yacht pulled back into Newport harbor two days later, everyone on board had an intimate knowledge of all the cast and crew. It was the single most entertaining weekend any of them had ever experienced. Vance laughed so hard his cheeks hurt and his ribs ached, something he was clearly not accustomed to.

As they were shaking hands and about to get into their separate cars, Vance, instead of shaking hands with Teddy, grabbed him and gave him a hug. "Thanks, Teddy," was all he said.

Jason and Alex looked at each other in amazement. It was doubtful Vance had ever hugged a man before in his life.

Chapter 50

GABRIEL HEADQUARTERS
October 5, 1985
11:45 a.m.

"You about ready?"

"Give me thirty seconds," Jason replied as he looked up to see Alex leaning into his office, one hand on the doorknob, the other on the doorjamb.

"Take your time." Alex let go of the doorknob and leaned against the jamb.

Jason made a couple of notes on the top sheet of an inch-thick sheaf of papers, grabbed the bunch and tapped them on the top of his desk, then placed the straightened stack in his out basket and stood. "We're outta here!"

"How are we doing with the *Times* acquisition?" Alex asked offhandedly as they waited a few seconds for the semi-private elevator.

"Don't know yet, gov. The Brits apparently keep a tight bottom lip to go along with their stiff upper, as it were," Jason said in his best English accent. "Should know more tomorrow morning, however," he said, resuming his normal voice.

Alex laughed. "I think you've been spending too much time with the Londoners."

11:50 a.m.

The two of them slid into Jason's Mercedes located on level A of the underground garage and no more than twenty feet from the elevators. On the wall in front of the car, the plaque said in bold letters, MR. GOULD. Jason drove out of the underground garage into the bright sunshine, turned right and headed north on Pacific Coast Highway. One of their favorite places for lunch was about two miles up.

"Saw Teddy's new movie last night," Jason remarked as he turned into the restaurant's parking lot.

"Oh really? I wish you had gone to the premiere with us. It was something."

"Would have been there if you hadn't sent me to London."

Alex smiled. "Well, what'd ya think?"

"I think that our friend Teddy is going to get an Academy Award for his efforts; that's what I think."

Jason drove to the valet parking area. Both men exited the car, leaving the keys in the ignition.

"You really think so?" asked Alex, holding the restaurant door open for Jason.

"The man is brilliant, and I'm not just saying that because he's our friend. And the movie was a perfect vehicle for his talents."

"Two for lunch, gentlemen?" asked the smiling hostess.

"That's why we're here, Peg," Jason replied.

The hostess smiled again. "Right this way, please."

Both Alex and Jason couldn't help but let their gaze drop momentarily to Peg's shapely fanny as she led them to their table. *Boy, that is really nice*, thought Alex.

She sat them at their reserved table with its commanding view of the ocean. "Enjoy your lunch," she smiled and walked off.

"Can I get you something from the bar before lunch?" the beautifully tanned waitress asked as she walked up to their table. She was looking directly at Jason, her perfect teeth shining brightly.

"Iced tea for me," Alex responded.

Jason looked at her nametag located just above her left breast. "A beer, Susie, thank you."

"My pleasure, Mr. Gould." With that, she smiled, turned and

walked toward the kitchen area.

"I believe that young woman would like a hunk of you, my friend," Alex smiled.

Jason picked up his menu. "All she has to do is ask."

"I think she just did." Alex changed the subject back to Teddy. "So give me your impression of Teddy's movie."

Having lunch with Alex normally involved business to some extent, but when it came to Teddy or family, business was usually put aside; but you had to know him well to know that.

"Well first, I was sorta surprised how good the movie was. Actually it was wonderful," said Jason. "He had me laughing so hard I almost wet my pants. Then five minutes later, I was crying. Jesus, what a talent! Teddy truly dominated the screen."

"He's coming into his own. This movie will make him a household name for sure." Alex made no attempt to hide his pride in Teddy.

"He'll be able to write his own ticket from now on."

"He was so excited when he got the lead in '*Tangle Foot*', I could hardly make out what he was saying when he called to tell me about it."

"Who's that you're talking about?" asked Susie as she placed the tea on a coaster in front of Alex and the beer in front of Jason.

"Teddy Oldaker," Jason answered.

"You mean Theodore Oldaker in the movie '*Tangle Foot*'?

"That's the guy."

"He's just a doll! My roommate and I went and saw '*Tangle Foot*' last week and both fell in love with the man." Susie paused for a second, "He's not as handsome as you two, of course, but I've never seen anyone cuter." She smiled at Jason.

"Well, you're looking at his best friend." Jason nodded toward Alex.

"No!"

"Wouldn't lie to you, Susie."

Alex just sat and smiled. His thoughts were on Teddy as a child, and his incredible gifts that were apparent even then.

...Teddy's here to see you, kid...he's on his way back..
"You're his best friend?"
"We're like brothers," Alex replied earnestly.
Susie looked over at Jason for verification.
"It's true," he nodded.

Part Two

Chapter 51

GABRIEL HOME
December 15, 1985
9:55 p.m.

"*Alex*!" someone screamed into the phone.

"Yes, who is this?" All Alex's senses went into full alert at hearing this high-pitched scream.

"Alex, you've got to come quick. Oh hurry, Alex, please hurry."

"Who is this?" he asked in a loud voice. He couldn't quite make out what the caller was saying, or who she was, but her hysteria was becoming contagious. Alex's pulse rate went way up.

"It's Jennifer. Oh! Alex, Teddy's horribly hurt. Come quick! Please hurry!"

"*What*?" Alex jumped up from the couch. "Calm down for a minute; just calm down!"

"Ok, ok...it's Jennifer. It's me; it's me!"

"Ok, I got that. Now what about Teddy?"

"You gotta come quick..." she screamed again.

"Please, Sis, calm down, please." Something was terribly wrong. Jennifer was not given to hysteria.

"Ok, ok. I'm in a hospital in Hollywood, and Teddy's hurt really bad, really bad. You've got to get here now, right now. Hurry, hurry. Oh, Jesus!"

"What hospital, Jennifer?"

"I don't know. Wait..."

Alex could hear her asking someone. He could barely hear the response; it sounded like Cedars-Sinai.

"It's Cedars-Sinai! Hurry, Alex!"

"I'll be there as fast as humanly possible, Sis." Alex hung up and quickly dialed another number.

"Hello," responded the voice on the other end.

"Neil, its Alex Gabriel."

"Yes, sir!"

"Get over to the building right now and get the chopper warmed up, and I mean right now! Call Cedars-Sinai Medical Center and see if we can get clearance to land on their heli-pad. Tell them it'll be just a touch and go. If they refuse, you'll be dropping me off in their parking lot. I'll be at the building in fifteen minutes."

"Yes, sir!"

Alex again hung up and dialed another number. "Jason, meet me at Cedars-Sinai Medical Center in Hollywood as soon as possible, and call Vance. Teddy's been hurt."

"Oh shit, Alex! Is he hurt bad?"

"I think it must be real bad. I'll see you there."

Alex slammed the phone into its cradle and ran to the study where he knew his parents would be.

"What is it, Alex?" asked Marian, at the same time hitting the mute button for the TV.

"Jennifer called from Cedars-Sinai Medical Center in Hollywood. Teddy's been hurt badly."

"Oh no!" Both she and Norman jumped up.

"I'm going to take the helicopter over. It would take over an hour, even at this time of day, to drive it. I want you to call Teddy's folks and tell them. Do whatever you can to help them in any way. Tell them I'm on my way to the hospital and should be there in twenty-five minutes."

"Is Jennifer okay?" asked Marian.

"I assume so, but I don't know any more than I told you."

"We'll need to get hold of Chuck," said Norman. "He's in

Helsinki at a conference. Not due back for a week."

"Jesus, I'd forgotten about that. You'd better get him back here, Pop. Jen may need him."

"I'll handle it, Son."

"I'll see you there." Alex turned and ran for the garage.

Oh please God, let Teddy be all right, prayed Alex as he climbed aboard the helicopter. *Don't let him...* He couldn't finish the thought.

"Couldn't get permission to land on their roof, Mr. Gabriel," advised Neil. "They say they're so busy, because of accidents, their chopper will be in and out of there all night."

"All right, so drop me off in their parking lot!"

"That's against the law, sir. They'll pull my ticket if I do that."

"No, they won't. I won't let them."

"But..."

"No buts, Neil. You're dropping my ass off in their parking lot!"

"Yes, sir!"

"Can we call the hospital from this phone?"

"Yes, sir!"

As it turned out, the clearest area was the top of the north-parking garage adjacent to the main hospital. Not a single car was parked there that evening. The drawback was that it was on the fourth floor.

Alex jumped and ran from the chopper, his heart pounding so hard he barely heard the helicopter take off. It took a full minute for the elevator to arrive and at least that long for the trip to the first floor. "Come on, come on," he repeated several times. The elevator was moving at a snail's pace. "Shit!"

The elevator finally opened on the first floor, and after quickly looking at the direction signs, he headed left, at a dead run.

Alex burst through the door leading into the emergency reception area and nearly ran over Jennifer.

She grabbed her brother in a bear hug and started ranting and crying at the same time. "Oh Alex, it was horrible, horrible!"

Alex, with a great deal of effort, managed to pry Jennifer away and held her by the shoulders at arm's length. He was stunned; her dress was ripped, bloody and dirty, her right eye was swollen nearly shut and her top lip was split. "My God, Jen, you're hurt."

Jennifer's eyes had the look of a crazed animal. Her whole body was shaking violently. She started to calm down as she looked into her brother's eyes. "Teddy's, Teddy's, he's, he's all messed up, Alex!"

"Where is he now?"

"They're operating on him. Oh Jesus, Alex, it was horr..." her voice trailed off; the color drained from her eyes as they rolled back into her head. She started sinking slowly to the floor. Alex pulled her to him and kept her, with some effort, from falling. She had held on for as long as she could. She was out cold.

"*I need help here*!" yelled Alex. He didn't need to yell, as there were a doctor and nurse within a few feet and they were at his side in a second.

The doctor helped Alex lower Jennifer gently to the floor. "Looks like she fainted," said the doctor. He looked to the nurse. "Let's get a gurney over here, now." A gurney and two orderlies appeared within ten seconds. They gently lifted Jennifer and placed her on the gurney. The nurse put a pillow under her feet to raise them above her head.

"Let's put her in room 'D' until she comes around." The doctor was checking her pulse while placing his stethoscope on her chest. "She'll be fine, sir; not to worry," he looked up at Alex. "I'm amazed she didn't pass out sooner." He took the stethoscope from his ears and hooked them around his neck. "I tried to get her medical attention but she wouldn't hear of it until you got here. We'll give her a sedative when she comes around."

"I'm Alex Gabriel." Alex extended his hand.

"Dr. Koehn. I'm chief resident here, Mr. Gabriel." He shook Alex's hand.

"Do you know anything about Teddy Oldaker? My sister must have come in with him," asked Alex.

"Yes, sir, why don't we..."

"Are you Alexander Gabriel?"

"Yes." Alex looked to his right. There were two men, both in wash-and-wear suits, standing just a few feet away. The one talking was displaying a police badge.

"I'm Detective Brown and this is my partner, Detective Hargrave. I wonder if we might have a word with you?"

"Yes, you can, but not until I find out about my friend."

"I'm sorry sir, but we'd like to talk to you now, if you don't mind."

Alex turned to face the detective straight on. "I'm only going to say this one more time, Detective. I'll talk to you later."

Detective Brown's eyes narrowed. "You'll talk to us now..."

His partner cut in, "That'll be fine, Mr. Gabriel. Please let us know when you're ready."

Detective Brown turned to look at his partner and got a "drop it" look from Hargrave.

Alex turned to the doctor. "Is there a place we can talk in private?"

"Why don't we walk down to my office, Mr. Gabriel," suggested the doctor. "I'll fill you in on what we know so far."

"Thank you. Let's go."

The doctor led the way down the long hall and to the right, stopped, opened the door and let Alex pass in front of him and closed the door behind him.

"Have a seat, please."

Alex walked over to a straight-backed wooden chair and sat facing the doctor's desk.

The doctor walked around the desk and sat. He looked Alex straight in the eye. "Your friend was severely beaten."

"What?" Alex was shocked; he'd assumed it was a car accident. "Who?... I don't understand." *This can't be*! His mind began rejecting this information.

"I don't know anything about who or why, sir."

"Nobody would hurt Teddy... not Teddy."

"It's worse than that, sir." The doctor paused, looked down at his hands for a moment, then back at Alex. "We don't expect him to live."

It was as though a physical blow had hit Alex in the chest. He rocked backward; his eyes grew large. He said nothing for a few moments; he was completely stunned. "Please," he began in a weak voice, "Please tell me Teddy isn't going to die. I'll give you anything if you'll tell me that."

"Mr. Gabriel, Teddy is being operated on right now and I suspect he'll be in the operating room for a couple of hours. The damage is quite extensive. If he makes it through the operation and for another day or two, he might have a chance." The doctor paused but didn't take his eyes off Alex. "Frankly, sir, I believe you should be prepared for the worst."

Alex was dazed and didn't know what to say. He was helpless. Tears began filling his eyes and he looked down at his hands; he could no longer look at the doctor. He didn't want to know the horrors inflicted on his dearest friend. That would make it worse. There would be plenty of time later, after Teddy was well on the way to recovery. *Oh God, please*, he repeated over and over in his mind.

The doctor said nothing, leaving Alex with his own thoughts.

After a minute, Alex looked up, still unable to speak.

"Would you like a sedative? It'll make this a little easier."

Alex shook his head, got up, nodded at the doctor and left the room. He walked in a near trance back to the room marked "D" and walked in. Jennifer was lying propped up in a cot. The two detectives were sitting close by with note pads and pencils in their hands. All talking stopped as Alex entered.

"Sorry, Mr. Gabriel," said Detective Brown. "I didn't realize who you were when we talked earlier."

Alex didn't even look in his direction. He walked over to the cot, sat on the edge and took Jennifer's hand in his. "How are you feeling, Sis?" he whispered.

"Better, now that you're here. They gave me a sedative... I guess

I went off the deep end."

Alex could do nothing but nod; tears were dripping down his cheeks.

"Do you know how Teddy is?" she asked, her speech slowing markedly.

Alex shook his head, "I don't know. He's still in the operating room," he managed to get out.

"I'm tired, Alex. I'm going to rest my eyes for a little bit, okay?"

"Sure, Jen." He pulled the sheet up to his sister's neck and kissed her gently on the forehead. "Pop is getting hold of Chuck, Sis. It will take him a while to get here from Helsinki but I'll bet he'll be here by early tomorrow."

"Thanks, Alex, I'm going to need him." Jennifer's eyes filled with tears. "Poor Teddy."

"You get some rest, Jen. I've got it from here."

"Okay."

He stood and turned toward the detectives. "Now why don't we have a talk?"

The three left room "D" and walked out to the waiting area. The two detectives sat on a couch; Alex sat on a chair facing them.

"You two know more about what happened than I do, so why don't you fill me in?"

Detective Hargrave opened his notebook and began. "Apparently your friend, your sister, and another lady.."

"What other lady?" Alex interrupted.

"According to your sister, there was a Miss Julie Bashford with them."

"I don't know a...wait, yes I do. I know who Julie Bashford is. Where is she now?"

"We don't know. Your sister thought the boys who attacked them probably dragged her off after they beat your friend. We have half our precinct scouring that neighborhood. Last report, they hadn't found her."

"Oh my God!"

The detective resumed his report. "At any rate, the three of them had just left a restaurant on Hollywood Boulevard and were walking down a side street, heading for their car. According to your sister, six young men, all but one with shaved heads, came up behind them and started giving them a ration of crap. According to your sister, they kept calling your friend a spick, greaser, wetback -- that kind of shit."

"Teddy's not Mexican."

"We know, but these assholes aren't known for their brains, sir. They were probably high on something, and it was pretty dark."

"She said none of them said anything, just kept walking, until the punks started saying nasty things about the ladies. Your friend stopped and confronted them. That was a mistake."

His mind flashed back to when he and Teddy were eight years old, right after the accident.

.... *I was real scared, Alex...almost ran away...*

Alex was holding onto his emotions with everything he could muster. *I wish you had run this time, Teddy.*

"Are you sure you want to hear this, Mr. Gabriel?"

Alex looked at the detective, "No I don't want to hear any of it…this is a nightmare." Alex paused for a moment, "There will be a lot of people here shortly and they're going to need answers," he said sadly. "So, go on."

"Your sister can't remember all the details, but it sounds like three of the punks jumped on Teddy and started punching and kicking him. Your sister says Teddy got in a few licks himself and again, that was a mistake. Another of the punks hit Teddy with a pipe of some sort and he went down. Then they all started kicking him. The one with the pipe grabbed Miss Bashford and started dragging her up on a lawn. Teddy managed to get to his feet and grabbed the guy with the pipe, pulling him away from the young lady." The detective paused for a second, reading his notes. "Your sister said that she tried to pull the punks off Teddy, but they hit her and she fell. Said she got up again and jumped on the back of the one with the pipe and believes she scratched his face pretty good; then she was hit again."

"Jesus, Jen."

"She said she started screaming for help from the time the first punch was thrown. She said that after she was hit the second time, she ran back to Hollywood Boulevard to get some help. Screaming all the way. When she finally managed to get some college kids to go back with her, Miss Bashford was gone and Teddy was unconscious on the sidewalk."

"Oh Jesus," Alex whispered.

"We got a call at the station at 8:59 p.m. from a party who lives on the street. A black and white arrived on the scene at 9:03 p.m. and immediately called for an ambulance. The ambulance picked up Teddy and your sister at 9:23 and brought them here."

Alex sat looking at the floor. For one of the few times in his life, he didn't know what to do. He felt helpless and useless.

After a few seconds, he looked up at the detectives. "Thank you for filling me in. Now, what information can I give you?"

Within the next half-hour, everybody arrived at Cedars-Sinai. Jason and Vance were first to arrive and Alex filled them in with what he knew. Jason reacted with shock, concern, and sadness. Vance's reaction was somewhat more stoic. There was an almost palpable hardening of an already granite-like demeanor; his eyes became very cold. Vance and Teddy had virtually nothing in common, other than Alex, but to everyone's amazement they got along like two peas in a pod. Nobody could recall Vance ever laughing out loud until he met Teddy. Perhaps he saw in Teddy everything he wasn't. And Teddy, inexplicably, really liked Vance. "Go figure!" Jason once remarked.

"Who's in charge of the investigation?"

Alex looked into Vance's eyes and felt a chill. "I talked to Detectives Brown and Hargrave of the Hollywood precinct."

"Would that be Clarence Hargrave?"

"Don't know, Vance. Hargrave is all I heard."

"I'll go see if there's been any word on the young lady, Miss

Bashford. Be back soon."

"Mr. Gabriel?"

Alex turned to see Dr. Koehn walking toward him as Vance walked away.

"Any word, doctor?"

"Not much, sir. Looks like another hour or so in the operating room."

"*Alex*!" called Sandy and Bob Oldaker as they rushed into the waiting room, looking as one might expect under the circumstances. Sandy had been crying and Bob was trying to maintain his composure.

Sandy hugged Alex tightly. "How's my boy?" she asked with a hoarse voice.

"We don't know yet, Sandy." He held Sandy and looked over at Teddy's dad. He could see Bob was sick with worry and he knew exactly how Bob was feeling. But it was time for him to be strong; no time to break down. Alex's voice was calm, almost detached; even he was amazed that his voice betrayed none of his inner terror. "This is Dr. Koehn. He's the chief resident here and will be able to answer your questions." Sandy released Alex and turned to the doctor.

The doctor was suggesting that they all gather in his office just as Marian and Norman came rushing into the reception room. Marian immediately went to Sandy and gave her a hug.

"Bob," said Norman. "How's it going? How's Teddy?"

"Don't know yet, Norm. This is the chief resident, Dr. Koehn. He is about to fill us in."

"Let's all go to my office; it'll be more private."

The doctor relayed everything he knew about Teddy's condition and the possible prognosis for his future. The prognosis was bleak. Teddy's skull had been fractured in two places; his right arm broken in three, one being compound. Five ribs were fractured and his left lung was punctured and had collapsed. Those were the main injuries. The skull fractures were the greatest concern. "The brain is swelling, and that's not good," explained the doctor. "The surgeons are doing everything possible to relieve the pressure. Time will tell if they succeed."

Marian sat next to Sandy on the doctor's couch. She held Sandy's left hand and Bob held her right. All the while the doctor was talking, Sandy sobbed quietly. Other than the doctors, there wasn't a dry eye in the room.

After leaving the doctor's office, Sandy and Bob returned to the waiting room to wait for word on their son. The Gabriels and Jason went to room "D" to check on Jennifer and found her still asleep.

"You didn't tell me Jen was hurt, Alex," Marian whispered. She sat, as Alex had, on the side of the narrow bed and brushed Jennifer's hair gently back from her bruised and swollen face.

"Didn't know it until I got here, Mom. The doctor tells me her injuries are superficial and won't be a problem."

"Superficial?" Norman said softly. "What about all the blood on her dress?"

"I don't think much of that blood is hers," Alex replied sadly.

"Ah shit!"

Alex looked down at his sister. He looked at her battered face and the dried blood on her torn dress. *Jen actually fought the assholes that did this*? he thought with some pride. *And some fucking piece of shit animal punched her*. His mind raged momentarily, then softened as he watched his mother tenderly stroking Jennifer's hair. *How did this happen? How could this possibly happen?*

Chapter 52

CEDARS-SINAI HOSPITAL
December 16, 1985
12:38 a.m.

Alex sat quietly with the Oldakers and Jason in the waiting room, his mind in turmoil. He was having trouble holding any one thought for more than a few seconds. His concern for Teddy, his empathy for Sandy and Bob, his rage against the pieces of shit who did this to his sister, Teddy, and her friend Julie was almost unbearable.

Vance entered the waiting room, and walked over to where Alex, Jason, and the Oldakers were sitting.

"Sandy, Bob," Vance greeted the Oldakers. "I can't tell you how badly I feel about what's happened to Teddy."

"Thank you, Vance. We're praying he'll be all right," Sandy choked out.

"Me too." Vance was displaying a soft, gentle side that few had seen. His sympathy for the Oldakers was deeply felt. He turned toward Alex. "They found Miss Bashford twenty minutes ago."

"Oh, Jesus! How is she?" asked Alex, concerned.

"Not good. It seems she was raped repeatedly and beaten. They are treating her now."

"Oh, that poor girl." Sandy started crying again. She told the detectives all she knew an hour earlier. "Teddy was going out tonight with Jennifer and a blind date, a friend of Jennifer's.

That's all I know."

"Where did they find her?" Jason asked.

"In an alley garage about a block from the scene."

"Do you know the extent of her injuries?"

"Just that they don't seem to be life-threatening." Vance excused himself after a moment and walked to a bank of phones.

Everyone stood up as Dr. Koehn came into the waiting room. "Teddy's out of the operating room and moved to our critical care unit."

"How is he?" asked Alex and Bob simultaneously.

"He survived the surgery. That's step one. Step two, hopefully, will be regaining consciousness, and soon. This is critical," the doctor was expressing deep concern. "He'll be monitored from head to toe twenty-four hours a day."

"Can we see him?" asked Sandy.

The doctor paused for a few seconds, obviously weighing the wisdom of that request. "Okay, but let's keep it to no more than two people at a time in the room. I've got to warn you, your son looks bad. He has tubes and wires leading in and out of everywhere."

"We understand," said Sandy.

"You and Bob go in first," suggested Alex, fighting his dire need to see his friend.

"Okay," Bob agreed. "Which way, doctor?"

"Why don't you all follow me? I'll show you to the critical care waiting room and then take you two to Teddy's room."

After they arrived in the waiting room and Sandy and Bob had gone in to see Teddy, Alex asked Jason to call Teddy's studio and inform them as to what was going on. They put a PR man on it right away. "*Tangle Foot*" was the number one box-office draw right now and the press began swarming the hospital.

Later that morning, Alex was alone with Teddy's parents in the waiting room and was just finishing a long conversation with them.

"I've already talked to the doctor and he agreed, if you two sign a release, to do the procedure. I must tell you, however, he didn't think much of the possibilities for now or the foreseeable future." Alex held onto Sandy's hand and looked deeply into her sad, soft brown eyes as he spoke. Bob sat beside his wife and listened intently. "But I know in my heart," continued Alex, "that it will be possible someday, and even if it isn't, there will be no harm done."

The Oldakers sat in silence for a minute or two, each with their own thoughts. "Teddy once told us," Bob said quietly, "that you have never been wrong about anything. That if you told him to jump off a cliff, he would, because he would know he wouldn't be hurt. Our son has you on a pedestal, Alex; always has, and I suspect, always will." Bob looked at his wife and could see she was in agreement. "There is no question that Teddy would agree to this if he were conscious, so we'll sign any release you want us to." Sandy nodded.

"I'm sure it won't be necessary, but I'll feel a little better just knowing there are possibilities."

12:30 p.m.

Sandy and Bob headed to the cafeteria for some much-needed nourishment, leaving Alex alone with his dearest friend. Anytime Alex was alone with Teddy, he spoke to him constantly, all the while holding his hand. He desperately needed to believe Teddy could hear him and be comforted, knowing he was not alone, that his best friend was with him. This time he told Teddy a condensed version of his life before the accident, and everything after. He had, years ago, stopped trying to tell this unbelievable story to anyone; he simply couldn't speak the words. But today he was able to tell Teddy. He knew that if Teddy could hear him, he would accept his story as the truth and quite possibly say, "I knew it was something like that. Geeze."

2:10 p.m.

Alex, Sandy, and Bob were in Teddy's room together when he started to moan quietly and move his head slightly. All of them jumped up and started loudly encouraging him to wake up, hoping it would help him regain consciousness, but it didn't. He stopped any sound and movement after just a few seconds, and fell back into silence.

"Oh Son, come back to us. Please, Teddy, wake up," Sandy pleaded.

"Come on, Teddy, you can do it Son," encouraged his father.

Alex silently prayed, *Please God, let this wonderful person wake up and be well. Please, I beg you!"*

There was no further sound from Teddy. The momentary excitement faded with each passing second. The sounds of the monitors with their rhythmic beeping and buzzing seemed to become louder as the minutes ticked away.

Marian and Norman had taken Jennifer home as soon as the doctors gave their okay. Other than the swollen eye, split lip, and a couple of scrapes, she was physically fine. It would take some time to heal her emotional wounds, however. She desperately wanted to visit Teddy and Julie before leaving the hospital, but Marian convinced her that it wouldn't do her, Julie, or Teddy any good at this time.

Jason, at Alex's suggestion, went home around 2:00 a.m. and would head to the office later that morning. Someone had to help mind the store. He and Alex remained in nearly constant contact throughout the day.

Norman called Walt and Colleen earlier in the evening, telling them what happened, and informing Walt that Alex wouldn't be coming in the following morning. He had to convince them to stay put -- that there was nothing they could do for now, except pray.

Vance's stoic, crusty persona was taking a beating. Nobody realized how much this man, this battle-hardened rock of a man, cared for the tender, loving Teddy. Even with the turmoil Alex was suffering, he couldn't help but notice the tenderness Vance was displaying. When Vance entered Teddy's room for the first time and looked down at that battered body, his sadness and concern permeated the room.

3:15 p.m.

Vance and Alex walked down the now-familiar halls, toward the cafeteria, for the fifth time that day.

"I assume you're checking with the police occasionally for any word on the punk bastards?"

"No point, Alex. Hargrave promised he'd get a hold of me the second anything breaks. And he will."

"What do you think the chances are of catching those assholes?"

"Considering the phone calls you made, Teddy's celebrity and his studio's pull...100 percent. They've got more people on this than fleas on a Mexican dog. You'd think some dipshit took a shot at the President. Add to that, these punks either live in the neighborhood or I'll wager live within a half a mile of it. Cowards like that don't venture outside their neighborhoods." Vance paused to push the door to the cafeteria open for Alex. "Little doubt they'll have records, and there are sure to be witnesses," he continued as they headed for the coffee bar. "It would be a good bet the police already know who they are. It's just a matter of rounding them up."

"Really?"

"Yes, sir!"

5:35 p.m.

"Son!" exclaimed Bob.

Sandy and Alex automatically looked at Teddy. His eyes were open! Just slightly, but they were open. He was looking at them. First he looked at his dad, then his mother. As the seconds passed, his eyes closed. Then, in a few more seconds, opened again. They had a dull faraway look, but he was looking around. The oxygen tube had been removed from his mouth but a tube was still feeding oxygen into his nose.

"You're going to be all right, Teddy," Bob told his son.

"I love you, Teddy," added his mother, barely able to talk.

"Teddy!" said Alex.

Teddy's eyes moved to Alex. They were clearing a little.

Alex had given a lot of thought as to what to do when Teddy came around. He knew that if he were in this condition, he'd want to know right away what was happening.

"You've been hurt and are in a hospital. You've been in a coma for nearly a day. Do you understand?"

Teddy stared at Alex for a moment, then nodded his head ever so slightly. He didn't try to speak.

"I'll get the doctor," Alex said. He walked over and pushed the call button. He reached down and took Teddy's hand and gave it a squeeze. "Welcome back, buddy."

"You're going to be all right, Son," repeated his father, tears of joy pouring down his cheeks.

"Do you hurt bad, Teddy?" asked Sandy.

Teddy crossed his eyes.

Alex smiled.

December 18, 1985
10:00 a.m.

It had been sixty-two hours since the attack and forty-one hours since Teddy regained consciousness. He was responding to treatments as well as could be expected. He'd been taken off direct oxygen and upgraded from critical to serious.

Bob Oldaker went home around midnight to feed the cat, and catch a few hours' sleep. He planned to check in with SARC in the morning.

"Bob, get your butt back to your family. I don't want to see you around here until Teddy is up and walking around," said his boss over the phone.

"Yes, sir -- and thanks."

During Bob's absence Alex had Teddy moved to a large private room where visiting was easier and a great deal more comfortable.

Bob Oldaker arrived back at the hospital around 9:00 a.m. He found Alex in Teddy's new room, sitting next to his son's bed.

"Jesus, this is nice." Bob looked around the room for a few seconds. "This room is something, I don't think I've ever seen a hospital room so big and luxurious." Bob looked over at Alex. "I see your hand in this."

"Hate being cramped."

"Have you gotten any sleep?"

"Just been here for an hour or so, Bob. Caught a few hours at the hotel. Mom and Jennifer brought me a change of clothes yesterday and left them at the hotel for me. Hell, I'm showered and shaved; feel like a new man." Alex stood up and moved to a small couch located ten feet to the right of the bed, allowing Teddy's father to stand next to his son.

"By God, you do look better. How's my boy?" Bob walked over to the bed and looked down at his battered son. His face saddened again.

"Well, he seems to gain strength with each passing hour," Alex offered lightly. "He managed to stay awake for nearly twenty minutes a while ago." He looked at Teddy. "If my calculations are correct, he'll be waking up again in a few minutes."

"Has he said anything yet?" asked Bob quietly.

"No, but you can tell he understands what's being said. He'll be yammering away in no time. Hell, we won't be able to shut him up."

Bob just nodded.

Teddy's mother didn't leave the hospital for the first thirty hours after Teddy regained consciousness, and only then, after she was assured by half the staff of Cedars-Sinai that her son was out of danger and on the road to recovery. Alex had secured hotel rooms within walking distance of the hospital for the Oldakers and himself. He gave Sandy directions and suggested she walk the three blocks for the fresh air and exercise. *...Just have to pick up a key at the desk...* After a quick shower, she dropped into bed. She was out for ten hours.

Sandy walked into Teddy's new room, looking quite relieved. She gazed around the room while walking directly to Teddy's bed. "My goodness!" She took one last look before taking Teddy's hand. "How you doin', Son?" she asked quietly.

Teddy was still asleep. The rhythmic beep of the monitors monotonously drummed out the beat of Teddy's heart. Alex, as he had done dozens of times, looked up at the monitor screens. The systolic and diastolic waves remained constant. Blood pressure seemed a little higher than it had been, but was probably normal under the circumstances.

Sandy stood for a few minutes looking down at her son. After a while she turned, walked over and sat next to Alex. She put her hand on top of his.

"Thank you, Alex," she said. "A better friend than you, nobody has ever had. You've made Teddy's life so much easier for him. And that makes our lives -- Bob's and mine -- much easier, too."

"There are no words to express our gratitude," added Bob.

"You two don't need to thank me for anything," Alex replied. "You gave me Teddy."

"You're going to make me cry again." Sandy squeezed Alex's hand.

11:00 a.m.

Alex was just returning from the cafeteria with rolls and coffee for the Oldakers and himself. Sandy was sitting on the right side of Teddy's bed with Bob on the left. They were talking to Teddy and he was talking to them.

Alex quickly set the coffee and rolls on a table and shot over to stand beside Sandy's chair. He looked down at his dearest friend and smiled. His emotions completely choked his voice; he couldn't talk.

Teddy looked up at Alex, his soft brown eyes the clearest they'd been. "Hi, Alex...whatchadoin?" he said in a weak, barely audible voice.

Alex still couldn't find his voice. He stared at his friend, his chin vibrating, tears welling up.

"Isn't it wonderful?" said Sandy without taking her eyes off her son.

"He woke up and started talking just a minute after you went for coffee," explained Bob.

Alex continued to look at Teddy, his relief and joy nearly overwhelming. He wanted to pick his friend up and give him a huge hug, but instead, he leaned over and kissed Teddy on the forehead just below the bandage.

"Geeze, I must be really hurt. Got heterosexuals kissing me!" Teddy's voice remained weak. He tried to smile, but it was a feeble attempt.

"Oh, Teddy!" smiled Sandy.

He squeezed his mother's hand.

"You been yakkin away for two days... Alex... run outta things to say... or what?" Again he tried to smile.

Alex slowly shook his head, spilling his tears. "Jesus, Teddy!" he managed to choke out.

"Are you hurtin', Son?" asked his father.

"Oh yeah," responded Teddy. He remained silent for a minute. "How'd I get hurt?"

Alex looked over at Bob, and shrugged.

"Well, Teddy...you kinda got in a fight," Bob said.

"Really?" Teddy contemplated that for a few seconds. "How's the other guy look?"

Alex and Bob looked at each other and smiled. Sandy clearly didn't understand the humor here; didn't realize Teddy was joking.

Although Teddy couldn't smile, Alex could see the sparkle in his eyes.

"You'll never change, Teddy," Alex blurted out.

"I'm a lucky man. I've got the greatest parents and my best friend is the richest man in the world." Teddy's voice was becoming weaker.

His mother didn't miss this. "Would you like to get some sleep, Teddy?"

"In a minute." Teddy looked at his mom and dad. "I want to tell you two how much I love you."

"We love you too, Son."

Teddy looked up at Alex. "If you promise you won't think I'm queer, I'd like to tell you that I love you, too."

"The feeling is mutual... my friend."

"We'd better let you get some sleep," Bob suggested.

"Okay," he nearly whispered. "But I need to ask Alex something."

"What's that?" asked Alex.

Teddy looked deep into Alex's eyes. "How old are you, Alex?"

Alex looked down at his dear friend, not comprehending his question at first. Then it dawned on him that Teddy had heard everything that had been said, or at least a great deal of it.

"What do you mean, Son?" asked Bob.

Sandy had a puzzled expression.

"I'm sixty-six, Teddy," Alex answered sincerely.

Bob and Sandy's heads snapped around.

"What?" Bob and Sandy questioned in unison. They looked at Alex. Alex didn't take his eyes off Teddy.

"I remember about that," Teddy said, his voice weakening. "When my friend Alex went away and Mr. Gabriel showed up." Teddy's voice was starting to tail off, "Thanks for tellin..."

Teddy's eyes suddenly got huge, his back arched, he started thrashing violently. The heart monitor stopped beeping and started screeching. Alarms on the other monitors let go in a horrible calliope of noise.

"*Teddy*!" yelled Alex.

"*Help*!" screamed his mother. "*Help! Help! Help*!"

His father grabbed Teddy by the shoulders to keep him from ripping out the IVs. "*Teddy, what's the matter*?"

Two nurses rushed into the room. One yelled, "*Everybody out*!" The other knocked Bob out of the way and started checking Teddy's vital signs.

Teddy abruptly stopped moving; his body relaxed.

"*Code blue*!" she yelled.

Alex was up against the far wall, paralyzed with fear.

Chapter 53

LOS ANGLES
December 19, 1985

"THEODORE OLDAKER DIES"

"The critically acclaimed star of the blockbuster movie 'Tangle Foot,' sadly succumbed to injuries received in a vicious attack on...."

The press was crawling all over themselves gathering information about Teddy. Vance put on extra security to keep the news-hungry reporters away from the Gabriels, and by Alex's request, the Oldakers.

The press spent the previous three days running the news of Teddy's attack. After the hospital spokesman reported Teddy's passing, the press and others disappeared from the hospital only to regroup in and around the Hollywood precinct. The pressure to make an arrest in this high-profile case became enormous. It didn't take the press long to make the personal connection to Alex Gabriel, which made the tragic incident even more newsworthy. The Gabriel home became besieged with reporters. One bold but not too bright reporter had come up the stairs from the beach to the Gabriels' pool area, but the unfortunate man was discovered by Vance just as he started across the patio. As Vance released the pain-ridden man on the street, he whispered into his ear, "I catch you on the grounds again, I'll throw you off the cliff. Do you understand?"

December 20, 1985
4:30 a.m.

"I'll be with you in a sec, guys," Teddy told a group of three ratty-looking hoods as they walked through the liquor store door. Teddy had on a clerk's apron and was stocking a shelf behind the counter.

"You'll be with us now, *Asshole*!" said the pudgy hood with greasy red hair and a stringy goatee as he pulled a huge pistol out of his coat and pointed it at Teddy.

"Asshole? Well, now you're getting personal," Teddy replied with a big grin on his face.

"You think this is funny, spick?"

"*Si, señor*." Teddy came out from behind the counter wearing a colorful poncho and a Charro hat. He threw the enormous hat on the floor and launched into a Mexican hat dance around it.

"What the hell do ya think you're doing," demanded the pudgy punk with the gun.

"I'm entertaining you, jerk-off. Whatdoyathink?"

The other two punks looked at each other and started laughing. "You hear what the spick said to Ronny?"

Ronny was laughing harder than anyone when he put the gun to Teddy's head and pulled the trigger.

Alex woke up screaming, drenched in sweat. He sat bolt upright in bed and shook. Then he cried. He cried for a long time in the darkness of his room. Teddy was dead again just as had happened in his first life. Now Alex remembered it all. He remembered getting a call from his mother at his office in Inglewood…

"Alex," she had said, "I have some terrible news..." Her voice was shaking. "Sandy Oldaker called a little while ago..."

Alex remembered his mother pausing, unable to continue. He remembered the adrenalin hitting his heart like a spear, his pulse pounding in his ears. Why would getting a call from his best friend's mother cause his mother this much emotion? Something bad must have happened to Teddy. There could be no other explanation.

"Did something happen to Teddy?" he had asked, nearly choking on the words; his throat constricting. Tears started flowing from his eyes even before he heard the answer to his question."Yes," his mother said almost unable to get the word our. "Teddy was shot... and killed last night in the liquor store where he was working."

Yes, he remembered it now. He often wondered why he and Teddy had lost contact so long ago. It never made sense. Teddy was always his best friend, as close as two people could be. *That was why I was frightened when I first saw Teddy after the accident. He'd been dead for many years.* The memory of that tragedy had been wiped from Alex's mind, as were the memories of other major events over the years. *Now Teddy has died again, as he had in my first life. Of course, it wasn't Rotten Ronny from their childhood who had pulled the trigger; that was just a quirk of the nightmare. It was some addicted asshole acting alone*. He was later caught and convicted.

The more Alex thought about it, the more he remembered. A shot of adrenalin hit his heart as he realized, *Teddy died on the same date both times*.

GABRIEL HOME
December 21, 1985
1:40 p.m.

Marian was sitting at the island in the kitchen staring out the window, seeing nothing. She was at an emotional low. The loss of Teddy had everybody in the household near despair. She and Norman were discussing Jennifer's mental condition and what, if anything, they could do about it. "She's taking responsibility for Teddy's death all on herself," Marian told Norman.

"Yes, I'm afraid she is," Norman agreed sadly.

They had both heard her say more than once, "If I hadn't set him up on a blind date, he would be alive today." She cried over and over, "And Julie -- raped and nearly killed." Jennifer was a wreck. "All we did was go out to dinner, that's all. We didn't hurt anybody."

Chuck had returned from Helsinki the afternoon after the attack and spent a few hours with the Gabriel family before taking Jennifer home. He grieved with her for the loss of Teddy while trying to convince her she was not responsible for the tragedy.

Then came Alex. Nobody had ever seen him in this condition. Not when Margaret Wallace and Victor Kula were killed and he was shot. Maybe his mental condition after the "accident" twenty-three years ago might compare with this, but that was a long time ago.

The doorbell rang and Maria could be heard shuffling slowly down the hall to answer it. Maria mourned the loss of Teddy as if he were one of her own. Marian told her to go home but she steadfastly refused, saying she needed to help, needed to be with others who loved Teddy. In a few moments, Vance and Jason walked into the study. Jason gave Marian a hug; Vance extended his hand.

"Mrs. Gabriel, how are you holding up, ma'am?"

"Not too well I'm afraid, Vance. My happy household isn't happy anymore."

Vance nodded in understanding, "Time heals all wounds, they say." The words sounded colder than Vance meant them to be.

"He's right, Marian. Nobody will ever forget Teddy, but the pain we're all suffering now will subside in time."

"I know...but Jesus, why Teddy?"

"Wrong place at the wrong time." Vance was being pragmatic, an obvious attempt to mask his feelings.

"How's Jennifer doing?" asked Jason.

"Other than Alex, she's taking it the hardest. Blaming herself entirely."

"Uh-oh!" said Jason.

"Chuck's been a trouper; he's stayed with her this past week," Marian's eyes filled with tears. "But I'm afraid she's going to need professional help before this is over."

There was a moment of silence before Marian spoke again. "Would you two please go and try to yank my broken-hearted son out of his deep depression… he's hurting so badly."

"Where is he?" asked Jason.

One or more of Vance's security team always had Alex in sight.

Vance knew where he was.

"Out on his rock," she answered, tears spilling out of her sad blue eyes. "He's not eaten since Teddy died and by the looks of him, he hasn't slept either. I took a sandwich and hot tea out to him, but he just set it on the rock beside him; it's probably still sitting there." Marian turned her head away from the two men and cried quietly. Jason stepped forward and put his arm around Marian's shoulder and gave her a hug.

In a moment, Marian regained her composure and Jason backed away. "Alex's attachment to Teddy was more than just friendship; it always has been. The relationship was hard to put a finger on. It was as if Teddy was Alex's own beloved son. Just the mention of Teddy's name always put a smile on his face."

"We'll go out and see what we can do. Maybe we can help," offered Jason.

"You're the only people I could think of; thank you."

"It's not like Marian to call for help," Jason remarked as he and Vance headed down the stairs to the beach. "She's one strong woman."

"That'd be my read on her, too. She's grasping at straws."

"Don't know if we'll be able to get the job done," said Jason.

"He nearly went crazy in the hospital." Vance held open the small gate at the bottom of the stairs for Jason. They headed across the short stretch of beach toward the spit of rock jutting into the harbor. Alex was sitting out on the far end, staring out across the Pacific.

"I heard," Jason replied. "Had to give him a strong sedative, I understand. I think Marian is afraid he'll overdose on Valium."

"He won't do that," Vance stated matter-of-factly. "Despite the fact that he can't seem to handle personal loss worth a shit, he's still a strong, responsible man. He'll come out of this."

Vance had told Jason one night, while they were having a couple of beers, that as Victor Kula was about to shoot Alex and Walt, Alex stepped in front of his uncle to protect him. That one act alone put Alex at the top of Vance's good guy list. "He didn't even think about it; he didn't have time. Hell, I've worked with some of the meanest, toughest combatants in the world and I'll tell you, here and now, most of them would have jumped for cover under the same circumstances. There's nothing wrong with our Alex. No sir, he's just a little too sentimental."

Jason glanced sideways at Vance. Here was as hard, controlled, and stoic a man as could be found, yet when Vance heard Teddy had died, he moaned and abruptly excused himself. He wasn't seen for a couple of hours afterward. Jason thought it wise to say nothing about that.

They climbed out on the spit of rocks. The tide was up, making the trip somewhat dangerous and a great deal more difficult than it appeared from a distance.

"Alex?" Jason called as they approached.

At first Alex didn't move or acknowledge he'd heard them. After a few seconds, he slowly turned his head. They were both a bit taken aback by his disheveled, miserable appearance."Jason, Vance," Alex acknowledged their presence. He turned back to look out at the ocean.

"Your mom gave me a call; she's worried about you. Thought Vance and I might be able to help."

Alex said nothing, but nodded slightly. He understood why they were there and who was responsible.

There was only room on Alex's rock for one person, so Jason sat on a lower rock a few feet away and Vance sat beside him.

"You look like shit, my friend," said Jason. "Marian tells me you haven't eaten or slept since Teddy's death. We're here to pull you back to reality."

"I appreciate what you're doing, guys. But I need to work through this by myself for a while." Alex wasn't looking at either of them as he spoke. "I've been going over all the times Teddy and I had together. He's been with me all my life. We grew up together, had our first experiences at almost everything at the same time. We went to our first day of kindergarten together, holding hands, for

Christ's sake." Alex paused and took a deep shuddering breath.

Jason and Vance remained silent; letting Alex talk it out. There would be nothing they could say to improve the situation.

"Teddy had so many qualities I lack; his sense of humor, his warmth, his carefree nature. His qualities somehow added to my own, making me more complete. I feel I've lost part of my character and I fear... " he whispered, "…it was the nice part."

Vance cocked his head slightly. What Alex had said apparently struck a chord with him. He looked away from Alex and Jason for a moment.

"I don't believe we will ever know another human being like Teddy, and our lives will be a great deal less fulfilled because of his absence." Alex stopped talking and continued to stare at the ocean. Then in a barely audible voice, he said, "I'd have given my life for him."

All three men remained silent, alone with their own thoughts. There was the smell of salt in the air, the sound of the waves lapping gently against the rocks, and voices could occasionally be heard drifting across the bay from Balboa Island. It was peaceful.

"They caught the motherfuckers!" Vance announced out of the clear blue.

Alex's head snapped around. "Did they now?"

Chapter 54

FOREST LAWN
December 22, 1985
10:30 a.m.

"THEODORE OLDAKER TO BE BURIED TODAY"

The sheer size of the funeral was a tribute to Teddy's effect on everyone he had ever met. There were nearly two dozen people who flew out from New York to attend the funeral. Everyone who was connected in any way to the production of *"Tangle Foot"* was in attendance. Inexplicably, cars actually joined the funeral procession as it progressed from the church to the cemetery. By the time the procession arrived at the cemetery, there were upwards of two hundred cars behind the hearse. Many of these cars were transporting new and saddened fans. How they managed to relay their intentions to other fans to join the funeral procession was a mystery.

Alex had just about concluded his eulogy at Teddy's service. His appearance was somewhat improved from the day before, but still drawn. He had shaved, showered, taken nourishment, and gotten a fitful night's sleep after the visit from Jason and Vance. The news of the capture of Teddy's killers yanked Alex back to the present.

"...Teddy had special gifts," Alex continued from the podium. "His gifts revealed themselves to people the minute they met him. His warmth and good humor were the first thing everyone noticed; then eventually, his remarkable gift for entertaining. When you next met him, no matter how much time had passed, he remembered your name and all about you. He seemed to be able to locate people's souls and somehow join with them. Everybody he met became his friend; there were no exceptions that I'm aware of." Alex stopped briefly and looked up at the heavy sky. He looked back down at the hundreds of mourners gathered on the Forest Lawn grounds. He could see Teddy's mother and father standing alongside his parents, with Jennifer and Chuck on one side and Teddy's grandparents on the other. Lesley Johns, the beautiful young woman Teddy had met at Julliard and brought to Alex's twenty-first birthday party, was standing just behind Teddy's mother. There was not a dry eye among them. Colleen, Walt, and Aidan were a little further back. "He could..." Alex paused, "he could pull you up from your deepest depths with just a few words.. I.." Alex again stopped and looked down at the podium. "I wish he were here now... I could use him." Alex looked up and smiled slightly. "Teddy wore his wonderful heart on his sleeve for everyone to see, but at the same time, he was deep, and very bright. The world has lost a remarkable person. I have lost part of me."

NORTH HOLLYWOOD PRECINCT
December 23, 1985

Alex and Vance drove to the Hollywood precinct to see the slimy bastards who had killed Teddy and raped Julie Bashford. Four of them, it turned out, were eighteen, one nineteen, and the youngest was just sixteen. All but the youngest, as Vance predicted, had records. Two had extensive records, including assault and robbery.

"One, the oldest, was suspected of killing a rival gang member, but insufficient evidence prevented him from being prosecuted," concluded Vance as they pulled up to the front of the precinct's entrance. Their chauffeur, a member of Alex's security team, was just about to get out of the limo.

"We'll get the door, Sam," said Vance as he opened the door and exited, holding the door for Alex while automatically scanning the area for any signs of danger. The two walked into the police station.

"Got a call from the mayor this morning. Asked me to give you two gentlemen every courtesy," said the overweight and balding captain, displaying just a trace of annoyance.

"I would appreciate that, Captain," said Alex.

Sergeant Hargrave came into the Captain's office. He and Vance greeted each other using first names and shook hands. Hargrave turned to Alex.

"Mr. Gabriel."

"Sergeant Hargrave," responded Alex as they shook hands. Alex turned back to the Captain.

"I understand the sixteen-year-old is being held at a different facility, Captain, but I would like the five assholes you have locked up here to be brought to a room where Vance and I can talk to them."

"That would be highly unusual, sir," the captain explained, "and frankly, against our policy."

"I appreciate that, Captain, but I really need to do this my way."

"I'm sorry, Mr. Gabriel, but..."

"May I use your telephone, Captain?" Alex interrupted.

The captain looked puzzled. "Yes, sir."

Alex walked over, picked up the phone, and pushed an unlit button. "Dial 9 for an outside line?"

"Yes, sir."

Alex quickly dialed a number, only briefly taking his eyes off the captain.

"This is Alex Gabriel. Connect me to the mayor, please."

No more than five seconds passed. "Henry? Alex here. I've made a request of Captain Mellin, which he seems reluctant to honor because of an internal policy. Would you mind asking the captain to oblige my request?... Thank you." Alex handed the phone to the captain. "It's for you."

Alex, Vance, Hargrave and Captain Mellin stood behind the two-way mirror as the five were brought into the interrogation room. All were in shackles, cuffs, and jailhouse orange jumpsuits. A razor hadn't touched their shaved heads for three weeks. They stood against the far wall facing the mirror. All looked stupid, and all were trying to look as tough as possible.

Alex turned to Vance, "Let's get in there."

"Go with them, Sergeant," ordered the Captain.

The three walked out the observation room door and into the interrogation room.

None of the prisoners had a clue as to who Vance and Alex were. They probably assumed they were attorneys by the way they were dressed. None, after the first look at Vance, had any desire to look at him again. Perhaps, in those cold brown eyes, they saw their dim future.

"Each one of you assholes state your name, starting with you." Hargrave pointed to the first man on the left.

Alex felt his soul grow colder as each said his name. He looked into their eyes in turn, trying to see what they were made of. He could deduce little, other than stupidity and blind hate. One in particular, a Stanley Waszak, was staring back at Alex with a look of sheer disdain. He was mean- looking. Beady, light blue, soulless eyes, pockmarked face, a deep scar on his right cheek and fading scratch marks running from his left cheek across a stylized swastika tattoo on his neck. This one had no soul at all.

"Which one of you used the pipe?" Alex asked in a conversational, yet icy tone.

He looked from one to the other; no one said a word.

"It was you, wasn't it, you piece of shit?" Alex was looking at Waszak.

"Hey, fuck you, prick! I don't have to answer shit without my attorney here!"

Alex said nothing as he slowly walked over to Waszak, staring into those vacant eyes; the hate within him was overwhelming. He slapped Waszak in the mouth as hard as he could. Waszak spun and hit the wall hard, blood pouring from his split lip. The other four quickly jumped out of the way, spewing as many expletives as possible.

"Hey!" yelled Detective Hargrave and moved to restrain Alex.

Vance grabbed him just above the elbow. "Let it go, Clarence."

Hargrave looked at Vance. "But.."

"Let it go!"

"Yes, sir."

"Alex," Vance said in an even tone, "be a good idea to let him live right now!"

Alex stood with his face just inches from Stanley Waszak's. Waszak's disdainful look was now missing, replaced by surprise, pain, and fear. Alex wanted to beat him to death, as Waszak had done Teddy. He could feel his soul screaming in all-out rage. All of his being wanted to inflict pain on this beast until he died. He suddenly turned and walked out the door.

"Clarence, I'd like you to leave the room for a minute and turn off the intercom, if you will."

"Vance, you know I can't let you kill these assholes while they're in custody," Hargrave half-joked.

The five punks displayed some alarm at this conversation. They looked at each other. *Who the fuck are these people?*

"I'm not going to kill them, Clarence," Vance said in a conciliatory tone, "just need to have a little talk with them."

Hargrave paused for a moment. "Okay!" He turned and left the room. As he entered the observation room, he walked over and turned off the intercom.

"What the hell do you think you're doing, Sergeant?" demanded his captain.

"Mr. Youngblood asked me to leave and turn off the intercom, sir."

"I heard him, Sergeant, but just who the hell is your boss here, Clarence?" the captain demanded.

"You are, Captain, but Vance told me he wouldn't kill 'em, and he's a man of his word."

"Kill them? There are five violent sociopaths in there with him. He's the one in danger, God damn it."

"No, sir. That man's in no danger at all."

The captain looked at Hargrave for a few seconds.

"My only concern is Vance might slap them around a bit," smiled Hargrave. "If you're unfortunate enough to get slapped by Vance, you're gonna stay slapped for a few days."

"Listen up, scumbags, and listen good," began Vance. "Every one of you better be looking me right in the eye because you don't want to miss a thing I'm going to tell you." Vance looked at each one of the prisoners. Satisfied they were paying attention, he continued, "What happened to this piece of shit, here today, never occurred." Vance gestured toward Waszak. "Is that clear? If I hear that any one of you said anything, to anybody, at any time, about today, I'll come back here and hurt you so bad your mothers will feel it. Now as dumb as you fuckers are, you just had to notice that we can get to you anytime. You have fucked with the wrong people!"

Vance moved in front of each one, in turn, and looked them in the eye. "Do you understand?"

"Yes sir," the first four answered without hesitation, damn near snapping to attention.

Vance stepped in front of Waszak. "Please tell me you don't understand so I can explain it to you."

Waszak briefly looked at Vance, then quickly at the floor. "I get it!"

"I'm disappointed!" Vance continued to look at Waszak for a few seconds, then turned and left the room.

January 12, 1986

The grand jury indicted the five adults for murder and bound the sixteen-year-old over to the juvenile authorities to be tried separately. All five were to be tried together, despite the efforts of their court-appointed attorneys to have separate trials. Two of the punks offered to turn state's evidence in order to get lighter sentences, but the Los Angeles District Attorney felt he had a strong enough case to get convictions without the two ratting out the other four. Over the objections of the defendants' attorneys the trial was set for February 16.

On February 12, just four days before the trial was to begin, the court-appointed attorneys were replaced, at the request of the defendants' parents, by three high-profile attorneys. These famous barristers volunteered their services in order to get these youths the "best legal defense possible." With the notoriety of the case, they argued, these "underprivileged" young men would have little chance of a fair trial. Once the attorney change was approved, the new attorneys filed two motions. The first, a continuance of thirty days for the three to get up to speed on the case, was granted. The second, requesting a change of venue because of the negative press in and around Los Angles, was denied. The trial was reset for March 16.

Chapter 55

PANTAGES THEATER
March 7, 1986

It was Academy Awards night. Outside the Pantages Theater was a sea of fans, celebrities, and the media. Limos were dropping off their precious cargo in front of the red carpet as the flashes from a thousand cameras lit up the area. A silver Rolls limo pulled up to the red carpet and a tuxedoed attendant opened the rear door. Alex, followed by Sandy and Bob Oldaker, exited and started up the aisle. Few pictures were taken of these strangers. The three walked, almost unnoticed, into the theater.

They sat in the third row center near the aisle in this historic old theater. On Alex's right sat Teddy's parents. On his left was Teddy's co-star, Julie Newman, with her date. Alex had met Julie at Teddy's funeral and found her a bit feather-brained and quite self-centered. It was quite an honor, Alex was told, for the family of a fairly unknown nominee to be allowed to sit in these prestigious seats. Only once before had the Academy posthumously nominated an actor for an Oscar, making this occasion high praise indeed.

Alex began thinking about his childhood with Teddy. He pictured little Teddy bursting into his bedroom right after the accident; of a scared Teddy in their confrontation with the local punks; bicycling with Teddy and some other friends while laughing hysterically. Alex remembered Teddy's introduction to his wealth via his first visit to the Gabriel Building. The stories Teddy shared with him,

Walt, Jason, Vance, on the making of "*Tangle Foot*," during their fishing trip just a few months ago. Tears were starting to drip down his cheeks. He took out a handkerchief and wiped them off.

Seldom was Alex nervous about anything, but tonight he was a wreck. He wanted so badly for Teddy to win. It would give a boost to Sandy and Bob's morale and it would be a great and lasting honor for his lost friend. Sandy and Bob requested that if Teddy won, Alex would go up and accept the Oscar on his behalf. He agreed, but insisted that if in fact Teddy won, they would join him on stage during the acceptance speech.

Alex wasn't a movie buff, but he went out of his way to see the four movies that comprised Teddy's competition. They were all fine performances and much to Alex's surprise, damn good movies. One actor in particular, Alex considered strong competition – John O'Carlin. O'Carlin had been nominated four times in the past and taken two Oscars home. Teddy had spoken highly of O'Carlin; he was clearly one of Teddy's favorites. After watching O'Carlin's performance in the action thriller, "*Cross Over*," Alex had a sinking feeling. He was truly a great actor and the Hollywood press had made him the odds on favorite to take the Oscar despite the deep sentiment for Teddy.

Three of the movies nominated for best picture included nominations for best actor in a leading role. *"Cross Over"* and *"Tangle Foot"* were two, and the epic *"Crusades,"* starring Walter Singletary, was the third.

All evening Alex sat on pins and needles. "*Cross Over*" had been nominated for six Oscars and had already won for Special Effects and Sound. *"Crusades"* had seven nominations and three were in the bank by the early evening: Cinematography, Costumes, and Best Supporting Actress. Clearly, momentum was on its side. *"Tangle Foot"* was nominated for only three Oscars: Best Picture, Best Director, and Best Actor.

Finally, the time had come. Snippets of the movies showing scenes of the five nominated actors were shown to the enthusiastic applause of the audience. It was apparent by the applause for

O'Carlin's and Teddy's performances, that they were the favorites. Sandy nearly lost her composure when Teddy's scene was up on the screen. Alex could hear a low mewing sound coming from her throat. Bob looked down at his tightly gripped hands.

Alex was wound tight as the presenter, the Oscar-winning actress from the previous year, opened the envelope. "And the Oscar goes to... Theodore Oldaker for *'Tangle Foot'!*" she announced with great fanfare. The audience went crazy and jumped to their feet. This was clearly the popular choice.

Alex and the Oldakers jumped up and hugged each other. Alex kissed Sandy and hugged Bob. Teddy's co-star grabbed Alex and gave him a big hug and bigger kiss. John O'Carlin and the other three nominated actors all stood and applauded enthusiastically. The standing ovation continued as Alex, Sandy, and Bob walked up the steps to the stage and walked across to the podium.

The Oscar-winning actress kissed Alex on the cheek and handed him Teddy's Oscar. She, in turn, gave Sandy and then Bob a kiss and stood back as Alex approached the podium.

"This is going to be difficult for me to get through so I hope you will bear with me for a moment." Alex looked down at the podium, then back up at the audience. "Teddy's parents," Alex turned and acknowledged the Oldakers, "asked if I would accept this award for Teddy, should he win. I agreed to their request with the provision that they join me up here so the world can see the parents of the... " Alex stopped for a few seconds. "Oh boy," he whispered, looking down at the podium. The theater was dead silent. Alex looked back up."...the parents of the nicest, warmest man in the world," Alex's voice cracked. He held the Oscar over his head and looked up. *This is for you, my dear friend; this is your night*. Tears started gathering in Alex's eyes, but he continued. "Most of you never had the chance to meet Teddy and that is a shame, because, if you had, your lives would have been better for it, as anyone who knew this wonderful man would attest. Many of you here would have gotten to know him in future years because, without question, he was to become a major star. Teddy was put on this earth to entertain and he did that exceedingly well."

Alex looked over the crowd of beautiful people. "I've spent little time in movie theaters in my life, but I've made it a point to see the movies that had the four best actor nominees. And I'll tell you; you four gentlemen all deserve an Oscar. I was particularly impressed with the performance of John O'Carlin. I feel that if this horrible tragedy hadn't occurred, it might be Mr. O'Carlin up here. I know Teddy would have felt the same. Mr. O'Carlin was his favorite actor." Alex held Teddy's Oscar in John O'Carlin's direction. O'Carlin acknowledged the great compliment by nodding his head and mouthing the words "thank you" to Alex. The crowd again applauded enthusiastically. Most of the women and a goodly number of men in the audience had tears in their eyes.

"I know the winners thank those responsible for the making of their movies, writers, directors, producers, fellow actors, etc. But I don't know any of the people connected with this wonderful movie, other than Miss Newman, yet I can assure you, Teddy wouldn't have forgotten a single person. I then will thank all of you for him from the bottom of my heart. He would have concluded by thanking the wonderful people standing behind me." Alex turned and acknowledged Sandy and Bob. "His parents."

Again the crowd was on their feet. Sandy was holding up quite well considering and managed a heart-rending smile, tears pouring down her cheeks. Bob, on the other hand, Alex could see, was about to lose control.

Alex quickly turned back to the audience. "I know that Teddy is in heaven looking down on this event, just bursting with pride. I thank you again." With this, he turned and handed the Oscar to Sandy and gave her a big hug, released her and hugged Bob. "Hold on for just a few more seconds, Bob," he whispered.

They managed to get backstage with the escort and the Oscar-winning actress before Bob broke down a little, but he regained his composure within a minute.

The entertainment press swarmed around Alex, Sandy and Bob Oldaker. Sandy had a tight grip on the Oscar and a permanent smile exposing her beautiful set of large, bright white teeth.

As the flash bulbs popped around them, Alex's mind again filled with images of Teddy and their sharing life experiences over the past quarter century. *I love you, my friend*.

Chapter 56

GABRIEL HEADQUARTERS
March 12, 1986
2:15 p.m.

Alex had just concluded a series of meetings with all his domestic department heads. He, Walt, and Jason were still seated at the board table in Alex's office, cleaning up some details concerning three pending acquisitions for Global Media. This was their first full-blown meeting since the tragedy. Alex had been, and still was, preoccupied with all the aspects of Teddy's death and the upcoming trial. Walt and Jason had managed to keep things running reasonably smoothly for the past three months with far less help and direction than Alex normally gave them. Most new investments and acquisitions were put aside for the time being.

"Mr. Youngblood is here to see you, sir," Carol's voice was heard over the intercom.

Walt looked at Alex, received a nod, reached over and pushed the intercom button. "Come on in, Vance."

Within seconds, Vance walked through the double doors, took a quick look around, and proceeded to the board table. His stoic features seemed a little drawn.

The three shook hands with Vance.

"Sit," Alex motioned toward a chair on the other side of Jason.

Vance stepped over, pulled the chair out and sat, looked at Walt,

Jason and then let his eyes come to rest on Alex's. "Julie Bashford committed suicide!"

3:05 p.m.

"What do you mean, this weakens our case considerably?" Alex had the phone on speaker so Jason and Vance could hear his conversation with the LA District Attorney.

"Well sir, obviously two eyewitnesses are better than one. Especially if the one left had been knocked about on a dark street."

"But Miss Bashford did pick out two of the assholes in a lineup, and that's a matter of record." Alex was starting to become agitated. "You also have the pipe and bloody clothes that match both Teddy's and Miss Bashford's blood, and practically a signed confession from two of the pieces of shit. What the hell do you need?"

"I'm not saying that our case is shot, Mr. Gabriel. I'm just saying her suicide weakens it."

"You said, 'weakens considerably'!"

"It's not just her testimony that we're going to have to do without, but the defense is starting to make noises about Miranda violations and illegal search and seizure."

There was silence on Alex's side of the line.

"Sir?"

"Are you telling me someone screwed up the arrest of these scumbags?"

"It's possible the arresting officers were a little overzealous at the time. There was a lot of pressure to capture the suspects. You added to that pressure as I recall, sir."

"Let me make a suggestion, Mr. Arbuckle." Alex's voice had a cold edge. "Were I you, I would see to it that all the T's were crossed and I's dotted on this case from now on. A failure to get a murder conviction on these five assholes could be catastrophic to the futures of everyone involved in the arrest and prosecution."

"Are you threatening me, Mr. Gabriel?" asked the District Attorney, indignantly.

"You can take my statement any way you wish, Mr. Arbuckle."

With that, Alex hung up.

LOS ANGLES SUPERIOR COURT
March 16, 1986

A remarkable amount of press was in attendance for the jury selection process. The high- profile defense team enlisted the help of two psychiatrists whose specialties were picking juries. The defense so far managed, with relative ease, to reject all Hispanic prospects and agreed to seat only three young white men by the middle of the third day.

Vance was on his cell phone in a courthouse hall, "I'm telling you the DA is giving the fucking jury to the defense. There isn't a single Hispanic or Black person." Vance was pissed. "So far they're about the same ilk as the defendants. Young white males of questionable character. The deck is being stacked, Alex and the DA isn't doing anything to stop it."

March 20, 1986

On the fourth day of jury selection, District Attorney Arbuckle stood before the Judge and announced he would be removing himself as a prosecutor and would be assigning two assistant district attorneys to prosecute the case.

"Who's going to be the lead prosecutor?" Alex's voice betrayed growing bewilderment.

"Oliver Hollis. Been with the DA's office three years," Vance answered as he watched the excited press call in to their papers to relay this astonishing news.

"Is he any good?"

"Looks like his success rate is just over eighty-three percent."

"Is that good?"

"Not really, considering most people arrested are guilty or they wouldn't have been arrested. Something over ninety percent would be closer to an acceptable level."

"Why the hell would the DA put a low-level prosecutor on this case?"

Vance could hear the confusion in Alex's voice. "The second seat is actually worse," Vance added. "She's never prosecuted anything. Just passed her bar three months ago... after two previous tries."

There was a notable pause before Alex spoke again. "This makes no sense, none at all. This is the highest profile case Los Angeles has had in years. Why jeopardize a successful prosecution and the positive press by putting in your second string?"

"There's a rat in the crackers here, Boss."

"Okay," said Alex after a long pause. "Let's run a deep check on Arbuckle. I want to know that man inside and out."

"Yes sir, got it started already,"

"Vance, I appreciate all you're doing," Alex said warmly.

"I'll stay on it, Alex."

Vance stood for a second, after disconnecting, staring at the phone. That was the warmest tone he had heard from Alex since Teddy's death.

If Arbuckle thinks taking himself off the case lets him off the hook, he's in for a wicked surprise, thought Vance. He couldn't help but wonder if Arbuckle was actually trying to sabotage the case. *If so, to what purpose?*

Vance felt his mood darkening. A mood that he hadn't experienced since the killing days of Viet Nam. *Don't these people know who they're fucking with?*

April 20, 1986

"The jury is, after ten days, made up of eleven young white guys and one solitary Black man. None of the whites are over thirty and all are just a step above the assholes they're judging, if that. The Black juror, I found out, had the shit beat out of him by a Mexican gang in East Los Angeles three years ago." Vance was clearly disgusted. "If I found this out, so did the defense, Alex."

"Why is the prosecution doing this?"

"Don't know. But I can tell you, if this jury had a fucking brain between them, they'd have it out kicking it around."

April 24, 1986

Within the first week, the defense made several motions and astutely had most of the physical evidence tossed because of shoddily written search warrants. The only piece of real evidence left was a blood sample found on Julie Bashford's dress that matched that of Stanley Waszak's. It was assumed that the blood came from the scratches found on the right side of his face when he was arrested. There was little evidence of those scratches now.

The prosecution's management of Jennifer's testimony was woefully inadequate. She was interrupted with defense objections no less than eighty-three times.

"It was too dark, your Honor; the witness couldn't have seen that."

"How could she tell who hit whom first, Your Honor?"

"That's hearsay, your Honor. There's no witness to back that up."

And so it went.

When it came time for the defense to cross-examine Jennifer, they did so to the point of cruelty, during which time the prosecution objected only twice. Even the judge seemed to be taken aback by the lack of protection the prosecution provided their star witness. At one point, he suddenly declared a short recess and called the prosecutors into his chambers.

Nobody knew what was said in the judge's chambers, but the two so-called prosecutors were noticeably more alert for the remainder of the day.

April 26, 1986

"You say the defendants kept calling Mr. Oldaker a spick, greaser, and other derogatory names generally connected with the Hispanic race?"

"Yes, but Teddy wasn't Hispanic."

"But the defendants didn't know that now, did they, Mrs. Kroll?"

"What difference does it make what race..."

"Your Honor, will you please instruct the witness to just answer my questions with a simple yes or no without editorializing."

"I object, even if the prosecution won't, Your Honor." Jennifer was getting more upset as the cross-examination progressed. "These people are intimating that had Teddy been a Mexican, it would be all right to beat him to death!"

"Objection!" expressed the defense attorney.

Jennifer glared at the two prosecutors. "You two want to start doing your job? God damn it!" she nearly yelled.

Enthusiastic applause came from the gallery. The press was eating this up.

"Mrs. Kroll, I can see where you would feel that way, but I must admonish you to please just answer the questions with a yes or no." With that, the judge gave the prosecutors a disgusted look.

"Well, God damn it, Your Honor. Those two numb-nuts are supposed to be on my side. What the hell's wrong with them?"

"Mrs. Kroll, another outburst like that and I'll hold you in contempt."

"I am in contempt, Your Honor. I'm in contempt of this entire trial."

"Mrs. Kroll, please!" The judge obviously didn't want to hold Jennifer Gabriel Kroll in contempt. The judge, it seemed, wished to remain a judge for many more years. He stole a quick glance to the gallery and spotted a stone-faced Alex sitting beside Vance.

There was no doubt now that DA Arbuckle was intent on sabotaging the case. Perhaps he was trying to show the powerful Alexander Gabriel he couldn't be intimidated. He surely had picked the assistant DAs because they would be totally inept in a case such as this.

The defense spent the next three days reviewing each of the defendants' lives, from birth to the fateful evening they were "attacked" by Teddy.

Each, it was made to seem, was brought up in the worst possible conditions. From childhood neglect, to severe beatings, to sexual molestation. These "poor young men," it seemed, were actually the victims here.

The trial lasted another three weeks. On May 20th, the prosecution spent no more than twenty minutes presenting their closing arguments and rested their case. The defense spent two hours and five minutes making theirs.

The jury was in deliberation for a total of four hours when they let the bailiff know they had agreed on a verdict. Because of the late hour, the verdict was held over until the next morning at 10:00.

LOS ANGLES SUPERIOR COURT
May 21, 1986
10:00 a.m.

The entire Gabriel family, along with Teddy and Julie Bashford's parents, were there at 9:00 a.m. Jason and Vance came in a little later. Just before 10:00, the five shackled and cuffed defendants were escorted in by three large deputies and sat at the defense table next to their attorneys. At precisely 10:00, the bailiff called the court to order and introduced the judge.

Everyone was on edge as the court was brought to order. After the usual shuffling and stacking of papers and files, the judge signaled the bailiff to escort the jury into the courtroom.

The tension was pervasive in the courtroom as the jury took their seats. The entire court was eerily still. A muffled cough could be heard toward the rear of the gallery and a dropping of a pencil somewhere in the front.

The Judge looked at the jury foreman. "Have you reached a verdict?"

"We have, Your Honor." The foreman handed a piece of paper to the bailiff, who in turn walked over to the bench and handed it to the Judge.

Marian held Alex's right hand and Norman's left. Teddy's mother had both her hands gripping Bob's. Jennifer had her hand on Chuck's knee.

"How say you, guilty or not guilty?" asked the judge.

"As to the charge of murder in the second degree we find the defendants not guilty, Your Honor."

The gallery was astonished and let out a loud protest. The judge was forced to bang his gavel hard for nearly ten seconds before order was restored.

"As to the charge of assault and rape of Julie Bashford," the foreman went on, "we find the defendants, Robert Bell and Stanley Waszak, guilty as charged."

The jury either bought the ridiculous self-defense story or just decided to stick it to the establishment; the latter was more likely.

The skinhead slimeballs would probably spend a paltry two to five years in the state pen for killing two innocent people.

The gallery let out another loud protest, some even jumping to their feet. Again the judge banged his gavel for several seconds before order was restored.

After the reading of the decision and dismissal of the jury, Alex stood and looked at the back of Arbuckle's head as he sat directly behind the prosecution table. As the judge left the courtroom, Lowell Arbuckle stood and shook the hands of not only his two assistant DAs, but the hands of the defense attorneys as well, apparently congratulating them on a job well done. He then turned and looked at Alex. He smiled slightly, gave a nod, turned, and started an animated conversation with the defense attorneys.

This, you son-of-a-bitch, will be the worst mistake you have ever made, thought Alex as he looked at the back of Arbuckle's head. *You're going to suffer; on that you can depend.* His thoughts went to Teddy. *Sorry, Teddy. We'll have to wait a little longer to make these assholes pay. And they will pay, my friend. They will pay. That's a promise.*

Alex stood there as most in the gallery were starting to leave the courtroom. His mother, father, Vance, Jason, and Sandy and Bob Oldaker also remained standing. Sandy was sobbing quietly as she bent over to pick up her purse. Teddy's father had tears streaming down his cheeks and was mumbling to himself. Jennifer was doubled over in her seat, rocking back and forth, her face buried in her hands. Chuck's face was drawn as he gently rubbed his wife's back.

The reporters had their cell phones to call in their stories; the flash of cameras was nearly constant; the din in the courtroom was loud and gaining momentum as Waszak and Bell were led off by deputies. The other three defendants were congratulating themselves; not caring one whit about their two friends who were being led away. *Fuck 'em, shit happens*.

Chapter 57

GABRIEL HEADQUARTERS
June 20, 1986
10:15 a.m.

In the three weeks since the trial ended, Alex had returned to work at a feverish pace. He was up an hour earlier than usual and stayed in the office until late in the evening. He made up for the neglect the trial had caused, and then some. The work helped take his mind off the trial and his lost friend.

"We got the fucker!"

Alex looked up in time to see Vance practically burst through his office doors. The smile on Vance's face revealed his mood.

Vance walked over to Alex's desk and casually tossed a sheaf of papers and a cassette tape on top of the desk. Subtlety wasn't Vance's long suit.

"What's this?" Alex gestured toward the material now sitting on top of several reports he was studying.

"I believe it to be DA Arbuckle's demise."

Alex picked up the papers; looked up at Vance, then back down as he started reading.

"Where in the hell did you get these?" he asked after quickly reading the first five pages.

"Let's just say I have connections at City Hall and let it go at that," Vance said with a trace of a smile.

Alex's left eyebrow lifted a little, as he looked Vance in the eye.

"He left this," Alex gestured at the papers, "where someone could get to it?"

"Our friend Arbuckle isn't the brightest star in LA's political sky. 'Course, we've known that since he chose to throw the case."

"And this?" Alex picked up the cassette tape.

"Oh, that's just confirming what is disclosed in the papers in his own voice." Vance was now, uncharacteristically, grinning from ear to ear. "What a dumb fucker!"

"Anybody else's voice on the tape?" Alex couldn't help but smile. He'd never seen Vance so obviously pleased with himself.

"Oh yeah."

Alex reached over and pushed the intercom button. "Carol, have Mr. Gould and Mr. Mallory join me in my office, ASAP."

10:50 a.m.

"What a dumb fucker!" Jason exclaimed.

"My sentiments exactly," Vance smiled.

Mallory sat back in his chair, his right hand rubbing his chin. "I have a feeling that this evidence," Mallory was looking at Vance as he gestured toward the papers and tape, "wasn't acquired with proper search warrants."

"Well... " Vance started.

Mallory quickly held up his left hand, palm forward. "I don't want to hear it."

Vance stopped whatever he was going to say.

Alex watched this exchange. There was little doubt now that Vance hadn't come by this information using legal avenues.

"I'll tell you this," Mallory went on, "if this material is considered illegally acquired, it will be thrown out of court. And without it, there will be no conviction."

"I realize that," agreed Vance. "I've been working on that, shall we say, challenge."

Alex smiled to himself.

"Have you?" Mallory was clearly skeptical.

"Yes, sir."

Alex looked over at Jason, then Vance. "How long?"

"Should be able to give you a yeah or nay in two days."

"Really?"

"Yes, sir."

Alex knew that the evidence, if tainted in any way, would be thrown out of court. The attorneys in this conspiracy would fight tooth and nail to bury this information. Their futures and fortunes would depend on it. Vance was the most resourceful person Alex knew. *This will certainly test that resourcefulness.*

Vance had, in fact, along with three of his men, simultaneously broken into Arbuckle's office and home. The typed papers were found in his office in a file headed "Kemple, Jackson, and Epley." The tape was found in Arbuckle's home sitting on a desk beside a tape recorder in his den.

June 21, 1986

As soon as he had the evidence in his hand, Vance ordered an expedited dossier on Arbuckle's secretary, a Mrs. Sylvia Morton. His instructions to his operatives were to gather what information they could in twenty-four hours and get it to him. The amount of information that could be gathered in such a short period of time was limited, but nonetheless, it turned out to be somewhat useful. In reading the report, Vance could see that Mrs. Morton was not averse to changing jobs. She had done so three times in the past five years and had always bettered her position. Her husband was a sergeant with the LAPD and evidently, squeaky-clean. They had two teenage boys attending Santa Monica high school. Vance highlighted the line stating that both boys were in the drama class.

June 22, 1986

Vance took a brief look at a picture of Sylvia Morton clipped to the upper right hand corner of the folder, replaced the file in his briefcase, and exited his black Mercedes, briefcase in hand. He quickly spotted the elevator that would take him to the lobby of the Bonaventure Hotel in downtown LA, and headed in that direction

Vance had posed as a headhunter with a lucrative job offer and managed to persuade Mrs. Morton to have lunch with him at a place of her choice. Her choice was the Bonaventure.

They had agreed to meet at 1:00 p.m. at a yuppie bar and grill just off the plush lobby. Many of the patrons had left or were in the process of leaving as Sylvia walked in the door. She was an average-looking, professionally dressed woman in her late thirties. Vance rose from a corner table he was occupying and walked over to introduce himself. He knew what Sylvia looked like but she wouldn't have known him from any other well-dressed ox.

Sylvia Morton spotted Vance as he approached. If she was intimidated by his unusual physique, she didn't let on. He had a nice smile on his face, which somehow didn't seem to fit his overall demeanor.

"Mrs. Morton," Vance held out his hand as he stopped in front of Sylvia. "I'm Vance Youngblood."

After the introductions Vance escorted her to his table, held her chair for her, and took his own. After the initial pleasantries, they ordered lunch and Vance cleared his throat. "Mrs. Morton, I've got to tell you, up front, that I lured you here under false pretenses."

There was an instant cooling of Sylvia's demeanor. "Really? Why would you do that?"

"I apologize. I couldn't think of another way to talk to you privately and face to face." Vance was being as tactful as he could manage. "I believe if you'll hear me out, you'll forgive me for the deception."

Sylvia looked into Vance's light brown eyes for a few seconds. "I'll tell you right now that if I hear anything I find offensive, I'll be out of here like the proverbial striped-ass-ape. Do we understand each other?"

"Yes, ma'am." Vance smiled.

"Well then, what's your story, Mr. Youngblood?"

"To be as direct as possible, I'll inform you that I represent Alex Gabriel and that we are investigating the trial of Teddy Oldaker's killers."

Sylvia noticeably stiffened. "Jesus," she whispered as she looked down at the surface of the table. "That was a terrible thing that happened to that young man." She looked back up at Vance. "My boys both cried when they heard the news. They went to see '*Tangle Foot*' three times. They thought Theodore Oldaker was the best actor in Hollywood."

"He was a lot more than that, Mrs. Morton. He was the warmest human being I have ever known." Vance abruptly stopped talking and looked down for a moment.

Sylvia's demeanor softened a little. "Mr. Oldaker was obviously a friend of yours. You're not just doing a job for Mr. Gabriel?"

"That's correct. He was a close friend of mine. He was a gentle and loving man. I miss him."

That statement caused Sylvia to pause for a second. "You surprise me, Mr. Youngblood. At first blush, I wouldn't have thought a big hulk like you would have many gentle friends. You, for lack of a better description, have the look of a hard case."

Vance said nothing for a few seconds. "I suspect most of us 'hard cases' have a softer side."

"I didn't mean to insult you, Mr. Youngblood."

"You didn't. You're being candid and I appreciate that quality in a person."

Sylvia smiled. "You want to start over?"

"Good idea."

"You believe I could help you with this investigation?" she asked apprehensively.

"You could be invaluable." Vance looked around the restaurant; it was clearing out. He and Sylvia were practically alone. He reached into his briefcase and retrieved copies of the typed evidence. He handed them to Sylvia.

Sylvia didn't read far before her face blanched and she looked up at Vance. "Where did you get these?" she asked in a near whisper.

"I'm afraid I can't tell you that. I'm sorry."

Sylvia's hands were visibly shaking as she handed the papers back to Vance. "What do you want from me?"

Vance told Sylvia what she already knew; that knowing of this conspiracy and not reporting it could cause her to be named a co-conspirator and that she, at the least, would be losing her job under appalling circumstances.

"That occurred to me." Sylvia, though still nervous, appeared to be beginning to relax.

Vance said nothing. He would have to be blind not to see that this woman was suffering a lot of guilt over this.

"I can't tell you the shit I've been carrying around. If you have a way I can make amends, both legally and to myself, I'd be grateful, Mr. Youngblood."

"I believe I do." Vance reached over and put a powerful hand on top of hers for a moment and squeezed gently. "Would you be willing to sign an affidavit stating that you not only typed the incriminating papers on the orders of your boss, Lowell Arbuckle -- which I assume is true -- but also, after typing the papers and realizing the truth, contacted Mr. Gabriel and gave him the incriminating evidence, which, of course, isn't true?"

She thought about that for a moment, "Why would I give the papers to Mr. Gabriel? Why wouldn't I contact the Attorney General?" she asked.

"Well," Vance reasoned, "you now know that the LA District Attorney, your boss, is corrupt and that he and the State's AG are friends. You just weren't sure of your ground. You felt sure Mr. Gabriel would be able to get the papers to the proper authorities."

She gave a slight nod. "That could work."

"And then there's the tape."

"What tape?"

"This one!" Vance pulled a small tape recorder out of his briefcase. "I would like you to listen to a few minutes of this."

"What's on it?"

"It'll be self-explanatory." Vance handed the small earphones to Silvia. "Let me know when you've heard enough."

After no more than three minutes, Silvia took the earphones away from her ears. "That rotten son of a bitch!"

"Our sentiments exactly," Vance agreed.

"Where'd you get the tape?"

"From you."

She stared at Vance for nearly thirty seconds. "Okay." She nodded her head. "That rotten son of a bitch," she repeated.

Vance again reached into his briefcase and pulled out a couple of papers. "I'd like you to read this over and then if you agree, sign and date it at the bottom."

Vance had the statement prepared by Mallory. He and Sylvia spent the following thirty minutes going over details of their conspiracy. When they parted company outside the restaurant, Sylvia reached up and gave Vance a big extended hug.

"Thank you, Vance; you've helped restore my self-respect."

"We'll get that rotten son of a bitch, Sylvia."

On the drive back to Orange County, Vance picked up a small recorder and pushed the "record" button. "Put a man on Sylvia Morton. She may need some protection."

Chapter 58

GABRIEL HEADQUARTERS
June 23, 1986
8:30 a.m.

Alex got up and walked over to the side table to refill his coffee. "Anyone else want a refill?"

"No thanks, boss," said Vance.

"Had all I need today," added Jason.

Mallory just shook his head and kept reading the paper in his hand.

"Alex, we're going to have to get hold of the State Attorney General for this." Mallory looked up from the papers. "They can prosecute Arbuckle, Kemple, and Jackson for obstruction of justice, corruption, and conspiracy, just to name a few."

"I like the way you think," Vance remarked. "I might point out that the Attorney General and the District Attorney are reported to be close friends."

"They won't be after this," declared Jason.

"That would be a safe bet," Vance agreed.

Alex sat down at the board table. "Mallory, you prepare these," Alex held the papers and tape up, "for the Attorney General and fly it up to him personally."

"Yes, sir."

"Jason, you get started with copy for the newspapers, TV, and radio. We'll go over it together when you're through."

"Yes, sir."

"The second Arbuckle is arrested, I want a full media blitz. Headlines in every one of our papers nationwide; lead story on all newscasts," instructed Alex.

"We'll bury them," declared Jason.

"I'll be making a few phone calls after the Attorney General has had time to look over the evidence."

"I'll bet you will." Mallory smiled for the first time.

"Vance!"

"Yes, sir?"

"I don't know how you did it, and frankly I'm sure it's better if I don't, but," Alex stopped for a moment, "you're the man of the hour."

"Just got lucky, boss."

June 24, 1986

After the Attorney General had a day to absorb the information, he had several phone conversations with both Alex and Mallory. When they were in agreement as to how to proceed, Alex called both the Governor and Mayor of Los Angeles. Warrants were issued for Lowell Arbuckle, Johnny Jackson, and Alan Kemple.

Arbuckle was arrested the following morning in his office in front of his entire staff, including Ollie Hollis and Sylvia Morton. Jackson was arrested while having lunch with two state senators at an exclusive men's club in Beverly Hills. Alan Kemple was handcuffed in front of the same court where the trial of Teddy's killers was held.

Bail was set at $1,000,000. each. An exorbitant amount by any standards, but the State's Attorney General argued that the three would likely be flight risks. The judge, without comment, went along with the AG's recommendation.

The State Attorney General and DA Arbuckle were, as predicted, no longer friends.

"This is some serious bullshit," declared Jackson.

"We're going to sue somebody's ass off," threatened Kemple.

"Flight risk? You can't do this!" Arbuckle screamed at the judge.

"Watch me!" exclaimed the judge as he banged down his gavel.

June 24, 1986

"LOS ANGLES DISTRICT ATTORNEY UNDER FULL INVESTIGATION"

...Los Angles District Attorney Lowell Arbuckle, along with high profile attorneys Johnny Jackson and Alan Kemple, have been arrested and charged with twelve criminal counts ranging from obstruction of justice to conspiracy. If convicted, these men could receive a maximum sentence of fifteen years to life.

"LOS ANGELES DA, LOWELL ARBUCKLE, AND FAMOUS ATTORNEYS IN CAHOOTS"

...Could it be that two of our nation's most famous attorneys, Johnny Jackson and Alan Kemple, teamed up with the Los Angeles District Attorney to throw the prosecution of the men accused of killing the Academy Award-winning actor, Theodore Oldaker...?

Headline stories ran across the nation in all Global Media's papers, scooping the rest of the national press. The lead story of every major network described the grounds for the investigation. All other networks not owned by Global Media picked up the stories and ran them as soon as possible.

Two days after Arbuckle was arrested, he was led down a long hall in his bright orange jumpsuit, to the visiting room.

Upon entering the room he found, standing on the other side of the room close to the visitor's door, Alex Gabriel.

Arbuckle involuntarily gasped. "What the hell?"

Alex smiled slightly, nodded his head, turned and left the room.

"*You-son-of-a-bitch*," Arbuckle screamed at the closed door.

Alex smiled as he walked down the hall.

September 12, 1986

The trial of Arbuckle, Jackson, and Kemple lasted nearly three months. It seemed there was no end to the bullshit the three men and their four attorneys could come up with to confuse the jurors.

The prosecution had, among others, pulled in the presiding judge from Teddy's trial. His testimony as to the conduct and professionalism of the prosecutors in Teddy's trial drove a few nails into their coffins. Ollie Hollis and his assistant were subpoenaed and added, involuntarily to be sure, a few more nails. But in the end, it boiled down to the physical evidence, tape and papers, backed up by the steadfast and believable testimony given by Sylvia Morton.

Jackson and Kemple were disbarred and sentenced to three to five years in a minimum-security facility and fined a quarter-million dollars each. Arbuckle was also disbarred and fined the same amount, but was given the maximum sentence the law would allow: eight to ten years in the same prison where Stanley Waszak was spending a paltry five to ten for the rape of Julie Bashford.

Within sixty days of the conviction, Alex brought a civil suit against the three men and the law firm where Jackson and Kemple were senior partners. He filed the suit on behalf of Sandy and Bob Oldaker and Julie Bashford's parents. The suit would eventually cause the collapse of the law firm and would nearly wipe out the fortunes of all three.

Chapter 59

GABRIEL HOME
December 3, 1986
7:12 a.m.

"It's for you, Son." Marian handed the phone to Alex. They were both sitting in the kitchen breakfast nook having coffee and rolls.

"This is Alex."

"Mr. Gabriel, this is Detective Hargrave of the Los Angles police department."

"Yes, Detective, I remember you. What's up?"

"Thought you would like to know that this morning, three bodies were found hanging in a garage located in our Hollywood Division."

Alex stiffened and felt his pulse begin to race. "Who are they?" he asked quietly.

Marian couldn't help but notice Alex's attitude change. "What is it, Alex?"

Alex held up his hand and listened intently. After a minute or two, he thanked the detective and asked Hargrave to keep him informed, as additional information became available.

"Yes, sir."

"Jesus!" Alex smiled as he replaced the phone on the receiver.

"What?"

"Seems three of the skinheads who got away with killing Teddy were found hanging in a garage this morning."

"Oh, my God!" Marian was shocked.

"They think it was gang-related. They were severely beaten before they were hanged and tagged with spray paint."

"Tagged?"

"You know, the graffiti you see on walls. Different gangs have different tags for marking their territory."

"Oh, sure, I know."

Alex sat for a few seconds. "Well, can't say this is the worst news I've ever had! Three down, two to go!"

Marian's face couldn't hide her disappointment because her son seemed to take pleasure in the fact that three human beings were viciously killed. "No matter who they were or what they did, dying a horrible death is not something for someone to relish, Alex."

"Sorry, Mom, but I can't consider this bad news."

"This isn't who you really are, Alex."

"Again I'm sorry, but those slimy bastards took Teddy away from us and their deaths please me." Alex saw how his apparent loss of compassion hurt his mother. He made a mental note to mask similar reactions in the future.

It was still difficult for Alex to get over the violent loss of his friend. His spirits had gained some ground after the conviction of Arbuckle, Jackson, and Kemple, and now the deaths of three of the killers brought him quite a way out of his funk.

8:00 a.m.

Alex called Jason.

"Have you heard the news?"

"I've heard a lot of news, but nothing earth-shattering," Jason said lightly.

"They found the three pieces of shit who were in on Teddy's killing hanging in a garage this morning."

"Wow, that is news… good news, actually."

"That was my reaction."

"I'll bet."

"And it was the same garage in which they found Julie Bashford."

Jason absorbed this unexpected news for about two seconds. "Is that so?" he said slowly. "Do you happen to know where Vance is?"

Chapter 60

May 12, 1988
12:35 p.m.

The three were well into their meal when Walt cleared his throat. "Alex, Colleen and I have something to tell you."

Alex looked up from his plate. "You're pregnant again?"

"No, no. We decided because of my advanced age, that we would stay with just one. Alexandra, your wonderful niece, our energetic daughter is -- and will be -- enough to handle for the rest of our lives."

Alex nodded knowingly.

"No, what we want to tell you… " Walt looked at Colleen and smiled, "…is that I'm going to retire."

Alex's smile disappeared. He quit chewing his food. He sat and looked at his uncle. It never occurred to him that Walt would someday want to retire.

Alex swallowed, "I don't know what to say."

"How about congratulations?"

"Sure…sure! I'm sorry. It just never crossed my mind that I would have to do this alone." Alex paused for a second. "That didn't come out right. I mean, we've always worked together. It just won't be the same without your counsel, your knowledge…Jesus!" Alex was at a loss for words.

"Alex, if ever there was a man who needed less support than you, I would like to meet that individual," Walt said sincerely. "Why,

Son, you haven't needed my help since you were ten or so."

Alex sat for a moment, looking at his iced tea. He looked up into his uncle's eyes. "I have been blessed having you as my mentor all these years, and you're wrong about me not needing your help since I was a kid. Your just being there was invaluable to me. You have, on a multitude of occasions, lent balance to my headstrong actions." Alex looked deep into his uncle's eyes. "I'm going to miss you."

"Hey, I'm not moving off the planet, you know. I'm going to be available to pull your nuts out of the fire at a moment's notice, for Christ's sake. Besides, Jason will fill my shoes with no problem."

"You've got some pretty big clodhoppers, Uncle. Jason's feet are going to have to grow a bit."

June 25, 1988

In the weeks following Walt's resignation as President of Gabriel International, Alex went through the restructuring of his top management. Top personnel would have to be moved or reassigned. He called a board meeting to announce Jason Gould as the new Executive Vice President of Gabriel International. In turn Jason to promoted his second in command, Jack Calloway, to President of Global Media; Jason remained as CEO. Vance was named Vice President in charge of Gabriel International's security, which over the years had become a monumental undertaking. It was a job he had been doing all along, but the title added to his clout and prestige within the immense conglomerate.

Chapter 61

GABRIEL HEADQUARTERS
January 11, 1989
11:45 a.m.

At 11:46 a.m., a pearl-white Rolls-Royce drove up the grand circular drive to the opulent entrance of the Gabriel Building. The driveway's extraordinary landscaping appeared to be designed with such beautiful automobiles in mind. The chauffeur stepped out, walked swiftly around, and opened the right rear door. A tall, distinguished-looking black man emerged, spoke briefly to his chauffeur, turned, and walked the fifty feet or so along the wide landscaped walk to one of the revolving doors and into the interior of the building.

Three young executives were about halfway through the grand lobby as Peter approached. He noticed them nudge each other simultaneously as they clearly recognized him as one of the world's movers and shakers. He nodded politely as they passed.

Standing a little over six feet tall, with a lean, fit-looking body, Peter Joshua moved in long, graceful and confident strides. Although he was in his late fifties, only the graying at his temples gave any clue as to his age. Time spent at an expensive haberdashery wasn't wasted. His dark gray pinstriped suit was tailored to perfection and his black alligator belt was a perfect match for his outrageously priced shoes. His ties were always on the cutting edge of style.

As it was the beginning of the lunch hour, most of the elevators were emptying into the lobby, and few people were going up. Peter walked right into the closest one. Vance just happened to be right behind, and followed him in.

"Good morning, Mr. Joshua," Vance greeted Peter.

"Ah, good morning, Mr. Youngblood. Nice to see you again."

"Thank you, sir."

"That store any good?" Peter said as the doors slid shut.

"Sir?" Vance responded as he pushed # 17 for himself and #33 for Peter.

Peter gestured toward the shopping bag Vance held in his left hand. The bag bore the name of the high-end men's store that was located in the building's lobby.

"Oh, yes sir, they have a good selection of ties, belts, and shoes. Haven't bothered to look at their suits. Haven't got an off-the-rack body."

"I'd say not," Peter laughed, "but it looks to me like you have yourself a mighty fine tailor. That's a nice suit."

"Thank you, sir." Vance paused for a second before continuing, "I assume you're here for the meeting?"

"I am."

There was a momentary pause in the conversation before Peter spoke. "You know I always look forward to these meetings. There is a strong underlying energy, almost palpable. Definitely addictive."

"An underlying energy seems to go hand in hand with whatever Alex is involved in," Vance remarked.

"Indeed," agreed Peter.

At the same time, somewhere down in the bowels of the parking garage, an old VW bus was creeping around. Professor Adam Texley was mumbling to himself as he searched for a parking space. The old bus suddenly backfired three times in rapid succession. "Piece of shit," he yelled as he banged the steering wheel with the palm of his hand, causing the cigarette hanging from the left side of his mouth to drop its ashes on his old cardigan sweater.

Peter Joshua and Professor Texley represented opposite ends of the economic scale and were 180 degrees off on social philosophy. Both men, however, were there to attend the same meeting.

Douglas Ito was first to step off the elevator on the executive floor. Alex was there to greet him.

"A pleasure to see you again, Ito-san." Alex smiled and bowed.

Ito smiled broadly and returned the bow as he took Alex's hand and shook it vigorously. "How are you, my friend?"

Alex liked Ito immensely, but he had trouble calling him by his given name, Douglas. The man didn't look like a Douglas. He looked exactly like what he was, a middle-aged Japanese businessman. Douglas was short in stature and impeccably dressed. His moderately cropped hair was graying and his heavy eyebrows reminded Alex of the cartoon character Yosemite Sam. Douglas Ito was in charge of Gabriel International's far-east operations.

The rest of the group arrived within ten minutes of each other. After a few minutes of greeting and engaging in informal small talk, everyone began taking their seats around the board table. Lunch would be served at 12:00 sharp. All, except Alex, would have beer or wine with lunch; only Peter Joshua would be served hard liquor, a martini. As always, the formal meeting would begin precisely at 1:00 p.m.

Of the three members of Alex's Consortium who were not employees of Gabriel Industries, Adam Texley was politically furthest to the left. Adam headed up the Sociology Department at the University of California, Irvine. That was where Alex first met the professor. Alex had attended a symposium held at the University entitled, "The Poor Among the Rich; an American Crisis." Professor Texley was the featured speaker. Although Alex disagreed with many of the conclusions Adam presented that day, he was impressed with Adam's knowledge and passion on the subject. Alex went out of his way to introduce himself to the professor that evening, and they maintained contact over the years. When Alex decided to put together a group of intellectuals to study the major problems of the world, Adam was the second one he called; Peter Joshua was first. It was Adam, at that point, who introduced Alex to Joan Hocket.

Joan Hocket was the Director of Social Services for the State of California. She remained left of center on most subjects, but when it came to today's subject, population control, she had, over the years, swung far to the right. Joan started her social services career as an extremely liberal Berkeley graduate some fifteen years before, setting out to right the multitude of wrongs that society was imposing on the less fortunate minority groups. She worked her way up from being a social worker in the barrios of East LA, and had seen it all.

The Consortium consisted of six people: three employees of Gabriel Industries, including Alex, Jason, and Douglas Ito. The three from outside the company were invited to join this group, not only because of their intellect, but also because of their diverse points of view. Each in the group was more than willing to defend their position and ideology aggressively. Alex respected them for their opinions, their thought processes, and their ability to express themselves.

Peter Joshua was this small group's staunch conservative. Peter had never been known to drift, on any subject, even slightly toward center. He considered Professor Texley a full-blown socialist. Alex assumed the truth, on almost any subject, lay somewhere between Peter's and Adam's points of view. Peter possessed, Alex believed, one of the brightest business minds on the planet. Peter's picture had appeared on the cover of *Business Week* and similar magazines countless times over the years. In his first life, Alex followed Peter's career closely and invested heavily in any enterprise with Peter's involvement. He never regretted it. Now, in his second life, he did the same. The only difference was that now he and Peter were friends.

This small group had been meeting for over two years, and at the end of each meeting, the subject for "debate" was picked for the following meeting. There were six major topics: world population, economics, crime and punishment, depletion of natural resources, world health, and world politics. Today's subject, world population, was the single most emotional topic, and the subject with the most diverse opinions.

12:10 p.m.

"As you recall," Alex began after all had been served their lunch, "we had Mr. Robert Parkerson, Chairman of the United Nations Commission on World Hunger and Disease, speak to us the last time we had a meeting concerning today's subject. At that time, we gained a great deal of insight and information on the state of the world's population, hunger, and disease. I assume that knowledge will help considerably with today's discussion."

"Quite enlightening," offered Douglas Ito.

"Indeed, I gained a great deal of insight and information on the state of the world's most miserable… a real eye opener," added Peter.

"I would bet, Mr. Joshua, you haven't lost much sleep over that startling information," Adam joined in.

Completely undaunted, Peter turned his attention to Adam Texley. "No, Professor, not a second. It sure wouldn't have helped those poor wretches if I had."

Alex and Jason looked at each other, sharing the thought that all was normal.

"So, Peter," Adam went on, "are you still advocating sterilizing anybody who has a chance of passing on serious genetic defects?" Adam stuffed another fork of salad into his mouth.

Alex smiled to himself. He spotted Adam's effort to feign nearly complete indifference to Peter's opinion. *Adam is anxious to continue the ongoing debate*, Alex thought, *but he sure doesn't want to give that impression*.

"You've got it wrong, Adam, my friend," Peter smiled graciously. "I favor mandatory sterilization of anybody who could pass on *any* genetic defect." He picked up his martini, still smiling. "A person has to be somewhat reasonable, of course. I wouldn't consider poor eyesight, short stature, or baldness genetic flaws that should be bred out." Peter let that statement confound Adam for a brief moment before looking up at Adam's thinning hair and continuing. "At least not for a century or so, anyway." Peter took a sip of his martini and sat the glass down. There was just a trace of a smile on his face.

"For a century or so? How kind of you," Adam responded in a condescending voice as he unconsciously rubbed his bald spot.

Peter does enjoy pulling Adam's chain. Alex smiled to himself.

Joan Hocket cleared her throat. "If this world is to survive, Adam, it better start acting like it wants to survive."

"Meaning what?"

"Simply that we, in the social services field, have a unique view of the subject at hand."

"It's a view," Adam cut in, "I don't know how unique, or for that matter, how it might qualify you as an expert on genetic defects."

"On genetic defects, little. On the economic and emotional impact of such defects on families and government, I know a great deal, Professor. God knows it's hard enough for these poor families to get along in the best of circumstances -- adding a seriously handicapped child makes it nearly impossible for a family to pull themselves out of poverty."

"I would think so," added Peter.

"Would it satisfy you two if only the people who cannot afford to care for their imperfect progeny be sterilized?" Adam asked snidely.

"You know better than that, Dr. Texley," Joan came back, none too pleasantly.

"A couple of problems with that, if I may," Peter remarked as he signaled to the waiter to replenish his martini. "One, it doesn't eliminate the lifelong pain and suffering the affected child will have to go through and two, although this child or maybe children, may not be a burden on the taxpayer, their offspring or some future generation surely will be."

"I guarantee it," said Joan.

A good point, thought Alex. He knew this issue burned in Joan's soul. She, as a young woman, had preached long and hard for the other side of this issue for the first few years after college, but the futility of it, the pain and suffering that beliefs such as Adam's caused, and the massive economic drain on the system, finally and totally changed her opinion.

"People have the right to have children, God damn it, you two. Reproduction is probably the single strongest instinct in all animals. To take that away would be imposing the cruelest of sanctions."

"I disagree with your basic premise here, Adam," Jason came into the fray. "I believe sex is the second strongest instinct, after survival, and propagation is simply a byproduct."

"Hear, hear!" Peter raised his glass, toasting that thought.

"Animals born with any defects rarely survive, making it impossible to pass those defects on to future generations," Joan declared.

"Wild animals don't propagate more offspring than their environment will support," added Jason.

"The destructive path the world is on can be attributed to one primary cause: out-of-control population growth," Douglas declared. "Wars, hunger, famine, disease, deforestation, unemployment, and crime can be attributed directly or indirectly to overpopulation."

"Even more important," offered Jason, "is the depletion of the world's resources. The planet can survive wars, crime, hunger, and disease, etc. -- and has been doing so for millennia. These things only affect, for the most part, the unfortunate people involved. But it cannot survive permanent pollution of its air, water, and land. It cannot survive the depletion of its forests, oil reserves, and minerals indefinitely."

"Quite frankly, Adam," injected Peter, "I truly believe it is you who has no heart. It's those of your ilk who seem to be willing to let the population explosion slowly destroy the world like a metastasized cancer." Peter paused long enough to motion to the waiter in attendance to bring him yet another martini. "People who believe as you do don't have the balls, or the compassion, to make the tough decisions."

The group sat silent for a moment, each with their own thought.

"Just who do you think should be in charge of deciding who

does and doesn't get to have children?" Adam asked caustically. "Just who gets to play God?"

4:41 p.m.

It was getting late in the afternoon and the top of the board table was cluttered with papers and files. The six around it were starting to look a little tired. Alex had the floor.

"Sheer numbers are the first consideration," stated Alex. "A world-body can bring together a group of the finest minds in sociology, anthropology, humanities, agriculture, geology, and many other fields to provide basic guidelines to oversee the development of individual nation's programs."

"Each country's needs differ, so each country needs to modify the basic guidelines to fit its circumstances," added Jason. "Countries such as China, India and most of the third-world nations, have a far greater need for farmers, ranchers, fishermen, and food processors to feed their vast populations than do industrial nations."

"They sure don't need many stockbrokers, bankers, or rocket scientists," said Peter.

"Third-world countries with huge populations are the ones who would use the most drastic means to control population in order to greatly reduce their numbers," offered Jason.

"If I might slip in a thought or two here," said Alex. "Public opinion, at this time in history, precludes any chance, in the free world, of imposing mandatory sterilization on almost anyone, no matter how justified. You won't find a single politician willing to take a stand on such a controversial subject, no matter what their personal beliefs."

"May I offer an idea?" asked Ito.

"You have the floor," said Alex.

"Supposing you could convince the press in each country to print periodically, say monthly, a... 'Doomsday' chart."

" 'Doomsday' chart?" asked Joan.

"Yes! As an example, the chart shows, based on scientific facts, assumptions, and extrapolations, how many years, months, and days their country has to survive until starvation, depletion of natural resources, war, or disease completely destroys them, or something like that."

There was silence for a few seconds before Jason declared, "That's an excellent idea."

"Perfect! I'll drink to that," said Peter and raised his glass.

"Absolutely!" said Joan.

"Thank you, Ito-san," said Alex as he bowed his head slightly.

Adam's silence stood out. Everyone turned to look at the one normally dissenting vote. What's he going to say this time?

Adam looked at the other five faces, then down at his hands on the table. After a moment, he looked up again. "I agree, it's a good idea!"

The others sat stunned.

"No shit?" said Peter as he pushed his chair back, walked over to Adam and extended his hand. Adam reluctantly took it.

"I never thought I'd see the day," said Joan as she fanned her face with her hand.

"We might think about starting a mild media campaign to warm the world up to the possibility of a need for mandatory sterilization," Jason suggested. "Maybe, to start with, as an adjunct to the Doomsday chart."

"To do that will take the cooperation of a great deal of the media, Mr. Gould," suggested Joan.

Adam leaned back in his chair, his face held a slight smirk, "Yeah, well, good luck with that."

"This is true," agreed Douglas. "The only way it could be done is if owners and editors of the papers, television, and radio could be convinced."

Alex smiled, "What needs to be done, and has been done to a great extent, is getting control of the liberal media -- or, at the least, the major and most respected of the liberal press."

"I'm sorry, Alex, but did I hear you say you are getting control of the liberal press?" asked Peter as he sat up straighter.

Alex looked over at Jason, then back to Peter. "As you may know, Global Media is a division of Gabriel Industries, but what you may not realize is the extent of Global's holdings. We happen to have the chief-in-charge of that organization here with us today. Jason, would you give us a rundown on how many newspapers, radio, and television stations Global presently owns outright, or in which it has a controlling interest?"

Jason pulled a file off the bottom of a stack and opened it. "As of yesterday, Global owns outright, 182 newspapers worldwide, and controlling interest in 36 others. These papers have a combined readership approaching one billion. Approximately a third of our papers are in the US."

There was an audible gasp from Adam and Joan. The normally unshakable Peter sat stunned for a moment before raising his now empty martini glass, "Hear, hear!"

Douglas Ito sat motionless and stared at Jason. His face was an unreadable mask.

Jason smiled a bit. "To continue, we have 205 radio stations, all with news-oriented programming. Most of these are outside the US. Here we have 58 TV stations."

"Excuse me," said Adam, "I don't believe the FCC rules would allow any one entity to control that many newspapers, to say nothing of the TV and radio stations."

"That's correct, Adam," answered Jason. "But we found a way around that hurdle."

"I'll bet you did," said Peter.

"So you've broken FCC regulations?" asked Adam.

"We've bent their spirit a little, I have to admit, but haven't broken any."

"My Lord!" said Joan.

"In addition, we own or have controlling interest in twenty-three news magazines world- wide."

"You're talking about controlling and manipulating the fourth estate?" The alarm was apparent on Adam's face. He obviously was having trouble imagining such power. He looked toward the head of the table, at the person in command of this unbelievable influence. "You are actually going to brainwash the citizens of the

United States into thinking your way, are you not?"

"Yes, I am!" Alex leaned forward. "Public opinion has been controlled by whoever owns the fourth estate since time began, Adam. I suggested some time ago that we change the ownership of this immense power to people who think with their heads, not their politics, their wallets, or their emotions. People who won't bend to political pressure; people who can and will plan past next week. I personally believe, as do millions of others I'm sure, it's way past time to 'brainwash' the citizens of the world with a new soap."

"I know you realize the power you have in your hands," said Adam. "That kind of power terrifies me."

There was another moment of silence around the table, all momentarily alone with their thoughts.

"Adam, my friend," said Alex, "you have known me for what -- three or four years now? You have been privy to my thoughts and beliefs on a variety of important subjects. Have you, in these past three years, felt in any way, that gaining or abusing power is my motivating factor? Do you in any way feel that I, or any of my associates, will abuse whatever power we have?"

Nobody at the table said anything or so much as took a sip of their beverage.

Adam sat for a moment, slowly spinning his water glass on the table before looking at Alex. "I owe you an apology. You are probably the one person in the world I would trust with such power. I know, without doubt, your motives are, for lack of a better term, honorable."

"I appreciate that statement more than you know, Adam. Thank you." Alex looked over at Jason. "Why don't you continue with your report."

"I might point out that most of Global's acquisitions have been papers with a liberal leanings," said Jason.

"Liberal? You're kidding of course!" exclaimed Joan.

"I'm not kidding," replied Jason, "and in those that lean to the conservative side, we slowly introduced a few liberal messages in order to attract some liberal readers. By the same token, we occasionally throw a conservative thought into our liberal papers. We have some conservative papers, large readership types, which we leave alone. Not much need to control papers that already agree with much of our philosophy."

"I don't understand," said Joan.

"If we begin a campaign, such as we are discussing, or any other subject that will surely infuriate the liberals, socialists, and do-gooders, we'd better conduct the battle on their turf. Liberal press, be it newspapers, TV, or radio, traditionally will be against almost anything we believe in. They obviously have been a powerful force over the past three decades. So we decided to buy the liberal presses. Just as simple as that."

"Just as simple as that?" queried Adam.

Jason smiled. "It's taken a lot of work over the years and a God-awful amount of money, but in a word, yep!"

"But the readers, viewers and listeners aren't going to buy a conservative blitzkrieg, for pity sake," said Joan. "Population control will slice into the nerves of people of all walks of life and all political views."

"It's all in the presentation, Joan," said Jason.

"I have to assume these newspapers are run by liberal editors. Reporters will also be a bit left wing. Just how in the hell are you going to persuade them to print your editorials?" asked Peter.

"We have been conducting regional seminars on a quarterly basis for the past three years for our editors, reporters and key copywriters," Jason explained. "Most of what is presented at these seminars are relatively normal subjects. We have also primed the pump with factual information, such as we discussed today. Facts on drug-addicted babies, welfare fraud, population explosions -- things we wish them to think about, but not act on. Our intent is to slowly sow the seeds of conservative thought."

"Jesus Christ," whispered Adam.

"You are quite devious, Mr. Gould. One of your honorable ancestors must have been Japanese," said Douglas, while displaying just the slightest smile.

"I've got to tell you that there have been times when we had to come down on editors and reporters to stop them from starting their own campaigns for mandatory birth control on certain segments of our society. And, of course, other sensitive subjects, on which we're not yet ready. You'd be surprised how many liberal editors and reporters are going to love to get a new directive from Global."

"When do you plan to begin this campaign, Mr. Gould?" asked Adam.

"Well, we've done all the research we can and there are just a few more ducks to put in a row. I would imagine it will be a week or two before we're ready."

The meeting continued for another hour with Jason and Alex fielding questions from the other four. All, with the exception of Adam, filed out of the office just before six. Adam hung back. He wanted to talk to Alex alone.

"So what's up, professor?" Alex asked as he walked back to his desk and sat down.

Adam plopped down in comfortable chair in front of Alex's desk. "The problem is, Alex, I'm beginning to agree with all of you on population control."

"Really?"

"Yes, God damn it! And it irks the shit out of me! That sanctimonious prick, Peter, will have bested me."

"Maybe you shouldn't think about this as a defeat, which in my opinion, it is not. You have kept hard liners such as Peter and Joan thinking and modifying their position these past two years. I do believe Peter would have summarily executed all the 'unnecessary people' two years ago." Alex gave Adam a big smile. "But now he seems content to just sterilize them."

Chapter 62

GABRIEL HEADQUARTERS
April 22, 1989
11:00 a.m.

Alex sat with his chair turned 180 degrees from his desk. Normally this would allow him to enjoy the view, but this morning he was engrossed in reviewing the minutes of the latest Consortium meeting, held two days before. The meeting was taped, and later transcribed by Carol. Carol had been Alex's secretary for fifteen years. She knew, when transcribing the minutes of any meeting, to filter out all that wasn't germane to the subject.

Crime and punishment was the subject of the last meeting, and Alex's original motivation for bringing this group of highly astute people together. His anger, distress, and subsequent depression after Teddy's murder, had a lasting effect on his life. He'd hoped the group would eventually come up with a plan to infuse some justice into the judicial system even if it meant completely changing it. However, after the first consortium meeting, some two-plus years before, it was apparent that the group wanted to branch out and discuss other major world problems. Alex smiled to himself; *they went beyond my wants in a hurry*. Alex continued to read the minutes:

> As the first order of business, Mr. Gabriel formally introduced Vance Youngblood to the group. He stated

> that Mr. Youngblood was a Vice President of Gabriel International and in charge of our National and International security. Mr. Gabriel added that, "Mr. Youngblood possesses an extraordinary ability to, as they say, cut through the bullshit."

Alex was surprised that Carol had left the last part in the transcription.

> Mr. Gould then gave a report on the progress of the population control campaign.... All but three states had already proposed legislation that would mandate sterilization for drug-addicted prostitutes. Fifteen states had taken the legislation even further, and included drug-addicted welfare mothers. All this within sixteen months from the beginning of Global Media's campaign...

We had not anticipated this kind of response, thought Alex. *Jason's management of the campaign, by all accounts, was nothing short of brilliant*. Alex smiled to himself.

> Mr. Gould further reported that the intelligence he was getting from his contacts around the world indicated that many governments would, at some time in the near future, start mirroring what the United States had begun in population control.
>
> Mr. Gould told the group that part of the unexpected success was directly attributable to Mr. Ito's "Doomsday chart." It was noted that most of the literate people in the world read the monthly Doomsday Chart religiously. The reported response was remarkable...

My friend, Douglas, was quite pleased, thought Alex.

Professor Texley brought up a danger he saw in the campaign. He stated that the campaign could get out of hand. He reminded the group that the motion of a pendulum never allows it to stop in the middle. He suggested they had better start putting the brakes on that pendulum's swing before it was impossible to stop.

All in the group agreed with Professor Texley.

Even Peter agreed with Adam. A landmark day, thought Alex.

The meeting then went on to the subject of capital punishment. Mr. Gabriel stated he specifically wanted each to express what they felt was the right length of time between conviction and execution, how many appeals should be allowed in the waiting period, and who should hear the appeals.

Mr. Ito started by asking why taxpayers, in any country, should pay twice the annual per capita income to keep a condemned person on death row, for an average of eleven years with unlimited, expensive appeals, before execution is carried out? Mr. Ito felt that six months between conviction and execution, with one appeal to the State Appellate Court, would be lenient enough.

Professor Texley stated he was against capital punishment altogether, and suggested that if the death penalty were eliminated, so would be the cost of appeals, and special care given to death row inmates.

Mr. Joshua suggested that if the guilty party was executed at dawn the day following the conviction, the cost would be even less.

> Professor Texley strongly suggested that wouldn't be much different than a lynching.

Again, Alex smiled; *Peter had no problem increasing Adam's blood pressure.*

> Mrs. Hocket felt that two years with three appeals, within the state, would be fair. She stated she had seen too many minorities railroaded by police and prosecutors, to rely on too short a time from conviction to execution.
>
> Mrs. Hocket stated that, at this time, a conviction could be appealed to the State Appellate Court, the State Supreme Court, and the US Supreme Court. If all these bodies uphold the conviction, the Governor of the state, in most cases, can take it upon himself, or herself, to commute the sentence; the will of the people be damned.
>
> Mr. Joshua said he was for a short waiting period, but he stated that the rest of the group, particularly Adam, changed his mind on carrying out the execution at dawn of the day following the conviction. He agreed that would be a bit hasty in most cases. Mr. Joshua said that he agreed with Douglas Ito; six months' delay in execution, and one appeal inside the state.

Professor Texley has gotten to Peter. Who would have thought? Alex was pleased with Peter's change of heart.

> Mr. Gabriel said that he and Jason both felt a one-year waiting period, with two appeals; none outside the state, was reasonable.
>
> Mr. Gabriel thought that if a medical reason, such as a

brain tumor, or improper medication, was proven to have caused the irrational behavior, he recommended that the person be treated, and if cured, possibly released.

Mr. Gabriel called for Vance Youngblood's opinion. (Sorry, Mr. Gabriel, I didn't filter out all that Mr. Youngblood said in the meeting. I have left in most of his dialogue, exactly as stated. I found it fascinating.)

Well! thought Alex. *She decided not to edit Vance*. Alex was aware that Carol, and most members of the consortium, hadn't heard Vance's opinion on anything.

Vance Youngblood: "Before I say anything else, I would like to thank each and every one of you for letting me sit in on your meeting today. It's been an eye-opening experience for me. Having said that, I will give you my opinion on today's subject... I believe, and have believed for many years, as all but one of you do, that there must be capital punishment. I believe the death penalty should include those who commit first-degree murder, aggravated murder, aggravated rape and child molestation where serious physical or mental damage is done, and any crime committed using a loaded firearm."

At this point, Professor Texley stated that Mr. Youngblood wasn't going to leave any bad guys alive.

"That's right. If some @#%&*$ holds up a store with a loaded firearm, it can be assumed that he plans on using it if necessary and sometimes when it's not necessary. That person is prepared to kill anyone who stands in his way. I call that premeditated murder."

Mr. Joshua thought that a good point.

Professor Texley asked, "What if they use a toy gun to hold up a store?"

Mr. Youngblood answered, "Then there is obviously no intention of killing anyone, and the perpetrator could be convicted of aggravated robbery only."

Mr. Joshua questioned Mr. Youngblood's stand on aggravated rape and child molestation.

"Why should we allow a pervert who causes great physical and mental damage to another, just to satisfy some cruel perversion he has, to serve a short sentence and be turned back into society? The damage done to innocent women and children and their loved ones by these monsters can be lifelong. It might help the victims if they knew these #$@%& would never be able to hurt anyone again."

And they thought Peter was a hawk! thought Alex. He wasn't surprised at Vance's suggestion that capital punishment be extended down to child molesters and rapists. He was quite surprised that Vance felt that much compassion, or cared that much about the victims of crime. Didn't seem to fit his personality. *The man's a lot deeper than anyone would suspect*.

Mr. Youngblood thought there should be one year between conviction and execution in most cases, with a maximum of two appeals. He said he further believed that the appeals should be limited to the State Appellate and the State Supreme Courts, and should never go to the Federal Supreme Court.

Mr. Youngblood said, "I feel strongly that the governor of a state should have absolutely no authority to grant pardons, or commute any sentence. Allowing governors that privilege can and does circumvent myriad laws. A man can be convicted by a jury of his peers, based on the laws of the land, only to have the conviction overturned by a governor, based on his personal beliefs. And that, I submit, is bull$@#%."

Mr. Youngblood continued. "How would these liberals feel if an @#%&*# was convicted of first-degree murder, by a jury of his peers, and given a life sentence, just to have the governor of the state issue an order to execute the son of a bitch at dawn the next day. If they have the right to go against the people's wishes and the law one way, why not the other?"

Mr. Joshua thought that was another good point.

Professor Texley asked what Mr. Youngblood thought about a man who has snapped, maybe has a brain tumor, a nervous breakdown, a horrible childhood, or something that could be treated and cured.

Mr. Youngblood answered, "I don't personally give a $#@% anymore why someone commits murder and causes mayhem. I'm tired of the legal system coming up with endless excuses for murder, assault, rape, and all other offenses to society. Bull$#@%! If a man kills another man, other than in self-defense or in defense of another, he himself should be killed. I don't give a $#@% about his childhood problems. I don't give a $#@% about his environment. I don't give a $#@% about his race, creed, or color. What I do give a $#@% about is getting back to a society where a person can walk down a street in their or anybody else's neighborhood without fear of being accosted in any way, shape, or form."

> Mr. Joshua suggested that Mr. Youngblood didn't have to soft soap his opinion. "We can take it."

At that point Alex knew Vance had just become a permanent member of the Consortium.

May 18, 1989

"Attorneys!" Vance grumbled as he replaced the receiver. "Why in the hell do they spend all their time telling you why you can't do something rather than finding ways you can?"

"Nature of the beast; covering their asses," suggested Alex as he looked across Vance's slightly cluttered desk.

"I feel like I've just stuck my head in a pencil sharpener." Vance rubbed his temples.

"One of ours?"

"No, actually, it's one of Peter Joshua's. I'd fire the negative son of a bitch if he worked for us." Vance gave a twisted little smile. "So what's up?"

"I'd like to get your input on something."

"Shoot."

"I'm thinking about starting a database of bad guys."

"Bad guys?"

"Yeah, murderers, rapists, child molesters, assholes like that."

"Why would you want to do that?"

"It's concerned me for quite a while that nobody keeps track of bad guys."

Vance looked confused. "Well, I have to assume most of those pieces of shit are in prison."

"Actually, I think the opposite. Most have either been released outright or are on parole. Only the recently convicted or lifers are in prison. And then I'll bet a good percentage of them are released every year."

"Okay, good point," conceded Vance. "Why would you want to keep track of what would be tens of thousands of the country's slimiest people?"

"Not just this country's, but the world's worst."

"Jesus, boss! I don't have to tell you that would be a monumental project."

"Maybe not so bad. We could, as an example, form an international organization for the express purpose of aiding law enforcement agencies worldwide."

"Oh, no problem," declared Vance, "I'm sure just about every country will jump at such an opportunity. We'll get each nation's underworked law enforcement system to feed information to a central data bank with basic information on every conviction, release, execution, or whatever in their country."

"That was sarcasm, right?"

Vance looked at Alex for a moment. "Please tell me you're not putting me in charge of this... new idea."

"Oh, hell no! You've got enough on your plate. I would like you to think about finding some bright go-getter who's maybe retired from the CIA or FBI; someone like that."

Vance sat for a moment, looking directly at Alex. "You still haven't told me why."

"I...I really don't have a specific reason. It's just something I feel should be done," replied Alex. "Not much of an answer, I know, but I feel quite strongly about it."

"You're the boss."

Chapter 63

GABRIEL HOME
June 1, 1989
1:35 p.m.

"I checked earlier, you're forgetting the kitchen sink." Jennifer was shaking her head as she looked at the three large suitcases being loaded into the limo by the Gabriels' chauffeur/bodyguard.

"Oh -- you're right; I'll have your dad yank it out for me." Marian reached over and gently pinched Jennifer on the cheek.

Norman came walking out through the garage door carrying a medium-sized bag. "Okay, that's it."

"What, you couldn't get all your stuff in the big bags?"

"I didn't get any of my stuff in the big bags."

Marian smiled as she stood aside to let Norman hand his bag to the chauffeur.

Norman and Marian were about to leave on their semi-annual vacation. This time it was a return trip to Turkey and Greece with an added week in Egypt. They hadn't been to Egypt before and were looking forward to seeing the marvelous sights. Egypt was last on the schedule. Marian was looking forward to it more that Norman. Chuck had to sit through hours of pre-Gabriel vacation briefing from Norman covering every possible contingency at Norman Research. Information, in many cases, he himself had given to Norman.

"You mind if I ride along?" asked Alex as he walked up from the pool area.

"Hey, glad to have you along, Son," Norman replied.

"You've obviously got nothing better to do, so come on," added Marian. She looked pensive for a moment. "I don't remember ever having said anything like that to you before. How odd."

"Yeah, what's up, Bro?" asked Jennifer.

Alex had been in an odd, brooding mood for days. He couldn't seem to stay focused on anything. He headed out to his rock that morning, but changed his mind just as he started to sit down. His rock was a place to meditate, to make plans, a place to put the pieces together, but for the past few days, he had no cohesive thoughts. He couldn't concentrate on anything. He walked back up the beach to the stairs and up to the patio. There he wandered aimlessly from one end of the pool to the other for nearly two hours, sitting occasionally just to jump up a few seconds later and repeat the process. Wasting time like this was completely foreign to his character.

Marian got in the back seat followed by Alex. He climbed in and sat on his mother's left. Norman entered from the other side and sat on her right. Jennifer pulled down one of the jump seats and sat facing the other three. The chauffeur closed the doors, slipped behind the wheel, and started the car.

As their limo pulled out of the driveway, the ever-present dark sedan pulled in behind. One of the occupants would be on the plane with the Gabriels. In addition, each time they arrived in another country, two additional local bodyguards would join them for added security and serve as guides during their stay. Marian had objected over the years, but to no avail. There was too much at stake to have lax security.

"To what do we owe the honor of your company today?" asked Norman. Alex had, in the past, just given his 'bon voyage' at home or called from wherever he was at the time.

Alex looked at his father for a moment. "Just a slow day, I guess."

Alex reached over, took his mother's hand and held it tightly.

"You're in a strange mood, sweetheart," said Marian smiling slightly, while looking deeply into her son's eyes, possibly looking for some clue to his unusual behavior.

"I know, I know, but I can't seem to shake it. I feel like someone's trying to sneak up behind me and whack me one. Probably something I ate," he smiled weakly.

"Well, if you get to feeling sick, go see a doctor," Norman advised.

"That might be a good idea," agreed Marian.

"Don't suppose I could talk you out of going on this trip, could I?" Alex blurted out.

"Why, Son?"

"Yeah, what's up, Alex?"

"Don't know."

Alex couldn't explain why he was antsy because he didn't know himself. He just knew that he had a foreboding he couldn't shake.

They rode quietly for a mile or two before Marian stated, "If you really feel we shouldn't go on this trip, maybe we shouldn't."

Alex sat silent for a few seconds. "I don't know why I feel anxious. It might not, and probably doesn't, have anything to do with your trip. It's just a strange feeling I have."

"It's probably nothing but a chemical imbalance," suggested Norman.

"Could be," responded Alex. "I guess you'd better go ahead and have fun in the sun and sand."

"If you're sure," said Marian.

"Not sure, but I don't have a concrete reason to call off your vacation."

"Okay, we'll go. But if anything starts to go wrong or we suspect anything, we'll come straight home." Marian smiled then started talking about the trip. She was excited about returning to Greece and Turkey.

In another ten minutes, they pulled into the Orange County Airport via the private aviation entrance. At one time, the John Wayne Airport had been the busiest general aviation airport in the country. After pulling into the hangar housing the Gabriel Industries Boeing 727C, the chauffeur went around, opened the door, and helped everyone out. He then went to the rear of the limo and opened the trunk.

Alex saw one of the bodyguards exit from the passenger side of the sedan, lean over, and say something to the driver, then walk over and take up a position at the rear of the limo. He gave Alex a short nod. This was one of Vance's handpicked people. Jake had served with Vance in the SEALs and other than Vance himself, this was the man you'd want protecting your loved ones. The sight of Jake with his crew-cut hair, and chiseled face and body, eased some of Alex's feelings of dread. This man looked tough to the core.

"Give me a second." Alex walked to the back of the limo.

"Jake, walk with me, please."

"Yes, sir."

The two walked toward the rear of the aircraft. "Jake, I have an uneasy feeling about this trip my folks are taking."

"Yes, sir."

"I doubt I need to say anything to you about being on your guard but, nonetheless, that's what I'm saying."

"May I speak frankly, sir?"

"Of course."

"I think the world of your folks, Mr. Gabriel. They're two of the finest people I've ever met." Jake's expression hardened. "So if any dumb sumbitch makes any sort of move on Mr. or Mrs., I'll fuck 'em up so bad their old pediatricians will feel it."

"Those are the words I wanted to hear, Jake." Alex stuck out his hand. "Thank you."

"No sweat, sir." Jake took the offered hand and shook it.

They returned to the foot of the stairs where Marian, Norman, and Jennifer waited.

"Well Son, looks like we're outta here."

"Looks like it."

Jake headed up the stairs and entered the plane.

"Be sure to check in with Chuck once in a while, Alex. Lot going on in the labs."

"Chuck can handle it, Pop, but I'll check in with him at least once a week anyway."

"Thanks, Son -- it just makes me nervous to be away."

"We hadn't noticed," muttered Marian.

Norm gave Alex a hug and pat on the back, and started to turn to do the same with Jennifer, but Alex held on to him and whispered in his ear, "Please be extra careful this trip, Pop."

Norm pulled away from Alex with wrinkled brow. "Sure, Son, we'll be careful."

Marian missed none of this. She reached up and wrapped her arms around her son's neck, looking him right in the eye. "I've never seen you so anxious before. Why don't you go see a doctor? Your dad could be right, it could be a chemical imbalance."

"I might just do that. I don't want to keep getting these adrenaline rushes, they're making me kinda edgy."

"Kinda?" remarked Jennifer.

Alex gave his mother a final hug. "Love you, Mom. Have a great trip."

Norman and Marian hugged Jennifer, turned, and headed up the stairs. They stopped at the top and waved to their children.

"We expect postcards just about every day," said Jennifer. "Bon voyage!"

"Call if you run out of money -- ha, ha!" called Alex. "Love you!" He wore a smile he didn't feel.

Chapter 64

GABRIEL HEADQUARTERS
June 11, 1989
8:00 a.m.

The anxious feeling started to ease up after getting calls from his parents from almost every town on their itinerary. The first calls came from various locations in Greece; then, in a week or so, from Turkey. The call early this morning was from the airport in Ankara, the capitol of Turkey. They were just about to board the plane and head to Egypt.

"How about buying your poor old uncle some breakfast and letting him in on the goings-on around here?"

"Uncle Walt!" Alex jumped up and walked rapidly around his desk to greet his uncle before Walt could get halfway across the office.

"God, it's great to see you," said Alex as he gave his uncle a big hug.

"Same here, son," smiled Walt. "I would imagine you have things pretty screwed up around here without my guidance."

"As a matter of fact, we had a bunch of screw-ups for a while but Jason, God bless him, managed to straighten most of them out." Alex hadn't seen Walt for over a month, since Colleen's birthday party. The sight of his uncle in his office was calming to Alex.

"So Jason's big feet filled my shoes, did they?" Walt looked into Alex's eyes. He'd gotten a call from Marian early that morning asking if he would drop in on Alex and check him out. He evidently saw little that would cause the concern Marian expressed on the phone.

"Jason wears a size fourteen, I believe, but that still leaves some gaps at the toes, I'm afraid."

"Jason's a good man. I'm glad you have him. Otherwise, I might have to come back to work and, I gotta tell ya, I like retirement. I like spending a lot of time with my wonderful wife, your gorgeous Aunt Colleen."

"Who the hell wouldn't?" Alex smiled. "Come on over and sit down for a minute. I've got a couple of things to finish up and then we'll head up the coast and I'll buy you breakfast."

"You've got a deal."

Forty-five minutes later, the two were sitting by a window overlooking the Pacific Ocean, sipping coffee. It was a beautiful morning. For the first time in weeks, the feeling of dread was completely gone from Alex's mind. Outside in a dark sedan sat one of Alex's security guards. His partner sat in the coffee shop not twenty feet from Alex and Walt. Alex was so used to having tight security around him, he actually gave it no notice at all. He and Walt ordered breakfast and were deep in conversation over the workings of Gabriel Industries.

"So Alex, tell me, what are we worth these days? I've been out of the loop for nearly three years, believe it or not, so I wouldn't have a clue anymore."

Nobody else would ask such a question -- and if they asked, they wouldn't get an answer. But this was his Uncle Walt. There is nothing he couldn't or shouldn't know.

"Not sure I have a solid clue myself." Alex briefly looked around the room. "I suspect it's approaching a magic number," he said quietly, and then with a slight smile, took a sip of coffee.

Walt stared at his nephew for a few seconds, his expression not changing a bit. "Jesus!" he muttered.

"Refills on that coffee?" the waitress asked as she walked up with a pot of coffee in each hand.

"Sure!" both Gabriels answered at once.

"Here you go; enjoy." With that, she turned and headed back to the kitchen.

"Say, I'll bet you'd like to see a picture of my pretty daughter, your young cousin, Alexandra."

"You bet I would! Happen to have any with you?"

"Oh, a couple I guess." Walt's face held a warm smile as he reached into the breast pocket of his jacket. "She's definitely a teenager."

"That just doesn't seem possible." Alex was reflective for a moment. "Thirteen?"

"Yep!" Walt laid five pictures on the table in front of Alex.

"Thank God, she looks like her mother," Alex remarked. In fact she was the spitting image of Colleen with the exception of her eyes; they were the vivid Gabriel blue, not the emerald green of Colleen's. "That hair is still something, isn't it?"

"Yeah, Jesus. Sometimes when she comes bouncing into the kitchen in the morning, she still scares the shit out of me!" smiled Walt as he picked up the pictures. "She seems to love that mop, though."

9:35 a.m.

Walt and Alex had just gotten off the elevator and were heading toward Alex's office when Jason intercepted them.

Walt extended his hand, "Jason, damned nice to see y..."

Jason cut Walt off, "Sorry Walt, we need to go into Alex's office, now!"

The color drained from Alex's face. He uttered no sound but looked pleadingly at his friend.

"Let's go in your office, Alex."

Alex felt as if he were walking in glue. It seemed to take several minutes to get into his office. Once inside, Jason closed the door and turned to face Alex.

"Alex, I don't know how to tell you this, but the State Department called just a few minutes ago." Jason paused a brief moment. "Jesus, Alex, your parents' plane was hijacked this morning at the Ankara airport in Turkey."

"*Oh my God*!" exclaimed Walt.

"First unconfirmed reports are that they are heading to Iran," Jason added. "Don't know any more than that."

Alex's heart rate leaped; his knees started to go rubbery. This was it. This was what he had been dreading. He started pawing the air with his left hand, looking for something to hold on to. He felt he was falling.

After Alex was helped to his chair, he gestured to Walt and Jason to let him sit without interruption. He sat for a full five minutes with his forehead resting in the palms of his hands, his elbows on the desk. He abruptly spun in his chair and looked out over the Pacific. He sat quietly for another couple of minutes and then turned back around. "Okay, let's get to work!"

"Yes, sir," said Jason; relief clear on his face.

"What can I do?" asked Walt.

Alex held up his index finger, then reached over and pushed the intercom button. "Carol, get Vance; I want him here yesterday."

"Yes, sir," her voice came back.

"And Carol, tell him my parents' plane was hijacked this morning at the Ankara airport in Turkey with the possible destination being Iran. We know nothing more than that."

"Oh no!"

"Also get a hold of Jennifer and Colleen and have them join me in this office."

"Should I tell them anything?"

"I'll call them," said Jason.

"Never mind, Jason will call them."

"Yes, sir."

"Next, Carol, put in a call to the President."

"Sir?"

"You heard me right!"

"Yes, sir."

Alex released the button. "Walt, get in contact with the American Embassies in Iran and Turkey. Find out what you can. How we should proceed on that front -- shit like that."

"I'm on it!"

"Jason, I would like you to make contact with all our business associates in the Middle East, concentrating on Iran and Turkey. Tell them we want to know everything they can possibly find out about these assholes. What they want, where they live, who their relatives are, where they bank, who they're attached to, everything."

"Offices will be closed. Probably 7:00 or 8:00 p.m. over there."

"You'll probably find them at home."

"No problem."

"Mr. Gabriel?" Carol's voice came over the intercom.

Alex reached over and pushed the intercom button. "Yes, Carol."

"The President's secretary is on line three."

Alex pushed the flashing button on his phone. "This is Alex Gabriel."

"Mr. Gabriel, this is Shirley Rosendahl, the President's secretary."

"Yes, Mrs. Rosendahl, may I speak to the President please?"

"The President has asked me to convey to you that he is presently in a meeting with the Secretary of State, Secretary of Defense, and the CIA chief. He said they are on top of the situation and he will personally call you at the conclusion of the meeting."

"Thank you, Mrs. Rosendahl."

"Mr. Gabriel?"

"Yes."

"On a personal note, I just want to tell you that I have you and your family in my prayers."

"I appreciate that, Mrs. Rosendahl, thank you. I'll be waiting for the President's call." Alex hung up.

Carol came back on the intercom. "Mr. Youngblood is on his way into the office, sir. Said to tell you he's getting a hold of, and I quote, 'every fucking contact he has on the face of the planet.'"

Within forty-five minutes, Jennifer and Colleen came rushing into the office. Colleen had a drawn expression but she was doing better than the clearly terrified Jennifer.

"What's happening, Alex?" Jennifer cried as soon as she came into the office.

Alex walked over and put his arms around Jennifer. "Nothing yet."

"Ah shit, Alex, what are we going to do?" She pulled back; her eyes were starting to look like they did the night that she and Teddy were attacked.

"We'll get them back, Sis. We'll do whatever is necessary."

"You knew, you knew!" She grabbed and hugged her brother. "Why didn't we listen to you?"

"I should have been more insistent. I wasn't sure...just wasn't sure." He squeezed his sister harder.

Jennifer started shooting questions, rapid-fire, at Alex.

"Whoa, Sis. I can't answer anything right now; we have no intelligence at all at this point."

Colleen went to Walt and gave him a long hug. "How you doin', sweetheart?"

"Too busy to think much about it right now, thank God."

"If we're going to get in your way, we'll be out of here right now."

"I'm staying, Alex," declared Jennifer.

"You stay as long as you wish, Sis." Alex held his sister out at arm's length. "We'll get through this, Jennifer."

Jennifer knew her brother, of all the people in the world, was the most capable, had the most resources, and would do everything humanly possible to get their parents back. She knew he and Vance would not overlook any possibility. This gave her great comfort, but she still was terrified of the possibilities.

She and Colleen found the quietest part of the office, dragged over a couple of board chairs and sat. "Don't forget you have a couple of 'go-fers' here if you need us."

At 11:15 a.m., the President called Alex as promised. The heads of the United States Government, as it turned out, knew little more than Alex already knew. The President did confirm that it was indeed Iranians who were behind the highjack. The highjacking occurred at approximately 5:00 p.m. Ankara time, 7:00 a.m. Pacific time. The Gabriel aircraft headed east-southeast to the Iranian border where it dropped below radar, making it impossible to tell where it might have landed. The President promised to keep Alex informed as new intelligence was gathered. Alex asked for and got the President's agreement to provide Alex with a Middle East specialist and upper-echelon honcho from the State Department.

June 12, 1989
8:35 a.m.

Little, if any, sleep was gotten by anyone that night. Alex, Walt, Jason, and Vance made contact with everybody they could think of who might be of the slightest help in the hours following the news of the hijack. Alex ordered the Executive Club be opened and manned to supply food and drink on a twenty-four hour basis. Just before midnight, Jennifer and Colleen left with the proviso that they would return early the next morning. They insisted on being called if anything happened while they were out of the office.

Jennifer and Colleen returned to the office at 9:10 the next morning and after being briefed, returned to their chairs at the far side of the office.

"Two gentlemen are here to see you, Mr. Gabriel."

Alex reached over and pushed the button. "Send them in, please."

Within seconds, a tall, fit-looking man in his early thirties with curly brown hair and a rather small, pug Irish nose walked through the door, followed closely by what looked to be an accountant. This smaller man was in his fifties, slight of build, sporting wire-rimmed glasses, a light gray slightly wrinkled suit and a maroon bow tie. The two stopped for a moment, looked quickly around the office, and then proceeded directly to the board table where Alex, Walt, and Jason were standing to greet them.

"Hello, I'm Sean Greenwood, with the CIA," said the younger man as he held out his hand to Alex.

"Stanley Pierce, assistant to the Secretary of State." He held out his hand.

"Mr. Greenwood, Mr. Pierce, thank you for coming. We need all the help we can get." Alex shook both hands in turn.

"Please meet Walt Gabriel and Jason Gould," Alex introduced the two. They shook hands in turn.

"You got here in a short time," said Walt.

"Happened to be in the neighborhood, as they say," replied Sean Greenwood.

Alex looked at Pierce.

"In the neighborhood, also, as a matter of fact. Met Mr. Greenwood, just seconds ago, in your reception area."

"Might I ask what your specialty is, Mr. Greenwood?" asked Jason.

"Middle East, sir."

"I would imagine that would be a tough area to specialize in," remarked Walt.

"Nearly impossible, as a matter of fact. Nothing seems to remain the same over there for more than a day or two," Sean smiled.

"And you, Mr. Pierce?"

"I'm here at the bidding of the Secretary, sir. I'll act as his liaison."

"Please be seated, gentlemen," said Alex.

There was a brief, polite knock on the door as Vance walked into Alex's office; right behind him was another man. The new man had similar physical proportions as Vance but on a smaller scale. He appeared to be about five years older, a little shorter, and was as bald as a tank helmet. His heavy, nearly white eyebrows all but covered his alert, deep-set, steel-gray eyes. He, with Vance in the lead, walked directly to the board table. Vance briefly looked at Greenwood and Pierce, then back to Alex.

"Vance, this is Sean Greenwood with the CIA, specializing in the Middle East." Alex nodded toward Greenwood. "And Stanley Pierce, an assistant to the Secretary of State."

The three shook hands and Vance set a folder on the table in front of Alex. "I would like to introduce everyone to George Jiepens. His friends call him 'Jeep.' Jeep and I served in the SEALs together. He has spent the past ten years of his tour in the Persian Gulf area, retiring last year. He now lives in Long Beach. There are few people in the world who know more about the Middle East than Jeep. I called him to help."

"You're most welcome, Jeep," said Alex.

"Thank you, sir," Jeep answered in a deep baritone voice.

Alex, Walt, and Jason shook hands with Jeep, while Pierce just nodded and acknowledged them across the expanse of the table. Sean Greenwood got up and walked around the table to shake hands with Vance and Jeep.

"Nice to see you again, Sean," Jeep smiled. "Been about four years, I believe."

"Closer to five," replied Sean with a smile. "You're looking damn fit for a retiree."

"I've been staying active."

"Why don't we get this meeting going," said Alex.

The six sat, Vance on Alex's left and Jeep on Vance's left. Greenwood and Pierce sat across the table.

"Vance, why don't you go ahead with your report?"

"This is what we have so far," Vance began with his usual directness. "One, it's assumed now there are a total of eight Iranians involved, two of whom, it seems, we mistakenly hired as backup security for Jake."

Alex closed his eyes for a moment, set his jaw, but said nothing.

"Apparently, they spent the entire week helping protect Mr. and Mrs. Gabriel during their stay in Turkey. Secondly, four of the other six were dressed as airport personnel, complete with proper identification."

"Excuse me, Mr. Youngblood," interrupted Pierce.

"Yes, sir?"

"Might I ask where and how you came by this information?"

"We have our sources, sir."

"I'm afraid I must ask you to reveal your sources to me, Mr. Youngblood."

"Not going to happen, sir."

"I'm afraid I have to insist."

Alex slammed the palm of his right hand on the desk. The sudden loud noise caused everyone to jump except Vance and Jeep.

"Mr. Pierce!" Alex said coldly, "if you wish to remain in this meeting, you will keep your mouth shut unless you have something helpful to add. If, however, you want to play some bureaucratic bullshit you can just get the fuck out of this office and I'll call your superiors and have you replaced with someone who doesn't have his head up his ass."

Pierce sat staring at Alex for a few seconds; one could nearly see the wheels turning. "I apologize, Mr. Gabriel and to you, too, Mr. Youngblood. Sometimes we forget the big picture and get our bureaucratic noses bent out of shape when civilians do our job better than we do. Again, I'm sorry."

Alex stared at Pierce for a moment, trying to decide if the man was sincere or just blowing smoke up their asses.

He looked back at his head of security. "Why don't you continue, Vance?"

"The Turkish police found four bodies about two hours ago in a remote hangar on the far side of the airport. They are, at this point, assumed to be the actual airport personnel." Vance paused for a moment while he consulted his notes. "The last two were disguised as Turkish police. Guns, badges, car, the whole works."

"Do we know how they got on the plane?" asked Jason.

"Right now it looks like it went down something like this: according to the witnesses, mainly airport personnel, the plane was being unhooked from the tow vehicle, as a Turkish police car came up in a hurry with its lights flashing. They signaled the pilot that there was some sort of problem. At the same time, the man from the tow vehicle, the man manning the stairs, and two more from a fuel truck advanced to the bottom of the stair ramp, gesturing loudly and arguing with the police. Within a minute, Jake showed up at the top of the stairs. The police at that point, say the witnesses, pulled their guns and pointed them at Jake while another man came from within the plane and put a gun to Jake's head. We assume that was one of the hired bodyguards. The witnesses weren't too clear about the next few seconds, but that's apparently when all hell broke loose." Vance consulted his notes for a few seconds. "Jake managed to throw the bodyguard off the stairs, pull his gun out, and start shooting. He killed one of the policemen outright and wounded the other. The four bogus airport personnel, by this time, had their guns out and dove for cover under the plane. Apparently, the first bodyguard staggered to his feet and started yelling at those under the plane to help him and he started up the stairs. Jake shot and killed this sumbitch and one of the airport personnel just as he started up the stairs. That's when the man who we assumed was the second hired bodyguard appeared at the door of the plane and shot Jake in the back of the head."

"Oh no!" exclaimed Walt involuntarily.

"Shit!" muttered Jason.

Vance said nothing. He continued to look at his notes, not looking up, not meeting anyone's gaze.

"To continue," Vance cleared his throat, "the three airport personnel headed up the stairs leaving their comrades lying in their own blood. They threw Jake off the top, pushed the stairs as far away from the plane as they could, and shut the door. What was happening inside the plane at this time is anyone's guess. The plane started taxiing within seconds, hitting and knocking over the portable stairs with its left wing as it went."

"How much time do you think all this took?" asked Greenwood.

"Hard to pin down to the second, but as close as we can put it together, one and a half to two minutes. It is apparent that this was a well-planned and well-financed mission. Had Jake not been there, it would have gone as smooth as silk."

"I assume the Turkish police are holding the wounded bogus cop?" asked Jason.

"Prison ward of a hospital; yes sir."

"Vance," said Alex, "I know Jake was a long-time personal friend of yours whom you served with I believe for what, twelve years?"

"That's correct, sir."

"I'm sure I speak for everyone here in expressing our sorrow for your loss."

"Thank you, sir." Vance was being formal, very military at this point. "Jake went down as a warrior, firing his weapon, defending what he was charged to defend." Vance's voice tightened just a little. "No greater honor for a soldier... I am proud of my friend."

"Mr. Youngblood," said Sean, "I too want to express my condolences for your loss, and tell you that at the conclusion of this meeting, I'll be on the phone to Langley insisting that your friend's body is on a plane heading home ASAP."

"Thank you, Mr. Greenwood, I would appreciate that."

"Is there anything else you have to report at this time?" asked Alex.

"No, sir, but we are lifting every rock in the Middle East to find out who, why, and where, sir."

"I'm sure you are," remarked Sean, obviously impressed.

"Vance, I don't know how you managed to gather so much information in such a short period of time, but I cannot express my gratitude enough."

"Yes, sir. Jeep and I got lucky with some friends in the area. Now if there is nothing more for me here, we've got a lot of work to do."

Alex held up his index finger. "Jason, have any of our associates in the region been of any help?"

"Not any solid information. A bunch of speculation of course, but that's all it is at this point."

Alex looked back at Vance. "I'm sure you know how much I and my family thought of Jake, and I know there is nobody on the face of the planet that could have done a better job."

"I appreciate that, sir. I know Jake thought the world of your family, too." Vance gathered his notes. "I need to get to work."

Vance and Jeep walked across the office and left.

"Why don't we take a short break?" suggested Walt.

"Fifteen minutes everyone," said Alex.

9:35 a.m.

Vance and Jeep came into the office, walked to the board table, and took seats. Vance put a file down on the table and said nothing.

"Do we know the condition of the wounded bogus cop?" Sean asked Stanley Pierce.

Pierce opened the thin file and after a few seconds, looked up. "Apparently the Gabriels' bodyguard, Jake, managed to shoot the top off the man's left ear, grazing his head and giving him a severe concussion. However, his wound is apparently not life-threatening. The authorities in Turkey feel he should be able to be interrogated by the end of the week."

"Is there any way our representative could sit in on the interrogation?" asked Vance.

"That would be irregular, Mr. Youngblood," said Pierce.

"Let me say something here, if you don't mind, Mr. Pierce," said Alex.

Pierce nodded. Alex continued.

"Vance is not only head of our security and a Vice President of Gabriel International but a retired, highly decorated captain from the Navy SEALs. He is without question the most resourceful individual I know of in this or any other country, when it comes to intelligence gathering. He has and will continue to provide us with intelligence our government cannot seem to acquire on its own."

Alex continued, "Jake Engstrom, the man who gave his life in an effort to protect my parents, was a long-time personal friend of Mr. Youngblood's, serving with him for twelve years in the SEALs. And finally, Mr. Pierce, Vance Youngblood is a close personal friend of mine."

Stanley Pierce sat for a moment absorbing this information.

Vance looked over at Alex and gave an almost imperceptible nod. Alex returned the gesture.

"So Mr. Pierce, I would suggest that you take it upon yourself to see to it that one of Vance's associates sits it in on that interrogation."

"There will be a lot of hoops to go through, sir. Our relations with Turkey have been a bit strained in the past several months, which won't help the situation any," said Pierce. "But I will take it upon myself to get your man in on the interrogation."

Chapter 65

ANKARA, TURKEY
June 11, 1989
5:00 p.m.

"Now what the hell?" Jake muttered to himself as he looked out the window.

Marian heard the remark and looked out to see what was miffing Jake. She spotted a police car approaching rapidly from the direction of the main terminal.

"Probably lost our flight plan or some such nuisance." Jake stood and headed toward the front cabin door. "I'll check it out."

"Probably nothing," said Marian and went back to reading a pamphlet on Egypt.

Jake hadn't gotten ten feet before he bumped into one of their Turkish hired guns, who was blocking his progress to the door. "Excuse me, Ali," Jake said to the burly man.

"We'll be leaving you now, sir," said Ali, continuing to block the passage. "Just wanted to let you know how honored we were to serve the Gabriels and you, sir."

"Nice to have you with us, Ali. Now if you don't mind, I need to check out the problem outside."

"Oh, yes sir." Ali stepped to one side, allowing Jake to slip by.

Before Jake stepped out of the plane onto the top of the portable stairs, he looked back at the Gabriels and could see the second hired gun was now standing by them. Marian was looking out the window.

As Jake stepped onto the platform, he saw the police arguing with some airport personnel. The police both turned at once with their guns drawn and pointed them at Jake.

"What the fuck?"

"You will put your hands behind your head, infidel pig!" said Ali from directly behind Jake.

Jake paused for a second, and then did as he was asked. But he did it so quickly Ali couldn't react fast enough. Jake's hand wrapped around the automatic pistol, his thumb blocking the hammer. At the same time, he twisted his body into the surprised man and threw him over his head down the stairs. This caused the two police to jump to one side, momentarily losing their sight of Jake.

Jake pulled his .45 automatic, squatted to one knee and started shooting. The first cop died with a bullet just below the right eye. The second round took the remaining cop in the left side of his head.

"Oh my God," exclaimed Marian, not taking her eyes off the horror going on outside.

Norman quickly found a window and looked out.

The second bodyguard bolted toward the front of the plane.

Marian and Norman both witnessed the airport personnel pull pistols out of their jumpsuits just before they vanished under the plane.

They could see Ali slowly get to his feet, his left arm hanging awkwardly. He limped, obviously in considerable pain, the ten feet or so to where his pistol lay on the tarmac, retrieved it and started yelling to his comrades under the plane.

The Gabriels couldn't see Jake because of the angle, but they had a clear view of Ali and another man as they started toward the stairs. As Ali's foot hit the bottom step, they again heard the loud report of Jake's pistol. Ali's head seemed to explode.

"Oh, my God!" cried Marian.

Then came another shot and the man behind Ali spun backward, a gaping hole exposed between his shoulder blades.

Another shot followed closely, but the sound was different. Marian and Norman then saw their protector, their friend

Jake, tumble halfway down the stairs. The back of his head was crimson.

Norman was the first to grasp the situation. He turned and looked at his beloved wife. "Sweetheart, we're in trouble."

Marian looked at Norman, clearly in shock.

"Let's get to the bedroom," urged Norman.

"What?"

Norman stood, reached down and pulled Marian to her feet. Pulling her behind him, he hurried to the master bedroom in the aft of the plane. He pulled Marian in and shut and locked the door.

In a minute or so, it became deathly quiet and then the engines could be heard starting. The plane started moving almost immediately. In a few seconds, a strange bump was felt and a crashing sound was heard.

There was a knock at the door.

Norman held his finger to his lips. They remained silent.

"Mr. and Mrs. Gabriel, this is Abdul."

"Is everything all right?" asked Norman.

"Yes, sir. The danger has passed. Feel free to come out whenever you want."

"Where's Jake?"

"He's up in the cockpit calling the Turkish authorities." There was a short pause. "I'm going up to help with the translation."

"Bullshit!" yelled Norman. "You killed Jake, you son of a bitch."

There was silence on the other side of the door.

After a long moment, Abdul's voice could be heard. His voice was no longer warm and friendly. It was cold and hard. "We have no intention of harming you or Mrs. Gabriel. We have other plans for you. But if you don't open the door in thirty seconds, I will personally cut the throat of the co-pilot.

"Jesus, Norm, what should we do?" asked Marian.

Norman thought about it for a few seconds. "Can't stay in here for long, I guess."

Norman opened the door and was greeted with a pistol pointed at his face.

"What the hell are you doing?" asked Norman just before Abdul hit him hard on the side of his head with the pistol. Norman went down on his knees and then toppled over on his side.

Marian screamed.

"You will not talk, you piece of pig shit," screamed Abdul.

Ali was his brother. Now Ali was dead along with three of his other comrades, including a nephew. Abdul was clearly in a rage. This was supposed to go off without a hitch. "That fucking Jake. You fucking capitalist pigs."

Marian went down to the floor on her knees beside Norman. "You son of a bitch," she said between clenched teeth. She cradled Norman's head in her arms. "Norm, Norm -- are you all right?"

Ali's foot shot out and caught Marian hard just below the ribs on her right side. She slammed against the bulkhead, the breath knocked out of her. She was gasping for air with searing pain in her side when Ali grabbed her by the hair and dragged her up on the bed.

"You will remain silent, you whore!" he screamed. He grabbed her throat with his left hand and slapped her hard with his right. "Do you understand?" Marian was still struggling to breathe, but managed to nod her head.

The Gabriels' plane was in the process of taking off as Norman and Marian were being roughly placed in handcuffs behind their backs. They were then blindfolded. Marian was left on the bed. Norman, head bleeding from the gash left by the pistol, was still on the floor.

Over the next hour, one or more of their captors would come into the bedroom every fifteen minutes or so to check on them. One, each time before leaving, would manage to put his hands all over Marian's breasts.

Chapter 66

GABRIEL HEADQUARTERS
June 12, 1989
1:12 p.m.

"They landed in Tabriz," stated Sean Greenwood while cupping his hand over the phone.

"Tabriz?" questioned Jason.

"Northwest section of the country," offered Jeep.

Vance was already at the large map of Iran laid out on the boardroom table as the others gathered around, looking over his shoulder.

"Is that bad or good?" asked Walt.

"Don't know yet," replied Vance, "we'll have to do a little research."

"At least it's not in Tehran," added Jeep. "The serious zealots hang their turbans in that hellhole."

"It's close to Turkey. That could be a benefit," observed Vance.

"Yes, sir," agreed Jeep.

"Okay," said Alex. "Let's get to work and see what their landing in Tabriz means to us. Mr. Pierce, Mr. Greenwood, we'll be looking to you for some good intelligence here."

"Already working on it," responded Pierce.

"Same here," declared Sean. "Going to call in some notes on this one."

"Got some calls to make, boss." Vance turned and headed out the door.

"I'll second that." Jeep followed Vance out.

3:05 p.m.

Everybody had just re-gathered around the board table after a short break.

"We don't have much of an intelligence network in that part of the country," admitted Greenwood, "but it has been confirmed by an eyewitness that the Gabriel Aircraft landed at the Tabriz airport at 8:25 p.m. Tabriz time. We're told the plane taxied to a large hangar at the far south end of the airport. Our witness thought the plane was pulled inside the hangar, but he wasn't sure -- he was on the opposite end of the airport. He didn't see anyone approach the aircraft or hangar, but again, it was over half a mile away, so he wouldn't swear to that."

"That's all you have?" asked Alex.

"For now, but our man is going to see if he can get a whole lot closer. We'll contact him again in about four hours."

"Thanks, Sean," Alex acknowledged the contribution.

"We need some photos from ground level, and from satellites," stated Vance. "Also want street maps of Tabriz."

"What are you doing, planning an invasion?" asked Pierce, half-joking.

Vance looked at him impassively. Jeep looked briefly at Vance, then back at the map.

"Now hold on, gentlemen." Pierce was showing his first real emotion of the day and it was clearly alarm. "There's no way this government is going to allow you to invade a foreign country. We have enough problems in that part of the world."

Alex gave Vance a small headshake, then turned his attention to Pierce. "Nobody said we were going to do anything of the kind," said Alex. "But the more intelligence we have, the more options may open up to us. Surely you can appreciate that, Mr. Pierce."

"I also appreciate that Mr. Youngblood is a military man and thinks like a military man."

"That's all true, Mr. Pierce, but he doesn't have an army to invade with."

"Oh! But he does, as you well know, Mr. Gabriel. You have a small army presently located in the Congo, if I'm not mistaken."

"That's a small security force to protect our GRI personnel," responded Vance.

"That's not what I've been led to believe, sir."

Mr. Pierce was well-informed. Gabriel Relief International did maintain a five-hundred-man security force to protect their hospitals and refugee stations in Third World countries from being raided and plundered. It didn't take a genius to figure out that all the humanitarian aid in the world would be of no use if the aid stations were constantly being attacked, food and medical supplies stolen, and personnel injured and killed. Whether the raiders were rebels, government forces, or just vicious gangs, the effect was the same. GRI's endeavors to ease the suffering of tens of thousands of refugees were fruitless unless a strong deterrent was put in place.

Three years before, with Alex's blessing, Vance started developing a small force to repel those brutal attacks. These security forces, out of necessity, had grown rapidly and were presently the best- equipped and trained private army in the free world. Pierce's information was a little inaccurate; actually there were GRI forces in three African countries. Besides the Congo, GRI built and maintained hospitals and refugee camps in Ethiopia and Somalia, all protected by a well-trained, heavily armed security force.

It amazed the world that the corrupt governments of these destitute nations would allow an independent organization, no matter how benevolent, to build and operate hospitals and refugee camps within their borders, let alone establish an armed force to protect them. But Alex was persuasive. After months of fruitless negotiation, he came to the realization that only by offering hefty bribes and terrifying threats in one package could the "leaders" of the respective countries be convinced to look the other way. Gabriel International had the power, these despots were convinced, to force the cutoff of all international aid. Truth be known, it was within Gabriel International's scope to heavily influence, through media and political pull, the distribution and portioning of international aid. It mattered little, to these despots, that a small percentage of the aid went to the needy as long as most went to fatten their bank accounts. After all, they knew that someday, sooner or later, they would be overthrown and they had better have money in the bank.

The GRI security forces did, in a short period of time, kill or wound hundreds of attacking natives in a relatively small number of skirmishes. They soon earned the reputation as efficient, effective, and professional killers. It didn't take many encounters before those who were inclined to raid the GRI compounds stopped doing so.

"I have to agree with Mr. Gabriel, Stanley," said Sean, "It is always a good idea to know everything possible about a situation. I hate to remind you that Ross Perot was successful in breaking two of his men out of prison in that country. Something our government could not accomplish."

"Or would not," injected Jeep.

Pierce looked over at Jeep, his face not changing expression. "That little operation was an embarrassment to our country. Something we do not wish to repeat."

"Mr. Pierce, I'm going to tell you something now so there is no misunderstanding later. The release of my parents, alive and well, is my only priority. I will do anything and everything to accomplish that goal. I'm going to give our government time to secure their release through political or any other means. By 'time,' however, I don't mean weeks, months, or years. The first time I even suspect foot-dragging, stalls, or any other form of bullshit, we'll be ready and fully able to take off in a different direction."

"You can't be serious, sir?"

"If and when you get to know me better, Mr. Pierce, you'll know just how serious I am."

The tension level in the room, already high, jumped several notches.

"Phone for Mr. Greenwood," said Carol over the intercom. "Line one."

Greenwood pushed the button and picked up the receiver. "Greenwood here." There was a pause. Sean started taking notes. "How much time, sir?... Okay, I'll tell them. Yes, sir. I'll get back to you shortly."

"We have their demands."

Adrenaline shot through the hearts of everyone in the room.

"Well?" demanded Alex.

"They want nearly two hundred political prisoners freed, and...500 million dollars."

All eyes turned to look at Alex.

"Where are these prisoners?"

"Israel, mainly. A few scattered around other countries. We, in the States, have incarcerated sixteen for various terrorists acts or conspiracies to commit same."

"Will Israel release these people?"

"Not a chance, I'm afraid," replied Stanley Pierce.

"Will we release our sixteen?"

"Again, I'm afraid not."

"How much time have they given us?" asked Alex.

"Three days," said Sean.

TABRIZ
June 11, 1989
6:10 p.m.

Norman was moaning on the floor of the bedroom in the Gabriel aircraft. The plane had been in the air for about two hours before the power started easing off and the aircraft began nosing down as if to land.

From the time the plane left the runway at Ankara, Marian had tried to get her husband to respond to her, but to no avail. The sound of panic had begun creeping into her voice. She was considering the possibility her husband could die from his head wound, and that she would have to take this terrifying trip into the unknown alone.

"Norm!" she pleaded for the hundredth time. "Please, sweetheart, wake up."

"What...what?" muttered Norman, his voice barely audible.

"Wake up, Norm. You gotta wake up!"

She listened to her husband start to struggle and move around on the floor. "What the *hell*!"

"Shhh, Norman. Don't talk too loud. Listen to me. Please!"

"I... I can't move...I can't see. What the hell is this?

"Listen, Norm. Okay?" she whispered.

After a moment or two she heard, "Okay."

"We've been hijacked by Abdul and Ali."

"What?"

"Shhh, listen. Abdul hit you with a gun and you've been unconscious for a couple of hours, I think. We're handcuffed and blindfolded. We're in the bedroom. I'm on the bed and you're on the floor."

"What bedroom?"

"On the plane."

"What plane? What the hell's going on?"

Marian's near panic began easing, as Norman became responsive.

"Think for a minute, Norm. We've been hijacked from the Ankara airport."

Norman remained silent for a minute. "Oh shit! Are you all right?" he asked.

"I'm fine. You're the one who got hurt. How do you feel?" Marian chose not to say anything about her ordeal.

"My head hurts like sin, kind of a big, throbbing, cheap wine hangover-type ache."

"I think we're in big trouble," expressed Marian, fear apparent in her voice.

After a moment, Norman asked, "Where's Jake?"

"I think Jake must be dead, Norm. Do you remember the shooting?"

Norm was silent for a moment, then quietly said, "Oh no."

Within minutes, they could hear and feel the engines of the aircraft slowing further. They could feel the plane descending.

"Where do you suppose we're going to land?"

"How long have we been flying?" asked Norm.

"About two hours, I'd guess."

Norm thought about that for a minute. His headache didn't help the thought process. "All things being equal, I'd say we're about to land in Iran."

"I think so, too. Oh shit, sweetheart."

"Don't be too scared, honey. We have a couple of people back home who aren't going to take kindly to this."

Marian knew that. She had already thought about what Alex and Vance had to be doing at this moment. Their son and Vance would have gathered together the best minds they could find and were probably devising some sort of plans. She knew that if anything happened to her or Norm, somebody would pay, and pay dearly. She could only hope that whoever was responsible was aware of this.

Chapter 67

GABRIEL HEADQUARTERS
June 13, 1989
6:30 a.m.

"It seems to me they would know that Israel won't bargain with terrorists and that neither will the US. So what is it they really want?" Walt had offered few opinions since this ordeal had begun. But his observation and question were foremost in everyone's mind and begged for an answer.

"That is the big question, Mr. Gabriel," replied Pierce. "We have yet to figure out who is behind this. If we knew that, we'd know more about their motives. It's possible they just want the money. That much money would finance a lot of terrorism around the world."

Sean looked at Pierce and shook his head slightly. This gesture wasn't missed by Alex. He made a mental note.

"So you know, Mr. Gabriel," said Pierce from State, "the Secretary has put in a call to the Ayatollah at the President's request. We have asked him to intervene with whoever is responsible for this travesty."

"Is there any reason for hope here?"

"I wouldn't count on it. Khomeni's people deny any knowledge of the hijacking."

"Is it possible they were left out of the loop?"

"Not likely in that country. Acting alone or in secret can get you hanged."

"Is it possible the government ordered or sanctioned this action?" asked Vance.

"Always a possibility. However, it's only been eight years since they returned the American Embassy hostages. I wouldn't think they'd want to re-irritate the world's opinion of them, but I certainly wouldn't rule it out," offered Jeep.

"I'm hoping to hear from some contacts within the next few hours. Maybe then we'll know who we're dealing with," said Vance.

"No way of pushing them along a little quicker?"

"They've been pushed, boss."

"I'm sure they have. Sorry, Vance."

"No sweat."

"It seems to me there can be some advantage to where they landed," stated Sean. "Being close to Turkey, a good part of the people there speak Turkish. Also, it's my understanding there are quite a few English, French, and some German-speaking people. But maybe the best advantage is that this part of Iran is probably the least political."

Vance got up from the table, ostensibly to stretch out a little. He managed to get Alex's eye without anyone else noticing and gave a look toward the door. "I'm going to check out some other sources of information. I'll be back in a few," he said.

Within five minutes, Alex joined Vance in his office. "What's up?" he asked.

"I'm not about to sit around with my thumb up my ass waiting for some dumb fucks from DC to fix this for us."

"No?"

"No, sir! I don't have much confidence in a political solution to this scenario, boss."

"What have you got in mind?" asked Alex as he leaned up against the door.

"A possible military action. Forced extraction. Just like the man said. They're missing the fact that southeastern Turkey is just a couple of hours away from Tabriz by jet and not much further away by fast-attack helicopters, Alex. This could be a big advantage to us."

"Could get my folks killed, you know." Alex had assumed that Vance would set other wheels in motion. He was a man to cover all contingencies.

"Alex, I've got to tell you this thing is looking bleak to me. If we continue to proceed the way we are, we're gonna use up a lotta time with bullshit. Not that we shouldn't continue on that course anyway, but we'd better start setting up a back-up plan or two."

"Agreed."

"We don't know who the assholes are, but we can be sure they're well-financed, trained, and cold-blooded. The ransom demand could just be a smoke screen. It's possible they're Muslim zealots with a fucked-up agenda that may or may not have anything to do with money or comrades."

Alex pushed himself away from the doorjamb, walked over and sat in one of the two chairs Vance had in front of his desk. He sat forward with his elbows on the desk, cupping his cheekbones in his hands, fingers on his forehead. He was, as were the others, at the point of exhaustion. He said nothing for a few moments.

Vance watched his boss and waited for him to talk. He was relieved by Alex's apparent coolness under the circumstances and, without doubt, encouraged to see that Alex had taken control. However, there was little doubt what would happen to Alex's control should anything happen to his parents.

"You've never given me bad advice, Vance," Alex stated as he leaned back in the chair. "So, how do we proceed?"

"Already started. Got our best men flying to Ankara from Africa. Also have a few old comrades who have gone into, shall we say, business for themselves, heading that way pronto."

"Mercenaries?"

"Yes, sir! And as hard as you'll find anywhere."

"I can imagine."

"Jeep is seeing who he can get into Tabriz and/or Ankara. We're not looking for a large force, just a good one. Fifty or so ought to do it."

"What do you need, Vance?"

"We have most of the equipment flying in with our African men. We'll need a few big pricey items, however."

Alex nodded as he got up and walked to the door. As he put his hand on the knob, he turned to face Vance. "You've got carte blanche." He turned to walk out but stopped and stood looking at the door for a moment before turning once again to look at Vance. "You think we ought to put some security on the rest of the family, just in case?"

"Done that, Alex. Got two men on your aunt and uncle and another on Alexandra, Chuck, and Jennifer. Put extra security on this building and at Norman Research."

Alex looked at Vance and realized how fortunate he was to have this man with him. He was invaluable. "Should have known.... Thanks."

Chapter 68

TABRIZ
June 13, 1989
8:45 p.m.

After the landing and a long taxi, the plane came to a stop and the engines were shut down. After a few minutes the plane began to move again under some external power; within two minutes, they stopped again. All was relatively quiet for about thirty minutes, but it was getting hot inside the bedroom of the aircraft. Occasionally, muffled voices could be heard and a couple of times something banged against the plane. After a long half-hour, the bedroom door opened.

"You will come with us now," Abdul commanded in his heavy accent.

He and a smaller man yanked Norman roughly to his feet and Marian was dragged off the bed and just managed to get to her feet without falling. The blindfolds were removed.

"Where are we?" asked Marian.

"We are in Iran, you cow!" answered Abdul.

After adjusting to the bright light, Norman looked at Marian.

"Oh shit, sweetheart. The son of a bitch hurt you."

Norman was pushed hard against the bulkhead. "You will remain silent! Do you understand?" yelled Abdul.

"Just a slap, Norm. No big thing," Marian said quickly. She felt that her eye and the side of her face had to be swollen, but the deep pain in her side concerned her more.

Abdul spun around to discipline Marian when the other guard grabbed his arm and said something quickly in Farsi. They exchanged a few heated words before the argument was settled; then they turned their attention back to the Gabriels.

They were roughly taken to the front of the plane, hurried out the door and down a makeshift ramp. From there, they were led to the back of a huge hangar. Other than the two men on the plane, there were at least fifteen more who could be seen. All looked to be heavily armed with automatic weapons. Vance had given all the Gabriels a crash course in weapons one afternoon at a shooting range, and instructed them in the basic use of several pistols. He also brought with him a variety of other arms just as a kind of "show and tell." Marian and Norm might have recognized the distinct look of the Uzis and AK47s under different circumstances, but not today. They were quickly moved toward a fairly large corrugated steel structure located at the rear of the hangar.

Off to the left of what must have been the office and against the inner wall of the hangar were the pilot, co-pilot, and navigator of the Gabriel jet. All three had hoods over their heads and their hands tied behind their backs. Blood could be seen on the shirt of one of the crewmen, and drenching sweat on the others. Marian and Norman were led over to that area. A video camera and lights were being set up facing the hooded men and there was a lot of shouting and scurrying around as their captors set the scene for something. After a minute or two, everyone seemed to agree on the set-up and Marian and Norman were moved in front of the camera and made to stand beside the plane's crew. They must have felt they were taken back in history about eight years to the embassy hostage situation in that country. Blindfolded and bound hostages were again going to be displayed to the world's press.

After a few more seconds, the video lights were turned on and one of the Iranians put on a ski mask and stepped forward into camera range as he removed the hoods of the three men. The bright lights caused the three to squint and blink rapidly. One of the Iranians behind the camera said something and the masked Iranian took an automatic pistol from its holster, cocked it, walked over, and stood in front of the navigator. All eyes, and the camera, were on this man. He put his pistol to the forehead of the navigator and pulled the trigger. Marian screamed; Norman yelled "*NO!*" as the navigator's head flew back and he dropped to the concrete floor, his body twitching in death throes. The Iranian then walked over to the pilot and placed the pistol to his head. Marian screamed at the man. "Please don't do that," she pleaded. "This man has three children, plea..." The Iranian pulled the trigger and the pilot crumpled to the floor. The co-pilot started crying and praying at the same time. The Iranian stepped in front of him as the co-pilot dropped to his knees and begged for his life. He was shot through the top of his head.

Norman looked over at Marian. "I love you with all my heart," he said in a strong voice, betraying the tears filling his eyes.

"I love you, too, Norm," she cried.

The Iranian stepped in front of Norman and put the pistol to his forehead. Norman suddenly stood straight as he could, his chest out and chin up.

The Iranian stood with the pistol at Norman's head for ten seconds before the man behind the camera said something. The masked Iranian uncocked the pistol and returned it to its holster.

The Gabriels just stood there, utterly stunned. They looked at each other, both terrified and confused. They were still alive? While the camera remained on the two, panning from Norman's face to Marian's, no one spoke a word. It seemed like an eternity standing in front of bright lights knowing they might be killed at any time. Were the others just waiting for the man in charge to give the command?

Marian tried to hold a brave face, but it was no use. Her chin was quivering uncontrollably as her whole face became a mask of terror. Her legs began shaking as if her bones had gone soft. It was a wonder she remained standing. The buzz of flies became louder as the seconds passed. The strong smell of body odor reeked from their captors and it mixed with a horrible stench coming from the dead men. The bodily functions of two of them had let go at the moment of death.

A word was given, the lights were turned off, and the cameraman picked up the camera, tripod and all, and moved away, back toward the plane.

Abdul and the other man who had led them off the plane and into this terror stepped in and roughly pushed them toward the office. Marian stumbled and fell; terror had drained her legs of all strength. She struck the side of her head on the concrete floor, knocking her senseless for a few seconds.

"Sweetheart!" Norman yelled as he tried to kneel by his wife, to help her in any way he could.

Abdul reached down and grabbed her under her arms and yanked her to her feet. "Weak capitalist bitch!" he screamed. "You fall again, I beat you!"

"*You piece of shit!*" yelled Norman.

Abdul spun and backhanded Norman hard across the face. Norman staggered backwards a few steps. "Is that as hard as you can hit, *you piece of shit*?" Norman was in a rage, momentarily losing his fear.

Abdul smiled and advanced to inflict a severe beating on Norm, but the man in charge -- the man who had given all the orders -- ran over and slapped Abdul hard in the mouth. Then he grabbed Abdul by the front of his shirt and pulled him close to his face. He screamed something in Farsi while continuing to hold him by his shirt front. Again he screamed and got a quick nod as an answer. He pushed Abdul, releasing his shirt as he did. The man in charge then turned and walked away.

Abdul was livid, but after a short conversation with the other man, took Norman and Marian by the upper arms and walked them to the office structure. After being ushered through the door, their handcuffs were removed from behind and replaced with their hands in front.

"You will stay here. There is sanitary facility back there," Abdul pointed to the rear of the office. "You will not try escape. You will be shot if you do." The two men turned and left the office. A lock could be heard being applied to the door.

Chapter 69

GABRIEL HEADQUARTERS
June 13, 1989
2:45 p.m.

"We have a videotape flying in from Iran. Should be in Langley in a couple of hours."

"Do we know what's on the tape?" asked Vance.

"No, sir," said Sean, "but if the Iranians follow suit, it'll probably show the captives bound and gagged and being led into some sort of prison."

"How are we going to view the tape?" asked Alex.

"We will set up a closed circuit transmission. We have the equipment heading this way as we speak. Beam it right into this office."

5:35 p.m.

"Are you ready?" asked Sean. He had a phone to his ear, his hand covering the mouthpiece.

"As ready as I'm going to be." Alex picked up the VCR remote so they would have a copy of the tape in the office. He purposefully excluded Jennifer and Colleen from the showing. He would show them the tape later if...

Sean and Pierce started to object to the taping but were cut off by Alex. "Gentlemen, I'm going to have a copy of the tape, and that's not open for debate."

"I could tell them not to transmit," Sean responded as he took the phone away from his ear.

Alex reached over to the intercom button. "Carol, please get the President on the phone, will you?"

"Yes, sir," her voice came back.

Pierce looked at Sean with eyebrows lifted.

"Jesus, you're not much on negotiating, are you, Mr. Gabriel?"

"No, Mr. Greenwood, I'm not."

"Do you think the President would intervene with our policy on your behalf, sir?" asked Pierce.

"I can assure you that would be the case, and if I have to go through the trouble of asking him to do so, I'll have both of you replaced at the same time." Alex looked from Pierce to Sean. "Your move!"

Sean, after a moment or two, put the phone to his ear. "Play it!"

Alex pushed the record buttons on the remote.

After a minute of flickering, the screen cleared up and produced a surprisingly clear picture. The picture was of five people standing side by side. Marian was the first on the left, with Norman standing to her left, followed by three hooded and bound men. No one else was in the picture, nor was there any sound.

Alex could see that his parents had been hurt. The left side of his father's face and hair were caked with blood. His mother's face was red on the right side and it was obvious she was extremely frightened. Alex's face displayed both fear and rage.

Within seconds, a man appeared wearing a ski mask. He walked over and roughly removed the hoods of the three. Alex, Vance and Jason recognized the co-pilot, pilot and navigator. All were trying to adjust their vision to the bright lights. The masked man took his pistol from its holster, cocked it and stepped in front of the navigator.

"Oh shit!" exclaimed Jason.

Alex said nothing. His body went rigid as adrenaline hit his heart.

The masked Iranian put the pistol to the navigator's forehead and pulled the trigger.

"*Motherfucker*!" yelled Vance.

"Oh my God," said Pierce.

Alex remained silent, unable to breathe.

The masked Iranian stepped in front of the pilot and killed him in the same way.

Alex began to make a moaning sound while involuntarily rocking in his chair.

Everyone in the room quickly looked at him, then back at the TV.

"*Fuckers*!" yelled Vance as he stood up, not taking his eyes off the screen.

"*Shit*!" added Sean, snapping the pencil he was holding.

The Iranian stepped in front of the co-pilot. You could see the man crying and saying something at the same time. Then he dropped to his knees and leaned forward. He was shot as he prayed.

The Iranian then stepped in front of Norman who seemed to be saying something to Marian.

Alex screamed and turned away from the screen. He was shaking so badly it was surprising he didn't fall off his chair. *No, no*, his mind screamed. *Please God, don't do this; please don't do this!*

After a few seconds that seemed like an eternity, Vance said, "They're not gonna kill your folks."

Alex turned back around just in time to see the killer uncock his pistol and return it to its holster.

"Oh, oh, oh shit. Oh shit." Alex continued rocking back and forth in his chair.

The killer walked off the screen and a few seconds later, the camera zoomed in to get close-ups of Norman's and then Marian's face.

Alex's heart broke when he saw his father looking lovingly at his mother, tears running down Norman's face. But the terror on his mother's face set him in a rage he would not have thought possible. *I will kill you all*, his mind screamed. Then the transmission ended.

No one in the room moved or said anything, their eyes still on the screen. Jason was the first to speak.

"I...I don't know what to do...I... oh my God!"

Alex jumped up and ran out of his office to his private bathroom. He didn't bother to shut the door. The sounds of violent retching could be clearly heard. The word "*MOTHERFUCKERS*!" was screamed out, then more retching.

Vance turned to Sean and Pierce. "You'd better tell your bosses they have little time to resolve this situation. Because I can tell you, my boss is gonna see to it that a lot of people die over this. You may have a real war if you don't get the Gabriels back safely -- and soon." Vance knew that a large number of Iranians were going die anyway, no matter what happened from this point on.

"You can't take matters into your own hands, Mr. Youngblood. I'm sure Mr. Gabriel will be reasonable and give us time to get this resolved through proper channels." Pierce evidently was not taking Vance's words seriously. After all, what could a private citizen do, no matter how much money he had?

Vance walked over and put his face just inches from Pierce's. "You had better listen carefully here. Mr. Gabriel is going to turn this into the biggest shit tornado you have ever had to deal with. I can't emphasize enough how you'd better convince your superiors of the extreme danger everybody involved with this incident is in."

"I doubt my reporting Mr. Gabriel's rage will convince my superiors to step up or change their efforts, Mr. Youngblood."

"Then they will live to regret such a decision, sir."

"Just what do you suggest we do, Vance?" asked Sean. Apparently, he was a great deal more astute than Stanley Pierce. He surely had observed over the past two days that Vance Youngblood didn't say or do anything that wasn't precise, something Pierce seemed to have missed. Vance wasn't given to panic, and he wasn't given to boasting. Sean Greenwood clearly was inclined to believe what Vance was telling them.

"If I were you, I would recommend to the President that he mobilize the 6th Fleet and move it into the Persian Gulf."

"You can't be serious!" replied Pierce.

Vance looked Pierce straight in the eye. "If I were you, I would recommend that the President get a hold of the Ayatollah Kohmeni and tell him he is being held personally responsible for the safe return of the Gabriels. I would recommend to the President that he inform the Ayatollah that he will order the complete destruction of Tehran, Tabriz, and maybe a few other places in that shithole country. That's what I would do, but then again, I know what will happen if all the stops aren't pulled and the Gabriels do, in fact, die."

"Mr. Youngblood," responded Pierce, "I don't know how you think a single man can force the President to act so irresponsibly. Do you really think Mr. Gabriel has the power to intimidate a President?"

"Mr. Pierce, power in all forms can be bought. And there is absolutely no end to the Gabriel purchasing power."

"Is that a threat, Mr. Youngblood?"

"Absolutely!"

Pierce sat for a minute before getting up and walking over to the board table. He started replacing files, recorded tapes, and notes into his brief case. When done, he picked up his case and headed for the door. "Tell Mr. Gabriel we will continue on the course we're presently on. I'm sorry, Mr. Youngblood, if you feel we're not doing enough." Stanley Pierce turned to walk out.

"I would strongly suggest you report to the Secretary of State exactly what I said."

"I'll take that under advisement."

"If you don't, I will remind you someday of the mistake you just made, Mr. Pierce."

"Vance, I'm going to help Alex," said Jason as he shakily got up and headed down the hall to the bathroom.

"Well, I, for one, plan on taking what you said seriously, Vance," stated Sean. "I don't know how much power Mr. Gabriel has, but I'm convinced he'll use it to the fullest extent."

Chapter 70

GABRIEL HEADQUARTERS
June 14, 1989
11:00 a.m.

Alex stood in front of a huge battery of microphones and cameras in the lobby of the Gabriel building; his face was drawn and tired. His eyes were red-rimmed and three days' stubble was clearly visible. He was dressed in a dark blue suit and white shirt – no tie.

All major networks, foreign and domestic, and local stations were in attendance. Behind Alex stood Jennifer, Chuck, Colleen, and Walt. Slightly off camera stood Vance's chief of in-house security, Bill Hitson. Hitson was in his late fifties with thinning red hair. He didn't look to be the physical threat that seemed to be the norm for Vance's men, but he must have possessed abilities that weren't apparent or he wouldn't have held the position of trust he did. Bill's eyes constantly shifted from one area of the lobby to another. In addition, there were a dozen members of Vance's security team stationed in the lobby.

Vance and Jeep had left for Ankara last night, leaving Alex feeling conflicted and vulnerable. Emotionally he needed Vance at his side during these horrible days as he had never needed him before. But intellectually, he knew Vance was putting himself where he had to be.

The shock of the hijacking, the execution of the plane's crew, having to deal with completely ineffective US Government agencies, and the almost total lack of sleep set Alex's mind in turmoil. *The fucking CIA has an annual budget of over thirty billion dollars to do little more than gather intelligence on our country's enemies, and I doubt most of the dumb sons-of-bitches even know where Iran is.*

He steeled himself and started. "My name is Alexander Gabriel." He waited a moment as the press settled down. "As you know, my parents' plane was hijacked three days ago in Ankara, Turkey, and flown to Iran. Within twenty-four hours, we received a ransom demand through the Central Intelligence Agency. The demand was for the release of approximately two hundred so-called political prisoners held in various countries around the world, mostly in Israel and the US and...500 million dollars."

The press immediately started shouting questions.

Alex held up his hand until the questions stopped, then continued. "They have given us three days to comply."

Again the questions came and again Alex held up his hand. "Three hours ago, a videotape was received from the hijackers by the CIA and viewed by me and my associates. I will play a copy of that tape for you now." Alex turned his back to the large-screen TV that had been set up just off the podium area. Walt, Colleen, and Jennifer also turned away from the screen. Colleen and Jennifer had not seen the tape, nor, after being told what it contained, did they want to. The men executed were not only employees of Gabriel Industries but had become friends over the years. They and their families had attended many social functions in the Gabriel home. As the tape played out, groans and expletives could be heard in the background.

At its conclusion, Alex waited for those gathered to regain their composure. He addressed the press once again. "Each network will be provided with a copy of this tape. I expect you to use it uncensored in this evening's newscasts." Alex paused briefly. "I will now take questions."

"Have the families of the men executed been informed?" a reporter yelled out.

"I personally met with the families an hour ago."

"There has been a report of a bodyguard also being killed. Can you verify that, sir?" came a question from another.

"...I think the world of your folks, Mr. Gabriel...so if any dumb sumbitch makes any sort of move on Mr. and Mrs. Gabriel, I'll fuck 'em so bad their old pediatricians will feel it..."

"Yes, I can," Alex answered after a moment. "Jake Engstrom was killed trying to protect my parents at the initiation of the hijacking. He shot and killed three of the terrorists and wounded a fourth before being shot from behind." Alex paused for a moment. "All four of these men and their families were personal friends of our family. We are deeply grieved at their loss."

The reporters paused for a moment, many scribbling notes before starting again with the questions.

"Mr. Gabriel, do you expect to give in to the terrorists' demands?" asked a young reporter.

"Most of the prisoners are being held in Israel and sixteen are being held in this country. The world knows, as do the terrorists, that the Israelis do not negotiate with terrorists, nor does the United States. I cannot give what I don't have, namely the prisoners. But I can and will give the 500 million dollars for the safe return of my parents."

There was a loud murmur in the crowd.

"Can you raise that huge amount of money in just three days?"

"It can be done."

"Do you believe the Iranians will release your parents if you pay the ransom without a prisoner release?"

"I don't know what to expect from the Iranians. I just know it would be in their best interest to do so."

"What do you mean by that?"

"I'm not going to elaborate."

"What's the US Government's position on this?"

"The State Department is following established rules of diplomacy. They are talking to the Iranian Government."

"How does the State Department feel about your intention of providing a half a billion dollars to a terrorist organization?"

"The government didn't know about my intention to pay the ransom until this minute. I expect they will not be happy with that decision."

"The government can forbid you to turn over such a large amount of cash to a hostile foreign terrorist group, can they not?"

"They can try."

"What does that mean?"

"Just what I said!"

"If the government orders you not to pay the ransom, will you comply with such an order?"

Alex's eyes scanned the throng of reporters and then he looked at Jennifer standing at his side. "I will do whatever it takes to secure the release of our parents. I don't believe that is the highest priority with our government."

"Are you saying you will not comply with such an order should it come?"

"I've already answered that."

"Couldn't the government freeze your assets, therefore taking away your ability to pay the ransom?" a portly middle-aged scribe yelled out.

"No."

The reporters were definitely eating this up. Here was a man who was not in the least intimidated by the most powerful government on the planet. Here was a man who planned on taking these raging monsters by the horns and the United States Government could just kiss his ass.

"Are you saying, sir, that you don't plan on complying with any governmental dictate concerning this matter?" This time it was a columnist from the *LA Times* with the query.

"I will comply with any suggestion, orders, or dictates that come from our government as long as they make any sense at all. I have no intention, however, of sitting back and watching our government ineffectively negotiate the release of my parents for days, weeks, or months. We have all seen how inept they have been in the not-so-distant past. I do not plan on watching my parents suffer for weeks or months while our government tries to solve this crisis diplomatically."

"It would seem to me, Mr. Gabriel, that you are, in fact, putting yourself in jeopardy. Why wouldn't the CIA or the State Department have you arrested either before or after you pay this huge ransom?"

"I expect that will be the government's intention. I would suggest, however, that an attempt to arrest me for trying to protect my parents will not bode well with the voters of this great country."

Alex paused for a few seconds. "I am, here and now, asking the people holding my parents to tell me if the ransom alone will be enough, and if so, how and where they want the money transferred. I assure them it will be done as soon as possible."

The reporters were writing furiously; they would certainly have a story today.

"How did your parents look to you in the tape, sir?" asked a young woman with a microphone in her hand.

Alex's face hardened. "They looked like they had been physically abused and were quite frightened." Alex's jaw was set. Those who knew him knew that his thoughts were black; knew he wanted to say more to the terrorists -- to threaten them -- but he remained in control. "That's all the questions for now. We will keep you apprised of any further developments." With that, Alex turned and took Jennifer's hand and walked to the bank of elevators at the rear of the lobby.

Chapter 71

GABRIEL HEADQUARTERS
June 14, 1989
3:55 p.m.

Alex listened to the speakerphone, as did the others in his office as Stanley Pierce told of his meeting with his boss, the Secretary of State, and the Secretary's staff. "The Secretary was unhappy at the idea of a private citizen attempting to dictate foreign policy, Mr. Gabriel."

"I'll bet he was."

"I told him I truly believe you will, in fact, attempt a military-type rescue if our efforts fail."

"What was his response?"

"He said, and I quote, 'They do that and I'll see to it personally that they themselves spend time in a federal penitentiary.'"

"He said that, did he?"

"Yes, sir."

"That would cause our government some really bad press, Mr. Pierce, press from which the administration will never recover," Jason offered.

Pierce ignored that comment. "The Secretary wished me to explain to you that these things can take months to work out."

"We've seen that act before, Mr. Pierce," Jason responded.

"I can guarantee you, Mr. Pierce, that will not happen in this case," added Alex.

"I believe that, Mr. Gabriel. I again tried to convince the Secretary that if we don't have a resolution to this incident within a few days, you would likely take matters into your own hands."

"And?"

There was a moments pause, "He doesn't believe you have anything other than a few mercenaries and that you wouldn't be stupid enough to charge a hangar in a foreign country in a rescue attempt." Pierce paused for a moment. "Might I ask where Mr. Youngblood is, sir?"

"You may not."

There was another pause, then from Pierce, "I see… The Secretary has requested a meeting with the President, sir. I'll keep you informed as to any decisions made."

"You do that, Mr. Pierce." Alex reached over and broke the connection.

June 14, 1989
7:05 p.m.

"They want the money transferred to this account at this Swiss bank," explained Sean as he handed Alex a sheet of paper. "I might add that I was told not to give you this information."

"By whom?"

"Stanley Pierce, acting for the Secretary of State."

Alex looked at the sheet of paper, said nothing, and handed it to Jason, whose eyebrows raised just slightly upon reading the information.

"I'm curious, Sean," said Alex. "Why would you risk your career and possibly your freedom by disobeying an order of this magnitude?"

"Boy… I've been asking myself the same question, Mr. Gabriel." Sean was being sincere. "I truly believe these terrorists will, in fact, kill your parents if their demands are not met. I've seen how the government works in scenarios like this. The government hates these situations more than just about anything else that comes down the pike. This is a no-win situation for them and they know it. To add to that, sir," smiled Sean, "I have acquired a great respect for you, Vance, Jason, and your family and staff in these past three days. I trust your judgment in this matter far more than I do our government's."

Alex looked at Sean for nearly a full minute. "I'll tell you this, Sean. If you lose or decide to quit your job at the CIA, you will have one here if you wish."

The offer plainly took Sean by surprise. "I appreciate that, sir, but I have to tell you I hate the fact that you're willing to give a terrorist organization a half a billion dollars with which to wreak havoc. That amount of money will create massive amounts of misery in the world."

"Sean, I appreciate that more than you know. The misery they will inflict with that amount of cash cannot be measured. It will set the demons of hell loose on the world."

Sean's brows furrowed. "You realize that, but yet you're willing to sacrifice possibly tens of thousands of innocent people to save two?"

"Sean, there is little in this world I wouldn't do to save my parents. Without elaborating, I will ask you to be patient with me for the next week or so. Things aren't always what they seem."

Sean Greenwood had seen much in his twelve years in the service of his country. He had seen atrocities committed by every side in the game. He knew of countless promises made only to be broken without so much as a blink of an eye. He knew the corruption that was rampant in the world, and that corruption certainly was not a stranger to Washington DC. But this man in front of him was not corrupt, not at all. This man in front of him could be trusted. Sean looked Alex in the eye. "I'm on your side, sir."

"I appreciate that, Sean. Thank you."

Sean looked over at Jason. Jason smiled a little and gave a nod. A new bond of respect and friendship had just been formed.

After a moment, Alex looked again at the piece of paper

containing the name of the bank and the account into which the ransom was to be deposited. "Then they have accepted the ransom money alone? They've dropped the demand for prisoners?"

"So it would seem," said Sean.

"Seem?"

"Well, you can't rely on anything these people say, sir. I wouldn't trust them for a minute."

"Just who is it the CIA is in contact with, and does the CIA know and trust this person or persons?"

"We have not been given any names. All communications have been made through the American Embassy in Ankara."

June 15, 1989
1:45 p.m.

"We have received word from Ankara that you have until noon tomorrow, the 16th, to make the deposit to the designated account," explained Sean. He looked down at a paper in his hand. He looked like a man who didn't like what he was about to do.

"You have something more to add?" asked Alex.

"Yes sir, I'm afraid I do." Sean continued to stare at a paper.

"Well, man, out with it," demanded Jason.

Sean looked at Jason, then Alex. "I have in my hand an executive order signed by the President. This order forbids you to pay the ransom." He reached over the desk and handed the letter to Alex.

Jason and Alex looked at each other. They had fully expected this. The President had made it clear on national television that he was leaning toward prohibiting the payment of this huge ransom. He made a strong and logical argument against such a sum of money being at the disposal of international terrorists.

Alex quickly read the executive order and smiled to himself. *These bastards won't be getting any money from me*, he thought. *Slow miserable fucking deaths, for sure, but no money.*

Alex, Jason, and Walt had spent the past two days accumulating the vast sum from Gabriel holdings around the world. No branch of the Gabriel Industries reserves was tapped for more than they could afford. The money was ready for transfer at a moment's notice for the past eight hours.

"We appreciate the fact that you were reluctant to give us this news, Sean," remarked Alex, "but I'm afraid I can't comply with such an order."

"Mr. Gabriel, I have been instructed to tell you that failure to comply with this Presidential order will result in your arrest and prosecution for treason against the United States."

Alex looked deep into Sean's eyes. "I appreciate you telling me that, Sean, but I'm afraid I will not be able to comply."

"I didn't think you would, sir. And I informed my superiors of that belief."

"Good! So you are aware, it is my intention to speak to the President about this matter. I believe we will be able to work something out."

"Really?"

"I believe so."

The more I know this man, the better I like him, thought Alex. *He's honest, intelligent, and has balls. Got to have him on our team.*

Chapter 72

TABRIZ
June 16, 1989
10:00 p.m.

Marian and Norman were startled awake by the sound of gunfire and excited yelling. Having no idea what was happening, they were terrified. They heard laughter and then more automatic gunfire. The sound was nearly unbearable even in their office cell. After a few minutes, the gunfire stopped, but the laughter and reveling continued. Something obviously had happened. Their captors seemed to be ecstatic. Nearly an hour passed before they heard someone unlocking the door.

"Maybe they have what they want and are going to let us go," Marian suggested weakly.

"Maybe, sweetheart," said Norm. "We'll see." Norm looked at his beloved wife. He would have to be blind not to see that this wonderful woman's health was rapidly eroding.

The day before, she had told him about being kicked in the side right after he was knocked unconscious. Norman had carefully lifted her blouse and was shocked to see a massive, ugly, multicolored bruise starting at the bottom of her ribs and continuing down past her hip bone and around to her lower abdomen. He dismissed her theory about a broken rib instantly. Broken ribs are painful, but this was much more than that, much more. He ran to the door of their cell and banged loudly until someone came and opened the door. He tried to explain to the guard that his wife needed medical care. He lifted her blouse and showed the guard the damage, pleading for a doctor. The guard said nothing, just turned and walked out. Within ten minutes, Abdul came into the office, walked over to the cot and roughly pulled up Marian's blouse and looked at the damage. "The capitalist bitch will have to endure the pain," he proclaimed as he turned and walked out the door.

But that was yesterday; now three men entered their holding cell. Two had grim expressions, but the third held a sickening smile. This was Abdul. This was the man who had masqueraded as their trusted bodyguard. This was the man who had shot Jake in the back of the head. This was the man who had viciously kicked a helpless, middle-aged woman as she tried to help her injured husband.

The two grim-faced men walked over and took Norman's handcuffs off and replaced them with his hands behind his back.

"*Get up*!" Abdul screamed at Marian. "*You weak American whore!*"

"Please handle her carefully, Abdul," pleaded Norman.

Marian tried to sit up, but was struggling just to get her feet and legs over the edge of the cot.

Abdul reached down, grabbed her by the hair and yanked her to her feet. "I said *get up*!"

"*You piece of pig shit*!" yelled Norman as he fought to get to his wife. But he couldn't break free of the two guards.

Abdul smiled at Norman, then turned to Marian, reached over with his free hand, and ripped her blouse off in one brutal motion. From halfway up her ribs to well below the waist, the right side of her body was swollen and nearly black.

Marian groaned and dropped to her knees. She would have fallen to the floor if Abdul hadn't been holding onto her hair. She was so weak that she barely kept her eyes open.

Norman was so enraged he could not speak. He wouldn't have thought it possible to hate like this.

Abdul gave an order to the two holding Norman and they turned and walked Norman out the door. Abdul, holding Marian by one arm, literally dragged her out the door. Two other terrorists came over and helped Abdul walk Marian across the concrete floor.

Chapter 73

GABRIEL HEADQUARTERS
June 16, 1989
11:00 a.m.

"The transfer has been made," said Walt as he put the phone down.

"The ball is in their court," muttered Jason.

Six of them were sitting around the board table. Alex was standing at the window with his back to them, looking out over the Pacific. He was strung as tight as a human being could get. He couldn't sit for more than a few seconds at a time, nor could he stand in one place. Truth be known, something was gnawing at him; something deep in the recesses of his mind, something he couldn't grasp. He turned back toward the table.

"Otto is ready?" Alex asked for the third time.

"No problem with him, Alex," responded Walt.

Alex appeared to have aged ten years over the past three days, not that anyone in the room was faring well through this ordeal. All the men needed a shave and shower. The women were better off. They had spent most of the time together at the Gabriel home.

An hour earlier, Vance had called from the staging area in southeast Turkey to give Alex an update on the force assembled. They were ready at a moment's notice to strike the Tabriz airport with a contingent of twenty men, two light tank/troop carriers transported by a C-5 Galaxy, and two Apache attack helicopters. The trip from the holding areas in southeast Turkey to the Tabriz airport would be less than forty-five minutes.

TABRIZ
10:01 p.m.

As Norman was being led out of the office, he kept looking back to see how Marian was doing. He witnessed her being dragged through the door. He tried to break free of the guards to get to Abdul, but one of the guards punched him hard in the stomach. He doubled over, gasping for air. He kept repeating, "You son of a bitch… you son of a bitch!"

"Look over there, you capitalist pig," ordered Abdul as he and his men continued to lead Marian across the concrete.

Norman looked up. There in that killing place stood a brightly lit makeshift gallows. On the gallows were two nooses. Assembled in front of the gallows stood at least three dozen masked Iranians with weapons in their hands. Behind the Iranians were a video camera and a bank of lights.

The guards led Norman, while Abdul, with the help of another terrorist, dragged Marian up a dozen steps to the platform under the ropes. She collapsed the second Abdul released her.

Abdul yanked Marian back to her feet and put the noose around her neck. One of the guards put the other around Norman's neck. Norman looked at his beloved wife and realized she didn't know what was happening. Her eyes were not focused and she was weaving back and forth. He didn't know what kept her from falling. Norman wanted to say goodbye to his wife -- to him, the most beautiful woman he had ever seen. The woman he had loved from the first cup of coffee they had shared so many years before. His special woman who brightened the lives of everyone whom she touched. He didn't see the bruises that now covered her face and body. He didn't see that she was nearly naked from the waist up. He saw only the most beautiful woman in the world and he knew she was about to die. She was going to hang in front of a gang of soulless monsters who believed in nothing but hate and terror. He was glad she didn't know what was about to happen. This wonderful, caring woman had suffered enough these past few days.

"Just so you know before we kill you," came the voice of the man who had been giving the orders -- the man who had slapped Abdul, the apparent leader of this sadistic group, "your son, the rich capitalist pig, Alexander Gabriel, has paid the ransom we demanded for your miserable lives. It will allow us to continue the work of Allah for years to come. Praise be to Allah!" With that, the assembled gave a loud cry.

As the revelry died down, the man gave another order and the trap beneath Marian's feet fell away. Marian fell, and the breaking of her neck could be clearly heard. The assembled gave another great cry of, "Praise be to Allah."

Norman let out a small cry as he watched his beloved wife die, but then he stood straight, his eyes clear, displaying no fear. He looked down at the monsters looking up at him. His eyes became fixed on the man in charge. "You have no idea what you have done today. You and all your families will, because of what you have done, die horrible deaths. You will have enraged the most powerful force on earth. Allah and his teachings will be poisoned in the minds of the world. His image will not be that of a God of peace, but a God of hate and terror. You will have greatly damaged what you profess to honor."

The head man looked into Norman's clear blue eyes, his expression suddenly changing from a sadistic grin to one of apprehension.

Norman looked straight at the camera. "Son, have your vengeance. Destroy them completely."

The man behind the camera paused for a second, uttered a command, and the trap beneath Norman's feet fell away.

Chapter 74

GABRIEL HEADQUARTERS
June 16, 1989
12:00 p.m.

Alex was sitting at his desk with his back to the office, looking out over the ocean. He spoke to no one. There was nothing more to do but wait. Sean and Jason were talking quietly at the far end of the board table. The two of them had taken a few minutes and managed to shower and shave in the private baths contained in each executive office. Walt, Colleen, Jennifer, and Chuck had left Alex's office twenty minutes earlier to stretch their legs and make some personal calls.

Time was moving so slowly that Alex felt he might start screaming in frustration. He was on the edge. His pulse was twice its normal rate since the money was transferred over four hours ago. He constantly prayed for the safe return of his parents. He made a pact with God. He promised that if they were returned safely, he would not take vengeance upon the terrorists. He would even let them keep the money.

Jason occasionally looked over at Alex. His concern for his friend was obvious and that fact was not missed by anyone in the room. Alex had said little during the past two hours; not a good sign.

There's something about the date, thought Alex; *something about the date*, he repeated again and again. *There's a big hole here. I can't see the day; I don't know what's going to happen*.

12:15 p.m.

For the past two hours, Sean had been in constant contact with his office at Langley. They had heard nothing, nothing at all.

"Line one for Mr. Greenwood," Carol's tired voice came over the intercom.

Alex spun in his chair, and along with everyone in the room, watched Sean quickly reach over, push a button and pick up the receiver.

"Greenwood here." He listened intently for twenty seconds or so before his shoulders slumped forward. "Oh, no!" he said quietly.

Walt involuntarily repeated the same, "Oh, no!"

"I'll tell them," said Sean as he shakily hung up the phone. He sat for a few seconds staring at the phone. He looked up, briefly looking at Jason, then over at Alex at the other side of the office. "It's bad," he said softly.

"No!" Alex whispered. His head began shaking from side to side. "No, please, no!"

"Oh my God! Those wonderful people," cried Walt. "Oh my God."

JUNE 16TH, 1991, Alex's mind screamed out, *THE DAY MY PARENTS WERE KILLED! THE SAME DAY MY PARENTS WERE KILLED...TWENTY-NINE YEARS AGO*. "They're dead?" he managed to choke out.

Sean nodded once.

Jason quickly stood and walked over to Alex's desk. Walt, Colleen, Chuck, and Jennifer came rushing through the doors at the same time, followed closely by Carol.

One look at Alex and Sean told them what they didn't want to know. Jennifer screamed and dropped to the floor on her knees. Chuck immediately knelt and cradled Jennifer in his arms, crying with her.

Walt stood stunned, not knowing what to do. He stood there, tears dripping from his eyes. His wonderful brother, his wonderful sister-in-law. Somebody had killed them on purpose? How could that be?

Colleen quickly walked over and put her arms around Walt. Her tears mixed with his as they ran down onto his shirt.

Alex tried to get up and get to his sister, but he was having trouble moving. He tried to speak but his throat had tightened so much he was having difficulty. *The same day! The same day! The same day*! his mind started to scream. *Stop it, Alex, you're needed now. No time for self-pity. Need to help Jennifer, need to help Walt, need to help Mom, need to help Pop. They're dead. Can't help; can't help. Please, God, let this be a horrible nightmare.*

Jason's face displayed his sorrow as he reached into his coat pocket and retrieved a small, flat metal box that Vance had given him just in case. He opened the box and pulled out a syringe already filled with a light amber liquid. He removed the protective cap from the needle and walked around Alex's desk.

"No!" Alex said, putting up his hand to ward off the needle.

"You're sure?" asked Jason.

"I'm sure," Alex replied just above a whisper. "Help me up, will you? I can't seem to move well."

Jason put the hypodermic down on Alex's desk, turned and spun Alex's chair a quarter turn. He reached down and took Alex by the arms and gently lifted him to a standing position.

Jason held on while Alex gained his balance. "Thanks, I've got it now," said Alex. Jason stepped back, keeping his eyes on his friend, ready to grab him if he were to stagger.

Jason looked over at Walt. "Vance gave me sedatives for you and the ladies. I would recommend you take them. Would be a good idea for you too, Alex."

"Got something to do first," he said, his voice becoming a little stronger. He turned and looked at Carol who was standing close to the door, tears pouring down her cheeks. "Get Otto Auchland on the line."

"Yes, sir." She turned and left the office.

Jason walked to Chuck and Jennifer. "Why don't we go sit at the table for a little while?" Jason was pale and he had a tremor in his voice, but he seemed to be in control of himself.

Chuck looked up at Jason. "Why don't you give me the sedatives?"

"Sure." Jason's voice was tight, displaying his grief. He handed a small prescription bottle to Jason.

"Got to make a couple of phone calls," said Sean, "I'll be back in a few." With that, he quickly turned and headed for the door.

Jennifer, with Chuck's help, managed to make it to the board table and sat. Jennifer put her head on her forearms and bawled like a baby. Chuck pulled another chair close to Jennifer's and put his arm around her shoulders, his head close to hers.

"Mr. Auchland on the line, Mr. Gabriel." Carol's voice was clearly choked as she spoke into the intercom.

Alex punched a flashing button and picked up the receiver. He paused before saying, "Otto?"

Alex listened for a moment. "No, the worst has happened, my old friend." He could hardly get out the words. He listened for another moment. "Thank you, I will do that."

Jason and Sean listened as Alex talked to Otto Auchland. Alex hadn't forgotten their plan in his grief.

"I need to hang up and help my family. You know what to do... and, Otto, thanks for your help." He replaced the receiver and walked over to where Jennifer and Chuck sat. He knelt down next to Jennifer and held her close, stroking her hair. After a few moments, he whispered, "Jennifer -- you, Colleen, and Walt need to take one of those pills; they will help you."

"Not me, Alex. You're going to need some help," said Walt, barely able to talk. His chin was quivering. He was such a gentle, loving soul; this tragedy was clearly tearing him apart.

Colleen looked at Walt with tears pouring out of her green eyes. "Your heart is broken, sweetheart; maybe it would be a good idea to take a pill."

"I have never been so sad in my life," Walt admitted, trying to maintain a tenuous grip on his emotions. "But I need to help here."

"Then I'll not be taking any, either," said Colleen. "I'll help as much as I can."

Walt looked at his wife, but could not speak. He just nodded his head.

"Walt," said Alex, his voice continuing to get stronger, "I wish all of you would take a sedative; then I need you two to help Chuck get Jennifer home. Between Jason, Sean, and me, we will be able to handle things here."

Carol came into the office looking as devastated as anyone in the room. She slowly walked toward the board table, grief written all over her face. Alex turned as she approached and pulled her into a tight hug. She broke down and sobbed.

"I'm so sorry, Alex, I'm so, so sorry," she managed to get out between sobs. "Such wonderful people."

Alex held her for a few seconds. "It's a horrible day, Carol… for all of us." Alex released his grip but held Carol at arm's length by her shoulders. We'll be needing your strength and help to get through this, so let's get to work, okay?"

Carol nodded, turned, and squeezed Jennifer's shoulder as she walked toward the door.

"Carol," Alex called after her. "Please have the limo waiting by the elevator in the garage."

"Yes, sir," she said in a stronger voice.

Alex turned back to Walt. "I really need you to help keep the home fires burning for a few days, Uncle. I need to know the rest of my... " Alex's voice broke and he looked away for a moment, then back at his uncle. "I need to know everybody is safe and cared for."

Walt nodded. "Okay, I'll do that," he replied, then after a moment's pause: "Maybe we should all stay at your place for a few days. I, for one, would like to keep my family... close."

Alex nodded.

Carol returned with a fresh pitcher of water and glasses, taking a tray over to the board table. She poured four glasses and returned to her self-appointed station by the office door. From there she could see what the people in the office needed and at the same time keep an eye on the phones.

Jason handed glasses of water to Colleen, Walt, Jennifer, and Chuck, and then gave each a small white pill.

"I won't be needing this," said Chuck. "I'll keep a clear head just in case." He put the pill in his jacket pocket.

The other three swallowed their pill. Within five minutes, the sedatives started taking effect. Jennifer quit crying, stood and gave Alex a long hug. "I'm going to go home now, Alex. You get on with what you have to do." With that, Walt came over and hugged Alex, saying nothing. He was followed by Colleen and then Chuck.

Five minutes after the four had left, Sean Greenwood returned to the office. He poured himself a glass of water before saying, "I talked to Jeep, sir. Vance wasn't near a phone. They'll be on their way ASAP."

Alex nodded in understanding.

"My boss wants me to convey his condolences." Sean took a long drink of water. "He's not a bad guy; he really is sincere in his sympathy."

Alex nodded again. "Any intelligence coming from that sector?" he asked quietly.

"Not really, sir," said Sean; then after a second or two, "I want to tell you how sorry I am for your loss. And I want to apologize for our intelligence community's complete ineptitude. Your people make us look like total amateurs."

"Thank you," Alex replied quietly.

"This country had better pull its head out of its ass, and soon, or we as a country are surely going to suffer," stated Jason.

"I absolutely agree," declared Sean. Then, after a couple of quiet moments, "I have to ask you a question on a professional level."

"The ransom?" asked Alex.

Sean nodded.

Alex looked over at Jason. "Tell him."

Jason looked at Sean, his sorrow giving way to anger, "The dumb slimy psychopaths had us deposit the ransom in our own bank. The stupid fuckers won't be getting any money. All they'll be getting is killed, no money."

Sean's face displayed just a trace of a smile.

ANKARA
June 16, 1989
9:15 p.m.

The small Gabriel attack force was on high alert as they waited in the dark just off the runway of a little-used private airport just twenty miles south east of Ankara. Hefty bribes to several Turkish ministries and local potentates had cleared the way, eliminating all interference from the government and curious citizens.

Their huge C-5 Galaxy was squatting like a massive winged toad at the end of the runway. It was fully loaded with two armored troop carriers, crates of weapons, ammunition, and explosives. All the crates were stenciled with, in Arabic, Machine tools or Farm tools. The twenty hand-picked men were all dressed in combat black, complete with hoods; their bullet-proof vests held a variety of personal weapons, knives, and grenades.

There were no sounds save the incessant chirping of crickets and an occasional bark of a dog a long way off. Two hundred miles to the east, in a small remote canyon, two fully manned and armed Apache helicopters sat silently in the dark waiting for orders.

A small command tent sat just fifty feet to the rear of the C-5. Inside, Jeep sat by himself at a field table studying a variety of maps. The field phone sitting by his right hand came to life; he picked it up on the first ring. "Jeep," he said. He listened for a moment before his head bowed slightly. "I'll tell him." He replaced the phone in its cradle and sat for a second before standing. He stood and turned just in time to see Vance burst into the tent. The question didn't need to be asked but it needed to be answered. Jeep shook his head. "The Gabriels have been killed."

Jeep had seen Vance's war face in the past, but nothing like this one. Vance's face quickly became monstrous and terrifying.

He let out a scream of rage so loud it could have sent a chill down a statue's spine. Even the battle-hardened Jeep involuntarily backed off a pace. The crickets went silent and every dog within a mile began to howl.

Chapter 75

GABRIEL HOME
June 17, 1989
8:00 a.m.

Alex arrived home from his office sometime after 2:00 a.m. and went directly to bed. He took several sleeping pills to aid in his sleep.

The next morning Colleen was in the kitchen with Maria preparing coffee and a light breakfast for whoever wished it. Maria had been crying almost constantly. Colleen twice told Maria to go home; take the week off, but Maria steadfastly refused. She desperately needed to stay and help.

Alex made an appearance in the kitchen shortly after 8:00 a.m. His eyes were bloodshot, his hair was tousled, and four days' stubble covered his drawn face. Colleen walked over and put her arms around his waist. "Alex, what can I do to help you?"

Alex shook his head and gave her a soft hug. "How are you doing?"

"As well as can be expected, I suppose."

"How's Jennifer?"

"Been in her room with Chuck since early last night. Chuck gave her another sedative."

Alex nodded. "Better get some more of those, I suppose." Alex remembered how sedatives helped him maintain his sanity after "the accident" so many years ago.

"One of Vance's men came by about an hour ago with a full bottle," said Colleen.

"Did he?"

"Yes. Vance is something, isn't he?"

"He's a Godsend as far as I'm concerned," replied Alex in a near whisper. "I couldn't handle this without him. I wouldn't know where to start."

Colleen turned and walked to the counter. "Cup of coffee?"

"Please."

Colleen brought Alex a big mug full of steaming black coffee.

"Some breakfast?"

Alex shook his head as he took the mug. "How's Alexandra handling this?"

Colleen's eyes filled with tears. "She can't stop crying."

Alex looked away for a second.

"She said, and I quote, 'Uncle Alex is going to have those assholes killed.'"

"She's right," replied Alex unemotionally.

Colleen said nothing for a second; then, "Are you sure you don't want some breakfast?"

"Not right now, thanks," said Alex as he took another sip of coffee. "I'll be staying home today. I... I need to be with my family." Alex was having a great deal of trouble keeping his emotions in check.

"Good," said Colleen, tears welling up. "We need to be together. We need to hold...each other. "Ah shit, Alex!"

Alex set the mug down on the counter and put his arms around Colleen. "We'll get through this. I promise you, we'll be all right."

"I know. But it's so hard... such wonderful people. My heart is broken."After a minute, Colleen pulled away. "I'm sorry, I know you're hurting more than anyone."

"We're all suffering, but I know the pain will subside in time." *I lost them before and felt this grief*, thought Alex. *I lost them before and recovered. We will all recover*.

"I know." Colleen put her hand up to Alex's face. "We're here for each other." Colleen looked over her shoulder. "I'd better give Maria a hand."

"I'm going outside for a while." Alex turned toward the patio door.

"Okay." Colleen watched Alex walk out and across the patio, heading for the stairs that would lead to the beach and onto his rock, but this time he stopped at the head of the stairs. After a moment, he walked to his right twenty feet or so and just stood, one hand on the rail, the other holding the mug. He stood motionless, staring blankly over the vast expanse of the Pacific Ocean. Colleen walked into the formal living room, sat on one of the couches, buried her face in her hands, and wept.

TABRIZ AIRPORT
June 17, 1989
1:00 a.m.

It was a moonless night as two men, dressed in black from head to toe, silently emerged from the shadows close to the airport's control tower. At the same time, nearly a half a mile away on the far side of the airport, two more black-clad men moved into position close to a large hangar. Each had, strapped to their chests, a knife, grenades, and a silenced Uzi carbine, and each of their backpacks was loaded with explosives and detonators.

Within a day of the kidnapping, at Vance's direction, these four ex-SEALs were air-dropped into Tabriz using the HAHO, (high altitude, high opening) system allowing them to glide, with specially designed parachutes, nearly ten miles to their target in Tabriz. A long-time friend and associate of Jeep's provided a run-down unused warehouse on the outskirts of Tabriz to provide them cover until such time as they might be needed.

The runway lights were off at this hour and there were only a few outside security lights scattered in various places around the airport. A light could be seen high up inside the tower, behind the glass, and a dim light lit the entrance.

The taller of the two SEALs at the control tower looked at his watch then signaled the other to move into the bottom floor of the tower; he quickly followed. Both silently climbed the stairs, their Uzis at the ready.

There were only two Iranians on duty at this time of day. One was asleep; the other was reading a magazine. The hapless man reading the magazine looked up just in time to see his killer pull the trigger, knocking him and his chair over backward onto the floor. The other died as he started to wake.

The taller SEAL again checked his watch, pulled out a transceiver, and pushed a button four times. Vibrators on the transceivers of the two SEALs near the hangar buzzed four times and simultaneously the lights of transceivers in the cockpits of the C-5 and the Apache helicopters blinked four times. The SEAL then sat down at a control panel and placed his transceiver next to a series of switches and levers while the other man set about planting explosives. When finished, the shorter man took up position to keep watch at the door, and the taller kept his eyes on his transceiver. Then they waited.

1:15 a.m.

The light on the SEALs transceiver blinked three times. He reached over and pulled three large levers in turn. The runway lights came on, lighting the early morning sky. At that same time, the two SEALs stationed at the hangar shot the two Iranian terrorists standing guard at the door before they could sound an alarm. They removed the robes and turbans of the slain terrorists, put them on over their black jumpsuits, and took up their station.

Within ten seconds the C-5 touched down at the far end of the runway. As it started to slow, the gigantic rear hatch was being lowered. Even before the lumbering plane came to a full stop the two armored personnel carriers roared down the ramp and headed toward the hanger.

The transceiver sitting on the control panel in the tower blinked twice. The SEAL reached over and shut off the runway lights and waited for the next signal.

The two armored personnel carriers approached the hangar at top speed. As they approached, one of the SEALs guarding the hangar door pointed a flashlight at the approaching vehicles and flashed three times. He received an answering three flashes from the leading carrier. The carriers slowed as they approached to make as little noise as possible. At fifty yards out they stopped and ten men quickly exited each. Vance was in the lead as the twenty men approached the hangar at a trot. The two SEALs guarding the door slipped out of the bloodstained turbans and robes. Vance signaled for four heavily laden men to set explosives around the exterior of the hangar. The two guarding the entrance were to stay put and the remaining fourteen slipped into the hangar.

The interior of the hangar was poorly lighted in the early morning hour. Just a few low wattage naked bulbs hung from the ceiling in the rear. Most of the terrorists were sleeping on cots; a half dozen were lying on blankets on the floor, their weapons beside them. At the far end of the hangar, at the base of the gallows, where Norman and Marian were still hanging, four terrorists were awake, talking and laughing quietly. The Gabriel aircraft blocked their view of the door and they didn't see the black-clad men enter. Nine of the Gabriel force quickly took up positions around the sleeping terrorists. Jeep, with two men, kept to the shadows as they headed quietly toward the four at the base of the gallows. Vance and two others went up the stairs and into the interior of the Gabriel jet.

Inside the Gabriel plane a terrorist was sleeping on one of the comfortable couches; another, Abdul, was sleeping in a reclining chair, an Uzi in his lap. Vance signaled as they slipped by. One of his men stood over the terrorist on the couch, the muzzle of his Uzi just an inch from the man's forehead. The other pointed his Glock .45 at the head of Abdul. Vance continued to the rear of the plane, to the master bedroom. The door was not closed but maybe it should have been. Maybe a second's warning might have saved the man sleeping in the Gabriels' bed a future of extreme pain. He might have gone for a weapon and been killed outright.

But instead, the first thing he heard was someone saying quietly in Arabic, "Wake up!"

One of the terrorists at the base of the gallows spotted Jeep and his men approaching. He let out a cry as he reached for his weapon. All four were killed within seconds in a hail of automatic fire.

The three dozen or so terrorists sleeping on the cots and on the floor were startled awake. Some reached for their weapons; they died. Others either froze in place or raised their hands in submission.

Inside the Gabriel jet, the man on the couch and Abdul quickly woke up. The one on the couch reached for his AK47 as a silenced 9mm round caught him just above his right eye. Abdul froze, his sense of self preservation on high.

In the aircraft's bedroom, Vance had the leader of these terrorists sitting on the side of the bed with his hands cuffed in back. "So you're the boss pig, are you? You shouldn't have picked this place to sleep. This place is for the wonderful people you killed." With that, Vance punched Mohamed Ashubah, so hard his jaw shattered and his mouth drooped lopsidedly as if it were melting. Blood poured out on the carpet as he fell unconscious to the floor. His blood and three teeth mixed with the dried blood left by Norman just four days before.

Outside, two hundred yards away, under cover of darkness, a commandeered Iranian truck was backed up to the cavernous opening in the rear of the C-5. The aircrafts crew was loading it with the crates marked "Machine tools." Once the transfer was complete, the two personnel carriers were driven back inside the C-5. Jeep and six of the Gabriel force herded the twelve surviving terrorists, including Abdul and Mohamed Ashubah, up the ramp of the huge cargo plane, chaining them in a standing position by their cuffs to overhead rails. Their cuffs were already digging into their wrists. It was going to be a long, horribly uncomfortable flight to Africa.

The Gabriel jet started and was being backed out of the hanger. The bodies of Marian and Norman were placed on the master bed and covered with sheets. Two ex-Navy pilots who were part of the Gabriel force flew the 727C.

Vance pulled out his transceiver and pushed one long and three shorts. The men in the tower turned on every light in their control at the airport, including the runway lights. Then they set the detonators on the explosives and ran down the stairs and out of the building. They ran as fast as they could toward the C-5 Galaxy. Nine men climbed into the canvas covered rear of the Iranian truck, and two, dressed in terrorists' clothes, got into the cab, started it, and drove off. At the same time, the Apache helicopters took off from a vacant field just three miles away and headed toward the airport. Vance and Sergeant Brawley quickly boarded the Gabriel 727C and secured the hatch as it taxied onto the runway. As the two SEALs from the tower ran up the ramp, the C-5 began its rollout behind the 727C.

Once the two planes were airborne and the truck had cleared the airport, all hell broke loose. Within seconds, the hangar, containing the bodies of twenty-two terrorists, was turned to scrap metal in a spectacular series of explosions. Then came the Apaches. Their orders were to destroy everything they could in and around the airport. There were six Iranian-owned American made F-15s lined up like ducks in a shooting gallery. The Apaches' 20mm cannons made short work of them. The Apaches then managed to destroy all other aircraft, and most of the hangars and support buildings in just ten minutes. Fires raged in every part of the airport. Lastly, the control tower disintegrated in a massive explosion. All remaining lights went out.

GABRIEL HOME
JUNE 17, 1989
8:24 a.m.

Walt came into the kitchen just as the phone rang. Maria picked it up. "Gabriel residence...jes, hee's heer. Ee's for ju, Señor Walt."

Walt took the phone. "Yes?"

It was Jason on the line. "Walt, how's everybody there?" Jason asked compassionately, concern apparent in his voice.

"Don't know; haven't seen anybody yet this morning." Walt looked up to see Colleen entering the kitchen. "Hold on a second. Have you seen Jennifer or Alex this morning, sweetheart?"

Colleen tilted her head toward the patio.

Walt turned to see Alex standing at the wrought-iron fence. "Jason, Alex is out on the patio. Don't know if he'll be in the mood to talk."

"It's all right. I'll tell you and you can relay the information when you feel the time is right."

"Okay."

"The shit has really hit the fan. We have CIA, FBI, NSA, and the State Department all over our offices. And being held at bay, in the lobby, is an army of press."

"I understand the press being there, under the circumstances, but what the hell are the government people doing there in person? Seems just a phone call to apologize for their complete incompetence, followed by their condolences, would be sufficient," Walt remarked bitterly.

"They're not here for that."

"No?"

"Apparently you haven't talked to Alex or had a radio or TV on this morning."

"God, no; just got up. It was a long night."

"Yes, of course. I'm sorry."

"We're all hurting, my friend, including you," replied Walt.

"Yes, sir."

"What happened, Jason?"

"Well, in a nutshell, it goes like this. There is a report coming out of Iran that a force of some sort hit the Tabriz airport early last night our time, and according to reports, completely destroyed it."

"Jesus Christ!"

"The report claims that dozens of Iranian citizens were killed or wounded. They say there was heavy damage done to some bridges and roads."

Walt was stunned. "Are they saying we had something to do with this?"

"Yes, they are."

"That's crazy! We don't have a fucking army, for Christ's sake!"

One of Colleen's eyebrows went up.

"When you talk to Alex, tell him we have a handle on the situation. Global has been activated."

"Global's been activated?"

"He'll know."

"I'll have him call you as soon as possible."

"That'll be fine, Walt. Please tell everyone I'm thinking about them."

"I will. I'll be talking to you later." Walt hung up.

Walt turned to Colleen and gave her a hug. "Be back in a minute." He turned and walked out the patio door.

Alexandra sauntered into the kitchen on long gangly legs with her shock of unruly red hair sticking out in every direction. There were dark shadows under her red-rimmed eyes and her young face was drawn. She went directly over to her mother, gave her a hug, and kissed her on the cheek. She said nothing.

"How are you doing, son?" asked Walt as he approached Alex.

"Not well, Uncle. Not well at all." Alex kept looking out at the Pacific. "Why?" he asked as tears spilled down his face. "Why?"

"I don't think there's a rational answer other than that there are some evil people in the world who don't give a shit about anything."

Alex nodded as he lifted the mug to take a sip.

"Jason just called."

"Oh?" The mug stopped moving.

"Said the shit has hit the fan. The Tabriz airport was completely destroyed last night and dozens of Iranians were killed. And to top that off, the dumbshits think we did it. Can you imagine?"

Alex took a sip of his coffee while continuing to stare off into the horizon. "We did do it."

GABRIEL 727C
June 18, 1989
5:23 a.m.

Vance had managed to get six hours' sleep on the flight back to Southern California. They had refueled in Hong Kong and again in Hawaii. He had used the shower in the master bath to wash some of the past few day's grime and blood from his body…and mind. Now he sat on the same reclining chair that had held Abdul just a few hours ago. Sergeant Brawley was in the shower. In Vance's hand was the tape from the video camera at the gallows. He would rather take a beating than watch this tape, but it could contain information he might need; he had to watch it. He stood, stepped to the entertainment center and inserted it into the VCR. He returned to the chair and sat. Within seconds the horrible images appeared. He moaned when he saw the condition of Marian. He moaned again when she was dropped through the trap, but what clearly affected him most was the incredible courage displayed by Norman at the moment of his death. Vance suddenly stood at attention and held a stiff salute when he saw and heard what Norman had told the unseen face behind the camera. After a few moments, he ejected the tape. He made the decision, then and there, to keep its very existence from Alex.

Chapter 76

GABRIEL HOME
June 18, 1989
3:15 a.m.

"Why are you crying, Son?"

"What's going on, Alex?"

"My parents were killed and my heart is broken."

"Aren't we your parents?"

Alex looked at the two people sitting on a sable-colored soft leather couch facing him. They were sitting on the other side of a beautiful granite coffee table. Behind them looked to be a large exquisitely decorated lobby of some sort. The two appeared to be in their mid-twenties, and nicely dressed. They sat side by side holding hands, both smiling with an inner glow, obviously happy. But they were not his parents. His parents were near sixty and they were dead. "You're not my parents! Why would you say that?"

"Think you'd better take another look, kid," suggested the young man.

"I don't need another look, for Christ's sake, and quit calling me 'kid.'"

"Take another look, Son."

Alex looked again at the two. The young woman was beautiful, slender with shiny dark hair, and warm blue eyes. The young man was blond; square-jawed, quite handsome with deep blue eyes. "Please God, not again," Alex whispered. He looked away.

"We need to talk to you, Alex."

"We're here to help, sweetheart."

Alex looked back. "Are you here to torment me? Have I not suffered enough? Please go away," he pleaded.

"Alexander, you need to listen to your father and me. We love you and will help you if you'll listen for just a little while."

Alex summoned all the control he could muster. He looked at his parents. "Okay, I have been though this before and I know there is nothing I can do about it. So talk to me."

"First you have to know we are as happy as we have ever been," stated Marian.

"You're dead. How can you be happy?" he choked out.

"Do we look dead to you?" asked Norman.

Alex looked again and could see them aging a little and then become young again. "This is a dream; it's not real."

"You are asleep, but this isn't a dream."

As he looked at his mother, she again aged, but she did so gracefully, as she had done in life. Alex could not speak as he watched in fascination. Then Marian slowly returned to the younger look.

"One reason for coming to you, Son, is to let you see we are not in pain and are happy."

"We wish to relieve you of the pain of our loss. You have to see us as we are now."

Alex looked at them at some length and suddenly he felt calm come over him in waves. His sorrow began to fade, the rage drained from his body, and his loneliness began to wane. The immense pressure of negative emotions that had consumed him for these past few days suddenly dissipated. He felt light, almost floating.

"Oh," he exclaimed. "Oh my!"

"Feeling better?" His mother smiled radiantly.

"Oh, my!" he repeated. "What -- what just happened?"

"You have been enlightened a little, Son."

"Enlightened?"

"There is much you must accomplish in your life, but you cannot do it if you're consumed with hate and anger."

"There is a profound reason for your being," added Marian.

"Alex," said Norman warmly, "you know I have always worried about what you would do with your vast wealth; it has concerned me greatly over the years."

"Yes… I know."

"I now know what you will do and I know it's something you must do."

Alex looked at his father, not understanding what was being said.

"Alex, we have seen the face of evil and it is hideous," said Marian, a great sadness in her voice. "You are the one to fight this evil."

"Alex," said Norman, "have your vengeance; destroy them completely."

Alex was shocked. Had his father, one of the most gentle of men, just told him to take vengeance? "Are you telling me to take the lives of the people responsible for your deaths?"

"Not only them, but destroy evil wherever it can be found."

Alex was stunned. "I don't have the power to accomplish such a task."

"You will, Son," responded Marian, "in time you will."

"Maintain your course, Alex; maintain your course."

"But?"

"We love you, Alex. Take care of your sister."

An air horn from a large yacht sounded. Alex awoke with a start.

3:30 a.m.

Walt experienced what could only be described as an epiphany about 3:30 on the morning of the 18th, two days after the deaths of Marian and Norman. He suddenly shot straight up in bed.

"What is it, hon?" asked a startled Colleen as she reached over and turned on the nightstand lamp. She hadn't been sleeping any better than her husband and she was in about a half-sleep when Walt's sudden movement startled her.

"I..." Walt didn't continue for a full ten seconds, obviously in deep thought. "I need to be alone for a little while." He suddenly threw his legs over the side of the bed, got up, and headed for the kitchen.

"You okay?" asked Colleen.

"I'm fine, sweetheart. Be back in a bit."

After half an hour, Colleen got up and joined her husband in the kitchen. "Okay, what's up?" She could see a legal-sized yellow note pad in front of Walt.

"I just haven't been able to take my mind off Alex all night. I've been thinking about the effect this tragedy is having on him."

"He'll be all right in time, Walt. We all will."

"I know we will, sweetheart, but this is different somehow. I've been recalling the effect Teddy's death had on him. It took a long time for him to return to his former self after that horrible event, and that return seemed to come in discernable stages, remember?"

"Some, I suppose."

"After the three punks were found hanging in the garage in Hollywood, Alex's mood became markedly lighter. Then nearly a year later, when the two who were convicted were gang-raped and beaten to death in prison, he became nearly giddy for a while."

"I remember."

"What do you suppose Alex will do to the people who tortured and killed his parents?"

Colleen shrugged her shoulders. "It won't be pleasant, I'm sure."

"His one weakness, his Achilles heel, has always been his obsession to get even. Remember Victor Kula?"

"How could I forget?"

"Well, what Kula did was nothing in comparison. There will be no way to dissuade Alex from taking some sort of revenge on the slimy bastards who killed Norm and Marian."

"He's already done that. They've killed everyone involved, haven't they?" asked Colleen.

"I don't think so, no," said Walt.

"Really?"

Walt sat for another moment, then without warning, he slammed his hand down on the counter. "By God, sweetheart, I believe I've had an actual epiphany!"

"What?"

"I have never had such crisp and clean thoughts. I know without any reservation, whatsoever, what Alex's destiny is and always has been. It's crystal clear."

"Whoa, big guy," exclaimed Colleen. "Better run those crystal clear thoughts by your opaque wife."

"Okay," Walt looked down at his notes, "Follow this. You know how our brilliant, caring nephew has never been able to say what he was going to do with his enormous wealth?"

"He says he's going to make the world a better place."

"Ah yes, but never anything specific."

"Well, he did create GRI which certainly made the world a better place for tens of thousands of people," said Colleen. "That sure as hell is specific."

"Yes it is, but he personally hasn't taken any great life-fulfilling satisfaction from that accomplishment. Don't get me wrong; there is no doubt he is damned pleased that GRI has been so successful, but I can tell you, categorically, it hasn't been the be-all, end-all of his life."

"I agree, it hasn't," agreed Colleen.

"But at the same time," Walt mused, "Alex hasn't been unhappy. He hasn't been, as far as I can tell, actively searching for the meaning of life. He seems content to continue to accumulate unimaginable wealth. I've always had a gut feeling that his vast fortune would be a means to an extraordinary end. But I've never had a clue past that." Walt paused for a second. "And for good reason. Alex doesn't have a clue, either."

Colleen sat and listened intently, saying nothing. It was clear her husband was on to something.

"I now know that Alex is, without a doubt, going to make the world a better place... if not a different place. All paths in Alex's life have pointed to the same focus." Walt again looked at his notes then ticked them off on his fingers. "The forming of his 'Consortium' after the death of Teddy is a major piece of the puzzle. That brain trust's directive was to find ways to better the world, and they have been meeting at least three times a year for many years now. I have no idea what they have come up with. Two, add the creation of Norman Research, seemingly out of the blue. At first, everyone close to Alex assumed this was an expensive hobby to placate his lifelong interest in science. But I'm sure now it's much more than that -- much more. Three, let's not forget Global Media, oh no! No other way to control the minds and emotions of the world's citizens than having control of the news media. Next, mix in Alex's unlimited wealth, his intelligence, and his obsession with vengeance. Now what has been left out?"

"What?" Colleen was clearly enthralled.

"A catalyst… and that has just been jammed into the pot."

"Jesus Christ!" exclaimed Colleen. "That's it!"

Walt nodded. "Yes, Alex is going to change the world, but I'd bet the farm his methods won't be as they have been in the past. I believe the shit is going to hit the fan worldwide. I think what happened to Marian and Norm will light a fuse to the biggest powder keg the world has ever seen. When the fuse hits the keg, it's going to be spectacular."

5:00 a.m.

Alex managed to slip out of the house unnoticed around 5:00 a.m. and headed for his rock. It was cold, dark, and foggy, but he'd bundled up accordingly. After an hour or so sitting on the rock, he smiled inwardly, stood, looked out over the horizon, turned, and headed to the house.

He was showered, shaved, and dressed by 6:30. He left two notes on the kitchen counter, one for Walt and the other for Jennifer. He then drove to the office.

He parked his car in his space close to an elevator and was immediately confronted by two large and heavily armed men.

"Mr. Gabriel?"

"Yes."

"Sorry, sir. We didn't expect to see you this morning."

"No problem, Sam."

"Sir?"

"Yes?"

"I just want to tell you how sorry I am for your loss, sir," Sam offered sincerely.

"That goes for me, too, Mr. Gabriel," added the other.

"I thank you both. It's a great loss for everyone who knew them."

"Yes, sir."

The elevator arrived and Alex stepped abroad. "Security at the top, too?"

"Yes, sir. Paul and Ken are up there. Six men at the lobby level."

"Thank you," said Alex as the doors closed.

7:00 a.m.

Carol couldn't sleep, so she decided to go into the office early and clear her desk before the phones started ringing. It was going to be another horrible day. Upon exiting the elevator on the top floor, she noticed that the door to Alex's office was ajar and the lights were on. She knew of the additional security in the garage, lobby, and executive floors, but still, as she looked to her left she was startled by the armed security. "Oh!'" she exclaimed. "I forgot you were going to be here."

"Sorry ma'am, didn't mean to startle you."

"That's okay. Who's in there?" She motioned toward Alex's office.

"Mr. Gabriel, ma'am."

"Walt?"

"No ma'am. Alex."

"He's here?"

Carol walked over and quietly stuck her head far enough into the office to see if Alex was at his desk.

Alex looked up. "Ah good, you're in early."

"What are you doing here?" Carol asked, before she could stop herself.

"Have a lot of work to do," Alex answered in a conversational tone. "Would you get hold of Mr. Gould and tell him that Mr.Youngblood has landed and would he join us here in one hour?"

Carol stood for a second before giving her head a slight nod. "Yes, sir!"

ORANGE COUNTY AIRPORT
5:40 a.m.

Vance had called ahead and had the Heavenly Angels Funeral Home hearse waiting at the Gabriel hangar to receive the bodies of Marian and Norman as they arrived at 5:40 a.m. He sent Sargeant Brawley off for some R & R, and then he called his message service.

His brow furrowed as he listened to the message. *Really?*

8:00 a.m.

When Walt walked into Alex's office, his eyes were red-rimmed and he looked tired. He and Colleen had gotten back to sleep somewhere around 4:30 or 5:00 a.m. "Got your note."

Alex stood up, walked around his desk, and put his arms around his uncle's shoulders. "Are you going to be all right?"

Walt just nodded in silence and patted Alex's back. "How are you doing?" he asked cautiously.

"I'm going to be all right."

"Really? What kind and how many sedatives have you taken, Alex?"

"None. I'll be able to get through this without chemicals."

Walt seemed puzzled. "Not sure I will," he muttered, looking into his nephew's eyes.

"What I have to tell you this morning might ease your sorrow somewhat."

Jason walked into the office.

Jason, like Walt, was prepared for the worst in Alex. "You're okay?"

"As well as possible under the circumstances."

"Really?"

Alex nodded.

The three sat down and Alex asked Jason to give a brief rundown of the events of the last twenty-four hours.

"Walt, I want to apologize for not clearing something up when I talked to you yesterday morning," said Jason.

"Clearing what up?"

"The fact that we did indeed raid the Tabriz airport. I thought it best under the circumstances not to discuss it over the phone."

Walt nodded. "Alex told me but gave absolutely no explanation. So," he asked, "just how in the hell did we manage to attack a sovereign nation? How could we do that?"

"Used our security forces from Africa for the most part," responded Jason.

"Africa... Africa! You had a bunch of security guys fly over to Iran and wreak havoc? That makes no sense!"

"Our African security force is made up of some damn tough, battle-hardened veterans," replied Alex. "Almost all are enlisted from mercenary ranks. The officers and non-coms for the most part came from our Special Forces, Rangers, and Navy SEALs. Although we don't have a large force, it's a good one."

"A good one?"

"A very good one, and very well-equipped," said Vance as he walked into the office. "Sorry I'm late; unavoidable."

"Not a problem," said Alex as he got up, walked around his desk and gave Vance a hug. "Damn happy to have you back safe."

Both Walt and Jason stood and shook Vance's hand.

"Why don't we go sit at the board table -- there's more room," suggested Walt.

The four walked over and took seats at the end of the table.

"There's some intel I need to give you," said Vance.

"Okay."

"Had your mother and father taken to the Heavenly Angels Funeral Home. You'll want to make arrangements as soon as possible."

Alex nodded.

Walt cleared his throat. "I'll take over that… duty if you want, son?" Walt almost lost control for a moment.

Alex looked over at his uncle. "Yes, please," he whispered.

The four of them remained silent for a few seconds.

"The other three bodies haven't been found yet," said Vance.

"Shit!" said Jason.

After a couple of seconds Vance said, "Just got off the phone with the Secretary of State.""Oh my God," said Walt quietly.

Jason cleared his throat. "And?"

"He wanted to know how we expect to get away with declaring war on a foreign nation."

"We didn't declare war. We haven't declared anything," said Alex.

"That's more or less what I told him," replied Vance lightly.

"That's technically true," said Jason, "but the State Department, nonetheless, is going ape-shit."

"I'll bet they are," acknowledged Alex, "but we have a lot of friends in DC and I'll wager they'll back us as long as public opinion is on our side."

"Did you tell the secretary anything else?" asked Jason, cautiously.

"Well… yes. First I asked the secretary if that mealy-mouthed little bureaucrat Pierce told him what would happen if anything happened to the Gabriels. I got an affirmative on that, and a lot of additional bullshit to boot, so I suggested to the secretary, that if you spineless, worthless bureaucrats had any balls and had done your jobs protecting the citizens of this country in the first place, we private citizens wouldn't have to do the job for you."

"Was that the end of the conversation?" asked Alex.

"Not quite," answered Vance, with just a hint of a smile. "I listened to a few more seconds of bullshit before I suggested he might just go fuck himself, and hung up. Could have handled that better, but… I'm not in a good mood."

Alex shook his head. "You don't burn bridges, you blow 'em up."

Walt nodded.

Alex turned to Jason. "Have we heard from the President?"

"Not yet, but the media coverage may have something to do with that. I don't believe there is a single paper, TV network, or radio station, other than those controlled by the Islamic States, that are expressing anything but support for what we did."

"Global has been activated."

"You got it," smiled Jason.

Walt nodded his head in understanding.

"I'm sure that's a major part of it, but also, I can't think of a time in our history when anything like this has happened. Our government has to figure out what crime was committed, if any, and just what the hell they can do about it," suggested Alex.

"The media is playing it as one of the most heroic events in modern history," smiled Jason. "This is the biggest news event since the assassination of Kennedy."

Alex nodded. "Jason, I know you have immense pressures on you now and I fear it is going to get worse before it gets better. Hope you can hang in there."

"Actually, Alex, I'm enjoying this more than anything I've ever done. Wouldn't miss it for the world."

Alex smiled at his friend. "Well, if you think its been fun so far, just hang in there for a while."

Walt tilted his head just slightly, as a dog might when paying close attention.

"Vance. I have to assume all went well with the raid?"

"Yes, sir; just about perfect. No deaths on our side and just three wounded, none life-threatening."

"Excellent." Alex smiled a little. "Vance, I cannot begin to express my gratitude for what you've done," he said. "I would be totally lost without you here at this time. You are truly a Godsend."

"Just doing my job, boss. A majority of the credit has to go to Jeep and his men."

Alex acknowledged that statement with a nod.

"Do we have prisoners?" asked Jason.

"Fourteen, including the assholes in charge."

The pencil in Alex's hand snapped. His countenance turned dark.

"Prisoners?" asked Walt.

"Yes, sir."

"I'd like you to give us a full report later today," said Alex.

"Yes, sir." Vance paused for a moment. "You seem to be holding up quite well, Alex."

Vance's confusion wasn't lost on Alex. "I'm going to be all right, Vance. Thanks for sending over the sedatives, by the way."

"Looks like they worked."

"Haven't taken any," responded Alex.

Vance didn't change expression, but he gave Alex a single nod.

Alex reached over and pushed the intercom button. "Carol, could you get some coffee in here; maybe some rolls, too?"

"Yes, sir, on the way."

Both Vance and Jason maintained quizzical expressions. Walt was watching his nephew with rapt attention.

"I can see you are confused about my apparent ease with this situation. I'm sure, based on my past behavior, you were expecting to confront a raging maniac this morning."

The three said nothing. Jason's right eyebrow rose a little.

"The three of you," Alex looked at each in turn, "know me better than anyone else. You know I am not subject to flights of fancy."

The three nodded nearly in unison.

Carol came in with a tray of coffee and rolls. "Had it coming already." She offered a cup to each and all took coffee, but only Alex took a roll. Carol walked over and put a large coffee pot along with the tray of rolls on a sideboard, then plugged the coffee pot into the electrical outlet. She turned and left the office, closing the door behind her.

"I'm going to tell you something that you may or may not believe or may or may not accept." Alex's tone was subdued. "I'm going to tell you this for three reasons. First, so you won't think I've had a breakdown. Second, to maybe ease your sorrow over the loss of my parents. And lastly, to hopefully assure you that what we are going to do is the right path to take."

Alex took a sip of coffee and set the cup down on his desk. "I suspect my biggest chore will be to convince you that I still have all my faculties."

The three sat staring at Alex, none making a judgment, all waiting to hear him out.

"Last night, I had what I first thought was a dream and I expect you'll feel that's just what it was. But I'm here to tell you it was no dream."

Jason's brow furrowed a bit further. Vance sat stone-faced, unreadable. Walt sat quietly, watching his nephew.

"My parents came to me last night," said Alex. "They came to me as young people, in their twenties, I'd guess. They told me they were as happy as they had ever been. And that was apparent."

Vance sat, not changing expressions. Jason's face gave away his skepticism, but Walt was attentive, like a man waiting to hear about the meaning of life.

"They told me I had much to accomplish in my life and I couldn't do it if I was consumed with hate and anger. They said that I had to see them as they are now so I could be relieved of my negative feelings." Alex paused for a second. "I tell you now, that being with them drained my hatred, my rage, and my despair."

Walt sat forward in his chair. His eyes were gleaming. Vance was noticeably more attentive. Jason's skepticism started to abate. Alex's behavior certainly wasn't what any of them, in their wildest imagination, would have expected.

"It's not that I don't feel a tremendous sorrow, because I do. I grieve. I will miss them terribly. But they are not dead; of that I'm sure. Just their bodies are gone."

Walt pulled out a handkerchief and quietly blew his nose.

"My mother told me that they had seen the face of evil and it was hideous." Alex's tone hardened a little. "She told me that I had to fight this evil." Alex paused for a moment. "I know I'm sounding like a lunatic, but please bear with me."

"You've got the floor," said Jason.

Vance was starting to lean forward in his chair, just a little.

"Then my father said something that was completely out of character."

Vance leaned a little further forward.

"He said, and I quote, 'Son, have your vengeance; destroy them completely.'"

Vance shot straight up, spilling his coffee and dropping the cup as he went. "*Oh, Jesus Christ*!"

The other three stood up, out of surprise.

"Vance, what's wrong?" asked Jason.

"You all right?" asked Walt.

Alex quickly walked around his desk and took Vance by the shoulders. "What is it, Vance?" he said urgently.

"I... I can't tell you right now." Vance was clearly shaken; something nobody in this room had ever seen. "I'll be fine; just let me be for a minute." He dropped back down and put his face in his hands. He was actually trembling.

Alex stood next to his friend. "What is it, Vance?"

"Fine, I'm fine. Not enough sleep, I guess. Go ahead with your story." Vance leaned down to pick the cup off the floor. "Made a mess of your carpet."

"No sweat." Alex returned to his chair.

"Want some more coffee?" asked Jason as he got up and headed for the sideboard.

"Yeah, thanks."

Jason returned with a new cup for Vance and a full one for himself.

Alex looked at Vance. *What the hell had set him off? Of the three, I expected him to discount my story as a dream or hallucination and let it go at that. This reaction is way out of character*, thought Alex. *He seems totally conflicted. He probably needs a lot of sleep to get his thoughts back to his comfortable black and white.*

"I can't believe Norm said that," said Walt.

"What?" asked Alex taking his thoughts off Vance.

"You said Norm told you to take revenge?"

Alex turned his mind back to the visitation.

"Yes, yes he did." Alex took another look at Vance, then turned his attention to his uncle. "I asked him if he was telling me to kill the people responsible for their deaths and he said not only them, but evil wherever it can be found."

"Jesus!" Jason was enthralled.

Vance sat quietly, his hands gripped tightly in his lap, his knuckles were white.

"I told them I didn't have the power to accomplish such a task. And my mother told me I would have -- in time, I would have."

"This is weird," stated Jason.

"And finally, my father told me to maintain my course; that I was doing it right."

Again there was a moment of silence before Walt spoke.

"Do you know what time you had this visitation?" he asked, his hands had a slight tremble."Yes, it was 3:15 this morning."

Walt nodded as if the was the time he expected. "Then I believe," he said, "I had better tell you about my epiphany."

"Epiphany?" said Jason.

"There would be no other word to describe it," said Walt.

Walt had everyone's attention.

"Well let's hear it," said Alex.

"Absolutely," agreed Jason.

Vance said nothing but he didn't take his eyes off Walt.

"At the same time as Alex's visitation," Walt started, "I had a crystal clear picture of Alex's life…"

Walt spent the next thirty minutes telling of his epiphany. "I can only conclude, by all we've heard here today, and the events leading up to this point, that we, led by Alex, are doing exactly what is intended of us. I have no more insight than that."

"Damn," said Jason as he slowly leaned back in his chair after being on its edge for the past thirty minutes.

Alex didn't take his eyes off his uncle while his mind tried to absorb this new revelation.

Vance slowly got up and started toward the door. He stopped halfway across the room, turned and said softly, "I'll need some time to myself." Without further word, he left the room.

After Vance's exit Alex looked at his uncle, then to Jason. "Let's all take some time to gather our thoughts and meet back here in an hour."

11:55 a.m.

The three rejoined Alex in his office after the hour break. Jason filled them in on the latest from the government and reviewed with them the extensive plans for an ongoing media campaign. By consensus of the three, his plans were inspired.

Walt spent the previous hour talking to Colleen and Alexandra. He told them of Alex's dream. Whether Colleen believed the dream or not, she was clearly relieved that both her husband and Alex not only believed it, but were greatly comforted by it. Walt asked Colleen to help him coordinate the funeral arrangements. She agreed without hesitation.

Alex spent the first quarter hour of the break watching CNN to acquire a feeling for the world's opinion of their action. He spent the rest of the hour talking to Jennifer on the phone and consoling her. He told her of his dream, his visitation. Jennifer, at first, was skeptical, Alex knew, but after a short time, he sensed, she came to believe him. He was sure she knew he wasn't a liar, nor given to exaggeration, nor crazy. He assumed she knew he wouldn't tell her anything that he himself didn't believe, and she wanted and needed to believe, with all her heart, that her parents' spirits existed and that they were happy. When he hung up, he knew his sister would be all right.

"Vance, I believe you need to fill us in on what happened in Tabriz."

Yes, sir. Yesterday morning at 01:15 Tabriz time, our aircraft landed at the Tabriz airport. Within ten minutes our forces had a perimeter set around the hangar. We knew that most of the terrorists had remained in the hangar after the news of the money transfer and the subsequent murders of Marian and Norman." Vance was doubtless uncomfortable talking about this with Alex and Walt.

"How would you know these people were still in the hangar?" asked Jason.

"We've had a mole inside from the second day after the hijack and two more on the outside."

"Really?"

"Yes, sir."

"The assholes stayed, I suppose, to celebrate the biggest victory any such group had ever accomplished," reflected Jason.

"That's our assumption, too," agreed Vance. "Probably couldn't imagine any threat. And that, by the way, makes us really suspicious of the Iranian government."

"Me, too," said Jason. "They should have been worried about their own government forces overrunning their position to secure the release of the hostages."

"Exactly," agreed Vance. "By the time we arrived, most were asleep. All our forces were equipped with silenced weapons. Our troops simply shot any who didn't surrender instantly."

"Jesus," remarked Walt.

"How could they not hear our aircraft as it landed?" asked Jason.

"It's an airport. Nothing unusual about aircraft landing and taking off. We had already taken control of the tower, so no warning could have been made."

"How'd you take control of the tower before you landed?" Jason was impressed.

"We infiltrated the area twenty-four hours after the kidnapping. Our men cut communication and subdued all ground personnel just prior to our forces' arrival."

"What else happened inside the hangar?" Alex asked.

"We knew, through our mole, that three were sleeping in the Gabriel jet, two of 'em the leaders. Two men and I headed straight for the jet, got inside, and had one dead and two subdued before any alarm went up. Those two assholes were the leaders, including Abdul."

"My folks' bodyguard?"

"Yes, sir."

"All captured alive?"

"Yes, sir."

Alex nodded.

"We rounded up all the able-bodied goat-fuckers and herded them into the transport."

"What'd they do with the 'goat-fuckers' that were no longer able-bodied?" asked Jason.

"We took all the IDs we could find and left them where they lay."

"Why their IDs?" asked Walt.

"We want to know who they were."

"Just so you know," Alex interjected, "Vance and I agreed that if the worst happened, we were going to punish these people to the maximum extent possible." Alex didn't feel it necessary to tell his uncle, at this time, that the punishment wasn't over, not by a long shot.

"We wanted to make sure that in the future, anybody considering a similar operation against us will think long and hard about it. These assholes seem to respect only power and savagery and we're gonna show 'em a lot of it," added Vance.

"There's more to come?" asked Walt.

"Yes, sir."

Alex looked at Vance. "There's something you're leaving out."

"Yes, sir."

"Well?"

Vance stared at Alex for a few seconds and looked down at his hands. "I don't want to appear evasive or flippant, but I think it's best if you remain ignorant here, Alex."

Alex sat, stone-faced, staring at his trusted friend. He had conflicting emotions. On the one hand, he wanted to know what happened to his parents, but felt deep down that he was better off not knowing. “How about just the basics?”

Vance shook his head. “I don’t think that would be a good idea, Alex.”

Both Jason and Walt sat quietly, eyes cast down at the top of the desk, both occupied with their own thoughts.

“Just something, Vance. Please.”

Vance couldn’t bring himself to tell this man or these men that the bodies of Marian and Norman were still hanging when the Gabriel forces entered the hangar. He wouldn’t tell them of the atrocities inflicted on the bodies after they were dead. He wouldn’t tell them of the videotape.

“Okay,” he finally said. “We found them in an office inside the hangar. They were lying side by side covered with blankets.” Vance looked down at his hands, then back at Alex. “The initial report says they were hanged.”

Alex spun in his chair and looked out the window.

Walt got up and walked to the other side of the office. He put his hands down on top of the desk, hung his head and cried.

Jason continued starring blankly at the top of the desk.

Vance remained silent.

After a minute or so, Alex turned back around. “Is that it?” he choked out.

“I personally carried them to the Gabriel aircraft and put them in the master bedroom for the trip home.”

“Thank you, my friend,” whispered Alex.

“I need another little break here.” Without waiting for acknowledgment, Vance stood up and headed for the door.

2:05 p.m.

The four men were just finishing a light lunch around the board table. Alex said little during the past hour. Vance was also quiet, only answering questions when asked. It didn’t take an astute observer to see that he was troubled.

"Jason," Alex suddenly said, "you are to take over the helm of Gabriel Industries and Gabriel International. You are, as of now, President of the whole shebang. I will remain as CEO. Walt, I will ask you to temporarily vacate your retirement and assist Jason as executive VP."

Jason was apparently surprised at the unexpected move. Walt wasn't.

"I'm going to have a lot on my plate for some time to come, and there simply won't be time to head up these companies."

"I'll do my best," said Jason.

"I'll stay as long as you need me, son," Walt added warmly.

"Thank you both. Vance, you need to get to the Congo to complete the operation there."

"On my way tomorrow morning, Alex. Need to wrap up some loose ends here first."

"When you get back, we'll talk about beefing up our military."

"Yes, sir."

"Next, gentlemen, we're going to need our own country," said Alex.

"Our what?" asked Walt.

"In order to accomplish what I plan, we're going to need our own country."

"You mean like the independent nation of Gabriel, for Christ's sake?" asked Jason.

"Something like that," said Alex.

"Well, just how in the hell do you expect to do that?"

"We're going to buy one."

"Buy one!" Jason was incredulous. "You're not kidding?"

Vance actually smiled. "Brilliant!"

Walt sat with his elbows on the table, fingers laced, holding up his chin. His face held a knowing look as he nodded approval.

Chapter 77

THE CONGO
June 20, 1989
8:15 a.m.

Vance had managed to relieve much of his remaining fatigue on the long flight from Southern California to Western Africa. In just twenty-four hours the Gabriel 727C had its carpets cleaned and the master bed replaced. There was no sign of the recent drama and violence. As he stood under the steaming and invigorating hot water, he marveled at being able to take a real shower while traveling at over five hundred miles an hour at an elevation of thirty two thousand feet. These were luxuries few in the world would ever experience.

"Thirty minutes to touchdown, Mr. Youngblood," came the voice over the intercom.

8:43 a.m.

The Kinshasa airport served the Congo's capitol city and was located near the Zaire River just ten kilometers west of the GRI Compound. After a brief stop at what served as a customs check for the Congo, which amounted to presenting his passport and a wad of cash, Vance was driven directly to the Gabriel hangar. He boarded a waiting small Bell helicopter which took off within seconds and headed west up the Zaire River. It would take only five minutes to cover the ten-kilometer distance. In four minutes, the

GRI Compound began coming into view beyond the tall canopy of the rainforest. Within a few more seconds, Vance could see the main hospital building, the administration building, the generation plant, and the recreation area. As they headed for the heli-pad located on the roof of the hospital, the off-duty Gabriel security forces could be seen enjoying the various aspects of the recreation area. Many were in or lying around the pool. Others were playing tennis and there were quite a number sitting under the shade of umbrellas at the restaurant/bar. This compound was outfitted as well as any five-star resort. If the Gabriel forces were to serve in one of the world's most vicious and backward hellholes, when not risking their lives, they would serve in comfort.

To the east, upriver, could be seen the living quarters for both the medical staff and security forces. To the west, down river about a quarter of a mile, was the compound serving as living quarters for hundreds of sick, injured, and starving refugees. This particular compound held six neat rows of eight large corrugated steel Quonset huts. Each of the forty-eight huts was forty feet wide and eighty feet long. Each hut could shelter as many as 100 of these poor souls. The entire compound, amounting to over 1100 acres, was surrounded by a four-meter-high chain-link fence. On top of the fence, razor wire was attached, and at 200-meter intervals, were fully manned and had heavily armed guard towers. The rainforest had been cleared back from either side of the fence to a distance of 100 meters. The interior of the compound was divided into sections by similar fencing, but instead of guard towers, there were manned checkpoints at each section.

After landing on the hospital roof, Vance followed a sergeant down the two flights of stairs and out into the steaming heat, to a waiting Jeep. They drove through two checkpoints to get to the refugees' compound, and proceeded to the hut located at the far end of the area. These huts were a sanctuary for hundreds of refugees who had fled from the seemingly constant civil wars being played out on the African continent. Although the GRI compound was designed as a place of care and healing, this one hut had been converted into something altogether different.

9:21 a.m.

"Right through here, sir," said the sergeant.

Vance passed the guards stationed at the door and walked through the door of the Quonset hut. The sergeant followed him in. The stench in the hot humid interior was nearly unbearable.

"Jesus," said Vance.

"Yes, sir," the sergeant replied.

Dressed in crisp camouflage combat fatigues, black combat boots, a Glock 45 sidearm, and a SEALs beret, Vance looked even more menacing than usual. As he walked, he looked briefly to his left, making a quick inspection of the twenty by thirty foot makeshift pen containing a dozen or so enormous pigs. On the other side of the pig enclosure, he could see five men shackled to the far wall, and an additional five were shackled to the wall on his right. He continued walking with a purposeful stride between the pigs and the captured terrorists to the far end of the building, stopping just five feet short of two miserable and terrified men. These two were chained to the wall in a standing position, hands shackled above their heads, ankles shackled to the floor. Both men looked in horrible condition. One had a grotesquely mangled jaw and both had damaged wrists and ankles where the shackles had dug in. And both had crimson stains on the front of their pants. These were the two monsters Vance had traveled halfway around the world to see one more time. He looked at each in turn, his brown eyes displaying nothing but deep-seated malice.

"I am Vance Youngblood, remember me?" he asked in a loud and clear voice while staring into the terrified eyes of Mohamed Ashubah. A soft moan could be heard coming from the man shackled next to him, the man they called Abdul.

"You are going to die the most horrible death we can devise," Vance continued. "You will die slowly. Your pain will be such that you will carry it with you into the next life. We will then bury you inside the rotting carcass of a pig."

"Please Mr. Youngblood," Mohamed managed to get out through his mangled mouth. He was nearly blubbering in fear. "I was not responsible."

"*Shut up*!" Vance screamed. "We know who is responsible, you fucking coward."

As Mohamed looked into Vance's eyes, he had to realize his end was near. These were truly the eyes of death. Mohamed now surely understood that what Norman Gabriel had said just before he died was true. That he, Mohamed, through his actions, would be responsible for the deaths of scores of his followers.

Vance turned to the sergeant. "Have these pieces of pig shit been made to suffer?"

"Yes, sir." The sergeant walked over and undid the button and unzipped Mohamed's, then Abdul's cotton pants, both of which dropped to the floor. The Sergeant stood back.

"Nice job of cauterizing the wounds, sergeant. What'd you do with their balls?"

"Fed 'em to the pigs, sir."

"What did these slime buckets think of that?"

"They cried like babies, sir."

Vance looked back into the eyes of Mohamed, then Abdul. "Guess you won't be able to service your seventy virgins, what with your balls turned into pig shit and all."

Abdul started crying.

Vance's face held a cruel smile.

"Please, sir," begged Mohamed. "I was only following orders."

"Whose orders?" asked Vance in a calm voice.

"I will tell you if you let me go. Please, sir."

"You will tell us anyway, but we will not let you go. We will, after you tell us, kill you. And believe me, you will want to die."

Mohamed started crying.

Vance turned to the sergeant. "Need to keep these two alive as long as possible; we want names from them. When they die, bury them with pigs for blankets"

Mohamed screamed.

"Yes, sir," snapped the sergeant.

Vance nodded. "Make sure the others see them die and buried. I want pictures and videos of these two and the others dead in their graves, with pigs wrapped around them."

"Yes, sir."

Vance turned around and was looking at the other ten captives. "Sergeant."

"Yes, sir."

"Do any of these others speak English?"

"Yes, sir; three I believe."

"Good. Keep two of them alive…your choice which. When we're all done here, give them copies of the pictures and videos and see to it they get back to Iran. Tell them if we find out that they didn't show the pictures and videos and tell everything that went on here, we will find them and they will suffer the same fate as their friends here."

"Yes, sir."

"*Please*!" screamed Mohamed. "*Please have mercy -- do not bury me with a pig!*"

Chapter 78

HEAVENLY ANGELS CEMETERY
June 22, 1989
11:10 a.m.

The funeral for Norman and Marian was a large and solemn affair. Hundreds of mourners from around the country and many from around the world gathered at the church and again at the gravesite. The President had sent the Vice President. There were senators and congressmen and their wives. Sean Greenwood and even Stanley Pierce were there, but not together.

Representatives from the three African GRI compounds were in attendance. Their leader, Marian Gabriel, was dead. The national and international press was in force. It was as if a Head of State was being laid to rest.

It was not possible to have an open casket ceremony so a large painting of Marian and Norman together, a painting that had hung above the fireplace in the library, was stationed at the head of their caskets.

After the invocation and prayers, and after the caskets containing the remains were lowered into the ground, Alex walked forward with Jennifer and Chuck, and together, they dropped a large bouquet of roses on their mother's casket. They stepped over to their father's grave and dropped a bouquet of carnations, his favorite flower. Jennifer could be heard crying softly, but Alex remained stone-faced, almost detached. Walt, Colleen, and Alexandra followed their lead and did much the same thing. All were weeping.

Alex turned away from the gravesite and walked purposefully toward an impressive array of microphones and cameras. He carried, in his demeanor, the look of cold, calculated determination. Vance walked just a few feet away, his eyes scanning the throng, not missing anything.

Walt, Colleen, Alexandra, Chuck, and Jennifer headed for the waiting limo. They knew Alex was going to make a statement about his intentions, and by prior agreement, they were to head to the protection of the limo and their security guards as Alex headed for the bank of microphones and cameras.

Alex purposefully waited until his family had arrived at the relative safety of the limo and security before beginning his statement. He knew he needed to get through this without displaying the emotion he felt.

"This will be short and brief," he started, "but I would suggest that all who would do such evil things as were done to my parents listen to what I'm about to say." The crowd became silent. "I will answer no questions."

"As of this day and until it is finished, I am going to dedicate my life to destroying all the people directly or indirectly responsible for this horrible act. Further, it is our intention, whenever possible, to extract any information these monsters have concerning any and all persons even remotely connected with the torture and death of my parents. And then we will deal with them also."

There was a loud murmur from the crowd.

Alex paused for a moment until the crowd was silent and then continued. "It is my intention to capture and rigorously question their families and their friends, wherever they may be. If we find any duplicity or prior knowledge of these despicable acts, we will summarily execute those people. We will destroy the homes and businesses of any and all involved. Make no mistake, when I say 'any and all,' I mean just that."

Again the mourners and press started talking animatedly among themselves.

Again Alex waited. When the assembled again became silent, he spoke. "There will be no further press announcements or communication of any kind concerning this matter until we have completed our task."

With that brief statement, Alex, with Vance right behind, turned and walked toward the limo. The assembled mourners stood in shocked silence, trying to comprehend the enormity of what was just said. The press didn't pause for a second and started yelling questions at the back of the retreating Alexander Gabriel.

"Is it true you have already killed or captured almost all the terrorists?" yelled a seasoned reporter.

"Where are you holding them, sir?" yelled another.

"Are you declaring war on Iran?"

"Is it true you have a private army?"

Several hurried after Alex but were abruptly stopped by his personal security force. They clearly were having trouble comprehending what they had just heard.

Another on-air reporter was speaking into a camera. "Has this man, this private citizen, just declared war on a sovereign nation? Rumors have been flying around for the past five days. There was a raid on Tabriz, they say, by forces controlled by Gabriel Industries. Dozens were killed, we're told. Dozens more were captured and hauled out of Iran. The Tabriz airport was completely destroyed. Bridges and roads were demolished. And so the rumors go…"

Another reporter was interviewing a senator. "We understand the Iranian government has, in fact, lodged protests to Washington and the United Nations Security Council. Is that true, sir?"

"Yes, I can confirm that," said the Senator.

"Is it also true that many Arab nations are calling for the arrest and prosecution of all involved in an attack on a nation of Islam?"

"Yes."

"Does Alexander Gabriel have a private army, Senator?"

"I can't comment on that at this time."

The majority of American and foreign newspapers and news programs backed what had been, and was being done, by Gabriel forces in Iran while seriously criticizing the lack of action of the US and Iranian governments. Accusations were hurled from the US Government to Iran and back. Most Arab nations sided with Iran, but not all. Some wished to remain neutral. One moderate Muslim nation actually accused the Iranian government of complicity in the affair.

On-air reporters continued talking to their cameras. They were asking the same questions. "Could it be, ladies and gentlemen, that a private army has the audacity and the power to attack a sovereign nation to extract vengeance? Will the United States Government be able to stop this? Does the United States Government *want* to stop Mr. Gabriel? These are questions that will have to be answered, and soon."

Other reporters were trying to get interviews with anyone of authority they could collar. The Vice President was besieged with reporters shoving and jostling for position. "I have no comment at this time," he repeated several times. "We and the State Department are trying to separate rumors from facts. Let's not jump to conclusions."

Two senators and a congressman openly supported whatever Mr. Gabriel wanted to do. One went so far as to say, "Any losses suffered by Iran or the people responsible for the atrocities committed are of their own doing. I personally feel the United States made a shambles of negotiating the release of these unfortunate people."

August 13, 1989

Information extracted from the captured terrorists led to eighteen additional co-conspirators. These co-conspirators in Iran, after being captured and coaxed vigorously, gave up an additional five. Two of these five led all the way to the Iranian government. Three, including the internationally known terrorist, Sheik Muqbel bin Shajea, had now taken refuge in Yemen. It was now known that bin Shajea was the mastermind, and had financed the Gabriel kidnapping. The Gabriel teams couldn't operate safely in Yemen; there was simply no reliable cover. They would have to wait to exact revenge on the sheik. Someday he would be vulnerable. Then he would die.

Late-night raids inside Iran continued and became the news of the day. The Gabriel forces were eliminating the co-conspirators, their homes and businesses, on nearly a weekly basis. There seemed to be nothing the Iranian government could do to stop it. The assassins were like ghosts. They came in, killed, destroyed, and were gone into the night without a trace. A creeping terror inside Iran was growing. Those involved, who could afford it, surrounded themselves with armed guards, but to no avail. Their guards were killed or run off.

After nearly three months of this reign of terror, the Iranian government arrested two high-ranking officials who, they said, were involved in the Gabriel hijacking and murders. After a short trial, these hapless government bureaucrats were convicted and publicly hanged. Immediately after that, the retribution stopped.

Part Three

Chapter 79

GABRIEL HEADQUARTERS
May 30, 1990
4:18 p.m.

Alex watched Vance take a seat next to Walt at the board table. He smiled to himself. It was obvious that Vance was excited about the prospect of forming a new country. And Alex couldn't help but notice that Walt, for some reason, was treating the whole idea as if he expected nothing less.

"This one looks like it will do the job," Jason continued after waiting for Vance to get settled. Jason, just short of a year ago, had put together a team of people with expertise ranging from anthropology to political science for the specific purpose of finding the ideal spot in the world to start a new nation.

"Let's hear about it," smiled Alex.

"Its name is Sao Tome, two islands actually. They're located in the Gulf of Guinea about 100 miles off the west coast of equatorial Africa."

"Africa?"

Jason picked up three file folders and handed them out. "Take a look at the map inside your file, if you will."

The three opened their file, retrieved the map and laid it on the table in front of them.

"We've looked all over the world," said Jason, "and this is the one that comes closest to filling the bill."

"I'm listening," said Alex.

"The two islands, circled on your maps, comprise a total of 386 square miles. You might note the smaller island is located about twenty-four miles north of the larger. The total population is at about 50,000, ninety-five percent of whom reside on the larger island. Of them, about eighty percent are African with the balance being Portuguese and Creole. The populous is mostly Catholic with a scattering of Islam." Jason briefly looked Alex in the eye. "They, as a nation," Jason continued, "have one of the world's highest percentages of illiteracy, which is to be expected for many reasons, not the least of which is their near total isolation, followed by a near total lack of government or infrastructure." Jason paused to take a sip of water. "In 1975, they gained independence from Portugal with, I understand, little objection from Portugal, and they are apparently still working on their constitution. Major resources consist of agricultural products -- copra, mainly -- and some tourism."

"What about the weather?" asked Walt.

"How's 75 to 90 degrees grab you?"

"Year round?"

"Highs and lows."

"You're kidding?"

"Nope, seems the ocean thereabouts runs with the Benguela Current, which is quite cold. It keeps the hot, humid temperatures confined to the African mainland. By the way, Sao Tome has a 6600-foot mountain on the big island."

"Language?"

"Portuguese."

"Annual income?"

Jason smiled, "$225. US."

"Ah, there we go!" stated Alex as he rocked back in his chair. "Why don't you and Vance take a trip and feel the place out."

"We're on our way."

Chapter 80

NORMAN RESEARCH CENTER
NOVEMBER 21, 1991
1:19 p.m.

"Hey, Dale." Vance poked his head into the Sensor Research lab. "How's it going? Haven't heard a peep out of you for a month or so."

"Mr. Youngblood." Dale looked up from a collection of electronic equipment, obviously excited about something. "Take a look at this."

"Could that contraption be what I think it is?" Vance asked, his voice betraying a trace of excitement.

On a stainless steel lab bench was an extraordinary conglomeration of computers, monitors, microphones, antennas, and what looked like miniature radar. All had wires and cables leading to a central collection terminal of some sort. The mechanism as a whole seemed to have a life of its own, complete with clicks, buzzes, beeps, and whirls.

"I believe this is the answer to about five years of work; that's what this contraption is!" Dale Isley was excited; his movements were animated and quick, even for Dale.

"You can pick anybody, anywhere in this complex and I'll tell you exactly where they are, even if they're in a room with other people."

Vance smiled at seeing Dale so excited. "What have you done...

miniaturized transponders and slipped them into everybody's coffee?"

"Heck no, didn't need to; every human already has his or her own transponder. I've spent the past five years combining six different sensors to read height, weight, body temperature, infrared and electrical impulses." Dale stopped fiddling with whatever he was doing and turned to look Vance in the eye.

"I know, so what's different?"

"What I eventually found was that I didn't need anything other than the infrared and electrical signatures. Each person has a unique electrical and infrared pulse. The variations are minute, but distinct." Dale walked a few feet to his left. "Until I designed sensors that were about a thousand times more sensitive than anything previously used, we couldn't tell there was any difference at all. It looks as if the electrical and infrared pulses are as individual as fingerprints or DNA."

"People have been touting 'aura' for decades. Could this be what you are measuring?" Vance was serious.

"Absolutely. I can't imagine, however, a human being able to detect this aura without the use of instruments, but I won't rule it out, not by a long shot," Dale smiled. "However, nobody has claimed to see an aura through a wall, I'll bet."

"You're saying that you can locate anybody no matter where they are in the Center?"

"Yes sir, and with no remote sensors!" Dale was making a minor adjustment on one of the instruments. "I ran everybody I could in front of these sensors for the past week, under false pretenses of course, and recorded that data. Give me a name."

"Chuck Kroll," Vance said quickly. He had just been with Chuck some fifteen minutes before so he knew Chuck was in the building.

"Got him in the database, watch this!" Dale typed "C. Kroll" on a keyboard and hit "enter." The screen flicked for a split second, and the gizmo that looked like a radar array turned slowly about sixty degrees. Three rapid beeps were heard, and the words "MEN'S

ROOM, LAB SECTION 5" appeared on the screen.

"Let's go!" Vance said quickly and started out the door with Dale in close pursuit.

Both ran as fast as they could through the halls, having to slow down for three turns and other personnel before reaching the designated men's room. Mail boys, office staff, and other researchers moved quickly out of the way, assuming there was some sort of emergency.

Chuck was just emerging from the men's room as the two arrived. Dale was completely out of breath and leaned up against a wall; Vance hadn't broken a sweat.

"Hey, where's the fire, guys? You been drinking beer or what?"

"I'll be damned, you've done it!" Vance was clearly pleased.

"I've done what?" asked Chuck, a half smile on his face. "Just took a leak, but I've been doing that for years now.

"Not you, the marathoner here." Vance gestured toward Dale.

"Okay, I'll bite. What's Dale done that causes you two to be so excited to see me?"

"Come on back to the lab and I'll show you," Dale puffed.

"You might want to consider a regular exercise program," Vance remarked as he looked Dale over.

Chuck looked at his watch, then quickly looked up and cocked his head. "You got it to work?"

2:05 p.m.

... so you see, when I combined the electrical signature with an infra-red reading, WHAMMO! Individuals stick out like the proverbial sore thumb." Dale was explaining his contraption to Chuck. "I notice that sometimes there is a flickering of the image, but that may be when they walk behind lead shielding of some sort."

All three men were looking intently at one of the computer screens. The graphics shown were the floor plan of the complex. They were picking individuals at random and locating them with Dale's sensor. The subjects showed up as blinking dots about the size of a BB within the room in which they were located. Other people in the room were also visible as dots, but much less bright and not winking off and on twice a second as was the subject of the search. Occasionally, a subject dot would disappear and reappear.

"There is a lot of lead shielding in that lab. They work with radioactive material in there. Watch as Bob moves from one part of the room to another." Dale was pointing to a part of a wall in the lab. "Right about here is their vault, lined with two inches of lead. There he goes -- he's disappeared behind it."

"Well, we know you can't see through lead, but then again, neither could Superman." Chuck was enjoying this.

"What's the range?" asked Vance, all his levity gone.

Dale thought for a moment. "Well, I know it works for the entire complex, inside and out. Let's see, the furthest distance inside the complex would be about 380 feet as the crow flies. To reach that point we're looking at breaching," Dale, using his finger to point, counted the walls on the screen, "seven inside studded walls and one eight-inch concrete wall. This doesn't include equipment or other bodies that would be in the path."

"Then we could assume that line-of-sight would be a lot further." It was a rhetorical question from Vance.

"Considerable," offered Dale.

Vance was being pensive. He walked absently to the other side of the lab and then back. "This device is not to be discussed with anyone at all. I'm taking the responsibility and classifying it 'top secret' and then only on a need-to-know basis. Dale, you get the privilege of informing the boss. You really have something here, my friend."

"Alex, I believe we have a breakthrough on one of your major goals." Vance was obviously pleased while he held the phone to his left ear.

"Tell me, old buddy, what have you got?" Alex asked.

"Not a chance, my friend. You'll have to come to the lab. This is something that you'll just have to see to get the full effect."

"Can't possibly make it until about 4:30. I'm starting a meeting in ten minutes and it promises to go on for a couple of hours."

"Okay, meet us in Dale's lab; we'll be here.

"Don't suppose you would want to give me a hint?"

"No, sir."

Alex laughed. "Okay, I'll see you at 4:30."

4:20 p.m.

Alex entered the Norman Research Labs lobby at 4:20 and greeted the security man as he approached the electronically controlled door. "Good afternoon, Gary, how are you today?"

"Fine, sir and yourself?"

"Great, just great."

A buzz and click could be heard and Alex used the lever-type handle to open the door and enter the lab area.

He walked down the long corridor with lab doors irregularly spaced down its length. As he walked, he could hear some animated conversations coming from those that had the doors open.

"Hello, sir," said a young man as he exited the lab to Alex's left.

"How are you today, Sam?" responded Alex as he continued on his way.

A mail boy hurrying along with his flatbed pushcart piled high with packages of all shapes and sizes nearly collided with Alex as he turned into the corridor.

"Hey -- careful, kid; you could kill somebody with that contraption."

"Sorry," said the young man without so much as slowing down or looking up.

Alex just shook his head and kept walking.

Alex knew what Dale had been working on for years and couldn't wait to see what he'd come up with. Alex smiled inside whenever he thought of Dale. This man was something for the books. Dale had matured into one of the nicest, most considerate people Alex had ever known. His absolute genius in the field of microbiology was by itself remarkable, but he was far from a slouch in physics.

He had been instrumental in the success that Chuck was having in heavy particle research. The two of them, their teams and their projects, were of paramount importance to Alex's future plans.

"Well, my friend, what's causing all this excitement?" asked Alex as he entered the lab at 4:23. He walked straight over to Dale and grasped his hand in both of his.

"Hi, Alex -- I'm sure glad you were in town so you could see this." Dale was grinning from ear to ear. "Come on over here and I'll show you what we have." He walked back to his project table. He'd cleaned and tidied the area around the sensor to make it look as attractive as possible.

Alex could see Dale was excited. Maybe he had succeeded with a project that had consumed his life for the past five years. Alex knew Dale considered him one of his best friends despite the fact that they spent little time together outside the lab. Alex, for his part, made sure that Dale was included on the guest list for any social gatherings held at the Gabriel home. Chuck had told Alex a few years back that Dale felt it was Alex who had added a wonderful new dimension to his life, the enjoyable interaction with other human beings. According to Chuck, Dale felt socially acceptable because of Alex, something he'd never felt before.

"We're back," said Vance as he pushed through the door, Chuck right behind him.

"Good," said Dale. "I was just about to demonstrate this gadget for Alex."

"It's your show; go for it." Chuck slapped him on the back.

"You know what I've been working on for the past five years."

"Indeed I do," acknowledged Alex.

"Well, I believe I have it done." Dale moved to one of the computers and turned it on.

5:15 p.m.

"How small can you make the input sensors? Does it take all this bulky equipment to do the job?" Vance inquired.

"Not at all. Now that I have all the principles down and know what programs to design, I can probably reduce the data-gathering sensors down to something not much larger than a video camera, and in time, smaller yet."

Alex was deep in thought and said nothing. He was just staring blankly at the array of computers.

"How about the locating sensor? How large would that have to be?" This time the question came from Chuck.

"Depends on how far away you would want to be when you use it. At the distance we have been using it, what we have here is sufficient." Dale was indicating two of the small radar arrays and another that looked like a miniature satellite dish about six inches in diameter. "I had Steve over in propulsion walk to the far edge of the parking lot a while ago and he started to fade out. That was about another hundred yards or so. The greater the distance, the larger the dish. I'm just guessing right now, but I'd say that we would probably need a dish about ten feet in diameter to spot someone from, say, a hundred miles away."

"Top secret! Only need to know." Alex came out of his trance.

"Done that already, boss," Vance responded.

Alex was now animated and obviously pleased. "Who other than we here know about this?" He turned his attention to Dale.

"No one knows how far along I am, except my team. But most at the center know what I've been working on and many have helped. You know how we work here," he smiled at Alex. "Share information, get ideas, let everybody put in their two cents." Dale paused for a second. "Actually, had it not been for Kathleen in propulsion, I might not be as far along as I am."

"Kathleen in propulsion?"

"Vance hit on it earlier today...aura! A couple of years ago Kathleen, who is into things like Tarot cards, bio-rhythms and such, and I were having lunch in the commissary and got to talking about what we're doing and she said something like, 'You just need to design a machine that can read people's auras.' She, in effect, was right. I was heading in that direction anyway, but she put a name on it and gave me a little more focus, believe it or not."

"If you say it, I believe it," smiled Alex. "But from now on, this project is only for those who need to know." He turned to Chuck. "I'd like you to gather together everyone who knows of this project, and explain to them that loose lips sink ships, or words to that effect."

"I'll get right on it."

NOVEMBER 22, 1991
7:25 a.m.

Alex was sitting behind his desk reading a report while two men sat quietly on the chairs in front. After Alex finished reading and set the report down on his desk, Chris Nauer reached down at his feet and retrieved his briefcase. Nauer looked like what he was, a research scientist. "Thought you also might like to take a look at the studies and history of the compounds that are the most promising to date."

"Our biggest challenge has been running tests without the use of human subjects," said the second man, Joe Martin. "We don't think any of the compounds are hazardous to humans, but of course, we can't try them on college volunteers."

"Inmates are ideal for our experiments, for obvious reasons, but we're having trouble with the California Corrections Department; the layers of bureaucracy are limitless," said Nauer.

"We have complied with all they asked. We have escape-proof facilities up and ready

to go, but still..."

Alex turned to Nauer. "Chris, I want your assurance that we are not be putting anyone at serious risk here. I want to hear from you two that you have run thousands of computer simulations, have tested every compound on all sorts of lab animals, and are all but 100 percent sure of what your results are going to be."

"We have done all that and more, Mr. Gabriel."

Alex sat saying nothing for a few seconds. Then he nodded as if coming to a conclusion. "Inmates are certainly ideal for your experiments," Alex smiled. "You two get everything ready, you'll have your inmates." Alex reached over and pushed the intercom button. "Carol, get the Governor on the line."

NORMAN RESEARCH
March 21, 1992

Alex had just finished reading the extensive report produced by Chris Nauer and Joe Martin. Vance was almost done reading.

"One hundred percent effective?"

"Yes, sir," smiled Martin.

"No exceptions?"

"No, sir," responded Nauer.

Alex looked at the report sitting on the desk in front of him. "I'm impressed, gentlemen. Very impressed."

Nauer and Martin looked at each other and smiled. They'd done it. They had created a foolproof truth serum.

"This will someday replace trials as we know them, that's for sure," said Vance. "There won't be any more bullshit."

"Going to put a lot of attorneys out of business," smiled Martin.

"That will be a real fucking shame," remarked Vance.

Chapter 81

GABRIEL HOME
July 15, 1992
10:00 p.m.

Alex raised his glass. "To Mariana, the world's newest nation." This was one of many toasts that Alex made during the evening. He was slightly inebriated and enjoying himself immensely.

"Hear, hear," said Jason.

"I'll drink to that... again." Walt turned and smiled at Colleen.

The crowd raised their champagne glasses in unison and toasted the new country. The festivities began three hours earlier and were winding down.

Alex's thoughts momentarily went to Aidan. He knew why. He wanted her to be here with him tonight, as she had been the last time he'd felt this happy. *My twenty-first birthday party, seventeen years ago*. He briefly reminisced about that perfect evening. *The ravishing Aidan had certainly put the topping on my cake*. He smiled to himself. He knew he had opted out of a wonderful, lifelong relationship with a marvelous woman, maybe the perfect woman for him. He realized this void in his life had been self-inflicted. But his life, his commitment to the massive task at hand, simply didn't allow time for that kind of happiness. *But*, he thought, *she needed and deserved a man who could at least spend some time with her enjoying life and its many wonders. I cannot*. She had, three years ago, met a man, an architect, who filled that role. The last time Alex had seen Aidan, she told him of her decision to break off their long relationship. "This decision nearly tore her apart," Colleen had told him. *My loss*, thought Alex, *my loss*.

"I've never been happier. I'll have dual citizenship," Alexandra said to her mother.

"Of a new nation… our nation," replied Colleen, a bit tipsy herself.

"It will be a perfect nation."

At sixteen, Alexandra was nearly as beautiful as her mother and a good two inches taller, making her quite stunning. Her looks belied the brain behind the face. When young men made the mistake of addressing her in a condescending or sexist manner, they were immediately set back on their heels by her quick biting wit and obvious intelligence. She was a serious young woman, goal-oriented and deeply driven. Some assumed her drive came from her direct contact with extraordinary role models. Others thought it was simply genetics. Alexandra was entering her second year of college in the fall and fully expected to graduate with a degree in business by the middle of her third year. She, like her cousin Alex, in his first life, had skipped two grade levels, putting her ahead of her contemporaries. Her plan was to continue school and earn a masters in international finance by the time she was twenty-one, a goal no one questioned.

The expansive patio was nearly filled with close friends, family, and political leaders. There were over 300 people who accepted the invitation for this black-tie event. After all, how many times in one's life can a person be present at the birth of a nation?

It had taken three years' negotiation to purchase the island nation of Sao Tome and receive the blessings of the United Nations. Many world leaders, particularly from Middle Eastern nations, objected strongly to the proposal Alex and his emissaries brought to the United Nations General Assembly. They pointed out the recent past activities of the Gabriel "gangsters," as they referred to the forces that wreaked havoc in Iran. They were terrified of the possibilities inherent in Alexander Gabriel owning his own country. Alex would have gone ahead with his plans without United Nations approval, but he much preferred being a member and, therefore, having some, if only a small influence in their decision-making.

Gabriel Industries ended up paying every man, woman, and child native to the island an amount equal to twice their annual income. For that compensation, each citizen signed over their interests in the island nation. For those running the country, the "payment" was somewhat higher, but for just over one hundred million dollars, Alex bought himself a country.

In addition to the cash payments, Alex promised them they would become citizens of the world's richest per-capita nation. He convinced them that their living standard would become the envy of all Africa and most of the free world. He promised them a near-Utopia and he was going to deliver on that promise.

At one point in the evening, Alex found himself briefly alone and standing at the patio rail. He looked down and to the left at the spit of rock where he had spent so many hours contemplating the future. He could hear the small waves breaking softly on the rocks and could smell the ocean. He raised his glass of champagne slightly. *Am I still on the right path*?

Chapter 82

GABRIEL HEADQUARTERS
March 14, 1994
1:45 p.m.

The board table in Alex's office was cluttered with maps, drawings, and aerial pictures. "The pier will be completed by the end of the week, sir," Norvil responded to Vance's question.

Norvil Winslet had been Gabriel International's head of real estate development for nearly eight years. He had overseen the construction of shopping malls, industrial complexes, golf courses, high-rise office buildings and a multitude of other projects over the years. His ability to juggle as many as ten projects, in various parts of the world at the same time, was nothing short of miraculous. Norvil maintained his Australian charm and accent despite the fact that he hadn't lived on that continent for twelve years.

"That's taken a while longer than we expected," noted Alex.

"About twice as long actually, but we'll see a more rapid progress as time goes on. We've learned a lot about working with the natives," Norvil paused to correct himself. "I mean, our fellow countrymen, while building the pier."

"Kinda like herding turtles with an attitude for a while, I take it," offered Vance.

"That's an apt statement," smiled Norvil. "In the beginning while building the airstrip, we needed nearly one overseer for every five laborers. But as time went on, many of them started to understand how to work with schedules and supervision. And they're developing skills along the way."

"I have to assume most weren't used to a 9:00 to 5:00 work day?" said Jason.

"Working together as a team with schedules and systems was quite foreign to them. Most have been doing it their way for generations."

"And not doing it particularly well, I might add," added Jason.

"No, their technology is pretty limited. About eighty percent are farmers or farm laborers. Punching a clock wasn't part of their day."

"Is language a problem?"

"Absolutely, particularly in the beginning. To find people with a working knowledge of both Portuguese and English was next to impossible. We've paid a premium to import skilled labor from other nations, most coming from Brazil."

"Are the English classes helping?" asked Jason.

"A wonderful idea, sir. That hour of English at the beginning of each workday is starting to pay big dividends. The natives are taking great pride in learning a new language. The fact that we're paying them to learn is a big incentive. I hear them teaching each other new words during the day. It's become a game to them. My English-speaking foremen help them whenever possible. It's obviously to their benefit."

"That's good to hear," said Jason.

"It will take a while longer to get organizational skills instilled in their minds, but we have a good start," Norvil continued his report. "By the way, any time we see an individual with leadership potential, we take him under our wing and see if we can keep him moving in the right direction. If he works out, we make him an assistant to a foreman and -- this is the important part -- we give him a different color hard hat."

"Giving 'em a stripe?" smiled Vance.

"You bet! We found that by making a big deal out of promoting standouts and giving them highly visible rewards causes many others to try harder."

"And if they screw up later?" asked Jason.

"That's happened, but not as often as you might think. When it does, we don't hesitate to demote them. We don't make any fanfare out of the demotion, just quietly take their hat away and put them back on the line, so to speak. If they get their act back together, we give them their hat back. But just one more time. They screw up again and they're permanently on the line. It's worked as an object lesson and has been quite successful. They learn quite quickly that there is no room for shoddy workmanship, irresponsibility, or showing up drunk, late, or not at all."

Alex knew Norvil Winslet was fair but stern, the man for the job. He stood and turned toward Norvil. "Norvil, you have a firm grasp of our vision of Mariana and the extraordinary ability to get the job done. So, these fine gentlemen and myself, after due deliberation, have made a monumental decision."

"Yes, sir?"

The other three men stood and turned toward Norvil.

"You, if you want the job, are to be the first Governor of Mariana," said Alex.

"I don't know what to say." Norvil was clearly puzzled. "I have a question."

"Just ask," said Alex.

"Is Mariana to be a democracy?"

All eyes turned to Alex. This question hadn't come up before. Alex looked at each man around the table. "No. The heads of the government will be appointed by the Gabriel International Board of Directors. At least for the foreseeable future, Mariana is to be run like a corporation."

"Then it's to be a dictatorship?"

"Yes. Benevolent to be sure, but a dictatorship nonetheless."

"Good! Then I'll be honored to take the job. I'm afraid I'd be a poor politician. Not much at kissing babies or arses."

"That would fit all the men here," said Walt.

Alex smiled. "Well, Governor Winslet, what's next?"

"Next?"

"Yes, next. What's the next step in building our country?"

"I'm sorry, you switched gears on me there," smiled the new governor. "Next, we complete the road to the airport from the pier."

"Then?"

"Everything! The total infrastructure, schools, roads, sewers, hospital, marketplaces, power plants, water plants, suburban housing, public transit, and about a thousand other things we haven't even thought of yet," answered Norvil.

"Time frame?"

"Three, four years... maybe."

Chapter 83

NEWPORT HARBOR
April 12, 1997

Alex managed to find his way out to his rock this beautiful morning; something he hadn't done for months. He needed a little time, even if it was just an hour or so, to breathe in the salt air and let his mind drift. It felt wonderful. He wished he could spend a whole day just indulging himself, doing nothing. But events and circumstances wouldn't allow him more than an hour at the outside to sit here and relax. He watched with considerable envy as a dozen or so boats left the harbor, the occupants not having to give a single thought to anything other than enjoying a day on the water.

His life, on the other hand, continued to become more complicated as the months and years progressed. The pace he set in the first few years following the "accident" was nothing compared to what it was in these past few.

But today was a very special day. Today was the day, thirty-five years ago, that his life changed. Today was the day of the "accident." *Today, thirty-five years ago, I was a successful forty-three-year-old single man on a skiing vacation. Then in an instant, I was an eight-year-old lying injured on a wet street in Inglewood. How did I ever cope with that?*

Alex reached into the recesses of his mind and pulled out the sequestered file he had successfully tucked away so many years ago. He now felt he had an answer or two to insert among the stack of questions contained within that terrifying file.

There was no longer a doubt in his mind that it wasn't an accident that placed him on this long, complicated road. It was by specific design. He was not dreaming nor hallucinating; he had not suffered any brain damage; he was not drugged. His time line had been purposefully and radically altered. He wondered now if his first life had just abruptly stopped at age forty-three or continued on in another dimension. Maybe his first time line ended at eight years old when his forty-three-year-old mind took it over. He realized he might never know.

The accident itself was the vehicle to move me from one time back to another. Brilliant, actually. How else could such a dramatic change in an eight-year-old's demeanor and intelligence be explained or accepted? By whom, what, or how, he still hadn't a clue. But the visitation by his parents after their deaths cancelled out all other theories. He had, for years, been concerned that maybe, on this day, he would be moved back to 1962 again or to his first 1997 to continue his original time line. But he was now sure that wouldn't happen. *Someone or something has me right where I'm supposed to be.*

Chapter 84

NORMAN RESEARCH CENTER
June 12, 1997

Alex was a great deal more excited and apprehensive than he appeared as he and Jason drove to Norman Research. Chuck and his team were going to make the first test of their "cannon" this morning. He knew that if Chuck could get the thing to work at all, it would be just a matter of time before it would be perfected. Dale had just about completed his project and it, together with Chuck's cannon, would constitute the capability behind Alex's future plans.

"What do you think the chances are of success this morning?" asked Jason.

"Depends on what we consider success. If the gun works at all, it will be a successful first step," replied Alex, sounding a lot less concerned than he actually was.

8:15 a.m.

"We built the tunnel to duplicate the atmosphere that is encountered in approximately 150 miles of this planet's atmosphere," Chuck was explaining. "By pressurizing the tunnel, adding steam and ozone, we have a way of testing the effect that distance, water molecules, and ozone have on our generated neutron particles."

"All you needed was forty feet?" asked Jason as he looked up and down the length of a four-foot diameter stainless steel, thick-walled pipe. It was flanged and joined with sturdy-looking nuts and bolts every four feet. Along its entire length were inserted a large assortment of gauges, hoses, valves, and wires.

"Absolutely. Actually, we could do it with less distance, but a tunnel this size allows us to add more condition-generating equipment as we progress. Originally, we were going with twenty feet, or five sections. But as we got into it, we came up with many other ideas, which required additional atmosphere-generating equipment, sensors, and cameras."

"What conditions do you expect to generate?"

"Thunderstorms, hurricanes, fog... you name it and we'll be able to know what to expect from our little gun."

Alex was delighted with the way Chuck and his team had solved what was considered a real problem -- namely, how to test heavy neutron particle beams through atmosphere...a lot of atmosphere.

"What are these?" asked Jason, pointing to regularly spaced protrusions running nearly the entire length of the tunnel and connected to each other by a heavy harness of multicolored wires.

"Those are the sensors and cameras. They will take pictures, if you will, of the progress of the particles. We can see how far they go and hopefully what stops them."

"Must have one hell of a shutter speed!"

"Indeed they do."

"And this, I assume, is the cannon itself?" asked Jason as he walked to the front end of the tunnel.

"That's our little shooter," agreed Chuck.

"Not as big as I thought it would be."

"Big isn't necessary... I hope."

"How are you able to analyze what's happening in there?" inquired Alex, nodding toward the tunnel.

"In the next room is the control center and the brains of the program. One mighty fast and real expensive super computer that's been dubbed 'White Lightning.'"

"Ah, that's where you've put it," remarked Alex. "If I recall, there are only two like it in the world."

"You recall correctly. Other than its twin in the Pentagon, White

Lightning is approximately 5,000 times faster than any other super computer, and has 20,000 times the memory. It can perform over a half trillion calculations a second."

"Get the hell out of here," responded Jason.

"It's true," Chuck smiled. "It should be able to give us incredible data in just a few seconds after a shot."

"Impressive."

Alex was looking up and down the length of this sophisticated tunnel. "How do you think your particles will fare against the atmosphere?"

"I would suspect not well to begin with, but that, of course, remains to be seen," answered Chuck. "This morning we just want to see if our theories will become facts."

8:35 a.m.

"Start the count down at minus twenty seconds."

Fourteen scientists, engineers, and lab technicians were at their stations. Alex, Jason, and Vance were placed in a space that would keep them out of the way, but still able to view the first heavy particle shot. There was a lot of tension in both labs. Chuck was at his station at the heavy glass window slanted at forty-five degrees overlooking the atmosphere tunnel. Sitting on his right was Dale Isley and on his left, a technician and an engineer. Down below, in the main computer room, were the balance of scientists, engineers, and technicians.

This first experiment was simply to see if the neutron particle cannon itself performed according to theory. There was almost no atmosphere at all in the tunnel. The system was capable of sucking out almost all air, refilling the tunnel with argon gas, as close to nothing as anything on the planet, and repeating the process. After repeating this "flushing" process three times, the tunnel was nearly a complete void, simulating space as closely as it was possible to achieve on earth.

At the far end of the tunnel, located dead center against the two-inch thick lead wall, was a balloon about the size of a grapefruit, filled with water.

As the countdown reached five seconds, high-speed cameras were set in motion, their shrill sound momentarily enhancing the tension in both labs. These cameras had shutter speeds of two nanoseconds -- or two millionths of a second.

"...three, two, one."

There was a soft pop, followed immediately by the shutting down of the cameras and breaths being exhaled.

"That was it?" asked Jason.

"What were you expecting?" replied Vance.

"Take a look at the balloon," suggested Alex, looking at the monitor on the wall.

"It's still there," remarked Jason.

"Looks a little droopy, don't you think?"

"It does for sure."

"Yahoo," yelled Chuck from his station, followed by a chorus of excitement from the others in the two labs.

"Holy shit!" Alex exclaimed.

"Take a look at the temperature!" Chuck called over the rail into the main computer lab.

The large dial displayed on the control panel indicated eighteen degrees centigrade.

"Oh, man," exclaimed Alex.

"What power was that?" asked Vance.

"1/100ths," replied Chuck.

"You two are way ahead of me on this project," declared Jason. "How about a little explanation?"

"The water temperature in the balloon was two degrees centigrade and was just elevated to eighteen degrees centigrade in a nanosecond. Using 1/100th of the gun's power, I might add," Vance explained.

Jason could do the math; he knew what this meant. Ninety-eight point six degrees Fahrenheit, plus anything more than eight degrees or so, equals a dead man.

Alex sat staring blankly for a few seconds. *It works*, he was thinking. *It really works. We've just taken a big step toward the end. I've got to be on the right path.*

August 1, 1997

"So it didn't work so well with atmosphere?" Alex said into the phone, disguising his disappointment.

"Didn't expect it to; not at low power, but we managed to penetrate 24 feet into the tunnel, at normal atmosphere, using 50 percent."

"How many real feet would that be?"

"Well, the first fifteen feet is pretty thin air, as you know. Equivalent to shooting from a 150 mile orbit down to 60 miles from the surface, 90 miles total. Each foot of the tunnel's atmosphere becomes denser as it occurs in reality. So the next nine feet is equivalent to only an additional twenty-seven miles," explained Chuck.

"That still leaves us thirty-six miles from the surface," replied Alex. "The last 36 miles will be harder to penetrate than the first 116."

"About twelve times harder, actually."

"And if you use 100% power?"

"White Lightning tells us we'll gain thirteen more miles. But please don't let these numbers get you down; we're just starting."

"I realize that, Chuck. I'm not concerned. I assume you and your band of merry men have quite a number of ideas brewing. You'll solve the problem."

"You're right, and thanks for not panicking."

"Not my nature, brother. Keep me informed."

Alex hung up. "Shit!" *If the damn thing won't penetrate thin air, it sure as hell won't be shooting through anything else.*

October 21, 1997

Vance sat quietly on a stool by a cluttered workbench in Chuck's laboratory. He'd been there for over an hour listening to exceptional people trying to figure out why the Neutron Particle Cannon wouldn't perform properly. Five of Chuck's team and Dale Isley were also either sitting on stools or standing around the same bench. All but Dale and Vance were making suggestions and offering ideas in hopes of solving the problem.

"So we're stuck nine miles up." Chuck was showing signs of despair. "And we're running out of fresh ideas. We've boosted the power to 170 percent of its original design. And still, even in a desert-like atmosphere, we stop at nine miles."

"I would suggest then, power isn't the answer," Dale came into the conversation.

"Then what?" asked the head of 'White Lightning's' programming.

"Don't know." Dale slid off his stool and sauntered over to the water cooler stationed at the far side of the lab. He started to reach for a paper cup, but stopped suddenly and turned toward Chuck. "Let's take another look at the pictures showing the progress of the particles."

Chuck went to a file, opened it, and retrieved two thick folders of photographs. He crossed the lab to a long stainless-steel uncluttered bench and began setting the eight by ten glossy pictures out in order.

Dale walked over and started looking from one picture to another in sequence, saying nothing. When he reached the end, he paused for a few seconds, obviously in thought. Nobody in the lab said anything. He turned and walked to another bench and retrieved a large magnifying glass. He returned to the middle of the first bench and started looking again, this time using the magnifying glass. "The visible little contrail of particles starts at about thirty miles up, relatively speaking, and continues for what, twenty-some miles? Interesting." He was talking to himself as well as the others in the lab.

"That's right, twenty-one miles," offered Chuck's top aide.

"If you didn't know what you were looking at, you might think you were looking at a jet at high altitude, certainly not a microscopic particle," added Chuck.

"The point is," said Dale, "the particle isn't stopped by the first molecule it hits. It actually destroys or moves out of the way thousands of oxygen and nitrogen molecules before it decays."

"No question about it, the pictures are worth a million words," Chuck agreed.

"Also, it seems not to be deflected." Dale again walked down to the middle of the series of pictures. "It decays as it continues to go straight."

"Yes, that's correct, straight as a string."

"Wait a second," Dale's voice rose a decibel. He remained silent for twenty seconds or so while rapidly tapping the magnifying glass against his leg. "What would happen if you tucked another particle right in behind the first and another after that and another, etc.? Kind of like guards in front of a running back. Each guard would take out as many opponents as possible and the next guard would take up the banner."

"Or maybe like closely-spaced machine gun bullets," Chuck suggested excitedly.

"Or a really thin spear that starts out six feet long, but has only an inch or so left when it arrives at the target."

"I like that one," the computer whiz remarked.

Vance liked what he was hearing.

"At least it'll give us a fresh approach," continued Dale.

"Fresh approach, my ass! That might just be the answer." Chuck's voice was displaying enthusiasm Vance hadn't heard for weeks.

"I'll get started on 'White Lightning' and see what it says," stated the programmer.

"Cool." Dale stood nodding his head.

"Hey thanks, buddy," said Chuck.

"You guys would have had it in no time," replied Dale.

"Gentlemen," Vance interrupted as he stood and walked toward the door, "I'll leave you to it"

Chapter 85

MARIANA
February 21, 1999
4:20 p.m.

The luxury coach pulled up to the entrance of the underground facility located on the eastern base of Mt. Norman. The occupants included Alex, Walt, Colleen, Alexandra, Jason and his wife, Rachael, Vance, Jennifer, Chuck, and the remaining members of Alex's Consortium. After they exited, they followed Governor Winslet past the guardhouse and into the security entrance to the mountain's interior. Adam Texley, the missing member of the consortium, had passed away just before Christmas last year after a surprisingly short bout with lung cancer.

The group, after exiting the elevator six stories down, went directly into the lounge adjacent to the cafeteria. After using the facilities and picking up refreshments of their choice, they all sat on the comfortable chairs and couches that surrounded the three large coffee tables.

The group had spent the past four hours touring the island nation of Mariana with the Governor providing a running commentary the entire time. It was difficult for any of them to believe all that had been accomplished in just short of four years. From the commercial pier, stretching into the Gulf over seven hundred feet, to the nuclear power plant, to the small but high-tech airport with its two ten-thousand-foot runways, the island was a sight to see.

"My God, Governor Winslet, you are a remarkable man," said Joan.

"You're being too kind. When a person can do things without government regulations or involvement, and that person has literally an unlimited checkbook, things can be done quickly and correctly."

"The Governor is being way too humble here," said Alex. "This man built an entire country's infrastructure in just over four years. He built a commercial pier, a modern airport, the nuclear plant and this extensive complex, which we will tour once we stretch our muscles a little. He built temporary housing for over two 2000 foreign workers, completely razed the capitol city and is replacing it with a two 2000-acre animal park. He's put in hundreds of miles of roads, power, water and sewer plants, and he is building entire towns to house our native population."

Norvil was smiling. "Again I refer you to that unlimited checkbook. We were able to hire the best possible help, and lots of it."

Peter was puzzled. "Why would you destroy their towns just to replace them? That has to cost a fortune."

"You had to see them, Peter. To say they were ugly would be kind," answered Joan. "If you imagine a ghetto in the States being an upscale neighborhood, these 'towns' would be a slum to them. In most cases they were nothing but a collection of shacks." Joan took a long drink from her Coke and continued, "Few had power, almost none had potable water, and virtually none had sanitary facilities, for pity's sake," added Joan. "The natives had never seen, let alone had, a modern bathroom with hot and cold running water, and sewer systems were unheard of. These people were among the poorest in the world; just a minimal existence."

"Five of the remaining six small towns are on schedule to be bulldozed. The citizens of three towns are being relocated to new communities located strategically throughout the island. Two other new communities are to be built on the same site as the old towns."

"Each community is self-contained," said Norvil. "The residences are built on streets laid out in concentric circles around a central park and community center. Each community center contains a medical facility, gas station, theater, police station, and a supermarket that sells everything from nails to lemons, shoes to beef roasts -- just about every product that is needed. In addition, each community has a school ranging from kindergarten to eighth grade. High schools are to be built at a later date. Currently few citizens are advanced enough scholastically to warrant any education past grade eight. Because ninety percent of the population is illiterate, we assume it will be at least six years before high schools are needed," Norvil concluded.

"I hate to be a cloud on the horizon here," responded Douglas Ito, "but to put such a backward people in such relatively plush accommodations is inviting disaster."

"How so?" asked Jason's wife.

"I don't see how we can expect these people, who are used to living on dirt floors, cooking in mud ovens, sleeping on rags or palm fronds, and relieving themselves wherever it is convenient, to be able to maintain actual homes."

"Joan?" said Alex.

Joan, at Alex's request, took a year's sabbatical from her duties as Director of California's Human Resources Department to set up a program in Mariana to educate the populace.

"We knew that would be a major problem, Douglas. We sure didn't want to build something beautiful just to have it turned into slums within a few short months, which, without question, is what would have happened. So we decided to take a multi-pronged approach. The first thing we built in each new community was the town hall and a model home. We bussed in the people who were going to live in the new community every Saturday and Sunday for a series of conferences. These conferences continued eight hours a day each weekend for three months while their new homes were being built. The purpose was, and is, to educate them on the proper care and upkeep of these modern homes from soup to nuts, so to speak."

"Really?"

"Yes, sir."

"How's the attendance?" asked Peter.

"One hundred percent!"

"Get outta here! How do you do that?"

"Simple. No attendance, no home," Joan replied.

"Have to tell you, after their first conference when they saw what they were going to get, how their life was going to change, we couldn't keep 'em away with a gun," added Jason.

"Interesting," said Peter as he walked over to the glass-fronted cooler to retrieve another beer. "Can I bring anybody anything?"

"I'll have another," responded Vance.

Everybody else was still nursing their first beverage. Peter handed Vance a beer and returned to his chair.

"Most of the education was done through films because of the effectiveness of that medium for teaching, particularly to people who have little or no exposure to movies or television. In conjunction with the films and lectures, we used the model home for hands-on experience. They were taught to use everything, including stoves and ovens, washers and dryers, toilets, showers, vacuum cleaners, all the way to lawnmowers."

"Really?"

"Yes, sir," replied Joan. "And they were tested at every phase."

Douglas was thoughtful for a moment. "Again I will play devil's advocate. Once these people move into their new homes, what is to prevent them from just letting the homes fall into disrepair?"

"We constantly drill a sense of pride into the people. We have movies that show pristine neighborhoods with people washing windows, mowing lawns, raking leaves, planting flowers -- all the while smiling and having a good time, of course. Then we show run-down neighborhoods with overgrown lawns, broken windows, paint peeling, trash all over the place, and of course unhappy, dirty-looking people. They must develop pride in themselves, pride in their personal home, pride in their street, and pride in their community," explained Joan.

"The third thing we did, after observing everyone in the class for the three-month period, was to pick out individuals we feel have leadership abilities, basing our choices on intelligence, attentiveness, and the respect of their peers. We picked five such candidates in each completed town; then at the end of the three-month indoctrination, we held an election. The rest of the community voted for their choice of mayor. The four other candidates became part of a community council."

"And?" It wasn't hard to tell that Peter was impressed.

"Then we have an honor system. It is drilled into everyone's head that in order to maintain the beautiful community they are given, everyone must work together. It is required that everybody be their brother's keeper. We spell out a simple plan of action. If, as an example, the neighbors see that a yard is becoming overgrown or that when visiting a friend, they notice the home is becoming less than what it should be, they are encouraged to talk to the offending neighbors and point out the error of their ways. If that doesn't work, they are to go to the mayor and ask for his help in squaring away the offenders."

"You actually think that will work?" asked Peter.

"It certainly hasn't in all cases. But it has in quite a few so far. It *will* work."

"Good luck!" expressed Ito, clearly skeptical.

"Don't believe in leaving such things to luck, my friend," said Alex.

"No indeed," added Joan. "If all else fails, we employ the last resort."

"Which is?"

"We left one town on the island as it was. Actually, it was the nicest of the six. We left it as a sort of Purgatory, if you will. If a family cannot or will not maintain their new home, they are evicted and moved -- lock, stock, and barrel -- to the old town. There they stay for at least six months. After that time, in order to return to the new community, they have to pass oral and mechanical tests concerning the care and upkeep of the new modern homes. If they pass that, then they stand before the entire community and ask for forgiveness."

"Jesus! Guess you don't believe in half-measures, do you?"

"There's never been success in half-measures that I'm aware of," remarked Alex.

"How's it working so far?" smiled Peter.

"Only had to move five families to the old town so far. None have yet completed their six months in exile. But the moving of the families certainly caused a buzz in the new towns," declared Joan.

Alex knew Joan was in heaven. Here was a woman who'd been beating her head against dozens of granite walls all her adult life in an effort to better the conditions of the less fortunate. A woman who, by virtue of her dogmatic approach to everything she tackled, along with her keen intelligence, had succeeded on many fronts where others had failed. But she could never, with all her skills and drive, bat down the walls of poverty, racism, and ignorance, within the giant welfare bureaucracy.

Alex recently invited Peter, Joan, and Douglas Ito to become citizens of Mariana. Joan enthusiastically accepted on the spot, Peter a week later. Peter needed to be sure he could maintain his US citizenship. Japan did not allow dual citizenship, and Douglas reluctantly declined the offer. Joan submitted her resignation to the state of California and was taking up permanent residence on the island nation as the National Director of Social Services. Alex was absolutely delighted. He knew he could never find anyone else as perfectly qualified for the job. Joan, for her part, was nearly giddy with the possibilities. She was like a gifted artist preparing to create a masterpiece on a huge unblemished canvas.

"I would like to say something here." Joan was solemn.

"You've got the floor," said Jason.

"I wish..." Joan paused, plainly having trouble expressing something. "I wish Adam could see this. He, I believe, would appreciate what's being done here as much as any of us... and I miss the arbitrary son of a bitch."

Peter stood up. "To Professor Adam Texley, the finest liberal I've ever known."

All stood and raised their glass. "To Adam!" they said nearly in unison.

March 3, 1999

There was a tiny island located about 900 yards off the northwest coast of Mariana. The island wasn't more than ten acres in size and possessed a jagged, rocky shoreline; there were no beaches. Half the island was semi-dome-shaped with its tallest point being no more than sixty feet above sea level; the other half was reasonably flat. Its interior had sparse vegetation -- just a few dozen coconut palms clinging precariously to the volcanic rock and soil, and a scattering of what the natives called elephant ear plants. There was little else.

Vance and Jason spotted the little island while touring the perimeter of Mariana by motor launch shortly after Alex completed its purchase. Out of curiosity, they motored over to take a closer look.

"Kind of a pretty little thing, isn't it?" remarked Jason.

"Wanna go ashore?" asked Vance.

"Sure, let's take a look."

They pulled up, anchored and with considerable effort, climbed ashore.

"Let's walk around it!" suggested Jason.

"Sure, I can use the exercise."

Their "walk," completing a full circle of the island, took a full hour and required considerable effort due to the broken and rocky terrain. As they approached their boat from the opposite direction at the completion of the walk, they spotted a huge, jagged rock starting about thirty feet up the shoreline and extending maybe forty feet into the water. The bulk of the rock lay in the shade of a dozen large palms. They both turned toward the rock without saying a word and within a minute, found a reasonably flat spot on which to sit. They sat on the rock in the relative cool of the shade and took in the view. From this vantage point, one could see Mariana's northwest coast, including the 6600-foot mountain that was renamed Mt. Norman. It was quite a special view. They could see the rocky shoreline at the base of the mountain, the dense rainforest to the east, and the vast expanse of the Atlantic to the west.

Jason and Vance sat for a few minutes enjoying the day and view, watching the distant waves breaking at the base of the mountain, the impact of the waves sending geysers shooting straight up twenty or thirty feet. They were on the lee side of this tiny island, where the ocean was comparatively calm, but they could clearly hear the waves crashing on the windward shore. Occasionally, the faint collision of waves could be heard on the distant shore of the big island.

"You know, I bet Alex would really like this place," Jason remarked.

"I was thinking the same thing," agreed Vance.

About a year later, without Alex's knowledge, the two arranged to have a small dock built about fifty feet east of the view rock, a place where a person could secure a small boat without risking life and limb. In addition, they had a comfortable bench, of sorts, chiseled into the face of the rock itself. Fifty feet into the interior, in the shade of palms, they constructed, of native rock, a small storehouse for bottled water and a few rations.

Chapter 86

NORMAN RESEARCH
October 10, 1999
11:25 a.m.

Dale, Chuck, and Vance were sitting around an uncluttered workbench in Dale's lab when Alex and Jason walked in. "Have a seat," Vance said as he motioned toward two empty stools next to him. The two men smiled and sat; their eyes went immediately to the lone object sitting in the middle of the bench. It was a small black carrying case.

"Can't wait to see what's in the case," said Alex without taking his eyes off the object.

Without further word, Dale released the latches, opened the case and retrieved the Auratron. He held it in his right hand at shoulder height.

"Here she is!"

"This is it?" asked Alex as he leaned forward and took the device from Dale.

"Yes, sir!"

"It looks like a video camera," said Alex as he turned the Auratron in his hands.

"It is a video camera," said Dale. "A good one actually. Made by one of your companies, 'SECLEAR.' It's their new deluxe model."

"Dale managed to shrink a lot of technology into that small package," said Vance.

"If he hadn't, the Auratron wouldn't be very useful," added Chuck.

"And," said Dale, "it's probably a good idea to have videos of our subjects as a backup for the other data."

Alex turned the devise around in his hand. He stopped turning the camera when he spotted a flat black circle about an inch and a half in diameter, slightly recessed just below the camera lens. "Could this be part of the sensor?"

"Good eye. That's just what it is," said Dale.

"Haven't seen any other camera with this feature."

"No, but we feel that if asked about it, the operator won't have a clue anyway. We don't think it'll be a problem. Few in the world know a damn thing about sophisticated equipment."

"Also, we built in a self-destruct mechanism."

"We did?" asked Jason.

"Yes, sir," replied Vance, "If this machine falls into the wrong hands, we have a problem. If some dipshit starts to dismantle the contraption, it melts all internal circuits."

"We had a bit of trouble getting SECLEAR's engineers to incorporate some unusual casing modifications," remarked Vance. "They didn't see any reason for the voids in the case. They considered them wasted space."

"They were right, based on their knowledge," remarked Chuck.

"Jason had a talk with them," added Vance.

"I ended up providing them with a written order before they would modify the mold," said Jason.

Alex smiled, "Good for them; they did the right thing."

"Full production will start next week -- without the special features this baby contains, however."

"SECLEAR is sending us 500 as soon as production starts. We'll add the special modifications here at Norman," Dale explained.

"Good," acknowledged Alex.

"As our subjects are scanned, the operator verbally, when possible, states the full name, DOB, nationality, and any other information she or he may have," Dale went on. "Actually, they may only have a name.

When the tape is returned to our labs, analyzed and entered into our data bank, the technicians will check and crosscheck all information available to assure a positive ID. Videos will certainly help.

"The data is recorded on a videotape?"

"Yes, sir. Digitally."

Alex, after sitting for a couple of minutes staring at the Auratron, looked up. "Well, I guess it's time to get the show on the road."

"I guess we've all been wondering about the same thing," said Jason. "Namely, where to start?"

Alex smiled slightly. "Prisons, I would imagine. That's where it's going to be the easiest to find the bad guys."

"You want to scan every prisoner in the entire country?"

"Nope, I just want violent people scanned. Murderers, rapists, those convicted of aggravated assault, child molesters. In short, bad guys."

"You don't want embezzlers?"

"Nope."

"Drug addicts?"

"Nope, unless they also fit the bad guy category."

"Thieves?"

"Nope -- and by the way, I'm talking about bad guys all over the world, not just the US."

"Ah hum," Dale cleared his throat.

"Yes?" acknowledged Alex.

"Do you have any idea how gigantic a database that's going to be?"

"Bigger than you think, because I'm not done yet," replied Alex. "I also want all politicians scanned from the state level on up. Again, worldwide."

"Holy crap!" muttered Jason.

"Not done yet."

"Oh shit!" uttered Vance.

Alex smiled as he looked at Vance. "That's right, I want every bad guy who has ever been convicted, no matter his or her present status, also scanned and placed in our databank."

"Do you have any idea how long it's going to take to do that?" asked Jason.

"Not a clue," answered Alex. "But I know we'd better start with 5000 Auratrons, not 500, or we'll never get the job done."

"Well, that brings up another question," responded Jason. "Just where in the hell are we going to get 5000 people to do the scanning?"

"Here I do have a clue," Alex smiled.

"Really?" Jason was surprised.

"Absolutely."

"Well?" asked Vance.

Alex smiled brightly, "How many people do you suppose we have working for us at Gabriel Industries and Gabriel International, worldwide, who would like a free video camera and some extra cash?"

Chapter 87

GABRIEL HEADQUARTERS
September 11, 2001
5:59 a.m.

Alex had just walked into his office when his private line rang. He walked rapidly to his desk and picked up the phone. "Hello!"

"Turn on your TV, Alex. The World Trade Center has been hit by a passenger jet."

"Oh my God!" exclaimed Alex as he grabbed the remote control and pressed the power button.

Within a few seconds, the picture of one of the twin Trade Center towers was clearly shown burning furiously. "Oh, Jesus Christ," whispered Alex. "What happened?"

"Looks like a horrible accident," responded Walt.

They both remained silent and watched in horror as the upper floors of Tower One burned, billowing huge clouds of thick black smoke.

"Jesus, Alex -- it's Tower One. Our offices are on the 95th floor, are they not?"

Alex did not respond. He could see that the plane hit below the ninety-fifth floor but the flames, the smoke and the heat were going up. *GET OUT*! His mind began screaming at the burning image on the TV.

Within three minutes, a second jetliner could be seen approaching the Trade Towers.

"What the hell's he..."

The aircraft slammed into the second tower.

"*OH MY GOD*!" both Alex and Walt screamed at once.

September 15, 2001

Alex sat, along with all department heads available, as Vance concluded his sketchy report of the tragic event. Alex's range of emotions went from rage to grief and back. Vance reported that fifty-six Gabriel International employees were missing in the terrorist attack on the World Trade Center. The East Coast Gabriel International offices were located on the ninety-fifth floor and few, if any, survived from the floors that were above where the plane hit.

"I know this is a massive loss for the country, its citizens and the families and friends of the people killed in this despicable act of terror," Alex spoke to those gathered around the board table. "We here at Gabriel may have lost as many as fifty-six of our own. Many of us had close personal friends in that office. I regret to inform you, those of you who don't already know," Alex paused for a moment, "that our head counsel, Bill Mallory, was on company business in New York... he and his wife are among the missing."

"Oh no!" could be heard from many of those in the room.

Alex looked down at the top of the table for a moment. "I would like to extend an offer that any of you who wish to travel to New York to attend funerals may do so, and at company expense."

"I might point out," Vance said solemnly, "it might be that a large percentage of the bodies will not be recoverable."

2:45 p.m.

"We're three years late with our project," said Alex, without preamble, as soon as their limo had pulled out of the Norman Research Campus. "Had we completed our goal, none of this could have or would have happened. I am, at once, deeply angered, frustrated, and saddened. Just three more years, that's all we needed!"

"We will be lucky if we have our project done before the

goat-fucking sociopaths attack again," stated Vance.

"The hate and fear generated in the world by the Muslim extremists and their terrorist organizations will soon cause the civilized masses to accept just about any form of retaliation and retribution that can be brought to bear against these monsters. This can be to our advantage when we're ready," stated Jason.

"The President has begun a well-planned and comprehensive campaign against the terrorists in Afghanistan, and he promises to rout out terrorists wherever they can be found," said Alex. "But I fear that unless his campaign produces results in a short period of time, public opinion of the war, particularly in Muslim nations, will start to erode. The support for any coalition the President can put together will soon disappear into the desert sands."

Jason nodded in agreement. "Some pundits are now suggesting, and I quote, 'that the retaliation against Osama bin Laden and his terrorist network be turned over to Alex Gabriel and his small but highly efficient army of killers.'"

"The sons-a-bitches," said Vance. "The politicians who publicly criticized us after we sent a few dozen Muslims to their just reward have miraculously changed their stories. You would think that they had backed our play against the terrorists from the beginning.... Fucking lying hypocrites."

Chapter 88

MARIANA
September 17, 2002
12:00 p.m.

"Is everything set?"

"All in go mode."

"How long?" asked Alex.

"Ten minutes and counting, sir," answered a technician.

This is it, thought Alex. *This is the test.*

Alex was anxious. This test determined whether or not the years of research and development would, in fact, work on a practical level. Alex knew that without a successful test here and now, his goals would suffer a major and lengthy setback.

The scientists, engineers, and programmers connected to the heavy particle cannon development were at their stations. Dale Isley and five of his staff members were fidgeting with their equipment, whether the equipment needed fidgeting with or not. The main control room was a buzz of various activities. The three dozen or so men and women in this spacious room were either shuffling from one monitor to another or sat busying themselves at their respective stations.

Alex, Jason, and Vance sat in the viewing area looking across and over the control room to the large monitors located on the far wall. Three separate monitors were showing the trajectory, speed, and altitude of a single satellite.

There were at least ten screens monitoring a number of lab animals. One showed ten rats in a single cage, each with an identifying tag around its neck; the cage itself was located inside a thick steel and concrete bunker. Other monitors displayed ten more rats, but these were in individual, numbered cages. Six other screens exhibited six separate cages, each containing one rabbit. All test subjects were under the cover of various materials, ranging from concrete to steel to several feet of water. Yet another monitor displayed a single, multi-colored, old cow standing in an open field with her head down, grazing peacefully. All the monitors had a clock showing hours, minutes, seconds and milliseconds.

"Satellite eight minutes out," said the voice over the PA system.

"Well," exclaimed Vance, "I believe my deodorant is starting to break down."

"There's a lot riding on the next few minutes," agreed Jason.

"The future of the world," Alex remarked offhandedly, as he reached over and picked up a glass of iced tea. A slight tremble in his hand belied the calm he was trying to project.

"Five minutes!"

Alex looked down into the control room and spotted Chuck going from console to console, checking with the operators.

On the other side of the room, Dale began flitting from one screen to another. *It looks as if he might want to cut back on his caffeine.* Alex smiled at the thought.

The central monitor showed the satellite and its relationship to the earth. The blinking dot could be seen approaching the west coast of Africa. Mariana's smaller island, located twenty-four miles to the north, was shown as a bright green spot on the monitor. The satellite was closing in on the small island at over 18,000 miles an hour.

"One minute!"

"Commands to be given in twenty seconds." Chuck's voice came over the intercom.

"Ten, nine, eight..."

Chuck sat at a central computer. When the voice reached "one," he pushed "enter" and watched his monitor.

"Ten seconds to shot!"

All eyes went to the monitors showing the animals.

"...three, two, one."

It seemed that within three or four seconds, twelve of the twenty mice, three of the six rabbits and the cow stiffened and fell over.

For ten seconds, there was dead silence in the control room; not a breath could be heard. Then "*PERFECT*!" yelled Chuck. Cheers, screams and whistles went up throughout the complex. Everybody stood and congratulated and hugged everyone they could get their hands on.

Alex sat motionless; his pulse rate, already high in anticipation, went higher. Nobody knew all that he knew. Few, save his inner circle, had the slightest idea of the enormity of what had just occurred. Nobody outside this room knew that the future of the planet was on a final countdown for a drastic alteration.

Chapter 89

NORMAN RESEARCH
August 19, 2003
3:50 p.m.

Vance got up to pour another cup of coffee while Alex, Dale, and Chuck continued to read the printouts that were scattered around the conference table.

"How many aura gatherers do we still have in the field?" asked Alex.

"We're down to less than two hundred. In another year or so, we'll probably have less than fifty," answered Vance.

"We're picking up the Auratrons as we retire their services, I assume?" asked Alex.

"We offer an exchange for them. We give them a brand new model with many new innovative features for the old ones. Had no problems at all," answered Jason.

"So you've collected nearly five thousand Auratrons?"

"Lost a few," Vance replied. "We had three fall in deep water, five burned in fires of one kind or another and eleven stolen over the years. Those stolen could be cause for some concern, but the self-destruct feature should eliminate any worry there."

Alex nodded.

"We've had to add nearly a million and a half gigabytes of memory in order to accommodate the data," stated Dale.

"If I'm reading this correctly, we have just over 230,000 people scanned and saved to memory," remarked Alex without looking up from the printouts.

"That's right," said Vance. "We can thank a lot of Gabriel employees for the success. We got the right people to do the job for little direct compensation."

"Especially retired people," added Jason.

"That was a stroke of genius, Mr. Gould," Alex smiled. "You, in effect, drafted a large force of totally innocent people, in just about every country in the world, to perform a form of espionage."

"I wouldn't call it espionage; maybe intelligence gathering is a better word," suggested Jason with a slight smile.

"As a whole, the people were delighted to do the job. Cash rewards for taking videos of specific individuals worked out well. And they enjoyed the challenge for the most part," said Vance.

"I actually think it added to the enjoyment of their trips," added Jason.

"And there were only three mishaps and they came out just fine -- thanks to the squeaky-clean backgrounds of the people involved," remarked Vance.

"How many of the 'A' list have we gotten?" asked Alex.

"We have most of them," answered Vance. "A goodly number of individuals in the Middle East and a few in Africa are giving us fits. As an example, it's impossible to get within twenty feet of the Sultan of Burundi or the Saudi Royal Family. Security is extremely tight in that part of the world."

"No way our gatherers can complete the list," added Jason. "And there are 516 left on the present list."

Alex sat for a few seconds with his elbows on the table, his chin resting on his laced fingers. "Jason!"

"Yes, sir?"

"We do a hell of a lot of business in that part of the world."

"Yes, we do; more than the next top three corporations combined, as a matter of fact."

"So what would it take to put together, say, a three-day conference on Middle East business affairs, followed by one hell of a big, lavish party for all the region's heads of state, their families, and their top brass?" Alex smiled. "I'd kinda like to have my picture taken with a few kings and sultans."

Vance nodded his head slowly, a knowing smile on his face. "That's why you get the big bucks, boss."

Chapter 90

GABRIEL HEADQUARTERS
January 22, 2004
11:30 p.m.

"I can't tell you how nice it is to see you again," Alex said as he gave Sandy Oldaker a big hug and then shook Bob's hand warmly.

"It's wonderful to see you, too, Alex," Sandy responded.

Alex noticed Sandy had put on quite a few pounds since he last saw her. Bob actually looked a little thinner. His hair was almost completely gray -- what was left of it -- and Alex assumed Sandy colored hers; there was no gray at all. Both had aged fairly well and looked a little younger than their actual ages.

It was tough for Alex to keep in mind that he was actually a good twelve years older than the Oldakers. He recalled them asking, during the trial of Teddy's killers, why he told Teddy, just before his death, that he was sixty-six. He explained that it was an inside joke with Teddy, and although he was tempted, he didn't feel right about telling them. They seemed a bit puzzled, but were willing to accept that explanation.

Alex had seen little of the Oldakers since the death of his parents. When Sandy and Bob, along with the rest of the world, realized the extent of Alex's wealth and subsequent power, they were clearly intimidated. They apparently felt they had no right to take up the time of such a powerful man.

Alex felt a strong emotional attachment to the Oldakers, not only because of his love for Teddy, but the fact that they had been part of his life in better and simpler times and they would always remain close to his heart.

Try as he had on many occasions, he could not convince them to just call once in a while; to let him know they were all right; to let him know if they needed anything, anything at all. But they would not. He nearly had to beg to have them join him for lunch or dinner once or twice a year. Today, other than the pleasure of seeing them, there was another reason. He needed to tell them what he had in mind. He was reluctant to go through with it without their agreement.

Seeing them brought back memories of Teddy, as it always did, causing Alex to experience a melancholy moment. He shook it off within seconds.

The three sat for an hour or so in Alex's office, catching up on each other's lives. Bob had quit SARC within a month of receiving the settlement from the lawsuit against Jackson, Kemple, and Arbuckle. The settlement amount was such that the Oldakers would never have to work again, allowing them the freedom to do as they wished. They had, over the years, become world travelers.

Up until Marian and Norman were killed, each time Alex and the Oldakers had gotten together, Sandy had brought along literally dozens of pictures of their travels, but after the death of his parents, she stopped doing that. Alex asked why, and was told they didn't think he would want to waste his valuable time looking at a bunch of silly travel pictures. It hurt Alex that he couldn't persuade Sandy to bring them again.

"I have something to run by you today."

"What's that, Alex?" asked Bob.

"Do you recall that when Teddy was in the hospital, we discussed extracting some material from him should he not survive?"

"Yes," Sandy responded sadly. She looked down at her hands

and then back up at Alex; this time her eyes had tears in them.

Recalling that terrible time was difficult for the three of them. But it was time. "Norman Research is a part of Gabriel Industries," Alex began. "Norman is a multi-faceted facility conducting research in literally dozens of fields. One of the fields is the study of human reproduction." Alex felt no need to tell the Oldakers that the research of human reproduction at Norman had been solely for the purpose he was about to run by them today. The research would eventually pay some dividends, but it would take a decade to recover the millions spent.

"I have read quite a bunch lately about in vitro fertilization. Is that what you have in mind?" asked Bob.

"Not exactly, Bob. Norman is well ahead of the rest of the world in cloning. We have, for the past few years, successfully cloned many animals, from mice to chimpanzees."

"Really?" remarked Bob.

"Yes, sir, but we don't publish our successes," said Alex. "You probably noticed the uproar over Dolly, the sheep the British managed to clone."

"Yes."

"Publicity would drag all sorts of people into our business, as Dolly has done to the British scientists. Most of the unwanted attention is from people who are, and will continue to be, a pain in the ass. We at Norman aren't looking for recognition of any sort; we're looking for results."

"Are you going to clone Teddy, Alex?" Sandy asked abruptly.

Alex looked at Sandy for a moment and then nodded his head. "We're going to try, Sandy, if it's all right with you and Bob."

"We have been waiting for years for you to tell us this," replied Bob, now with tears in his eyes.

"I… I didn't realize that. Had I known, I would have kept you informed as to our progress. I apologize."

"No need for an apology, Alex," said Bob.

"Can we be the grandparents?" asked Sandy, barely able to contain her emotions.

"I couldn't think of better grandparents on this planet."

Bob and Sandy looked at each other with broad smiles and teary eyes as Bob took Sandy's hand.

"How will you go about it?" asked Bob, turning his attention back to Alex.

"Without going into a great deal of detail I'll tell you that we have on a special list sixteen couples with fertility problems, who very much want a baby, but neither is fertile. We are going to have more interviews with them and I want you to be part of these interviews. I want your input as to which couple will have the honor of being Teddy Junior's parents."

"Teddy Junior!" Sandy exclaimed as she put her face in her hands and started crying.

Bob patted Sandy's back as tears spilled down his cheeks past his smile.

August 18, 2005
7:45 a.m.

"Sandy Oldaker on line two, sir."

Alex quickly punched the blinking button, hoping this was the news he was waiting for. "Sandy, have you any news?"

"Alex," giggled Sandy, obviously overjoyed, "Teddy Junior was born this morning and you've never seen a cuter baby."

I'll bet I haven't, smiled Alex. "That's the news I've been waiting for, Sandy." Alex had tears starting to form in the corners of his eyes. *So many years I've waited to get my friend back*. "What's the little fella's name?"

"William Theodore Stoddard," she said proudly. "Seven pounds, nine and a half ounces, and twenty inches long."

"Good-sized!" said Alex, his voice on the verge of cracking.

"Exactly the same size Teddy was," remarked Sandy as if she expected nothing else.

"Really?"

"Alex," Sandy chocked out, "it is Teddy!"

Alex sat silent for a moment; he could not speak. "We have him back," he whispered.

Chapter 91

MARIANA
January 12, 2009
6:10 p.m.

"It's been quite a day," remarked Walt. "We four haven't been out fishing for over twenty years."

"Not together," agreed Jason.

"*Should start to head back in, gentlemen*," yelled the captain from the deck of the flying bridge.

"*Take her in, Captain*," Walt yelled back.

Following a wonderful day on the equator, the four of them were sitting on comfortable deck chairs sipping cold beer and enjoying a balmy afternoon. The deckhands had already secured their fishing gear and had disappeared belowdecks. The boat made a gentle turn and they could hear and feel the speed increase as the captain applied more power. Walt's new fishing boat wasn't nearly the size of the yacht he kept moored in the Newport Harbor eleven thousand miles away, but this one was better adapted for fishing and, despite its relatively short sixty-five feet, quite luxurious. They were an hour out and now heading at full throttle back to Mariana. The tip of Mt. Norman could be seen protruding over the eastern horizon. About a quarter mile behind and slightly off to starboard was a heavily armed ultra-modern gunboat that stretched over 100 feet in length. It was one of four such boats that patrolled the waters off the coast of Mariana. Today it had been providing security for this little fishing party.

"Just one man missing," muttered Vance with a touch of sadness.

Just one missing, thought Alex, *our dear friend*. He remembered clearly just about every detail of that day over twenty years ago, a day he had thought about hundreds of times over the years. It was the last time he was able to spend a full day with Teddy. It was the single most enjoyable day he had ever experienced.

"That day was the most fun I've ever had," remarked Vance, echoing Alex's thoughts.

"I would have to agree," added Jason. "I can't think of a time when I've laughed harder, or longer."

The four of them sat in silence for a minute or so.

"Alex, do you believe in God?" asked Vance out of the blue as he took a long pull off his tenth beer of the day.

The three turned in unison to look at Vance. First, it was an off-the-wall question, considering the circumstances and the time and place. And second, it was Vance, of all people, who had asked it.

Alex's left brow raised slightly and he looked at his friend. "If you're asking if I think there is a supreme being sitting on a throne, sporting a flowing white beard, surrounded by angels playing harps, I would say that I seriously doubt that. That image was created by man to give himself a deity he could relate to."

Vance sat in silence for moment. "Do you believe there is any Supreme Being or beings?"

Alex remained silent for a few seconds, trying to form his response in an intelligent way. This was a question he had asked himself a thousand times over the past forty-six years. "I believe there is, without question, a being or beings, some entity or force or intelligence of some sort that has some control, be it major or minor, not only over this planet, but the entire galaxy and maybe the entire cosmos."

Now it was the other three looking at Alex.

"Really?" This admission clearly took Jason by surprise.

"I've known you all your life and I didn't realize you were a religious man." Walt was obviously puzzled.

"I don't believe I am," answered Alex matter-of-factly.

After a short pause, Jason said, "But you just said you believe there is a supernatural force exerting some control over us."

Alex smiled. "I didn't say anything about a supernatural force. I think whatever has this influence or power is probably quite natural. Can you imagine what man will be capable of in a million years, if we don't destroy ourselves first?"

"No, I actually can't imagine," replied Jason. "Do you feel we're being controlled or manipulated or influenced or whatever?"

Alex knew he wouldn't be able to tell them everything that had happened to him. After all, the only person he had ever told was Teddy and that, unfortunately, was just before he died. "I've had a couple of experiences that simply can't be explained as a natural phenomena. You three are aware of one."

"The visitation from your folks?" offered Jason.

"That's right."

"That *was* a visitation," expressed Vance.

"You sound positive about that." Walt remarked.

"I am positive, and I have been since the morning Alex told us about it."

"Really?" said Jason, again surprised.

"Yes, sir."

"Well, I'll tell you," said Jason, "I too, believed Alex's story simply because, as we all know, our friend is not given to flights of fancy."

Alex smiled.

"Also the effect the visitation had on this man," Jason nodded toward Alex, "was nothing short of a miracle."

Walt sat pensive for a few seconds. "Then, of course, there was my epiphany. Since the two events occurred at the same time and dovetailed seamlessly, my belief is rock-solid."

Vance said thoughtfully, "It all fits."

The four of them sat looking out over the stern, watching the foam from the twin props trail for a quarter of a mile aft on this calm day. The only sounds were that of the swish of the ocean as it was parted by the bow and the low hum of the twin diesels as they produced the power to drive the boat. They could see their escort boat was maintaining its distance, and were secure in the knowledge it was ready to jump into action at the slightest provocation. After another minute or so, Vance cleared his throat. "I have something to tell you about that same morning."

Alex looked over at Vance, and at the same time, felt a slight surge of adrenaline. "What?" he asked quietly. He'd never forgotten Vance's emotional reaction to his telling of the visitation, a reaction that was completely out of character.

Vance briefly turned his head to look at Alex, then back to the rear of the boat. "I didn't tell you the complete story of the raid on the Tabriz airport."

The three said nothing while waiting for the man in charge of their security, and their close friend, to go on with his story. It was a good bet that all their pulse rates were suddenly elevated.

"And," Vance went on, still absently looking out over the stern to the vast Atlantic, "I'm not going to tell you all I know now; it would serve no useful purpose. I am, however, going to tell you something you don't know about that horrible time."

Alex was tensing up but he remained silent. *What horror has he been shielding me from all these years*? He wasn't sure he wanted to know.

Vance turned in his deck chair and faced Alex. "There was a tape made of your folks' execution."

"Oh, Jesus," whispered Walt.

Alex quickly looked away, breaking eye contact with Vance.

Jason said nothing but moved his eyes from Vance to Alex and back.

Vance continued, "I bring it up now for a couple of reasons. One, it's been nearly sixteen years and the pain of that time has healed some. And two, the tape and the description of the visitation along with Walt's epiphany made a lasting and deep impact on me. It, in fact, caused me a faith I never had nor sought."

"Are you saying you became religious?" asked Jason.

"I don't know what I became, but I'm sure not the skeptic I was. I have, since that day, believed there is an intelligence far greater than ours."

"What was on the tape?" asked Alex.

"Again, you don't need to know everything...but I need to share one thing. The one thing your father said that will, unless I miss my guess, renew your resolve that what we plan on doing is the only path we can take." All eyes were now on Vance. He had their attention.

"No more than an hour before you told us of your visitation, I was watching the tape of your parents' execution." Vance paused for a second, clearly conflicted. "I saw and heard your father say, and I quote, 'Son, have your vengeance; destroy them completely.'"

"Ahh..." was all Alex could say as he turned and looked over the rail.

Jason was clearly stunned. His face went slack.

Walt nodded his head in complete understanding, tears flowing freely.

After a few seconds, Alex turned to Vance, his voice tight, "Why did you wait so long to tell us?"

Vance looked down at the deck for a moment, then back up at Alex. "For years, I felt you would demand to see the tape. That was something I could not allow to happen. Then, some time ago, I decided I would tell you just this one thing when the time was right. Today is that time."

"Why today?" asked Jason in a subdued tone.

Vance smiled, "I tell you this because we are just a short time away from attempting the most monumental undertaking the world has ever witnessed. I tell you this so you will know I have complete faith in Alex's judgments and direction, since that morning sixteen years ago. I am completely convinced that something or someone has chosen this man to straighten out this fucked-up world. I have a rock-solid faith that we, through Alex, are being guided along a particular path by some force, intelligence, entity, or something we have no way of understanding."

The three sat and stared at Vance, all clearly affected by what he had just said. Walt's beliefs obviously coincided perfectly with Vance's. Alex, himself, felt he was somehow being guided or influenced by an outside force. It was the only way to explain his life. But Jason, until this time, didn't have the faith the other three possessed. He unquestionably felt that what they were doing was the right thing to do, but probably never gave credence or thought to an outside force.

"Well," replied Jason, "I'm at a loss for words here."

"Not much more to say," said Alex. "Vance, I want to thank you for sharing your thoughts and most importantly, your faith. It will certainly bolster my resolve to keep going through what will surely be some trying and gut-wrenching times."

"I need to tell you one more thing about your father -- something you need to know," said Vance.

"Okay," Alex agreed cautiously.

"Your father, at the time of his death, was the bravest man I have ever seen."

Part Four

Chapter 92

THE TAKEOVER
June 30, 2010
2:00 a.m.
GREENWICH MEAN TIME

"PLEASE STAY TUNED!"

"Now what the hell is this?" muttered the fat man sprawled on an old, stained couch. "Can't this station go for twenty-four hours without fucking something up?" This expression was just a little louder than the first. "Helen, bring me another beer will ya?" he yelled over his shoulder. "Shit!"

An unfamiliar logo with bold letters "WGC" at the center appeared simultaneously on every active television worldwide. Every audio and visual frequency on the planet had been commandeered. Every radio began emitting a rhythmic tone, and then at ten-second intervals the words "Please Stay Tuned" were being repeated. The time was 2:00 a.m. Greenwich Mean Time, on June 30, 2010.

"All green!" the technician spoke into his headset.

"Copy that," responded another.

After approximately thirty seconds, the picture changed to an attractive, conservatively dressed young redheaded woman sitting at what seemed to be a conference table. She was viewed from the waist up and shelves of books could be seen slightly out of focus behind her.

"Exactly twenty-four hours from now," she began in a steady, somewhat commanding voice, "at precisely 2:00 a.m. Greenwich Mean Time, there will be an announcement of monumental consequences. This announcement is to be broadcast to every nation, on every continent, on every major and most minor audio and visual frequencies," she said matter-of-factly. "This announcement is simulcast in forty-two languages and will last approximately two hours. All broadcasting signals and frequencies worldwide will be controlled by the WGC tomorrow, as they are now. We request that if you know of people who have no way of listening to or watching tomorrow's announcement, that you make every effort to find a way for them to do so. This is an announcement that will affect virtually every citizen of every nation and will be the most far-reaching announcement in the history of the world."

She stopped speaking and stared into the camera for a brief second, then the "WGC" logo reappeared and then disappeared. Most screens worldwide returned to their normal broadcasting as if nothing had happened.

After a few moments of utter shock and disbelief, the communications world went ballistic.

"*Is this some kind of a fucking joke*?" the vice president in charge of programming for NBC screamed into the phone. He listened for a moment, then more quietly said, "Are you saying this was heard and seen over the entire world at the same time?"

"I don't know about that, Chief," answered the technician, "but I can tell you it seems to be a fact in Paris. Old Leblanc over there just about crapped in his beret. He did, in fact, drop the phone. They received the same announcement apparently, except theirs was in French."

Phone lines, throughout the world, were jammed within minutes, anxious callers asking anybody they could get a hold of, what that announcement was all about. Live talk-show hosts could be seen looking off-screen for some sort of direction. Studio monitors also carried the announcement. World leaders, politicians, and newspaper editors all scrambled for answers.

Within the hour, those stations that were able had their news teams assembled and broadcasting. Major network news anchors who weren't already at the station were called in. Heads of nations who hadn't heard the announcement were informed by their aides or awakened from sleep to be informed. In the United States, the timing of the announcement was 6:00 p.m. Pacific and 9:00 p.m. Eastern.

The Hanly and Jordan News Hour had just started its program. Bob Hanly was speaking "on air" to his co-anchor, Dan Jordan.

"I would like to believe that this is some sort of joke, Dan, but the amount of power and technology it would take to pull something like this off had better not be under the control of a practical joker."

"I don't for a minute believe this is any sort of joke," Dan Jordan replied. "Frankly, Bob, I find this quite disturbing. This is the sort of thing that can cause widespread panic in parts of the world. I can only imagine what the powers in Washington are thinking right now.

"Who or what is the WGC, then?"

"I have a feeling we're going to have to wait the full twenty-four hours to find that out. I only hope the answer will be comforting."

Similar programs were being watched or listened to in homes and offices, in every town, in every country in the world.

The initial WGC announcement was, predictably, replayed over and over on most stations around the planet. The face of the attractive redheaded woman making the announcement was, within hours, as recognizable as a movie star's.

Newspapers, in the process of printing their next issue, stopped the presses and rewrote the headlines: "*MYSTERY ANNOUNCEMENT WORLDWIDE*." A picture of the mystery woman as seen on TV appeared below the headlines. The conjecture worldwide went on continually through all news medias.

"What do you mean, you have no leads?" questioned the

President, who along with eight others, was in the Oval Office. The phone conversation was via speakerphone. "I want to know who, where, and how this was done, and I want to know before they do it again." The President didn't want to be perceived as ignorant by the citizens and more importantly, the voters. The takeover of the airways was huge news and the citizens were looking to his administration for answers. "I mean it, Charlie. Get me all the facts and get 'em quick!" The President reached over and hit the disconnect button. "That man couldn't find an outhouse door from the inside," he remarked offhandedly to those sitting close by.

Seven of the eight agreed with their Commander-in-Chief in various ways, ranging from a slight nod to "You're absolutely right, Mr. President."

"I think Charlie will come up with any information possible, Mr. President," remarked the eighth man. "He's spent most of his adult life in the intelligence community and you felt him capable enough to appoint him head of the CIA. I have every resource available working on this and we haven't come up with a single clue, either."

The president looked over at his National Security Advisor, Sean Greenwood, and held eye contact for a couple of seconds. "You're right, Sean; Charlie's a good man. I just hate not knowing what the hell is going on."

"Yes, sir. Me too."

July 1, 2010
2:00 a.m. GMT

The WGC logo reappeared at precisely the announced time. Again, within thirty seconds, the picture changed to the now-familiar young woman. Again it looked as though she might be sitting in a library as shelves of books could be seen over her shoulder.

"It is my pleasure to introduce Mr. Alexander Gabriel, Chairman of the Board of the World Guidance Council...Mr. Gabriel." She looked to her left.

Now the world knew what the initials WGC stood for and who

was behind whatever was going to happen.

"Jesus Christ, it's Alex Gabriel!" exclaimed the President. "Shit," he added quietly. His demeanor immediately changed from one of anger to deep concern.

Now the world would take seriously whatever they were about to hear. Alexander Gabriel was by far the richest and as such, arguably the most powerful man on the planet.

All remembered Iran. All remembered this man had the chutzpah and the wherewithal to invade a hostile sovereign nation. All remembered he ordered the execution of everyone remotely connected with the kidnapping and murder of his parents, and all remembered that those orders were fully carried out. Almost all remembered that not a single formal charge was brought against him for those audacious acts. In addition, the majority of the free world knew he was the President of Mariana, the world's newest nation. Few, however, were aware that he and his companies took on the burden of sheltering, doctoring, and feeding tens of thousands of the world's most destitute citizens. That rarely made any news. But all knew one thing for sure; this was not a man who would toy with the world.

Alex was dressed in a white shirt, stylish blue tie and a dark-blue pinstriped suit. He sat at the same table as the young woman.

"Thank you," acknowledged Alex as he looked to his right. He then looked straight into the camera. Alex held an affable expression as he began speaking. *This is it…* "I know that most people watching or listening to this broadcast are, for the most part, curious. Some will be annoyed, and others may be frightened. In the next two hours or so, I will attempt to answer many of the questions you have. During the next two hours, there will be several recesses, the reasons for which will become obvious."

Alex's eyes dropped briefly to his notes. "I believe most people watching or listening at this moment know who I am. Many, I assume, do not." Alex paused before proceeding.

The members of the WGC who were sitting at the conference table with him knew him well and could see that he was nervous.

But to those watching and listening around the world, he seemed quite calm.

"I am a man who has had a most unusual and extremely rewarding life. Rewarding, in this instance, means I have amassed a vast fortune." Alex paused briefly. "I tell you this not to brag, but to educate. Without going into any details, I will tell you that the Gabriel International and Gabriel Industries holdings are estimated to equal to nearly fifteen percent of the total world economy.

"I have, over the years," he went on, "shared some of my fortune by helping those we believe to be the least fortunate, no matter where in the world they live. We attempted to relieve some of the pain suffered by the hopelessly destitute. We have done so in various ways. Many of you are familiar with Gabriel Relief International -- or GRI as it's called. Some of you, no doubt, have been assisted in one way or another by GRI, and tens of thousands more will be in the future." Alex looked down at his notes. "Further, Gabriel Industries and Gabriel International provided and will continue to provide thousands of college scholarships annually throughout the world. We have and will continue to contribute millions of dollars annually for medical research. We distribute millions more to dozens of charitable organizations." Alex stopped talking for a moment. "I tell you these things now because I am aware that a sizeable percentage of the world's population are unaware of most of our activities.

"My life has been ideal by almost any standards. I have wanted for nothing. I enjoy wealth and excellent health. I also have the love of a great family and friends." Alex's face became a little harder; his eyes narrowed slightly. "However, in 1979 my dearest friend was viciously murdered. Six years later, in 1985, my wonderful parents were kidnapped and brutally hanged by Muslim terrorists." Alex's eyes displayed some sorrow. "Then, just shy of nine years ago on September 11, 2001, Muslim terrorists showed the world what I and my colleagues have known for years; that is, in fact, their hatred has no bounds and they have no souls. There are, unfortunately, a minority of people, be they Muslim, Christian, or Jew, who hate for hate's sake and do not hesitate to inflict pain, suffering, and death in the names of their various religions.

"These senseless acts of violence became life-altering, not only for me, but for everyone and everything I've been associated with since. These horrible acts were the catalyst that established my future. I, from the time I lost my dear friend in 1979, have dedicated my life to righting the multitude of wrongs committed by all manner of despicable beings.

"I give you this brief background so you will better understand what is about to be done. I want to assure the innocent people of the world that they need not fear; we will cause you no harm." Alex's face hardened. "But let those of you who have trod upon your fellow man be concerned. The world as you know it will be changed today." Alex stared into the camera lens for a few seconds, before continuing, "We're going to have a ten-minute break here." The WGC logo reappeared.

"Ten minutes, everyone," said a voice from the control room.

Alex looked down the long ebony and walnut semi-circular conference table. All eyes were on him. "It's started."

"What in the hell is he up to?" asked the Secretary of State.

"Does he think he's scaring anybody?" offered his assistant with unwarranted bravado.

"Well, I happen to be concerned," expressed the Treasury Secretary. "That man has the financial power to ruin most countries with a nod of his head. This country could be thrown into a deep economic depression if Alexander Gabriel wished it."

"How much is fifteen percent of the world's economy?" asked the Chief of Staff.

"Too may zeros for me to figure," responded the Secretary of State.

"I believe he gave the world that information to assure us that he has the ability to do anything and everything he says he's going to do," offered Sean.

"I agree with Sean, gentlemen," said the President. "Alex Gabriel has a reason for everything he says or does." The President was pensive for a moment. "I suggest that in ten minutes or so," the President continued without taking his eyes off the WGC logo, "we're going to get the shit scared out of us. Let me rephrase that." He looked at his cabinet. "In the next ten minutes or so, the world is going to get the shit scared out of it."

Televisions and radios around the world were on. Whether they were in homes, offices, churches, cars, prisons, or local taverns, they were on, and billions of people were anxiously watching and listening. The world was, without a doubt, paying attention. What in the hell was going to happen?

2:15 a.m. GMT

At precisely the appointed time, the image of Alex replaced the WGC logo. His face held no readable expression.

"Citizens of the world," he began, "you have presumably not heard of the World Guidance Council prior to this day, but let me assure you, the name will become familiar." Alex smiled. "In the coming minutes, hours, days, and weeks, you will learn much about the WGC." Alex's eyes were staring directly into the camera's eye. "The first thing you will need to know about the WGC is this. As of this moment, the WGC is assuming control of all the world's governments."

"What did that son of a bitch just say?" asked the President, suddenly shooting forward in his chair, spilling his coffee in the process.

"I think he said the WGC had just taken control of all the governments in the world, Mr. President," an aide answered in an abnormally high-pitched voice, his eyes not leaving the screen.

"They haven't taken control of this one, by God!" expressed the President, his eyes also glued to the screen. "Why doesn't he say something?"

"Probably waiting for the world's population to pick their collective asses up off the floor," suggested Sean.

Alex paused for a full thirty seconds to let what he just stated sink in. He continued looking directly into the camera's eye, but remained silent. "To continue," he resumed, "we, the WGC, have taken control of the world's governments without firing a shot or launching any sort of attack. We are doing so by virtue of this announcement alone." Alex paused again. "Just so there is no misunderstanding, let me assure you that the WGC has the ability to force the world to its knees, by economic manipulation and/or physical force." Alex momentarily took his eyes off the camera and looked down and then back up. "To accomplish this seemingly impossible task, the WGC has, over the past five years, placed seventy-eight satellites in various orbits around this planet. These satellites are of multipurpose design. Over the next few minutes, days, and weeks, you will learn some of their purposes and abilities." Alex stopped and seemed to take a deep breath. "One of the abilities, obviously, is to override every frequency, both audio and visual, worldwide. That ability is allowing us to do what we are doing at this moment."

"Did we not help this son of a bitch launch most of those satellites?" asked the President.

"About half, sir," answered the Chairman of the Joint Chiefs. "But Gabriel paid a fair price for our service."

"They developed their own launching system a few years ago, and far superior to ours, I understand," added Sean.

"Shit," muttered the Secretary of Defense.

Alex continued, "I will now tell you why we of the WGC are taking this drastic step; why we are being so bold and why this action has to be taken.

"The world, as we know it, is in the throes of destroying itself. Corrupt governments, run by greedy men, are raping economies, people, land, and seas without regard to the consequences. New and more restrictive laws and regulations are systematically replacing freedoms of so-called free countries. In the so-called 'free nations,' many of these new laws and regulations come under the guise of added security, and many freedoms have been systematically removed since the World Trade Center massacre. The United States, as an example, prides itself on being the leader of the free world. The fact is that the citizens of the United States have been losing freedoms at a steady pace for the past fifty years, and at an alarming rate for the past nine. Elected officials, in all democratic nations, listen to special interest groups, listen to the cries of the minorities and make their majorities pay and suffer. They pass laws and taxes to protect and aid the criminals, perverts, and shiftless with little or no regard for their honest, caring, and industrious citizens. They pass laws to protect the guilty, despite the suffering of the innocent. Their tax structures effectively make their citizens indentured servants. All so-called free nations are making the same mistakes."

"Crime worldwide is at epidemic proportions. Wars are commonplace in nearly every corner of the planet. Eighty percent of the world's population is within a two-weeks' food supply of starvation. The world's forests and seas are being stripped of all exploitable life. The air, ocean, rivers, and streams have been and are continuing to be polluted to the point of no return." Alex paused to consult his notes. "Based on our statistics, which I can assure you are accurate, this planet is becoming perilously close to self-destruction. Within the next sixty years, at the present rate of decline, it may well reach a point from which nothing can be done. We estimate that, without intervention, the planet Earth will start an irreversible downward spiral which will, within a mere 200 years, make it all but uninhabitable. We estimate that seventy percent of all species alive today will cease to exist." Alex again paused for a brief moment. "We are taking control simply because it is necessary to assure the survival of the planet. From this point forward, we will take strict control of all major world decisions and functions.

"I believe now is an appropriate time to take a fifteen-minute break."

The WGC logo once again appeared on the screen.

Alex looked at his colleagues and family sitting around the long table. He stood shakily to release some of the tension in his joints.

"Well, that ought to get some phones ringing," Jason said quietly.

"Get me Brozovich, Jung, Leguyonne, and Merrill on a conference call," demanded the President.

"Yes, sir."

"We're going to be ready to blow this megalomaniac off the fucking planet." The President looked at his Secretary of Defense. "Sam! DEFCOM 2, everybody gets mobilized... General!"

"Yes, sir."

"I want enough missiles retargeted to turn his piss-ant little island into a deep hole in the ocean."

"Yes, sir," responded the General. This was something he could sink his teeth into.

"Mr. President," Sean said calmly.

"What is it?" the President snapped.

"I think, before we start a war, we should hear what Gabriel has to say."

"He's said all I need to hear. And why wouldn't your ass be in gear? I want a DEFCOM 2 now!"

"I would suggest, Mr. President," continued Sean, "that there is little or no urgency at this time. We are not being attacked in any way that I'm aware of."

The President seemed about to fire his National Security Chief when he took pause. He stared at Sean for a couple of seconds. Sean, over the past couple of years, had been his most trusted advisor. He knew that Sean would always give him an honest and accurate opinion, and he had always been grateful for that.

"Your conference call is ready, Mr. President."

The President continued to look at Sean for a few seconds, his emotions clearly written on his now-drawn features. He was definitely in conflict. He took a deep breath, reached over, and picked up the phone.

The heads of the world's most powerful nations all wanted to give the President their opinion as to how to proceed, at the same moment.

"Gentlemen," interjected the President, "I suggest we hold off on any aggression until after we have heard what Mr. Gabriel has to say." He looked over at Sean. "We, as far as I am aware, are not being attacked in any way at the moment. Let's hear the man out before we decide on a course of action."

2:40 a.m. GMT

The screen again changed to Alex. "I have to assume that during this last break, a few governments started a dialogue concerning the destruction of the WGC, including the nation of Mariana. I cannot and will not fault them for that. I suggest, however, that they pay close attention to what I say next."

What was to happen next was the most emotional decision Alex had ever made.

Stay tough, stay tough, he repeated to himself. *You've gone over this moment a thousand times; stay on track.*

He steeled himself and began. "To demonstrate how serious we are in our world domination, and as a demonstration of another capability of our satellites, we are, starting at this moment," Alex paused and looked off-camera to his right for a few seconds; his face seemed to grow a little older, and he gave a slight nod. "We are now, with the use of these satellites, summarily executing the following persons: all people worldwide who have been convicted of aggravated or first-degree murder, including those who have served prison time and have been released. All persons who are guilty, in our opinion, of aggravated or first-degree murder, but have not been convicted for whatever reason. As an example, there are three famous sports figures and two actors on our list. Also on the list are a number of national leaders, politicians, and military persons past and present, who are guilty of political executions, torture, or genocide. The majority of these are from the Middle East, Africa, and Third World countries. We are also executing most, but not all, child molesters, rapists, and persons guilty of malicious aggravated assaults. Those being executed are, in our opinion, dangerous, amoral sociopaths who, left to live, will continue to destroy lives and wreak havoc. They will do so no longer. We, admittedly, don't know who all these people are yet, so many will live for a while. We would suggest to those people who may escape our initial justice to lay low and change your ways. Any future 'capital crimes' will not escape our judgment.

"We, in a future broadcast, will provide a list of capital crimes to the world. So there is no mistake, it is our judgment alone that determines who lives and who dies, and there is no appeal in our court." Alex paused and then added, "We will pause for thirty minutes to let what I have just told you sink in and to allow time for everyone to see that what I have said is true."

The WGC logo reappeared on the screen.

By Alex's direct order and by his design, tens of thousands of lives were being extinguished. Intellectually, he had convinced himself it was the right and just thing to do, but emotionally, he was hating himself for playing a demigod. But he knew that without the fear and caution that these executions would instill, the superpowers of the world would not hesitate to attack and destroy them.

Alex was fully aware that this moment was the culmination of two lifetimes of work and sacrifice. This was the moment he had been working toward since regaining consciousness on a wet street forty-eight years before. There was no question that his fate and time had been twisted for this moment. It was his sole purpose in life.

The world was dumbfounded. Tens of millions of people sat in shock or stared transfixed at their televisions or cried, or screamed, or ran around without direction. Hundreds of millions more rejoiced and laughed. The multitude listening to radios went through the same myriad emotions. Confusion reigned supreme in most national capitols and in eight countries -- as of this moment, there were no living leaders.

Alexander Gabriel, possibly the most respected man in the world, a great humanitarian and philanthropist, strong of character and will -- the man who had built dozens of hospitals in Third World countries and provided the funds to staff, supply and protect them; the man who was first to offer help wherever a disaster struck

-- this saint of a man was now killing how many? Thousands at least, maybe tens of thousands.

"Get me a prison warden on the phone right now!" ordered the President.

"Which prison?" asked an aide.

"*I DON'T GIVE A SHIT WHICH ONE*," yelled the President, "as long as it has a death row." Sweat beads appeared on his forehead.

The President called in his entire cabinet to watch the WGC announcement in the Situation Room. None, except Sean Greenwood, had any idea of the subject of the announcement. The rest, as of this moment, were in various states of shock, fear, and confusion.

All over the world, people, the majority of them men, were dying right where they sat or stood. Two men walking down the street -- one dropped to the ground while the other looked on in shock. Men tumbled off their couches, dead. In showers, in churches, they fell dead. No matter where they were or what they were doing, their life was ended.

Their loved ones, if any, were screaming and crying as they cradled their relatives, friends, or lovers. Others, who were not with their doomed loved ones, were in anguish. Could this be true? Could this really be happening?

"Yes, Mr. President, they're all dead... yes, sir, the guards on duty tell me it looked like an electrical jolt and they just fell in a heap, limp as a rag."

"No pain, no sounds, Warden Gillespy?" asked the President.

"Apparently not. One guard told me that the bodies seemed quite a bit warmer than normal, however. I've got the prison doctor on his way to the 'row' now. It's not just the inmates on the 'row' who are dead, by the way, sir; there are dead bodies all over the prison... yes, sir; I'll give you a full report within the hour," agreed the warden.

"You do that, Warden." The President hung up. "Holy shit!"

THE WGC

3:20 a.m. GMT

"Thirty seconds!"

Alex did not speak during the thirty-minute break. His father and mother's last words began reverberating in his mind. It was as if he were back in the dream. *"You are asleep, Son, but this isn't a dream,"* he remembered his mother had told him. *"You have been given a gift, Alex,"* his father had said. *"There is much you must accomplish in your life, but you cannot do it if you're consumed with hate and anger."* Alex could still feel the compassion and love his parents had displayed so long ago in the darkness of his room. Tears started forming in his eyes. *"I know now what you will do, and I know it's something you must do,"* his father told him.*"We have seen the face of evil and it is hideous...you are the one to fight this evil.... Maintain the course, Son. You're doing the right thing."*

Alex again became aware of Vance and Jason at his side. He took a great deal of comfort in having such loyal and capable friends. But now he must remain completely focused on the task at hand. He looked up at a monitor on a far wall, the one displaying the activities of the satellites.

"Ten seconds," said the technician.

Jason and Vance moved back toward their seats

"...five, four, three, two, one."

The image of Alex reappeared on the screen.

Alex continued to show no emotion. "We have to assume that you now know we have, in fact, already executed many of those we described. So you know, the exact number to be executed at this time is 157,580. You should also be aware that over 23,000 of this number have been executed in the past 32 minutes."

Alex paused and set aside some notes and replaced them with others.

"We also realize there are thousands of people around the world who have taken advantage of and seriously damaged others without having committed capital crimes. Trusted officials, politicians, power brokers, investment counselors, bankers, attorneys, and con men of every description. We know of many corrupt political leaders and in many cases, we know how much money they embezzled and extorted from their respective countries and citizens. We are in the process of confiscating every asset these criminals have and whenever possible, returning funds to those who lost it. Where that cannot be determined, the funds will be returned to the city, county, state, country, or province that suffered the loss. Not only will these criminals be wiped out financially, but they will be arrested and spend a great deal of time in prison. We consider corrupt politicians, persons in positions of trust, who steal from their fellow man, on a much lower rung than ordinary thieves.

"To that end, we have effectively sealed, as of the beginning of the week, the bank accounts and other assets of all such persons. This includes banks and other financial institutions whose records have historically been impossible to access."

"23,000 killed in 32 minutes -- holy mother of God! What kind of weapon do they have?" asked the President.

"Not known, sir," offered the Secretary of Defense. "But if I were to guess, I'd have to say it has to be some sort of laser or heavy-particle beam. There haven't been any reports of explosions, fires, or for that matter, any kind of sound." Manning paused. "These people are just dropping dead no matter where they are or what they're doing. We haven't gotten a single report to the contrary."

"I think as important as the weapon is, how the hell are they aiming it," remarked the Chairman of the Joint Chiefs. "They're hitting specific individuals under cover of large buildings from space, for Christ's sake."

"Yes," said the President, "they are."

Phones could be heard ringing in the background, excited voices talking.

Alex continued, "Now we feel is the time to share our goals with you."

The screen turned a deep blue. Alex's voice stated the goals as they appeared in white lettering, one at a time on the screen.

"We will:

1. FORM A CENTRAL WORLD GOVERNMENT WITH THE EXISTING NATIONS BECOMING AUTONOMOUS STATES WITHIN THE NEW GOVERNMENT.
2. ELIMINATE ALL WARS.
3. PUNISH CRIME TO A POINT THAT IT WILL NO LONGER BE A VIABLEALTERNATIVE LIFESTYLE.
4. RESTORE FREEDOM WHERE IT HAS BEEN TAKEN AND INSTALL FREEDOM WHERE IT HAS NEVER BEEN.
5. CONTROL THE WORLD POPULATION.
6. ELIMINATE HUNGER WORLDWIDE.
7. PROVIDE HEALTH CARE TO ALL THE WORLD'S CITIZENS.
8. BEGIN RESTORING THE PLANET TO A HEALTHY CONDITION.
9. CREATE A SINGLE WORLD MONETARY SYSTEM."

The screen returned to Alex.

"You must understand these are not goals that we hope to accomplish. These are goals we will accomplish. We know exactly how long some of these goals will take. The balance will be accomplished as soon as humanly possible." Alex glanced at his notes. "We will take a twenty-minute break." The screen returned to the WGC logo.

The world's citizens were of mixed emotions. Many were terrified, but many more rejoiced. Some were happy; some were heartbroken. All were bewildered to one degree or another.

The Situation Room was, for the most part quiet, each man in the room deep in his own thoughts and emotions. The President himself seemed dazed. He had turned in his chair and was looking absently at a bank of monitors. His world, as it was for billions of others, had been turned upside down. This man who had sought and fought for power all his life felt absolutely helpless.

Sean got up and walked behind the President and placed his hand on the President's shoulder. "Mr. President, I would like to suggest to you that it is not Alex Gabriel's intention to remove you or most other heads of state from office. You will, I believe, remain President of the United States."

The President turned and looked at Sean and nodded his head. "Yes, that may be true, but at his pleasure, not at the pleasure of our citizens and certainly not at mine."

3:40 a.m. GMT

Again Alex's image returned to the screen.

Alex started without preamble. "I told you earlier that we knew how long it would take to accomplish certain of our goals. One goal is well on its way to being accomplished, the elimination of most crime. All criminals or would-be criminals, still alive, had better pay close attention to the following." Alex stared even deeper into the camera's eye. "Almost any crime committed within the next sixty days will be considered a capital crime. So, take heed.

"The second goal we will accomplish today is eliminating all wars." Alex leaned slightly forward in his chair. "Warring nations and warring people are hereby ordered by the World Guidance Council to cease all aggressions immediately. Those leaders of nations who choose to ignore this order will be executed. This includes leaders of nations that back terrorism or condone and encourage such activities. If we observe continued aggression anywhere in the world, we will begin executions of those responsible within forty-eight hours." Alex maintained a serious expression. "We expect and require all armies to be ordered to retreat from battle as of this moment. We will not tolerate any dragging of feet in this matter. If you want to live longer than forty-eight hours, remove your troops from any and every conflict!" Alex paused for a few seconds.

"It is assumed that some nations will get together and plan an attack on the WGC. I will say this now and will probably repeat it to some extent over the next few days and weeks. Any act of aggression against the WGC will cause the immediate death of the leaders of the nation or nations who order such an attack." Alex stopped for a few seconds. "The executions presently being carried out will convince all but the incredibly stupid that we can and will single out anybody in the world no matter where they are or what they are doing, and cause their instant demise. We sincerely hope these national leaders realize their continued survival is a great deal more important and useful to their nation's futures than their deaths. To order an attack of any kind on Mariana, the WGC, or any person, organization, or company that is in any way connected with the WGC or Gabriel Industries has the same effect as suicide on those who order or condone such an attack." Alex paused and continued, "As an example, if the President of the United States, his advisors, or any member or members of the Congress or Senate advocate or vote for hostilities against WGC… they-will-be-executed." Alex again paused.

All his cabinet was looking at the President, wondering what his reaction would be to this additional threat. They didn't have to wait long.

"Gentlemen, since we have to assume that Mr. Gabriel and The 'World Guidance Council' cannot afford to bluff at this point, and, in fact, are proving that they can and will take lives -- a lot of lives -- I am hereby ordering any and all hostilities in which The United States is involved to cease until further notice."

"Mr. President," said the Secretary of Defense, "you can't let this man dictate policy to the United States."

"Really, Paul?" the President responded sarcastically. "I would suggest that you give Mr. Gabriel a call after he's done with this proclamation, and personally tell him you want him to kiss your ass, and that 'you' voted to ignore his warning."

Sean sat passively watching this exchange.

Alex was growing weary. The emotional strain was taking its toll. He told himself that this first day was almost over and with it, the worst he would have to endure. He wanted to sleep.

"Further," he continued, "you must be made aware that the WGC has the ability to destroy all ballistic missiles as they are launched, submarines no matter what their depth, and aircraft no matter what their altitude. We are, in a word, invulnerable.

"We will avoid, whenever possible, the taking or endangering of innocent lives. We consider armed forces, ordered into battle against the WGC, innocent people. Because of this, we will attempt to immobilize any armies sent against us without lethal force. We will, however, execute those who ordered those troops into battle.

"To prove to the world that we can do all these things, and as a further demonstration of our capabilities, we will allow each of the following five countries -- The United States, Britain, Russia, China, and France -- to launch a limited attack on our position. Each country is to use a single missile of their choice, fired from any location, and at any time, within the next four days. You may choose to launch all five missiles at once, or you may choose to launch them at separate times or any combination thereof; the choice is yours. It is a requirement that you remove the atomic warheads for your own protection. These missiles will be destroyed shortly after their launch and there is no point in spreading radioactive material anywhere on the planet." Alex looked down and then back to the camera. "Be warned, only one missile each, and no other sort of attack will be tolerated. We do not wish to harm anyone. Within the next three months, the dismantling of all nuclear weapons will begin. They will become a horror of the past." Alex looked down at his notes.

"It is not our intention to have control of the everyday operations of any governments, individual nations, or the lives of the individuals in those nations. We do not have the manpower to occupy even the smallest of countries; nor will it be necessary to do so. Changes will, however, be made in the leadership of twenty-three nations because of the absolute and deep corruption that these nations are suffering. To this end, we have had in training, for the past eighteen months, over a thousand citizens from these twenty-three separate nations. Some of these trainees are the legally elected heads of state and other officials who have been exiled from their countries by the despots in power. The depraved heads of eight of the twenty-three nations and most of their henchmen have been executed today. The new heads of state and their support staff are within hours of returning to their respective capitols. The remaining fifteen ineffective and corrupt leaders will simply be removed, jailed, and replaced with the citizens of their countries who have trained with us. Most trainees will be returned to their countries within the next two days and will take control of their respective governments.

"I must give a note of warning here. The people who have been training with us have had no idea as to our activities or plans. They are, most likely, even more surprised and shocked than most of you. Be that as it may, there will be those in their countries who will blame them for what has happened today. There will be those who will seek revenge on these innocent people. To those who would harm these people, I say this: Do not harm them in any way, for you will be executed. We know that many religions teach that sacrificing one's life in the name of their deity secures a place in heaven. If you are ignorant enough to believe such lies, and you harm in any way your new leaders, we will immediately execute you, and then you can judge for yourself whether you've gone to heaven or hell.

"We realize that right now, there are literally tens of millions of frightened people around the world. We do not wish to frighten you, but it is unavoidable for the time being." Alex's eyes softened as he spoke. "If you listen carefully to what I'm going to tell you over the next few minutes, I believe I can relieve the fear the vast majority. There is, however, about one percent of the world population who will not be relieved of their fear, and frankly, we have no intention of making these people comfortable.

"As stated, our number one goal is to form a New World government and have all nations become distinctive, autonomous states within that new government. This New World government will be called the World Guidance Council. The WGC will provide laws and guidelines for all nations and their citizens to follow. From that moment on, the WGC will oversee the individual nations' governments to be sure the basic laws are followed. I must stress this clearly. We are not interested in changing the world's religions in any way. Your religious beliefs are your right. But heed the fact that your neighbor has the same right to believe as he wishes. There will be, in all nations from this day forward, a complete separation of church and state. The new laws will, for the most part, give much greater freedom and a great deal more safety to the world's citizens.

"Your nations remain independent nations. However, as of this moment in time, all nations are republics. You vote for the people whom you wish to manage your government's affairs. It will not be the WGC. As stated, we, of the WGC have no interest in controlling your everyday lives. There will be no storm troopers banging at your door in the middle of the night. There will be no arrests made on trumped-up charges. There will be no abductions and torture. These are some of the atrocities that we have just eliminated. Those of you who have been living in fear of your government can sleep easy tonight. Those governments are gone forever." Alex smiled for the first time. "You are not a conquered people; you are an emancipated people."

"It is our intention to change the disastrous direction in which the world is going and correct the multitude of major injustices and errors that individuals, corporations, and governments of all nations have made and continue to make.

"We know that over the next few weeks, you will hear of little else besides what has happened here today. I hope you keep an open mind and listen to your hearts. There is no doubt there will be many doomsayers, but hopefully, many more who will recognize the good in what has happened. Listen to them all, but think with your own mind. We can assure you that what we have undertaken here today is what is best for you and our planet."

4:06 a.m. GMT

The screen lingered on Alex for a second and then switched to Alexandra.

"Our next scheduled broadcast is one week from today, at the same time, but it's highly likely that we will need to be in communication with the world prior to that time. Until then."

The WGC logo reappeared for a few seconds and then went off.

Alex remained seated with his elbows on the table, his face in his hands. He had never been so emotionally drained. His mind was nearly devoid of thought. He could hear the commotion going on around him, but it seemed surrealistic somehow, not connected to him.

"Alex, how are you doing?" Jason was squeezing his shoulder, trying to get his friend's attention. "It's over, Alex; this day is over."

All the members of the WGC board and others were standing, milling about, and congratulating each other. All knew the first, and by far the most critical step, had been taken. Most people in this room had labored and sacrificed for years, some even decades, to accomplish what was started here today.

Alex raised his head from his hands and looked up at Jason. He smiled a weak smile."Well." He stood up, a little shakily, shook hands with Jason, and gave him a hug. After releasing Jason, he shook hands with and hugged Vance, his Uncle Walt, and Colleen. After a few words with each, he moved to the center of the table and tapped a glass with a spoon. "I want to thank each of you. Without your labors, sacrifices, and dedication, we could not have accomplished this. Thank you again." All enthusiastically applauded and raised their glasses to Alex.

After shaking hands with the last of the council, Alex again addressed the entire group. "I need to be alone for a while. I can't tell you how tired I am at this moment, but I'm sure a few hours' sleep will do me a world of good. In the meantime, Jason will take the helm. He and Vance can oversee the intelligence reports coming in and take the appropriate action. The rest of you have your assigned duties for the next few hours and without question, you will be busy. We will meet back here tonight at 8:00. I ask that each of you be prepared to give a full report on your area of responsibility. If, in the meantime, there is a major catastrophe, I am available in my quarters."

All nodded in the affirmative. "We can handle it for a while, Alex," said Jason. Alex nodded and walked slowly out of the conference room. He felt as if he were walking waist-deep in glue.

Chapter 93

MARIANA
July 4, 2010
9:15 a.m.

"They've launched," a surprisingly calm voice came over the PA system.

"Copy that," came another voice.

It was three days since the WGC announced their takeover of the world's governments. It was three days since Alex invited the five superpowers to attempt an attack on Mariana. There was no doubt that the five superpowers would make the attempt; they had no choice.

The control room was abuzz with activity. This would be the final test of the WGC's power. They knew that if just one of these missiles got through, all was lost; the superpowers would destroy the WGC. However, if all five missiles were destroyed, the world would have to concede to the WGC.

The launch was coming from five different locations and all at the same time. The Chinese were launching from their base in Nanning in the south. France, from an airbase near Grenoble at the base of the Alps. Russia was launching from one of their mobile launch pads in western Siberia. The Brits dropped a cruise missile from a high-flying bomber as it flew along the coast of Senegal, barely three hundred miles north of Mariana. The United States launched from a nuclear sub just fifty miles off the coast of Mariana.

Alex sat passively with the rest of the WGC in the situation room, located deep in the bowels of Mt. Norman. They were watching the huge world monitor located on the opposite wall. Five blips appeared within seconds of each other.

"Here they come," voiced Jason as he watched the monitor in fascination.

"Take 'em out," ordered Vance over his headset.

Within eight seconds, all five blips flashed and went off the screen.

"There they go," exclaimed Alex as he let out a deep breath.

All the members of the WGC breathed a sigh of relief.

"Ready to go live," came a voice over the intercom.

Alex readied himself as the cameras were moved into position in front of the council podium. It was time to tell the world about the results of the coordinated launch by the five superpowers.

"*ALERT! MORE INCOMING*," said a voice over the PA system.

"Display them," ordered Alex.

One blip flashed on the monitor only to disappear. The location was over Central Africa, in southwestern Chad. Again a blip appeared, then a second, only to vanish without a trace. All in the control room had their eyes locked on the monitor. Dale was at his station closely monitoring the technicians in his section. Chuck was doing much the same in his area. Seconds passed with no sign of the blips. Then a brief flash and out again. A full minute went by with no reappearance.

"What's the deal, Dale?" asked Alex.

"Unknown, sir."

"Wait...there they are."

This time there were three blips and they looked to be in an incredibly tight formation. They were moving slowly, particularly in comparison to the ICBMs. Again, within two seconds, they disappeared from the monitor. There was no doubt in which direction they were heading.

"Three aircraft moving at about 300 knots." Dale's voice could be heard over the intercom. "All carrying nukes."

"Time till they get here?"

"At present speed, sixty-eight minutes, sir," replied Vance.

The WGC satellites could detect an aircraft at any altitude, but no alarm was triggered unless the aircraft were carrying nuclear weapons. At least three such aircraft were now heading directly for Mariana.

"Where'd they originate?"

"Checking our surveillance. Might take a while."

"Is there any way to disable them without destroying them?"

"No, sir."

"Shit!" Alex expressed angrily. First, he knew the pilots were following orders from some political egomaniac, and second, by destroying the aircraft, there was a great risk of spreading radioactive materials over Central Africa. And lastly, he was going to have to order the deaths of more human beings.

"What's their altitude?"

"Tree top, sir."

"That might help contain the radioactivity to a smaller area," remarked Jason.

"Looks like the flight originated in Southern France, probably Nice," said Vance.

"The sons-of-bitches," exclaimed Vance.

"Why did it take us so long to spot them?" asked Alex.

"Unknown, sir. Maybe they have the payloads wrapped in a lot of lead."

"Sir?"

"Yes, Dale."

"It's possible they have a number of planes flying above them with lead shielding stuck to every available place," offered Dale looking up to the podium from his position, talking into his headset. "Kinda like a big lead umbrella."

"Could be the reason they're flying so slow," suggested Vance.

"And also why we're able to pick them up occasionally," added Jason. "Their cover is exposing gaps only once in a while."

"I'll reset our sensors to pick up all aircraft in that area," said Dale.

Alex thought about the situation for a minute. "Can we contact the pilots directly?"

"Not likely," answered Vance. "Their shielding will probably prevent that."

"How about the cover aircraft. Can we send a message to them?"

"We could certainly direct a satellite to override their communications and try to warn them off."

"Do it," ordered Alex. "Tell them we see them and know their mission and we know where they came from. Tell them that we will destroy the entire flight within the next five minutes if they have not turned around by that time." Alex paused for a few seconds. "Tell them that after we have destroyed their mission, we will be executing the entire political and military leadership in France."

"Yes, sir."

"And, Vance?"

"Yes, sir."

"Be sure the message is received in France at the same time."

The minutes passed and as they did, the control staff adjusted the sensors in the satellites and managed to get a full reading of the flight of aircraft heading in their direction. There were over sixty aircraft holding an unbelievably tight pattern at five different elevations. It was assumed most were large transports, but many had to be bombers and fighters. The nuke-carrying aircraft were flying just below their umbrella.

"Sixty!"

"Yes, sir! At least."

"Coming up on two minutes," an announcement came over the PA system.

"No word yet, Alex," Jason remarked.

"Alex?" It was Dale's voice.

"Yes, Dale."

"We have lost the lock on all but three of the French military chiefs and top officials."

"Fuckers must have gotten under some lead," responded Vance.

Alex thought for a moment. "Do we have their last locations?"

"Yes, sir."

"Where were they?"

"Almost all at an air field outside of Nice. I believe Vance has pegged it; they've ducked under some shielding."

Alex sat silent for another minute. "Chuck?"

"Right here, Alex."

"How long will it take you to get one of the big guns in position?"

"Not sure, but number eleven is presently over Western Europe. We'll need to make some course corrections...I'll get back to you in ten."

"One minute left, Alex," stated Vance.

"How much longer for you, Chuck?"

"We can have the satellite in position in five minutes."

"Delay the destruction of the planes for that long," ordered Alex.

"They're gonna be gettin' close, boss," stated Vance.

"I know. Get ready to broadcast."

"One minute," said the technician.

Alex again readied himself before the cameras.

"In five, four, three..."

9:25 a.m.

"Just over ten minutes ago, the five superpowers launched five missiles from various locations around the world in an attempt to reach this location. All five were destroyed within eight seconds of their launch." Alex stopped briefly. "Approximately six minutes ago, we detected a flight of over sixty aircraft, three carrying nuclear bombs, heading toward Mariana. These aircraft took off from France in direct violation of our mandates given three days ago. We do not wish to destroy these aircraft for two reasons. One, it will involve killing the pilots and crews, whom we consider innocents and secondly, it may spread nuclear material over a large section of Central Africa." Alex paused for a second. "If within two minutes, those aircraft have not turned around and headed back to France, I will order their destruction, and the execution of the entire French military from the rank of colonel up, and the entire French Parliament, including the Prime Minister. They believe they are safe under cover of lead shielding at a Nice airport, but," Alex looked up at a large clock, "in one minute and forty-five seconds, if those aircraft are not diverted from their present path, all I have described will be dead." Alex stopped talking.

The WGC logo reappeared.

Ten seconds went by. You could nearly hear the heartbeats of those in the control room.

"They're still coming," said Vance.

All eyes were on the large monitor. The entire flight was now clearly visible as a mass of flashing blips. All could see that their speed and direction had not changed.

Time to arrival at Mariana was chillingly shown on a digital clock above the monitor. The clock was counting down and was now at eight minutes.

"They're turning!" Colleen proclaimed excitedly.

A cheer went up all over the control room.

Alex rolled his eyes back in his head. "Looks like they got the message."

"They're breaking formation," informed Dale Isley.

All looked back at the monitor. It was apparent that the cover planes were no longer trying to conceal the bomb-carrying planes. The bombers were now three steady blips on the screen and were pulling away from their cover at a rapid pace and heading directly away from Mariana.

"How soon can we talk to Sean?" asked Alex.

"I'll get a message to him right away," Jason replied.

Alex nodded to Jason, then turned to his council. "Thoughts?"

None said anything for a few seconds, but all were fully aware of what advice Alex was looking for.

"Seems to me, Alex, they got the message," Colleen spoke first. "No point in taking more lives."

"I agree," added Walt.

Again there was silence.

"Some of the French are out in the open again," said Dale.

"All of them?"

Alex could see Dale studying the screen in front of him.

"Nope, but quite a few."

"Let me guess," Vance said sarcastically. "Still under cover are the Prime Minister, his government's upper echelon, and General Lamoureux and his chief flunkies."

Dale studied the screen for a few seconds. "You're right."

11:45 a.m.

Alex put down the phone and sat silently for a full minute before speaking. "Sean says he just left the briefing room. Seems the President knew of the French plan, but kept it to himself."

Alex was not happy.

"What was he thinking?" asked Jason.

"He was undoubtedly thinking if the French took us out, the world would remain in status quo. But if we caught them at it, he could deny any knowledge or culpability. We would retaliate only against the French," Alex replied wearily.

"But we also know who in the French government and military were in on it," said Jason. "We had it right, with the exception of one general, Taluse Piche, and his staff. They weren't in on it."

"Alex," uttered Colleen.

"Yes?"

"I don't want you to execute the President."

2:00 p.m.

"Get President Lockhart on the phone."

"Yes, sir."

All eyes were now on Alex. The monitor was clear of any further threats. All French aircraft were still heading to Nice. What was Alex going to do?

"President Lockhart on line one, sir."

Alex pushed the button and picked up the phone. "Mr. President?"

"Yes, Mr. Gabriel."

"Your response to the following will determine your future, sir. Do you understand?"

There was a long pause. "Yes."

"We have requested that a French TV crew be sent to the Nice airport."

"I'm aware of that," remarked the President, the fatigue obvious in his voice.

"Then I suggest, sir, that you pay close attention to what happens next." Alex looked over at Vance and nodded.

"Send the message, Dale," ordered Vance.

"Yes, sir."

All screens in the world were now showing a single, large, low-profile building located a hundred yards off a runway on the Nice Air Force Base. The cameras were located half a mile away and the view of the building was slightly distorted due to the heat shimmering off the runways.

The message was heard all over the world as the camera's eye remained on the building housing most of the French government and military leaders. "The following individuals are to exit that building within the next three minutes: all individuals who are not in a policy-making position in the French government, all military personnel who are below the rank of colonel, and General Piche and his staff. All others may remain in the building or come out; it matters not," said Alex.

"Mr. Gabriel," said the President.

"Yes," Alex answered, replacing the phone to his ear.

"I'm going to ask you not to execute those people."

Alex paused and stared at the monitor. Dozens of people could be seen running from several exits located on every side of the large building.

"Thirty seconds," informed Vance.

The control room was deadly quiet except for the sounds of the monitoring equipment and computers.

"Ten seconds."

"Please, Alex," pleaded the President.

Alex took the phone away from his ear and looked at Vance.

"Five, four..."

"Hold firing, Vance."

"*ABORT*," Vance yelled into the mike.

All eyes in the control room were fixed on Alex. It was apparent he was conflicted. After a few seconds, he looked at the director. "Put me back on the air."

The screen switched to the image of Alex. "This is a notice to the French. Those remaining in the building are to come out immediately and your lives will be spared. You have thirty seconds." The screen again showed the large building.

Within a few seconds, an additional two dozen or so people could be seen running from the building, a few falling as they ran in panic.

"All out except eighteen," said Dale.

"Which eighteen?"

"The Prime Minister, General Lamoureux, and their staffs."

Alex put the phone back to his ear. "Mr. President?"

"Yes, Mr. Chairman," answered the President using, for the first time, Alex's proper title.

"I will spare these lives because you have asked me to. However Prime Minister Cherzan, General Lamoureux, their advisors and staff have apparently chosen to remain in the building. I can only assume they don't trust us and feel safer under their pathetic cover. That's unfortunate, but they have dug their own graves for the second time today. Their time has run out. So be it."

"I understand, Mr. Chairman, and I thank you for your compassion."

"You will not see it again, under these circumstances, sir."

"There will be no further attempts on the WGC if I have anything to say about it, Mr. Chairman."

"Goodbye, Mr. President." Alex hung up. "Continue the countdown, Vance."

"Starting at T-minus-ten," said Vance.

"Three, two, one.."

A loud humming sound began emitting from the building and grew in intensity over a six-second period. The building began to glow brighter by the millisecond until it was nearly impossible to look at; then it collapsed in on itself.

All in the council room were transfixed on the screen; all knew what the "big gun" was supposed to do, but to see it actually happening was almost surreal. The site where the airport building had stood radiated immense heat and within seconds, everything within a thirty-yard radius seemed to explode into flames. Trucks, cars, aircraft, and three other buildings went up almost simultaneously.

"Jesus," whispered Walt.

"My God!" cried Colleen.

Vance and Alex remained silent and just watched the monitor.

People who left the building just minutes before were seen running in panic from the new peril. The fuel tanks of the burning vehicles began exploding and something inside one of the burning hangars blew and most of its roof went skyward in a pillar of flames. It seemed to take a full twenty minutes before the first fire-fighting units came into view of the cameras. The people in the council room were relieved to see an effort was finally underway to control the damage. All members of the WGC knew the world was watching as they were. Hopefully, this violent sight would dampen the aggressions of any other would-be foes of the WGC.

After a half hour or so, most of the fires were extinguished or were under control. Alex stood and made a feeble attempt to stretch. "That should do it."

"I can't imagine anybody else making an attempt to do us harm," expressed Colleen.

"I would think not," agreed Walt.

"Jason, would you make another announcement informing the world as to exactly what happened today. Tell them we will not tolerate any further aggression toward the WGC. Tell the world we intend to get on with our agenda."

"Yes, sir."

"I don't think I'll be needed for a while -- so if you don't mind, I'm going to take a little time off."

"We can handle it, boss," Vance replied.

Alex turned and walked over to where Colleen and Walt sat. They both stood as he approached. He gave Colleen a gentle hug and kissed her on the cheek. He gave Walt the same. "Thank you both for staying with me." He turned and left the room.

Chapter 94

MAJOR NETWORK- NEWS ROOM
July 30, 2010

Dan Jordan's serious countenance was in close-up on the screen as he spoke to his audience. "It's been a month since the hostile takeover by the WGC and the world remains in a somewhat confused state. But what most were initially calling the definitive hostile takeover, are now calling a benevolent takeover. The frantic buying of survival gear such as food, water, camping gear, candles, guns, and ammunition has all but disappeared, as have the runs on banks." Dan smiled slightly. "The churches, mosques, temples, and synagogues that were filled to overflowing every day for the first two weeks are now nearly back to their pre-takeover attendance. It seems the population is coming to realize that nothing really sinister has been introduced to their everyday lives."

"So it would seem," said Bob Jordan. "The stock markets around the world have quieted down considerably, although they are still way off their pre-takeover highs." Bob turned to look at his on-air partner. "The incredible adaptability of the human animal never fails to amaze me, Dan."

"I attribute that quick change in attitude to the continuing positive reporting by the world press. It's a brilliant public relations campaign by the WGC."

"And the cooperation of the heads of state, and their

positive speeches, have definitely had a calming influence on the population."

"I have to tell you, Bob, I'm beginning to believe this kind of takeover was secretly…or maybe subconsciously might be a better word, wished by the majority of people."

"Really?"

"If we look at the facts they would go something like this. There are no wars anywhere. At no time in recorded history could that be said. And there is almost no crime of any kind… anywhere. And again, at no time in history could that be said. I personally feel better about almost everything and I suspect that feeling is spreading rapidly."

"There are a few notable exceptions, Dan, mainly the Muslim nations. They cannot seem to stop their mantra of hate. Now it's directed at the WGC."

"That, I suspect, will be a very unhealthy stance to take."

Spurred on by religious zealots in those poorest of nations, where illiteracy prevailed and religion, it was believed, provided the only hope, civil unrest had started and the unrest soon grew into demonstrations, small at first but growing dramatically in size as the days passed. Muslim clerics, bolstered by the rapidly growing hate directed at the WGC, began suggesting a Jihad, a holy war against the WGC. In Kabul, Afghanistan, Islamabad and Faisalabad, Pakistan, and two nations on the African continent, all-out riots exploded in the third week.

MARIANA

August 8, 2010

"We've got to squelch this soon, boss," expressed Vance, not taking his eyes off the screen.

"I know," responded Alex as he rubbed his temples with his index fingers. "Are our people on site taking videos?"

"Yes, sir, with a direct link to the satellites."

Alex sat in thought for a moment. The lives he would now take weren't, as far as he knew, guilty of anything other than ignorance and inciting public opinion against the WGC. But these acts would surely, sooner or later, lead to more terrorism. That innocent people would again get killed in the name of Allah was a certainty. So, Alex knew, these acts had to be cut off at the head and soon.

"We need to make these executions dramatic and highly visible," said Jason.

"I agree," stated Vance. "We need to set several examples."

"Need to get a bunch of the instigators in front of a lot of cameras at the same time," suggested Jason.

At the beginning of the tenth week, in full view of thousands of followers and a worldwide television audience, eleven clerics, dressed in white robes and turbans stood on a large platform located in a large plaza in central Riyadh, capitol of Saudi Arabia. They called for a Jihad.

"Take em out!" said Vance into his mike.

All eleven stiffened and fell over in a heap. The effect on the crowd was immediate. Thousands began running away from the platform. Three younger clerics managed to mount the platform, took up the microphones and began imploring their fellow Muslims to have courage. "Do not flee in fear from the devil Alexander Gabriel." Three more young men joined them and again began shouting for a Jihad. The crowd began to turn back.

"These people are actually terminally stupid," scoffed Vance, without a trace of humor.

"Have we got them?" asked Alex solemnly.

Vance spoke into his headset. "Do we have 'em?"

A few seconds went by. "Well?" demanded Vance, his impatience obvious.

Alex waited passively, watching the large screen across the control room. *Damn it*!

"We got 'em, boss."

Alex looked over at Vance, paused for a second, and nodded.

"Take 'em out!" ordered Vance.

As the six young men collapsed to the platform, the crowd fled screaming in all-out terror. There were no further demonstrations in Riyadh this day.

This basic scenario was repeated in six different countries that day and spaced within an hour of each other. The world's news media repeated showing the films of the executions at every opportunity. The following days, far fewer suicidal followers of Islam attempted to rally a crowd. The total executed before it was over came to one 163. The crowds began to dwindle, the large demonstrations stopped, and even the civil unrest became all but nonexistent.

"Seems the Muslim world is running thin on zealots willing to lead their fellow Muslims against the WGC," Vance declared on the fourth day.

August 22, 2010

Vance walked past Alex's secretary and directly into Alex's office.

"Turn on your television, Alex."

Alex picked up a remote and pushed on. Within seconds the picture was on and showing Freetown, the capitol of Sierra Leone. There is a riot going on. Through the riot, men could be seen wielding machetes and hacking at bodies lying on the ground. Another camera was catching other bodies being dragged behind old Jeeps. The people were cheering as the bodies passed them.

"That's our transition team, boss," said Vance, barely able to control his rage. "They've slaughtered them all before we could stop them."

Alex was stunned for a moment, but his shock soon turned to anger. "Execute everybody involved, starting now. And I mean anybody within fifty feet of the bodies."

Vance gave Alex a curious look and didn't move to relay the order Alex had just given him. "I don't think you want to do that, Alex. There will be innocent people in the crowd."

"I gave you a direct order… now…" Alex stopped talking for a second. "Jesus, what am I doing?" Alex got up and walked to the far side of his office. There were no windows to look out of, here in the depths of Mt. Norman, but the painting his father had commissioned for his birthday when he was a kid was hanging here. He looked at it for a few seconds before turning to face Vance.

"Thanks, Vance. You take out who you feel is responsible. I'll leave it to your judgment."

Chapter 95

GOVERNING HALL-MARIANA
October 30, 2010

In the third month, the WGC requested all Heads of State to come to Mariana. They were to provide their own transportation to a central collection point in Accra, Ghana. From there they would board a Gabriel Boeing 757 for the thirty-minute flight to Mariana. The ten nations with the largest economies were the first to spend two days at the New World Headquarters before being flown back to Accra. Every two days after that, twenty heads of state arrived to spend their time on Mariana until all nations had been represented. All were there for indoctrination and to personally receive their nation's copy of The New World Constitution, along with a book containing the Laws of the WGC.

Alex was standing behind a short podium that was sitting on the apex of a large semi-circular board table. This table was in a beautifully appointed room with dark walnut paneling surrounding a large colorful painting of the world. On either side of Alex were the members of the WGC, nine in all, counting Alex.

"It is our intention to monitor and oversee the world's separate and autonomous states as compassionately and intelligently as possible while making sure each maintains a clear focus on the WGC's laws and goals. Because of our need to operate as a single cohesive unit in governing and controlling the world's states for the first two years, none of the 200 separate nations will have a vote nor voice in the WGC. After two years, however, it is our intention to invite five heads of state to join the WGC Board. These individuals will serve on the WGC board during their tenure as heads of their governments."

Chapter 96

MARIANA
November 23, 2010
2:00 a.m. GMT

Alex sat behind a table in the small conference room located in the interior of Mt. Norman. He continued skimming his notes as a lighting technician held a meter next to his face. Seemingly satisfied, the tech moved away.

"Thirty seconds, sir," said the director.

Alex acknowledged with a nod. He put his notes down and took a deep breath. *This is going to be a tough sell*, he thought; *this is the last one*. He took another deep breath. *This is the last of the hard ones*.

The world had settled down remarkably since the takeover five months before. Now, Alex knew, it was about to be shaken again. *Hopefully, Jason's efforts will have eased the impact some*.

Jason, for three months, had been using Global Media in an effort to soften public opinion on the subject of sterilization. His campaign began slowly -- just short articles placed strategically off the front page in all the major and most minor newspapers worldwide. Included were articles describing the ease of childless living for the millions of men and women who had voluntarily become sterilized. Then, after a week or so, thirty-second TV clips began, showing couples on a Caribbean cruise, playing tennis, golfing, or swimming with no children in sight. The articles and the short clips were all creatively designed to reveal the positive sides of being a childless adult. After a few weeks, people-on-the-street interviews concerning sterilization began showing up on television news shows. Radio talk shows began discussions on the positive and negative aspects of sterilization.

"How do you feel about the rumor that the WGC intends to sterilize a large percentage of the world?" a passerby would be asked, usually by a pretty, smiling young woman holding a microphone up to his or her face. "Had I been sterilized, I would be retired by now, with a lot less gray hair, too," one would say, maybe tongue-in-cheek; maybe not. "Children... a bunch of ingrates," responded a haggard-looking woman. "Who needs 'em?" From a teenage couple, "They'd probably treat us like we treat our old ball and chains." "About sixteen years too late for me," said another. In one out of five testimonials, Jason would insert a positive side of having children. "I can't imagine my life without my children," a mother would say. Or a middle-aged man would say, "Who will care for us in our old age?" The campaign grew in intensity as the days and weeks went by. By that evening, the world had been subjected to the word "sterilization" used in a positive manner dozens of times a day.

Alex was aware of the rumors circulating throughout the world. He knew the fears being expressed. What was the WGC going to do? How was the WGC going to impose their will? How were they going to control the population of the world? Would there be extermination camps? People would fear the worst, he knew. *They're not going to get the worst, but they're going to hate it anyway*.

"Ten seconds."

Alex cleared his throat.

"Three, two, one." The director pointed at Alex.

"Citizens of the world," he started, "I now have the unenviable task of explaining our next major goal. That goal is worldwide population control. Of all our goals, this is, by far, the most difficult to explain and it will be the most difficult to accomplish, but we feel it is the single most important goal." Alex was looking directly into the camera's eye.

"I will first try to summarize the years of study and discussion we have gone through. In this summary, you will be given numbers and statistics. You will be given explanations and conjecture. You will be given projections and hypotheses. You will be given the facts. You will not be lied to or misled in any way.

"We realized many years ago that the explosive and disastrous growth of the world's human population could not be contained unless we had control of the population. Five months ago we did, in fact, take the necessary control." Alex paused for a moment.

"I will start by giving you a number of statistics." Alex looked down at his notes, then back up into the camera's eye. "The human population is presently growing at the rate of over 90,000,000 people a year." His eyebrows furrowed. "Let me put that into some sort of perspective. Consider the fact that the average population for every country in the world, including India and China, with their massive populations, is about 22,000,000. The world, in effect, is producing enough people to populate over four average-sized nations each and every year. That is 7,500,000 more people a month; 1,700,000 a week; 245,000 a day or 10,000 additional people, enough to populate a good-sized town, each and every hour. We have accelerated past six billion and are rapidly on the way to seven billion people on this little planet. Of these, over five billion are trying to survive in the poorest regions on the planet, the so-called Third World countries. In countries, I will add, whose only means in the past of controlling their population has been by war, starvation, and disease. At the present rate, the world population will grow to eight billion in thirty years, and more than ten billion in fifty short years. Some studies suggest that at some point late in this century, the explosive growth will peak and then start to decline, but we are not convinced of that. We know that in just thirty years the populations will outstrip food supplies in eighty percent of the countries, but despite massive starvation, the population will continue to explode. Diseases and plagues will develop and kill millions, affecting all nations, yet the population will continue to explode. We, the WGC, have effectively eliminated the wars over territory, food, and water. Those inevitable wars would have killed additional millions, but now those people are left to flourish and propagate.

"Because of this unchecked growth of the human animal, thousands of other plants and animals are presently and will continue to be driven to extinction. The human is like a cancer on the planet; it consumes everything in its path in favor of its own survival. We suggest that the world cannot continue this explosive growth rate. We suggest that the world cannot continue to support even six billion people." Alex paused for a few seconds, checking his notes.

"Over the years, it has been suggested to us, and in a few cases intelligently argued, that the total human population should be reduced to no more than one billion. This would allow the planet to recover most of its resources and beauty in a relatively short period of time. Our studies, however, indicate that this planet can support a great deal more than that. Let me stop here for a second and put an unfortunate rumor to rest before I continue." Alex put down his notes and looked into the camera. "The WGC is not going to execute a single person in our quest to bring the population to a proper level. There will be no internment camps, no gas chambers, and no ovens. There will be absolutely no execution of innocent people. Please listen to what I have to tell you for the next few minutes and you will know the facts." Alex picked up his notes.

"The World Guidance Council, after twenty years of study, has come to the inescapable conclusion that the human population must be reduced to no more than four billion by the year 2060, and half of that by the year 2120. When the world's population hits two billion, our goal will be accomplished!

"The only way to accomplish such a drastic reduction in population, short of massive extermination, is by the use of effective birth control. There is only one effective form of birth control and that is, of course, sterilization." Alex paused for a few seconds, ostensibly to look at his notes, but in reality, he wanted to give what he had just said time to sink in.

"The WGC put together a world body of the finest minds in sociology, anthropology, humanities, agriculture, geology, and many other fields to provide basic guidelines. This group made an extensive study of every nation, from every possible perspective, to determine the number of people each nation can support. The study was based on the following criteria: the nation's present population, its present and projected food supply, its present and projected economy, its natural resources, its fresh water supply, its soil make-up, its weather, its topography, its access to a seaport, and its location in the world.

From this information, they developed a maximum viable population for each nation, and the number of people that each nation can support indefinitely." Alex again stopped to review his notes.

"We are going to ask that each nation appoint a board of their brightest citizens for the express purpose of developing practical demographics for their populations based on their nation's unique needs. It will be their task to pick the people who, and in what number, are to be sterilized. As an example, most nations with huge populations will require a far greater percent of its population to be food producers. Maybe as many as fifty percent will be farmers, ranchers, or in agriculture in one form or another. Many industrialized nations, such as the United States, will require, as they do now, less than five percent of their population in agriculture. Such nations may have a greater need, for skilled factory workers, electronics, medicine, research, teachers, etc. Over the years demographics for each nation will undoubtedly change, and adjustments will be necessary.

"Some nations will be required to sterilize up to thirty percent of their populations within two years, others maybe only ten percent. There are certain peoples within some nations, however, that will not be required to be sterilized. These people, such as the Bushmen in Africa, Aborigines in Australia, and other nomadic peoples who live with the land and do no permanent damage to the land are to be left alone." Alex stopped for a full ten seconds.

"We fully expect to be contacted by representatives of every major and most minor religions condemning our stand on this issue. We are certain we will be threatened by most of these religious leaders, including everything from massive worldwide riots to massive hunger strikes." Alex stopped for a few seconds. "So there is no misunderstanding, I issue the following warning." Alex looked deep into the camera's eye. "We will not tolerate any attempt to incite violent acts in protest to our efforts to control the population. We will execute all leaders of riots or any civil disobedience that cause any physical injuries, deaths, or property damage whatsoever." Alex's blue eyes pierced the lens of the camera for a few seconds. "This goal, as with all the WGC's goals, is absolutely non-negotiable." Alex put some papers to one side and picked up another set.

"Within the next two weeks, we will deliver to each head of state the number of people to be sterilized in their jurisdiction. Along with that number, we will provide guidelines for creating the demographics necessary to accomplish that goal. That is it for now. Thank you."

The cameras and lights were turned off. Alex gathered his notes, tapped them together and placed them in a neat pile on the left side of the desk. With that done, he stood.

"Well done, my friend," offered Jason as he came out from behind the camera's position.

"That's the last of the big ones," added Vance, who had been leaning up against a bookcase off to the side.

Alex nodded in acknowledgment. "That's the last one that will hurt anybody."

"Now we'll see how the world handles this," said Jason. "Global will continue its campaign for as long as necessary."

"Well, you can bet the shit will be hitting a lot of fans... starting now," suggested Vance.

MARIANA

June 25, 2011

"Our biggest and continuing problem, as you all know, is population control," said Alex. "The major religions began an uproar that even exceeded our expectations, but at the same time, the leaders are careful to preach non-violence." Alex looked at Jason. "Few religions anywhere can solicit any cooperation from the press... thank you, Jason. And of course without the support of either local, national, or international press, their opposition to birth control is gaining no momentum."

"Passive resistance is their means to defy the WGC's mandate and this passive resistance is very effective," said Jason. "Fully a third of the world's governments have done little or nothing to gather the necessary demographics. And naturally it's the nations with the largest populations -- the nations who are still highly influenced by their dominant religion -- who are thumbing their noses at us. The dragging of their feet can be heard all the way to Mariana."

"Time to get harsh, boss."

September 17, 2011

The now familiar WGC logo again appeared on the world television screens. The world was told twenty-four hours earlier to expect an announcement. The screens, at the prescribed time, switched to Alex. His demeanor was quite cold as he began his announcement.

"It has become apparent that many of the world's governments have decided not to gather or provide the information necessary to begin an orderly, fair, and logical sterilization plan. The task now falls to the WGC. But the WGC doesn't have the manpower nor the inclination to select who in each nation should be sterilized. So we decided to simply start at the top and work our way down."

"Following this announcement, the Presidents of each non-cooperating state will receive an email. This email will contain a list of people including themselves, their sons, daughters, sisters, brothers, mothers, fathers, aunts, uncles, and first cousins of not only the

President, but of his First Lady as well. The e-mail demands that all people on the list gather on October 30th at a given time and location, normally the executive mansion or palace, for immediate sterilization. Those who decide not to show up at the proper time and place will be executed. Then, thirty days from that date, we will do the same at each level of government. Thirty days from that date we will move on to captains of industry and on down until the required number of people are sterilized."

The WGC logo flashed on all televisions around the world and then went to regular programming.

The Hanly and Jordan News Hour was in progress.

"Well, a person cannot accuse Alex Gabriel of being wishy-washy," remarked Dan Jordan.

"No, no you can't. That, together with the indisputable fact that Mr. Gabriel has never been known to bluff, makes for a very interesting next few weeks."

"I'll bet my meager pension that the WGC will have all the demographics it requires before sunset on the 30th of October."

"No bet."

"At least the actual sterilization is quick, painless, and safe. That certainly helps," remarked Dan.

"Just a simple shot. Norman Research scientists developed the serum over twenty years ago, using mutated human hormones as I recall. It's been used for years on a limited basis," added Bob. "You'd almost believe Alex Gabriel was planning this takeover for a long, long time."

Chapter 97

GOVERNING HALL -- MARIANA
November 25, 2011

In the year following the takeover, a legion of major and minor challenges were addressed and, for the most part, overcome by the WGC with the cooperation of the majority of nations. This cooperation was sometimes given willingly and even eagerly; other times it was extracted under duress and intimidation. Despite the edict of the WGC, in many nations, particularly those where religion still played a major role in politics, the cooperation was generally antagonistic, if at all.

Inside the Governing Hall on Mariana sat the members of the WGC board. Douglas Ito was concluding his report.

"It is taking massive amounts of Gabriel resources to modernize, streamline, and stabilize many governments. The corruption and ignorance is so deep-seated in some, it has at times, seemed all but an impossible task. In some states it's taking near-constant supervision from WGC teams to educate the highest government officials down to the lowest level of workers. It is slow, perplexing work, but progress is being made." Douglas put a stack of papers to one side and picked up another. "On the bright side, the political instability that has always been a deterrent to economic growth in many parts of the world is no longer a factor. Investments in Third World countries have begun growing at a healthy pace. The vast bureaucracies that controlled and stymied so many economies have been dismantled. The shackles of red tape have been cut, allowing people to freely pursue their fortunes." With that, Douglas bowed slightly and sat down.

"Thank you, Douglas," said Alex. "Might I ask how much of the Gabriel resources we have spent?"

Douglas consulted his notes, found what he was looking for and looked at Alex. "No way of calculating exactly, but I believe we have provided something over 400 billion so far."

Alex nodded, "Well, that's what its for." He smiled. "I assume we have a couple of dollars yet to spend?"

"Yes, I'm afraid so."

"Let me know when we're broke."

Douglas gave a rare smile. "I will do that."

Alex turned to Vance. "Vance, how is the legal community taking our introduction of truth serum into the justice system?"

"In the old days they would have sued." Vance smiled. "The tens of thousands of legal sharks, who have made their ill-gotten gains through lies and deceit, are effectively out of business. And they're pissed. You can only imagine how badly that makes me feel," Vance said sarcastically.

"This is completely changing the judicial systems," said Jason. "The need for juries to determine guilt or innocence has been eliminated for most criminal cases. Our team of legal scholars is working on a new, practical justice system. It will be interesting to see what they come up with."

"I might add that Jason's idea of making all crime big news and then the quick and harsh consequences for the perpetrators even bigger news, has certainly helped in keeping the crime rate down," said Vance. "It shows that even dumb sumbitches can be trained."

Toward the end of the first two years, the WGC invited the leaders of the United States, Great Britain, Indonesia, Russia, and China to join the WGC board of directors. That brought the number on the board to thirteen. To everyone's delight, the addition of these new members had a calming and reassuring effect worldwide. As the years passed and elections were held, these five board members would be replaced by either their successors or, at the WGC board's option, a head of state from a different country.

In the third year, the WGC began promoting a single world currency, named WECS, World Economic Currency System. It was estimated it would take three years before the transition to WECS would be completed. The European Union's transition to the Euro in 2002 was a helpful guide in the process. Also, in the third year, the WGC mandated that all primary and secondary schools, worldwide, start teaching English as a second language. It was hoped that within two generations, a common language would facilitate better communication among the nations and help bring the peoples of the world closer together.

GOVERNING HALL -- MARIANA
March 4, 2012

The WGC logo appeared on televisions worldwide. And, at a prescribed time, Alex's face appeared. He was seated at the semicircular council table. On his right were Jason, Vance, Douglas Ito, and Peter Joshua. On his left were Alexandra, Walt, Colleen, and Joan Hocket.

"This will be a short announcement." Alex paused and smiled slightly. "Over my lifetime there have been a great many changes in the world. Some good, some bad, and some that could only be described as truly evil. The evil was, in fact, gaining in power and influence at an alarming rate, and had to be stopped. Something drastic was required. So, after decades of planning and building we, just under two years ago, took over all the world's governments. We have, in these past twenty-three months, eliminated most of the horrors and evil the world had been subjected to. The WGC will, I assume, continue its efforts for decades to come. However, not with me at the helm." Alex smiled. "Although my birth certificate shows me to be fifty-eight, I can assure you I feel as if I've lived twice that. This will be my last address to you as Chairman of the WGC. Again

Alex paused. "The Board of Directors have unanimously elected Jason Gould to take my place as Chairman." Jason's image filled the screen. "And Alexandra Gabriel will become the WGC President." Alexandra's face replaced Jason's for a few seconds, then switched back to Alex. "So, at last, I bid farewell to the citizens of the world. May an intelligence greater than ours continue to provide a fruitful and bountiful planet for this and all future generations."

Alex's image remained on the screen for a second before switching briefly to the WGC logo and then to the news pundits around the world.

Everyone around the council table stood when the camera went off. All had smiles as they gathered around Alex.

"Well, you've done it. How do you feel?" asked Jason.

Alex looked at his friends, smiled and said, "I feel wonderful."

"Really?"

"I haven't felt better or happier since my twenty-first birthday party...and the formation of Mariana." Alex smiled. "I'm done."

"Just like that!" smiled Vance.

"Just like that."

Colleen was first to give Alex a big hug. "I still remember the ten-year-old I met in your Uncle Walt's office so many years ago. You were special then and you still are. What a ride you have taken us on."

"I remember that day quite well. And I still have a crush on you," Alex smiled and gave Colleen a short kiss on the lips.

Uncle Walt managed to be next in line to hug Alex. "I felt like you were my own son all these years." Walt choked up and could say no more.

Alex gave him a big hug and patted him on the back. "I was a very lucky man, I had two wonderful fathers."

Alexandra was next. She hugged Alex tightly. "I promise you, Cousin, that what you started will be continued as long as I draw breath."

"I have no doubt," said Alex. "None at all."

Alex then shook hands with Douglas and Peter, and hugged Joan.

Alex looked fondly at Jason and Vance. These were two of the most capable people he had ever known -- the two people who stood by him during his greatest heights and deepest lows. He kept smiling. "Gentlemen, ladies, I'm going out to the island. I'm probably going to spend a lot of time there for the next few days. While there or here, I don't plan on doing one damn thing that doesn't add to my pleasure or comfort. In other words, I'm leaving the world we created up to you to oversee." Alex smiled brightly, turned and walked out the door.

Jason and Vance were clearly amused as they watched their friend leave.

As Alex exited the entrance to Mt. Norman, the security guards on duty gave him a snappy salute. He got into the Jeep that was kept there for his use, and started the engine. He enjoyed the eight-minute drive on the beautifully landscaped road from the entrance of Mt. Norman to the wharf where his small powerboat was tied. He unconsciously held a slight smile as he untied the boat and climbed aboard. He maintained the smile as he stood behind the wheel, guiding the small craft across the light chop of the Atlantic toward his tiny island. The feel of the salt spray exhilarated him as it came over the bow during the 900-yard trip. He instantly became aware of a gunboat as it roared around the west end of the island under full power. *Bless your heart Vance*, Alex smiled to himself. As soon as the gunboat pulled up to within 200 yards, it reduced power and shadowed him as he motored across this short stretch of ocean. Alex knew the gunboat would, after his arrival, take up station on the far side of the little island. He knew he was never left unprotected. After securing his boat by bow and stern, he walked to the end of the small dock and then, breaking his normal routine, walked to the right instead of left to the rock bench.

He had never felt better. The immense pressure he placed on himself so many years before and lived with all his life seemed to have just floated away. He felt almost buoyant. He began absently walking around his little island, stopping every few feet to admire a flower or look around. Today he enjoyed the multitude of plants and flowers that had been planted years ago, as he never did before. Orchids of every description were abundant. An infinite variety of flowers were everywhere and floral scents permeated the salt air. Narrow gravel walks and tiny bridges were built to make a walking tour around the island safe and comfortable. *Are these new additions, or have I just never noticed*? he wondered. He could see that the papaya trees were heavy with fruit and an unbelievable number of coconuts were clustered in the palms. He stopped occasionally to admire a particular flower or to look high up into a towering palm. At one point, he stopped and picked up a fallen coconut. He turned the thing over in his hands a few times trying to figure out how in the hell one got the husk off. It seemed impenetrable. He held onto it like a running back with a football as he continued his stroll through this beautiful garden. The warm floral-scented breeze, along with the gentle slapping of waves on the north shore, gave him a feeling of peace he had never experienced or imagined.

After a couple of hours, he found himself within a few feet of his rock bench. He smiled broadly as he thought back to the day Jason and Vance escorted him out to this tiny island. *Fourteen years ago, was it? They were pretty damned pleased with themselves*, he remembered fondly. *They were like little children showing off to a parent as they proudly pointed out all the flora and fauna, the fruit trees, and this bench they'd had carved into the rock*, *each trying to point out things to me before the other did*. He recalled the warm feeling he had as he sat on this bench located in the shade of these majestic palms for the first time. He remembered looking across the short stretch of ocean on that day, to his island country. He remembered being nearly overcome with the sight. It was truly beautiful.

He walked the last few feet, sat down, and placed the coconut gently on the bench beside him. It was a remarkably cool day for this season on the equator. He looked out across the now-familiar stretch of water to the island of Mariana. His gaze took in the heights of Mt. Norman and the rainforests to the east. He could see no waves breaking at the base of the mountain; the ocean, other than a mild chop, was calm today. As he sat, he began lightly reflecting on the past. *It started for me in pain and terror*; he smiled whimsically, *fifty years ago. What in the universe could have done that? What awesome power had started a sequence of events that put me on this rock, on this tiny island, in this place and at this time?* He didn't have any more of a clue now than he'd had when it all began, but he had rock-solid faith that someday he would come to know the answers.

Alex had somehow been chosen to drastically change the course of human events; to instill order in a chaotic world. As he sat staring out at the horizon, he was fully aware that he had all but completed the massive task that someone or something had thrust upon him so long ago. He was, for the most part, done. There would be an abundance of challenges, large and small in the weeks, months, and years to come, but they would pale in comparison to what had already been accomplished. The primary goal, the principal reason for his being, was completed, and he was totally tranquil for the first time he could remember. He wasn't making any plans, or developing any strategies, or giving any thought about today's monumental action; he was simply enjoying the day.

EPILOGUE

The Gabriel mansion on Mariana sat on top of one of the low foothills situated between the ocean and the base of Mt. Norman. It was a magnificent structure reminiscent of the Gabriel home in Newport Beach, but several times its size.

There was a party in progress on the great veranda that overlooked the landscaped grounds as they rolled west toward the Atlantic Ocean. Walt, now in his late seventies with thinning gray hair and a slight paunch, sat with Colleen and the Oldakers at a table next to the striking granite railing where they had a perfect view of the superbly landscaped estate. Jennifer, Chuck, Governor Norvil, and his wife are standing close by, talking animatedly with guests dressed in the traditional garb of their African nations. A white-haired Peter Joshua was talking to an equally white-haired Douglas Ito and his wife. Joan Hocket and her husband were laughing as they made one of many toasts of the day. There were at least two dozen other dignitaries from various nations around the world in attendance, keeping the colorfully uniformed waitstaff continually on the move serving refreshments.

Sean Greenwood and Alexandra Gabriel were off to one side, holding hands while looking into each other's eyes. The two were the subject of a lot of conversation around the island.

"I'm just saying," said Alexandra, "considering how unique and special they both are, it's not a bad idea to have the option; we certainly have the technology." Alexandra turned and took both of Sean's hands in her own.

Sean smiled as he looked in her eyes. "You realize that would make you your cousin's mother."

"Just an option for the future. Not set in stone."

Sean gave Alexandra a quick kiss on the forehead. "Can you imagine being Vance's mother? Jesus!"

"Look," said Walt as he nodded across the expanse of the landscaped lawn. There, at the far end, were two men and a young boy playing catch with a football. From this distance, it was difficult for him to make out the faces but he could hear faint laughter from all three. One of the men looked toward them and waved. The four at the table waved back.

Alex looked up for a second to see his Uncle Walt watching them; he waved. He smiled as he saw the entire table wave back. Alex was breathing hard and had beads of sweat on his forehead as he turned back to his two companions. Vance bent over and picked up a football and threw it to young Teddy, who deftly caught it on the run and proceeded to zig-zag across the lawn as if dodging opposing players before diving, head first, across an imaginary goal line. Teddy got up, doing a hysterical victory dance. He was all smiles as he turned toward the two men, revealing his huge white teeth and soft brown eyes. He threw the ball to a huffing and puffing Alex. He then put his hands on his hips.

"You pilgrims might be a gittin' a little old for this game, ya know," he said in a perfect imitation of John Wayne.

Those on the veranda could hear the laughter coming from Alex and Vance.

Sandy Oldaker smiled brightly. "Teddy always looks forward to these visits. He has an uncanny affection for those two remarkable men. He talks about his 'friends' all the time."

Walt had tears of joy in his eyes. "The birth of Teddy Jr. has put a lot of joy back in the lives of us all, but, aside from you and Bob, Alex and Vance have benefited the most. He's put all the heart back in them. I haven't heard Vance laugh like that for many, many years." Walt paused for a moment. "Does my old ticker good." Want took a handkerchief from his pocket and blew his nose.

Colleen reached over and patted Walt on the knee. "He sure keeps those two amused."

"That he does. That he does," said Walt nodding to himself. "The boy's a natural-born entertainer."

THE END

LaVergne, TN USA
26 December 2010
210093LV00002B/4/P